THE PURGATORY INN

Terry Lloyd Vinson

A Wings ePress, Inc.
Suspense / Thriller Novel

The Purgatory Inn

Approximately thirty-one hours later saw LeAnn's arrival. The weather conditions...clear, sunny and practically breezeless, were in stark contrast to the previous day, as was the level of difficulty involved in transporting her limp frame from the chopper's cramped cab to the lobby. Wherein a two-man transport team had barely strained in hauling Jorgensen's slim, muscular frame, this despite sloppy terrain and gusty winds, it had taken a herculean effort to relocate visitor two. The forty-to-fifty yard distance from landing pad to lobby had included numerous pauses to readjust their grips on the fold-out gurney. Once inside, they'd been forced to practically roll her atop the larger of two couches, their necks, arms and foreheads littered with pulsating veins from the effort.

Much like Jorgenson, the initial symptoms of her reawakening were a spastic flutter of the eyes and equally jerky movements of the limbs. Unlike Jorgensen, she didn't as much rise to a sitting position as collapse into one, as in onto the tiled floor with a pained grunt, nearly flipping the massive couch end-over-end in the process.

Shaking her head vigorously from side to side, she ran splayed fingers through a comically puffy doo before depositing a wet cough into a curled palm.

THE PURGATORY INN

Terry Lloyd Vinson

A Wings ePress, Inc.
Suspense / Thriller Novel

Wings ePress, Inc.

Edited by: Jeanne Smith
Copy Edited by: Joan C. Powell
Senior Editor: Jeanne Smith
Executive Editor: Marilyn Kapp
Cover Artist: Richard Stroud

Wings ePress Books
http://www.wings-press.com

Copyright © Terry Loyd Vinson 2014
ISBN 978-1-61309-817-2

Published In the United States Of America

Wings ePress Inc.
3000 N. Rock Road
Newton, KS 67114

Dedication

To Liza; my wife, best friend and the light of my life.

Prologue

The fine art of self-preservation

The instinct to survive, it's been said, is inbred in all living things. It is, seemingly at birth, hardwired. I have to agree, though with some slight reservations. For example, I have no doubt those species lucky enough to earn a top-twenty spot atop the interplanetary chain are born with a natural propensity to save their own hides when faced with grave danger. I speak, of course, mainly of human beings and their animal brethren. On the flipside of the survival coin, I just can't rationalize a dandelion purposely leaning to one side to avoid a rapidly descending boot-heel, or an aged elm somehow sidestepping the sharp end of an axe blade via some magical uprooting tap dance.

But I digress, meaning backtrack to those so woefully uneducated, to the *homo sapien* masses and their well-documented prowess in dodging the reaper's sharp-edged scythe, whether it be out of skill, luck, greed, white-knuckled fear, or a combination of same. Infinite are the factual yarns throughout human history that speak of unmatched determination and a 'never say die' mentality that allowed those involved to defy insurmountable odds to live another day.

From a South American soccer team stranded in tundra conditions for months on end and forced to consume human flesh—to an elderly couple buried underneath a mountain of avalanche-driven snow and thus trapped within an overturned automobile for weeks on end—to a teenager so hopelessly lost in the wilderness a search is eventually called off, only to reemerge alive and well, having lived off rainwater, grub-worms and berries for the better part of three months, there is no shortage of documented evidence. Look no further than the chaos that was, is and will presumably always be the chaotic Middle East...dig deep beneath the rubble for all manner of die-hard survivalists. Go ahead then, pick a century, pick a scenario, pick a potential victim of disaster, man-made or natural, crime scene or war.

Imagine the unimaginable, the ultimate in cliffhangers, the inescapable trap from which certain death appears inevitable. History has shown there is no...such...thing, as no matter how dire the circumstances, such uniquely human traits as determination, perseverance and grit have tipped the scales to the side of the living. Call it a triumph of will. Call it divine intervention. Call it blind-assed luck, sometimes driven not by bravery but chicken-shit cowardice. Regardless, it's a fact that the majority of the population will not only fight like the dickens to avoid going belly-up, but also lie, cheat, steal and toss their fellow man under the proverbial bus in a New York blink of an eye.

On the bravery front, motivations for doing so are many and varied, self-preservation being the most obvious. Many more use their loved ones, the ones they'd be leaving behind, to fuel the inner fire. Still others, a tiny minority at best, are given a choice to either perish via unnatural means or to survive and begin a new lease on life—their slate wiped clean, their past sins forgiven and forgotten. On the flipside, cowards need only surrender to their fear and run...like...hell.

To face the challenge of survival in the face of insurmountable odds is a rarity in modern society, thus most have not an inkling how they'd react.

Such was the rare opportunity afforded not one but two individuals of similarly shady backgrounds. Individuals whose rather questionable mettle would be sorely tested in the name of revenge...in the name of greed...but ultimately, in the rebirthing of souls once deemed hopelessly lost.

~ * ~

Kung-Fu fighting

"Mister Hanley says hello, Jorgy. Apparently he didn't regard your capture and subsequent interrogation worthy of his precious time. Still, I've rarely seen the man so openly annoyed when dealing with a low-level scum-sucker such as yourself. You think by now he'd have grown accustomed to your kind."

The rotund, barrel-chested man paced frantically, a well-chewed stogie pinched tightly between jagged, shark-like teeth that remained magically clamped even as his growling rant continued. Myron G. McKinley, aka "The Tracker," as he was referred to by subordinates, peers and enemies alike, leaned slightly forward as he waddled about, eyeing the source of his dialogue through floss-thin slits.

"Were that he requested we simply snap a few bones and toss your welching carcass into the nearest dumpster, but nooooooo! Mister Hanley has had, in your particular case, an epiphany of sorts."

The hired muscle manning opposite ends of the pool table snickered in unison, each coughing into a curled palm to mask the effect, lest they experience the considerable wrath of the man responsible for said outburst. The rarest of breeds was their boss, a *"Mic-Spic."* Being of Irish father and Hispanic mother, McKinley had nonetheless ascended the ranks of enforcers due to a pit-bull attitude and, more vital, an almost supernatural ability to track down whatever prey the family deemed of fugitive status.

"Ah yes, Mister Hanley has a plan for you, fella. A plan...and an offer, if you will."

The short, round man halted in mid-step, reaching over and down to land a moist palm atop the shoulder of their guest—a guest lying flat on his back atop the pool table, blood seeping freely from both nostrils and a deep gash on the underside of his chin. His vision littered in narrow, pulsating waves, the man could just make out a canvas of dark stains on the ceiling above, a wide, purplish blotch that spread like a spider's web from all directions.

"Mister Hanley won't allow I divulge further, except to assume it's an offer he figured you'd be more than open to, that is, considering the alternative."

The prone man grumbled incoherently, reaching up to smear the back of his hand with pooled leakage from his bushy mustache.

"Oh, pardon me all to hades, Jorgy. I see you're struggling to regain a sense of balance. Sometimes I just plain forget how an unexpected bludgeoning affects a person," the dialogue continued, its originator leaning against a far wall with his stubby arms crossed.

"Watch 'im close, they said. Martial arts bad-ass, they said, with Chuck Norris skills. Yeah, *right*...Chuck Norris my a...um, eye," the younger and bulkier of the two hired muscle spewed with a grin, peering down at the splayed man with a devilish grin, "more like *Catherine* Norris. You hear 'im cry, boss? For a dude that spends so much time in the gym, punk sounded just like my kid sister when I used to goose her butt cheek."

Before his superior could reply, their victim intervened while struggling to roll over onto his left side and nearly fell off the table. Somewhere in a far distance, he heard muffled voices, no doubt originating from outside the establishment's thick-walled perimeter. He'd spotted maybe five or six bodies loitering about the pool room just before his lights had so abruptly gone dim from the initial blow.

"I'm g-guessing that served as f-foreplay in your f-family?"

The muscle lunged forth and snarled, rearing back a fist as to strike.

"Fucking wise-ass punk."

"Kerry, keep it cocked where it is," the boss blurted, halting his subordinate's intended blow with the casual raising of a hand.

"But Mac, you heard what that fuck…" the muscle whined, his fist already uncurling near his left ear.

"Mister Hanley doesn't want him *over* battered, Kerry, only sufficiently bruised. By the way, that's a ten spot for the pot when we get back to the grounds."

"Ah….shiii…shoot, Mac! That ain't fair, boss. He baited me," the muscle cried, slapping his own forehead with an open palm. A devout Catholic, Peter Hanley did not tolerate profanity from those in his employ, stressing to all in supervisory positions to maintain an active *profanity pot* to punish offenders, the fine a hefty five dollars per curse.

The older man paused to relocate the severely gnawed cigar from one side of his mouth to the other, all the while eyeing their victim with squinty-eyed curiosity.

"No excuses, my boy. A ten spot and that's that. If I'm not allowed to vent, *no one* is."

Leaning up on his left elbow, the target of their aggressive actions blew a reddish nose-bubble that evaporated upon his speaking.

"W-well, since I'm e-employed elsewhere, I can s-safely refer to the l-lot of you as chicken-shit, cock-sucking a-assholes."

The man peeked casually over to the younger muscle and winked playfully, the right side of his mustache dripping a thin, maroon stream onto the pale blue tabletop.

"Na-na-na-na-nah," he concluded before spitting out a small chunk of silver filling from between bloodied teeth. Peering briefly at the jade-shaded concrete floor, he noticed a half-dozen dark-maroon splatters he logically deduced as his own.

The muscle on the opposite side, tall and lanky with numerous facial scars, slapped a hand over his lips, a half-hearted gesture that did little to muffle an ensuing giggle-fit.

"Clam up, McGinty," the boss said with a stern stare the gangly muscle's way. "One more smarty-Marty remark like that, Jorgensen, and I'll give Kerry here the green light for an additional jab to the ribs."

Struggling mightily, the man eventually pushed himself upright, his legs still splayed out in front with the feet protruding off the pool table's far side. His light green cotton tee was spattered from collar to belt, his blue jeans equally stained in abstract leakage. He heard a car horn, then another. Inaudible whispers followed, probably the same weak-kneed cowards that had witnessed the ambush and subsequently taken the high road to avoid conflict. Sirens wailed in the far distance, only to gradually fade in lieu of gaining volume.

Brief hopes of outside intervention quickly faded upon the realization that nary a one of the aforementioned yellow-streaked nut-sacs possessed the courage to call the proper authorities. Minutes earlier, he'd witnessed McKinley openly threaten to 'crease the knee-caps' of a pair of unfortunates who'd accidently sauntered in. One had started to argue, a deep-voiced biker type with multiple tats and piercings, only to depart meekly enough upon the hired muscle's glaring insistence. Jorgenson bristled internally, his disdain for the city and its low-grade inhabitants growing by leaps and bounds yet again, a regular occurrence of late.

"Ye-yeah? Promises, promises, squat. Real b-brave grease-ball m-micks, y-you are...as l-long as y-you're sneak...sneaking up to cl-clothesline a guy a-across the choppers with a s-steel pipe."

Casually removing the stogie from between clamped lips, the man in charge leaned forward and delivered a casual pat atop his prey's right shoulder.

"What'd you expect, tough guy? We crawl into a squared ring with a ref dancing between us? We're not exactly in the 'fight fair' business, pal, 'specially with a man of your reputation. Now, on your feet, lover-boy. We have a lengthy drive ahead and you've got a flight to catch."

Through a single open eye, the other so grotesquely swollen the lid appeared to have literally been sewn shut, the man regarded McKinley with a sour smirk.

"And w-what if I say I'd prefer not to?"

This time, it was the younger muscle's giggle that echoed forth.

"In that case, Jorgy old salt, we'll have to insist," McKinley replied, scratching his double-chin with the backside of one hand.

"No shit, squat. F-flying seriously freaks m-me out."

"As opposed to floating face-down like driftwood in the city sewers...driftwood sporting so many holes you'd think a flock of woodpeckers had a fucking field day."

The younger muscle flashed a wide grin, raising a finger airborne.

"Ahhhh, got'cha boss."

Said grin transformed to a warped frown upon viewing his superiors' predatory stare.

"Upon further review, Kerry my boy, I'd say *you* only owe the pot a single fin, dig?"

The young man swallowed hard and nodded his acknowledgement.

Reaching over, McKinley attained a loose grip on the back collar of the injured man's tee.

"Hoo-kay, enough delay, tough guy. Let's roll before traffic on the turnpike begins its usual afternoon snarl."

Stepping down with a groan, Brian Jorgenson's knees trembled on the verge of collapse just as the hired muscle took up position on either side of his slumped frame. McKinley meanwhile had slid his left hand from their quarry's collar to the small of his back, shoving gently forward as if navigating a small child. The unlit stogie pointing upward from his cinched lips, "The Tracker" had just begun to move his free appendage forward in order to check the time when a sudden jolt propelled his wrist at an upward trajectory, forcing his pursed lips to greet the ascending Rolex and splitting each in the process.

Tumbling away with both stubby arms pin-wheeling, freshly mutilated lips and the gnawed remains of a badly smashed cigar jammed into his left nostril, McKinley rammed shoulders-first into a far wall just as the hired muscle had lunged forth to regain control of their wounded but suddenly feisty prey.

Attempting a clumsily executed bear hug, the taller of the two, McGinty he'd been called, barked in agony as a perfectly aimed knee-cap mashed his groin. His arms fell limp and his eyes widened just a split-second before an open-handed chop to the back of the neck forced him to his knees.

Leaning in, the shorter and more stoutly built muscle, Kerry Cleaves by name, tossed forth a vicious left hook that found nothing but air; ditto a roundhouse right that barely grazed the intended target's scalp upon its rapid descent. Thrown slightly off-balance from the effect of the double-whiff, he swung around awkwardly and yelped just as his left knee was bent backward with a sickening crunch. The next blow found the underside of his chin, the sharp retort of chattering teeth preempting a backward flip that saw the back of his skull break the fall.

Brian Jorgenson sprang forth from his battle-crouch and gave Kerry Cleaves, squirming and groaning while grasping his wrecked knee with one hand and bruised noggin with the other, a final once over before lunging toward the pool room exit.

A mere three steps in a wild sprint and something snared his left ankle, sending him toppling chest-first into a nearby poker table as multi-colored chips sailed airborne and a trio of accompanying high-back chairs scattered like bowling pins.

"Oh n-no ya don't, fancy b-boy," Jorgenson heard a voice grumble as his combat-roll from the tabletop concluded with a fairly painless thumping of his left shoulder and hip. It was McGinty, crawling toward him like the reanimated dead on all fours and sporting a bloody grin.

"Where t-the fuck ya think yer goin'?"

Tossing the table roughly aside, Jorgenson struck a decidedly defensive pose, both arms raised in full block mode and feet planted firmly for potential impact.

"Damn if you mick goons aren't gluttons for punishment. Listen, sport, just spare yourself further humiliation and step...well, roll aside."

Machismo aside, McGinty struggled to rise, briefly staggering back before executing a clumsy two-step to right his stance.

"Y-you fight as pretty as ya talk, slick?" he said, winking playfully while striking a classic pugilistic pose, "Ya done used up your one element-of-surprise chip, so just hoof on over h-here and dance with daddy, sissy-boy."

The exit door looming in McGinty's considerable shadow, Jorgenson sighed heavily and waded in.

McGinty threw a series of short, compact jabs, all of which were slapped harmlessly aside, before barreling forward like a raging bull with his slickly-waxed bald head acting as a flesh and bone battering ram.

In textbook toreador fashion, Jorgenson stepped aside at the last possible blink before adding to the lanky man's already substantial forward momentum by planting an elbow to the back of his sweat-slickened skull. Propelled airborne at impact, McGinty was helpless but to endure the flight that concluded with his upper body crashing into and ultimately submerged partially *within* a far wall whose stucco construction provided little resistance.

Jorgenson whirled gracefully about on his left heel in the direction of the room's lone escape route, only to collapse to one knee before the initial step was complete, unable to catch his breath as his vision was blurred by an onslaught of black and red dots that flashed like miniature strobes. Bowing his head, he closed both eyes and sucked in a fresh lung-full in preparation for yet another attempt at flight.

The sensation of cold steel pressing the bony slope behind his right ear was at first strangely comforting, like a probing digit at the outset of a rigorous massage. The feeling passed just as abruptly as increased pressure transformed pleasure to discomfort.

"You so much as twitch a testicle, karate-boy," a gruff voice blurted, each spoken word punctuated by the slight push of gun-barrel against flesh-and-bone, "and Mister Hanley will have to be satisfied with viewing your corpse. Minus a sizable chunk of skull, o' course."

Croaking, semi-nasal vocals aside, there was no doubting the originator as the scent of stale cigar tobacco filled the surrounding air.

"Just try me, Jorgy. Just give me...a reason. Make that...another reason."

Whatever energy Jorgenson held in reserve instantly ebbed away, his entire frame deflating like a punctured balloon.

"Kerry, get up and go pull McGinty's limp ass outta that wall, will you?" McKinley barked, sounded less angry than merely exhausted. He'd pulled the Glock nine mil back nary an inch from the neat circle its barrel-end had dug into Jorgenson's flesh.

They exited the rear door of Shooters Suds N' Spuds less than three full minutes later, a trio of limping men in dark, somewhat ruffled suits trailing behind a similarly gimpy individual adorned in a blood-spattered muscle tee, blue jeans and high-top sneakers.

"You reimburse the management, boss?" McGinty inquired wearily, sporting a golf-ball sized knot on his forehead.

McKinley grunted, a napkin tucked to his torn lower lip.

"Enough to redecorate that shit-hole in gold-plated billiard tables."

"Figured he'd go quietly enough after the beating we put on 'im, Mac," Cleaves chimed in, his left leg noticeably stiff and lagging behind its twin.

"Never with these marital arts clowns," McKinley replied, seeing fit to reach forward and lightly shove their captive with an open palm, then flinching back upon recalling the last time he'd dared attempt such casual contact.

Hobbling down the trash-strewn alley past a handful of wide-eyed on-lookers careful to maintain a safe distance, they soon piled into a slickly waxed black SUV with equally opaque windows.

"Um, you mentioned something about air travel?" Jorgenson inquired as they'd merged onto the interstate beneath the blazing rays of a noonday sun. Lodged between McGinty and Cleaves, he'd leaned forward to address McKinley, who peered up at the rearview through dark shades while casually navigating the vehicle around a chain of semis.

"Yep, that I did. Still wetting your pants at the mere mention, are we?"

"I just don't see the need," he replied after a short pause, squinting through the windshield at the moderately clear four lanes ahead, "I mean, hey, it's a beautiful day. Sun's out, traffic's light. Nothing more relaxing than a good, old-fashioned road trip, am I right?" His hands wriggled and flexed at the pit of his back, the wrists bound by a set of plastic cuffs.

Beside him, McGinty snickered before wincing in the aftermath, the underneath of his left eye having swollen and turned a light shade of purple.

"Chicken shit cracker. What say we toss 'im out at 'bout twenty-thousand feet, boss? Minus the parachute, o'course."

McKinley licked his swollen upper lip while studying the side mirror and guiding the Escalade into the far left lane.

"Wanna watch 'im scream 'n flap his way towards pancake city, huh McGinty?"

The other man sneered devilishly.

"Surely...maybe strap a camera to his ass and then post it on YouTube. Maybe call it 'flight of the kung-fu fairy.'"

To this, the other muscle openly groaned.

"McGinty, you are to comedy what an un-wiped ass is to romance."

To that, they all shared a hearty laugh, including Jorgenson, whose roaming eyes had locked on a state trooper car a few hundred yards ahead, parked so very conspicuously beneath an impending underpass. His mind raced in a frantic attempt to formulate a plan to somehow gain the trooper's attention as they passed. It would involve leverage, he knew...leverage his present positioning made an impossibility.

"To be fair, Brian, I understand your hesitation in boarding one of those flying Greyhounds," McKinley practically shouted, staring into the rearview while steering the truck past a sputtering mini-van wagon filled with waving, gyrating juveniles.

"I'm a *terra firma* man from waaay back. I mean, you realize none of this is personal. I don't know you...only know tidbits *about* you. The pains you've inflicted. So, I can sympathize. All that said," he concluded with a shrug, "what the boss man wants, the boss man gets."

It began as a faint sting just above his left elbow, escalating into a substantial burning sensation. By the time Jorgenson fell back into his assigned space, McGinty had pulled the syringe free, its pointy tip glistening as a final teardrop-sized pool held firm.

"Ah, that just ain't right," he snarled as a heavy cloak of paralysis took immediate hold, "you could at least w-warm...warn a g-guy."

His eyelids grew leaden, closing despite stern mental orders to the contrary. His thoughts were hazy, scrambled. Something about a state trooper or perhaps an eight-ball tournament. He thought of Sandra...no...Wanda...it was Wanda...flopping about the Jacuzzi with those perfect tits balanced mere inches from his face. He was asking her when her husband would be home. She giggled, her eyes ablaze with seductive mischief.

A ringtone chimed in, the theme to a recent TV show or movie, snapping him to...and McKinley reassuring a mystery caller that *yes indeed*...the quarry was ensnared and on its way to the nest.

Floating into a blissful realm of unawareness, Jorgenson's last thought was, surprisingly, free of self-pity in that life as he knew it had surely just ended. There was, in fact, a queer measure of relief in the resignation.

The quarry's entire frame appeared to briefly tense before total deflation, his otherwise haggard visage sporting the faintest of smiles.

~ * ~

Stretch Pants and Beam

Awoken by her own thunderous snores, LeAnn fought the numerous blankets holding her captive and rolled over, inadvertently backhanding a coffee mug from the lamp table. Flaring her nostrils, she caught a stout whiff of last night's night cap—a pungent scent of scotch and soda, woefully short on fizz.

Temporarily discombobulated, it took several frenzied moments of wide-eyed, slack-jawed concentration to recognize her surroundings...Pop's infamous "guest house," to which few ever actually visited save the occasional relocating relative or, in her case, a relative in dire need of a space to crash. At three-thousand six-hundred square feet, the two-story Colonial had originally been constructed as an upscale bed and breakfast. In the two decades since falling under Pop's ownership via, as legend told it, the previous owner's penchant for picking the wrong bang-tails at Saratoga, its main use had been as an oversized guest room for wayward kin.

Kicking herself free from the entanglement, she flopped onto her back and groaned as a thin ray of sunlight shone through the curtains to find her eyes. Balancing a forearm across the bridge of her nose to block the unwelcome intrusion, she worked her tongue across the roof of her mouth in attempt to build saliva in the soured desert terrain found there. Her stomach growled loudly, a concerto of mass cravings barely muffled by the buildup of bedding.

She'd managed to nod off despite the assorted maladies fighting for her sole attention when a thumping at the door, incessant and stern, broke the fragile spell.

"Miss LeAnn, its past ten. You need to think about preparing yourself for travel."

It was Miss Jennings, her curt, impatient tone no doubt a result of being held back from initiating the wakeup call hours earlier. An old-school domestic in every conceivable way, from her "up at dawn, concede at dark" work ethic to her unwillingness to accept anything other than perfection from the rest of the staff, Beatriz Jennings had been in the family employ for just under three decades. LeAnn could only deduce she'd been instructed to babysit until such time for Pop's inevitable scolding and/or lecture, be it via landline, cellphone or webcam (a technology he'd only recently discovered and grown quite fond of).

Soon enough, the deafening pause was shattered by yet another series of rattling thumps.

"All right...all right already...I g-got it...message received," LeAnn grumbled before burying her face into her pillow.

"Breakfa...brunch is warming in the oven as we speak, yet *again* I might add. It won't take another and still be consumable. All, that is, save the daily servings of Advil and Alka-Seltzer."

Twisting her head to the side, a tuft of strawberry blonde locks shading her eyes, LeAnn's growling reply easily drowned out the squeaky fart she'd released in perfect unison.

"Un-der-stood, Jennings. Allow me a few precious moments to get my bearings, yes?"

Pausing to endure yet another insufferable rebuff, LeAnn squeezed out an additional pocket of intestinal gas (*butt biscuits-fully baked* she mused, forcing a pained smile).

Satisfied that Jennings had relocated from outside the suite door, she wrestled the blankets free from her upper body, struggled to sit up, then paused to belch—a sour, sickly moist emission that reeked of the previous night's feast. A feast that had consisted of, in no particular order of consumption: several servings each of three-cheese lasagna, chicken parmesan, unlimited breadsticks and at least a half-dozen JB scotch and sodas. Stepping onto the cool hardwood, she stood shakily and wobbled into the bathroom. Cupping both hands, she slashed several handfuls of faucet water onto the dry sponge serving as her tongue before dropping trough and collapsing onto the toilet with an exasperated sigh.

"Oh, don't give me that now..." she barked between strains, "...as much as was deposited at one end, there has to be a healthy withdrawal forthcoming from the other..."

She departed the suite a half hour later, donned in red sweatpants, flip-flop shoes and a Green Bay Packers jersey, the lengthy trek to the kitchen and connecting dining room akin to a 10K marathon.

The scent of freshly brewed coffee and warmed-over sausage and eggs permeated the spacious dining room, initiating a fresh spasm of midsection rumblings.

"Miss Jennings, I care not what others spout...you are indeed a goddess," she warbled between lengthy sips of ice water, with which she gulped down a pair of black and white striped tablets she'd surmised were the aforementioned headache remedy. Several slurps of steaming java followed once it was obvious no reply was forthcoming.

The first floor of the spacious home was deathly silent, echoes of LeAnn's greedy gorging the lone evidence of life. Upon forking in a final, heaping helping of eggs and washing it down with the last of the coffee, she casually raised a thigh and farted yet again, a booming effort the echo of which reverberated throughout the otherwise eerily silent trappings.

"Whoops...stomped on a duck," she quipped, the high back chair squeaking its disapproval as she pushed back and surveyed the damage.

"Not too shabby for a midday snack. Gonna have to amp it up for din-din. Hey Jennings! What's for supper, old girl? Gotta tell you, I'm thinking b-b-q ribs or maybe a roasted chicken or two...what say you? I know Pops probably instructed the low-cal menu, but hey, what he don't know won't hurt him, correct o'mundo?"

Her knees snapped and crackled upon standing, and still, as she wobbled forth and exited the dining area for the living room, no verbal reply materialized.

"You desert me already, Jennings? Ha! No pun intended...get it? De-sert me? Speaking of which, a freshly baked apple pie would sure hit the spot....peach or cherry cobbler maybe...half-gallon of French vanilla ice cream melting on top...and allll around. Jennings? You hiding somewhere in this damned mausoleum? Jennings...damn it, woman...show yourself!"

Collapsing across a black leather couch, LeAnn peered out a nearby picture window to see the bright morning sun had been sufficiently cloaked by a mass overhang of ominous black clouds.

"Awww, nix the avoiding and come on out, will you? I'll see to it that Pops doubles your salary just for sitting here and shooting the horse manure. Come on, Jennings, my eyelids are growing heavier by the minute!"

As testimony to said claim, LeAnn's attempt to rise to a sitting position at the sound of distant footsteps was a colossal failure as a wave of severe dizziness saw her flail back with a resounding moan.

"Whoooaaa, Nellie...guess the Beam is still working some overtime," she mumbled, laying the flat of one hand against her forehead, which possessed a cool, clammy feel. Shutting her eyes and taking short, shallow breaths, she hoped to accelerate healing from the sudden onslaught.

The approaching footsteps pulsated weirdly, sounding distant and adjacent all at once.

"J-Jennings...I'm not...f-feeling so sh-sharp... you... you got another a-aspirin...or...b-better yet...a Xanax lying ar-around?"

Her stomach churned a sudden disapproval, seemingly on the verge of cramping.

The footsteps halted...replaced by what sounded like a chorus of sighs.

"Y-you there, old g-girl? I'm....really f-feeling like danced –on d-dog s-shit. C-come to think...of it...that s-sausage d-did smell...kinda...r-rank. Y-you...there, Je-Jennings?"

Something stung her upper arm...twice...a third time. LeAnn was instantly reminded of a bee sting she'd suffered as a young teen. A wasp had left its stinger imbedded behind her left ear. Easily the most abrupt dose of physical pain she'd ever endured in all her thirty-one-plus years.

Drifting on the very edge of unconsciousness, she was faintly aware of a smattering of voices which faded in and out like a badly tuned radio.

"Good god....ter than just a few weeks...need a blessed crane to lift..."

"How long...dative last?"

"Six, seven hours...ty of time. Flight from...only three hours, tops."

"Need...change clothes...sweats are fine...shirt as instructed..."

"Help me lift...nings, her bag packed?"

"Indeed...sitting in the foyer. You'd best make haste...

"Damn if she doesn't...a fucking ton...ripped my pants!"

"Hush that language...-ley doesn't appreciate such vulgarity, you know."

"My apologies, ma'am...to the door."

LeAnn's nostrils flared yet again as a soothing wave of blackness poured over her senses....the thick scent of antiseptic strangely soothing.

One

The Wage(r)s of Sin

Notes to the Boss (*General Entry*):

There was a distinct pre-arrival vibe concerning one Brian Jorgenson long before his arrival. It was less than positive. Understand, pre-conceived notions are frowned upon, but in studying the man's file, it was going to be nigh on impossible not to approach with extreme caution. Actually, it would be damned foolhardy. The words spoke for themselves. Emotionally, he was not to be trusted. Physically, he most certainly was to be feared.

The Helsinki chopper made landfall in the nick of time, touching down on a mostly dry landing pad soon to be awash in a cold, torrential downfall to the tune of five to six inches in less than an hour.

Early March in this particular neck of the woods showcases quite the buffet of schizophrenic weather conditions—an eccentric mix of all four seasons often overlapping with the most violent of consequences. Case in point—the previous evening rain was replaced by a sleet/snow mix that essentially cancelled all incoming flights, thus Brian Jorgenson's scheduled roommate would not arrive until a full forty-eight hours later. Actually, this turned out to be a godsend of sorts, a chance for the assigned staff to adequately acquaint themselves with the man labeled by their employer as the ultimate conman, a conscienceless serial liar and loose cannon personality on whom one did not dare turn their back.

Upon arrival amid merely a light sprinkle, Jorgenson was hauled from the copter and into the lodge's neat, capacious lobby. There he was administered a loaded syringe of B-12 before being unceremoniously dumped onto a spacious leather couch, damp clothing and all, and left to awaken at a snail's pace. The copter had touched down at precisely nine-thirty-six p.m. on the third of March. He'd been laid to rest some fourteen minutes later. The Helsinki re-pierced the rumbling skies just as Jorgenson's eyes began to flutter, the fingers of each hand racked with spasms. Leaning up, he reached up to gently massage a purplish bruise beneath his left eye and a similar wound on the right side of his jaw. Dried blood caked both nostrils. His short-cropped coif lay matted in several sections by similar leakage and stood out like porcupine quills in others. Despite these numerous drawbacks in appearance, a rugged handsomeness still existed, thus justifying at least a portion of the man's reputation with the opposite sex. If forced to provide an old-school Hollywood comparison, I'd say he resembled an early eighties Burt Reynolds—the thickly mustachioed, slightly haggard version, just past his box-office prime, only with the chiseled physique of a much younger heartthrob.

Several moments passed until Jorgensen arose wearing a mask of befuddlement at precisely ten-o-eight p.m., rolling off the couch onto the slickly waxed floor as if from a drunken stupor. Even in such a weak, vulnerable condition, standing with all the vitality of a wobbling infant, the man still managed to maintain an outward aura of menace. Despite being decked out in a comically oversized zip-up windbreaker, there was no completely camouflaging the trim, muscular physique beneath.

A tall pitcher of ice water and prefilled glass had been left on a nearby coffee table, along with a package of saltines and a serving dish possessing sliced cheeses and cubed ham. Peering around cautiously as his gait gradually stabilized, Jorgenson took note of the refreshments but initially passed them by in lieu of taking a walking tour of the lodge.

Obviously still fighting the effects of the sedative, he sporadically reached out for support while lapping the circular room's outer perimeter. Every few steps, he would peer through the slightly tinted glass walls, where moderate rain was fast mutating into a full blown squall. Once, side-stepping carefully around a rocker recliner and accompanying footstool, he placed both hands to the side of his face and squinted through the glass into the cloaking murkiness, where visibility was practically nil. Backing up, he twisted around and side-stepped clumsily to avoid tripping over a tile-topped, v-shaped coffee table. He stumbled forward, his scalp brushing the lower edge of a colossal flat-screen plasma hanging suspended from the coffered ceiling. Snatching a remote from a nearby lamp table, he tried in vain to power up the set, aiming and punching the power button for several frustrating moments before discarded the clicker with a casual toss. Frowning, he glanced briefly toward the rear of the room at a flat panel door positioned at the center of a sleek, veneer brick wall.

Eventually resigned to his exact location remaining a mystery to solve another time, Jorgenson eventually made his way to the brick and marble bar centering the room. He picked the center of three bar stools and sat tentatively, unzipping and removing the windbreaker and draping it over the seat to his left before lowering his head as if fighting off a sudden dizzy spell. He remained slumped, taking in several deep breaths, before rising yet again and making a beeline toward the snack spread. Lifting the glass of sparking ice water to eye level, he began to twirl it about, studying it with great intensity before parking it between flaring nostrils. Apparently satisfied of both its validity and lack of poisonous ingredient, he sipped timidly before emptying the contents with a half dozen greedy gulps. Peering about as if perpetrating some heinous felony, he ripped into the package of crackers with such fervor several saltines flew free and scattered about the slickly waxed hardwood floor. Instead of layering the crackers with the prepared cheeses and ham, he consumed them separately, taking in large mouthfuls of each and rarely pausing to chew before swallowing. Discarding the glass, he instead slurped directly from the pitcher, soaking his green muscle-tee from neck to beltline and thus clearly outlining an upper body so meticulously cut and defined it appeared a *faux* mix of air-brush and CGI technology. The sparse remains were poured over his head and upturned face, after which he used splayed fingers to comb through his blood-stiffened do.

He'd fallen to one knee, the empty pitcher hanging loosely from one hand and his head bowed as if in deep meditation, the moment of tranquility so rudely lost as an overhead speaker blared from above. Jorgenson openly flinched, tossing the pitcher aside and oblivious to it shattering against the side of the brick bar a few feet away, shards of glass raining down on his crouched form.

"Whoa there, partner... pardon the Dolby effect. Now reel in those brittle nerve endings...though you might heartily disagree, things are just as they should be," a voice chimed, echoing within the stony glass chamber as if originating from all directions simultaneously.

"I can imagine you're a bit...discombobulated 'bout now, but not to worry, partner—it only gets worse," the gruff male voice exclaimed with obvious glee, a voice drenched in a deep southern drawl. "Seriously, I'm thinkin' you're just chompin' at the bit for an explanation. That's where I come in...well, me and a few other folks servin' as your of-fi-cial welcomin' committee. Apologize for the skimpy pickings as far as the food tray goes, but...well, you'll soon understand the logic to the madness....or...maybe understand ain't the right word."

Stone-faced and stiff of limb, Jorgenson backed toward the lodge's double-door entrance and filled each palm with a handle. At his back, rain-spattered glass trembled from gusting winds that grew increasingly vicious.

"Pull and tug all ya want, partner...she's locked tighter than a bass drum. Ain't worth the hernia, but if ya feel ya must, by all means give 'er a go."

Turning casually about, Jorgenson gave the handles a series of stout jerks to no avail. Releasing his grip, he briefly stared into the swirling blackness before again facing front. The frustration was etched in his pained expression, clenched fists and stiffened posture. Men such as he weren't at all accustomed to failure in terms of physical challenges.

"Fine then...allow me to inquire the where, what, who and whys," he said wearily, bowing with the palm of each hand propped atop a slightly bended knee, "as in...*where* the hell am I...*what* the hell am I doing here...*who* the hell are you...and *why* the fuck am I here to begin with?"

There was a slight pause, wherein the building storm's full fury could be heard in the incessant pounding of the surrounding walls and a constant thumping from above.

"Fair queries, I'd have to say, and not the least bit surprisin'. A certain level of...frustration is expected, though I gotta say that all the salty language serves no purpose but to showcase a woeful lack of vocabulary skills."

Stepping gingerly forward, Jorgenson neared the marble bar and halted with the palms of both hands propped atop the center bar stool.

"Tell you what, Foghorn..." he began calmly enough, "...excuse me for not really giving a steaming *rat turd* that any of my forthcoming rants being littered with profanity offend you and whoever else is watching and listening. You see, understating the damned obvious..." he paused for a heavy sigh, the resuming tone several decibels louder, the tone laced with a building anger his slumping pose belied, "...I don't think I'm being at all unreasonable in desiring an explanation...post haste, considering several A-list felonies were perpetrated before I ever laid eyes on this fucking place."

"And an explanation you shall receive, partner. First things first... now that you're energy level seems to ha..."

"*Answer my question, mother-fucker*!" Jorgenson shouted, pulling the bar stool free from its bolted stance with a combination twist/pull motion that saw a trio of steel bolts snap free and spin across the room, "where the fuck am I and what the fuck am I doing here?"

He held the metal stool by its padded seat, his shoulders, biceps and forearms noticeably pumped—his neck and forehead riddled with bulging veins.

"Just calm down, partner...there is the matter of protocol here, and you ain't exactly in a position to dictate same."

"Protoco...son of a....*bitch*!" Jorgenson spat wide-eyed before shifting position in a fluid blur of motion and heaving the bar stool full-force at the glass wall just to the left of the entrance. The follow-through saw him collapse onto all fours as the metal stool struck its intended target and bounded harmlessly away without leaving as much as a streak on the glass. Of course he would have nary a clue it would take nothing less than close-range shell-fire from a Sherman tank to dent that clear barricade.

"Shatterproof, partner...that is, less ya have a bazooka tucked away in your ass-crack. Now, how 'bout we move on with the process? Times a wastin', and believe me when I say, this here situation is all about timing."

Repositioning until he sat on his backside with each forearm resting atop a bended knee, Jorgenson glanced over at the warped bar stool lying a few feet to his left.

"Doesn't take a genius to know who's behind the situation. Are you in there, Hanley? Getting your jollies, I'd wager, no doubt savoring every second of this pathetic shit."

"Um, partner...it's better if we just move on with th...."

Jorgenson's tone was controlled—surprisingly calm, as he gradually re-achieved a standing position.

"Assault...kidnapping...forced imprisonment...yep, real Hanley family specialties..."

"Take my word for it, partner, we're gonna cover all the particulars just as soon as you..."

Jorgenson began to pace, slowly at first but with increased fervor, his hands tucked neatly at his lower back—bringing to mind the Roadrunner of Looney Tunes fame, but only if that particular feathered friend had bulked up significantly.

"...probably hand out special family diplomas for degrees in extortion..."

"Mister Jorgenson, this can all be jawed over in the initial sessi..."

"...signed in blood by Peter 'the Mic Prick' Hanley himself."

The voice cleared its throat noisily.

"Enough is enough, Brian...we really need to move on."

To that, Jorgenson strolled over to the entrance doors and struck a crouching pose famously known in the annuals of Kung Fu masters as the "Eagle Claw."

"Think I'll pass, Hanley...thanks just the same."

The voice snickered, albeit a bit nervously.

"Don't kid yourself, partner, what are fists an' feet gonna possibly do that *steel* wouldn't?"

Springing forward, Jorgenson bombarded the glass with a furious combination of straight punches and kicks, effectively and efficiently alternating fists and feet like the well-oiled martial arts machine so well-advertised prior to his arrival.

"Shatterin' various bones ain't servin' no purpose, partner."

Backing away with bloodied knuckles tucked to his chest, he charged forward and executed a textbook roundhouse kick, stumbling gracefully back in the aftermath before surging forth to deliver yet another kick, this of the double-flying variety. Landing cat-like on all fours, Jorgenson's limbs coiled, the knuckles of each hand clearly shredded from the earlier flurry.

"...satisfied, Bruce Lee? Can't knock ya for effort but I wasn't just tuggin' your chain about the strength of that glass. Now, how's about we converse like civilized men?" the voice concluded smugly, the last few words drowned out by a predatory growl that increased dramatically in both volume and intensity before reaching its crescendo—a throaty, battlefield howl that ended only as its originator planted his left shoulder at the center of the double door. Ricocheting back, Jorgenson again paused, bowing slightly with his arms crossed over his chest while appearing to search out a new target area in the circular glass encompassing the whole of the lodge.

"...ahhhhhh mule muffins...ya ain't about to cease the tantrum, are ya, pard?"

Lifting both battered hands airborne, Jorgenson casually flipped a double-bird.

"Didn't think so. Damned shame it has to come to this. Not *surprised*, mind ya, but a man can hope."

Sauntering over to a brown leather Ottoman sectional, Jorgenson bent down and scooped up the larger of the trio of units and hoisted it overhead.

"So be it then...see ya on the other side..." the voice concluded with woefully *faux* sincerity, "...actually, bein' as it appears those mitts 'a yours resemble scrambled sausage, I'd expect an infirmary visit is in your immediate future. Regardless, we'll jaw again soon enough."

Heaving the unit at a section of glass just to the left of the entrance, Jorgenson had already turned to seek out a new potential projectile even as the first bounded harmlessly away.

Freezing in his tracks while reaching for the largest of a trio of nearby footstools, he tilted his head slightly to the left as a pronounced hissing sound filled the lodge.

"Nighty-night, pard. See ya on the other side...well, eventually."

"Wha-the-fuck?" Jorgenson mumbled, taking note of a rather sizeable ceiling vent and its fluttering panels. His nostrils flared as he hurled the footstool to still another previously untouched section of glass wall, seemingly apathetic to its plight as he lurched toward the rear of the room in a mad sprint.

Reaching the brick barricade, his head rotated wildly as if on a swivel, his eyes wide with fear.

"Breathe easy, pard..." the voice consoled blandly as Jorgenson clamped an open palm over his nostrils and mouth, darting along the smooth brick perimeter while running his free hand against its smooth service. By the time he reached the flat panel door, curling a gnarled hand around its oblong handle, he'd collapsed to one knee. A weak tug...a feeble pull later...both knees met the tiled floor.

"Oh, *now* he tries it the easy way. Little late in the game now, partner...little late in the game."

"Op-open t-th-th-the d-door...y-you s-s-som ma ma ba-b-baatccch," Jorgenson muttered, sliding down the panel, his left hand hanging stubbornly even as his torso and head descended into a trembling heap.

"Yep...a *damn* shame," the voice concluded with a mournful sigh. Not that it meant squat as the big picture was concerned, but a sliver of hope had been held out that the in-processing phase would come and go without such drama. So much for taking the glass-half-full approach.

~ * ~

Approximately thirty-one hours later saw LeAnn's arrival. The weather conditions...clear, sunny and practically breezeless, were in stark contrast to the previous day, as was the level of difficulty involved in transporting her limp frame from the chopper's cramped cab to the lobby. Wherein a two-man transport team had barely strained in hauling Jorgensen's slim, muscular frame, this despite sloppy terrain and gusty winds, it had taken a herculean effort to relocate visitor two. The forty-to-fifty yard distance from landing pad to lobby had included numerous pauses to readjust their grips on the fold-out gurney. Once inside, they'd been forced to practically roll her atop the larger of two couches, their necks, arms and foreheads littered with pulsating veins from the effort.

Much like Jorgenson, the initial symptoms of her reawakening were a spastic flutter of the eyes and equally jerky movements of the limbs. Unlike Jorgensen, she didn't as much rise to a sitting position as collapse into one, as in onto the tiled floor with a pained grunt, nearly flipping the massive couch end-over-end in the process.

Shaking her head vigorously from side to side, she ran splayed fingers through a comically puffy doo before depositing a wet cough into a curled palm.

"Ohhhhh my achin' globe. *Betty's boobs*, what a bender," she moaned hoarsely, leaning forward and glancing out the double doors with a flat palm parked at her brow as if to ward off the effects of the morning sun's blinding rays. Crawling forward on all fours, she paused only to dry heave before resuming a gradual creep around the overturned couch to the glass wall beyond.

Her breathing labored, she leaned a shoulder against the cool, clear surface, the intrusive brightness causing an outbreak of rapid blinking as she surveyed the surrounding scape through a tight squint. Knee-deep sea grass swayed and pulsated in oceanic splendor as far as her bleary eyes could see, the asphalt of the neighboring landing pad standing out like tar-black carpet at its center.

"Jeepers creepers," she muttered, pausing to lick horribly chapped lips, "where forth hath he planted thee this time?"

Leaning a pale cheek flush with the glass, she took note of the thickly forested perimeter serving as the perfect background matte, painted in towering cottonwoods, bulky cedars and black walnuts pregnant with the flowing entrails of late spring.

"Long Tall Sally, methinks the middle of blessed nowhere be yon answer."

Pushing herself upright with the assistance of a marble table lamp (left arm) and solid oak underside of the overturned couch (right arm), LeAnn stood on wobbly, wide-set feet—feet enveloped by a pair of soft-heel slippers that appeared every bit as alien to her as the rustic prairie landscape. Taking in her reflection from the mirrored surface of a nearby coffee table, she frowned in apparent disgust at the less-than-fashionable ensemble provided sometime during her premeditated coma. Baby-blue sweat pants with an elastic waistband that felt as if it were slowly feeding off the flesh it so effectively creased, a lime green sweatshirt, the collar of which had already scratched a reddish grove into her neck and sleeve-ends so stunted they would have required another two to three inches just to reach her wrists, instead chafing the center portion of each forearm. A polite description might describe the look as overly snug. It crueler, less politically correct twin: a pregnant sea lion packed into scuba gear.

Turning toward the lodge interior for the first time since the reawakening, her eyes first bypassed, then retreated and finally locked on twin serving trays taking up a wide birth atop the slick marble bar.

"Ahhhh yes..." she practically purred, lumbering forth with the outstretched arms of a chronic sleepwalker, "...even the most wicked of little girls require nourishment, right boss? Can't take the chance of *premature expiration,* oh heavens to Sigmund Freud nooooooo...not with a laundry-list of lectures and butt-chapping scoldings yet to endure."

Peering down at the tray to her left, she squealed with the unrestrained glee of a pre-teen girl, her eyes practically gleaming as she reached to gently cup her initial treat of choice.

"Of course..." she paused with the donut's outer chocolate glaze poised mere inches from parted lips, "...these little beauties could be poisonous."

Eyeing the remaining five treats: two each Boston creams and glazed crullers and one remaining chocolate glazed, she applied a cautious lick to the donut in hand, simultaneously sniffing as to possibly capture a questionable scent. Alas, such timid caution officially noted as the initial similarity between Jorgensen and herself.

"But then, there are definitely worse ways to go," she concluded before practically inhaling the cream-filled dessert in two ravenous bites.

Engulfing one of the Boston creams with equal fervor, she then took a large bite from a cruller before pausing to fill one of two tall glasses provided with vitamin D milk poured from a frost-coated glass jug. Chowing down on the remainder of the cruller, LeAnn smacked her lips noisily between chugs, her eyes occasionally rolling back in ecstasy.

The final two treats were soon finished off in good measure, washed down with three additional glasses of milk. Apparently spent from the feeding frenzy, the duration of which lasted less than four full minutes, LeAnn belched loudly before sauntering lazily over, kicking off the sandals and collapsing onto the centerpiece of the nearest sectional.

Leaning back, she frowned sourly while surveying the lodge interior a final time before shutting her eyes and allowing her multi-layered chin to dip. She drifted quickly away, a bubble of saliva collecting at the left corner of her mouth. Her head lolled about as if on a swivel, at once point completing two full circles before a spastic jerk of the neck initiated an abrupt reversal of rotation. The sudden intrusion of the voice had little effect save a mild batting of the eyes.

"Ugh, Miss? Excuse me? Helllll-ooooooo..."

LeAnn grunted in disapproval and resumed the impromptu power nap unabated.

"As much as it pains me to interrupt, I gotta point out you're hardly in need of any further downtime. Seriously Miss Garner, I'd think the previous forty-plus hours would've filled that particular quota for days to come."

Rolling over onto her left side, LeAnn lifted a leg and farted loudly in response.

"Damnnnn....now that's just plain rude. Probably don't give off a rosy scent neither. Miss Garner? Snap out of it now. We ain't got all day. Well, actually we do, though accordin' to the original in-processing itinerary, we're already a half-day in the red."

"In-process...bingo..." LeAnn croaked while using extended forefingers to massage the blur from each eye, "...just as I'd suspected. Worst fears realized. Par fudgin' course. You know, mystery man..." she continued, pushing herself upright with great effort before tying her shoulder length hair into a tight ball atop her scalp.

"...for a moment, possibly even two or three, this girl coveted the notion that perhaps...just perhaps...I'd been magically transported to a day spa for some much-needed R and R. You know...massage...facial...manicure...the works."

"Sorry to disappoint, Miss Garner, but then again, logical thinkin' would dictate such a far-fetched notion would indeed be one helluva stretch," the voice retorted in a shoulder-deep drawl, concluding the thought with a brief, comical snort.

Having peered upward as to pinpoint the voice's exact location, LeAnn quickly surrendered the effort, lame as it had been, as fruitless.

"Hey, can't blame a girl for dreaming."

"If you say so, Miss Garner. Enjoy the snacks, I take it?"

Checking her hands and fingers, apparently for leftover glaze or chocolate residue, LeAnn licked her lips and flashed a toothy smile that provided proof of both, the latter ingredient having stained several of her teeth a dark brown.

"An understatement of colossal magnitude, Colonel Sanders. Those juicy little jewels were nothing short of orgasmic."

She paused, raising her arms in mock surrender with the palms of each hand fully displayed.

"Um...pardon the rather crude southern stereotyped reference—totally uncalled for. My sincere apologies. Just a tad grumpy, you understand, from the whole...abduction thing. You'd think family would be treated with at least a microscopic twinge of respect."

With that, she dropped her head in and stared blankly at her own feet bare feet.

"Apology appreciated but not necessary. Um, you up for a little tour or do ya need an additional minute?"

Sighing wearily, she maintained her slumped pose.

"Is he here?"

"Ma'am?"

"My father...is he in...on site?"

"Miss Garner, at this time I ain't...that is, it ain't...well, let's just say I'm not at liberty to divulge any info outside set guidelines. Hope ya understand....it'd be my ass."

Following another resounding sigh, LeAnn flashed a tiny smile, forced as it may have been, and lifted herself from the couch wearing a pained scowl.

"No need to elaborate. The...your boss's penchant for dolling out unwarranted punishment is old news."

She slipped on the flip-flops without bending down to guide their way before regarding the high ceiling with a casual shrug.

"So...you mentioned a tour then?"

"Yes, ma'am, that I did. One thing: there is a bit of walking involved. You sure you're up to it? I mean, another five or ten minutes ain't gonna affect..."

She nodded impatiently, a lock of hair slipping loose from the curled bun atop her noggin to essentially cloak her left eye.

"No worries. I may resemble a major stroke victim waiting to happen, but I'm in better shape than I look."

The giggle that followed was laced in solemn resignation.

"Guess my standing upright proves that particular point. Okay then, mystery man with the confederate twang, point me onward to whatever grisly fate awaits."

Stepping toward the rear of the lodge, she closed to within an arm's reach of the panel door when it popped open with a low click.

"Be my pleasure, Miss Garner...just follow the path provided if ya please."

Stepping back, she gripped the oblong metal knob and gave it a gentle tug before taking the initial step inside. Moments later, the door reclosed with a sharp snap, soon to be followed by a relieved sigh that echoed throughout the lodge.

If nothing else, optimism could be found in the relatively event-free intro of houseguest number two. If only such tranquility could be counted on for the duration.

Two

The Purgatory Inn

Notes to the Boss (General Entry):

"Mr. Jorgensen, again may I remind you that I do not...*do not*, mind you, serve as the complaint board of this facility. My name is Darwin McClintock. My specialty is family practice med..."

"Yeah, yeah, I heard you the first three times. Tell you what...I'll agree to balk on the bitching rant only if you agree to cut to the chase as to exactly why I was bludgeoned, kidnapped, and doped up, not once but *fucking twice*...apparently so you can communicate to me via voice box how healthy I am? Riddle me *that*...riddle me fucking that!"

"There is no need for such blatant crudity, Mist..."

"And while you're at it, Doc-tor McKay...riddle me something else. Am I considered such a threat by your jerk-wad boss that he doesn't dare place an actual human body in the same room? First I get Johnny Fucking Reb barking at me from above, and now a *video* sawbones no less? I must be one very baaaaaad man indeed!"

A short pause ensued, wherein the overhead voice issued an irritated snort. Leaning forward from an unpadded high-back chair with each elbow propped atop what was essentially an oversized TV tray, Brian Jorgensen wore a stone mask of smoldering discontent while squinting directly into the garish projection. His hands, particularly the knuckles of each, were littered in assorted Band-Aids. He would sporadically curse under his breath while eyeing the bandages.

Constructed in the same circular style, the room appeared even more spacious than the lodge, though this was perhaps due to an overall lack of furnishings. Other than the TV tray and chair Jorgensen occupied, it resembled any standard physician's treatment room, complete with adjustable bed, digital scale, a portable blood-pressure monitor and a large rolling cabinet filled with assorted med supplies. The otherwise bland, beige-painted walls were spruced up somewhat by the sporadic, equally insipid painting, most of which showcased pastoral scenes. The thick carpeted floor, a somewhat foreboding dark red, was the lone paradox from the lodge's stony surface.

"McClintock, Mister Jorgensen...Darwin *McClintock*. As I've stated and restated, my dealing with you in your...stay here are solely medical in nature. I'm paid to evaluate, exam and advise in order to see you meet your goals."

Scooping up a glass pitcher of water from the center of the spindly tray, Jorgensen refilled the plastic mug provided before emptying its content in two lengthy swallows. Casually tossing the mug over his left shoulder, he again retrieved the half-filled pitcher and stared into its swirling mix as if entranced by the bright yellow reflection. In the fluorescent glow, his grim smile screamed dementia. Decked out in rubber-soled medical slippers and comically baggy, dark maroon sweats, upon waking he'd rolled up the sleeves to discover a small gauze bandage taped on the inside of his right elbow.

"My goals? Just what in the fuck are you talking about, Bud? Could someone...*anyone*... refrain for just two fucking seconds from talking in conundrums? Priceless...from Goober Pyle the greeter to Sigmund the Sawbones. You just can't make this shit up. What's with the cockney twang anyhow? They ship me all the way to Jolly ol' England? Didn't figure Hanley would deem me worth the freight cost."

"For your information, though it matters little, I do originally hail from Whitechapel, though I migrated to the US in my late teens."

"Whitechapel?" Jorgensen grinned devilishly. "Just my luck...a doctor from the hometown of Jack the fucking Ripper no less. Probably trained in the same med school."

The projection snickered before coughing into a curled palm in a failed attempt to mask the effect.

"The ripper being a man of medicine is mere speculation...urban legend, I believe you Yanks refer to it. Regardless, I don't see where th..."

"Don't take it personal, bud. Just yanking your chain to test the sensitivity waters, so to say."

Whirling about gracefully on his right heel, Jorgensen executed a flawless three-sixty spin. He regarded his surroundings with a sour smirk, gesturing wildly while slinging the pitcher about as if it were a fleshy attachment he was unable to shake free.

"Who the hell designed this place, doc, some NASA egghead turned crack addict? Feels like I'm locked inside a fucking Pringles can."

"I'm...um...not at all certa..."

Jorgensen cut off his non-present host with nothing more than a combination snarl/stare, the latter of which was delivered through a narrow squint.

"Now, for those answers, Darren....I'll ask nicely *just...this...once.*"

"It's Darwin, Mister Jor...um, regardless, the constant use of profanity is quite unnecessary. Your anger is woefully misplaced. I advise you save the brunt of your....building resentment of the situation for the next phase of in-processing."

Introduced as a full-sized image, the good doctor appeared strangely compressed, as if his outer aura had been somehow whittled away via a low-grade projection. Thin-faced, spindly of build and sporting a bushy, gray-tinted mustache and matching mop of curly bangs, he was practically being swallowed whole by a bulky lab coat. Furiously stabbing a forefinger into the hidden keyboard of a palm-sized digital device, he only occasional aimed his glance Jorgensen's way, peering through narrow-lensed bifocals that bloated his otherwise beady-brown eyes to mutant-bug proportions.

"Shove your advice. Don't think I don't know what's going down here," Jorgensen ranted, pacing the wide, circular space while cradling the pitcher to his chest, "this sadistic shit has Pete Hanley's prints smeared allllll over it. Soooo, what say we bypass all this role-playing horseshit and get his ass out here to spell it out in simp..."

"I must inform you, Mister Jorgensen," the projection interrupted sternly, tucking the device behind his back while simultaneously jutting his pointy jaw and pumping out his scrawny torso, "if you had simply cooperated at Phase One, Phase Two would have included a tour of the facility, during which time you could have expressed your displeasure *ad nauseam.* Unfortunately, the...forced sedation that ensued caused a...riff in the planned itinerary. Thus, this particular briefing...normally Phase Three...was pushed up a slot in order to give your body and mind the opportunity to properly reset. Now, if we could *please* proceed wit..."

The pitcher pierced the projection at chest level in a whitish blur, exploding into an army of wet, microscopic shards upon impact with the wall beyond.

"Where the fuck are you, Hanley?" Jorgensen shrieked, his face beet-red and his neck and forehead encased in pulsating veins. "Enough of this juvenile shit, old man! I'm not one of your fucking stooges. We both know what this is about. Let's settle it without the sideshow, what say?"

Doctor McClintock bowed his head, shaking it slowly from side to side. From a distance, he appeared every bit the stereotypical mad scientist pacing and pouting over a failed experiment.

"Mister Jorgensen, please...there are two, only two choices here. We can proceed as planned...or another regrettable postponement via sedation will commence. Either way, you'll wake up to find yourself at square one yet again. I can only give you a minute or so to decide."

Maintaining his combative pose for well past the doctor's sixty-second deadline, Jorgensen relented in gradual increments, his balled fists uncoiling coming as the final sign of resignation.

"Just say what you have to say, Bud," he mumbled, reaching down to reclaim the chair he'd kicked over during the initial tantrum, "obviously I can't do jack-shit to stop you. Whatever gets me some face time with Hanley the fastest, 'cause I'm pretty damn sure that's scribbled on your precious itinerary somewhere."

With obvious relief, the doctor brought forth the palm device and studied it with great intensity.

"Fine...good to hear...a wise choice I must say. You'll be relieved to hear this won't take very long, Mister Jorgensen. It's a summary really...a beginning stat sheet for comparison with future numbers."

Jorgensen shrugged wearily, perhaps drained from his previous rant.

"Stat sheet...yep...future comparisons...whatever you say...uh-huh."

Seemingly oblivious to the sarcasm, the doctor continued with renewed enthusiasm.

"Unfortunately, due to your...sedated condition, several elements of the physical had to be...to use the vernacular...scrapped. I was, however, able to gain an overall picture of health. I must say, Mister Jorgensen, you are indeed an amazing specimen in terms of overall fitness. Fact is, I felt compelled to retest your blood sample just to quench my own curiosity."

Leaning forward with his elbows propped atop his knees, Jorgensen balanced his chin on clenched fists.

"You hitting on me, doc?" he said with a smirk.

"Seriously, how does one reach such stratospheric heights of near perfect physicality?" McClintock asked, having either ignored or simply not heard the jabbing query.

"Yep, thought so," Jorgensen added with a wink, "you a closet butt-bobber?"

"First off, the exterior numbers...height is six-one...weight one-eighty-three. Measurements as follows: Chest...forty-four inches...waist is thirty-one..."

"Bet that isn't all you measured, right doc? Just itching to collect a sperm sample, I'd wager..."

"...body fat measurement is an amazing six-point two..."

Jorgensen muttered along while carefully pulling narrow strips of tape from his inner elbow, allowing the squared piece of gauze to fall away.

"...bet you even took the time to count my pubes..."

"...body marks are limited to normal mole distribution and a single tattoo on the upper left bicep. Numerous scars, to include fresh cuts and abrasions in and around the knuckles of both hands, each of which were cleaned of dried seepage and properly sanitized. Also scarring noted on each elbow and assorted other areas to include the left kneecap, lower right ribcage area and upper left shoulder, none of which are shocking considering your profession. I observed more recent bruising about the lower back, both forearms, and the back of the skull, no doubt...obtained during capture and transport."

Picking at the needle mark with a forefinger and thumb, Jorgensen winced between barely audible mumbles. Meanwhile, McClintock's voice cracked with excitement, as if reciting from some ancient, history-altering scroll, the hand which held the palm device noticeably trembling.

"...hope you at least kept those greedy mitts off my rear end and those skinny-ass fingers outta my poop shoot..."

"Now for the interior findings: equally impressive I must say, if not more so."

"I get the feeling you're about one more *impressive finding* from whacking off beneath that lab coat, doc."

"Total cholesterol level at one-thirty...LDL at seventy-five and HDL at fifty-five. Due to sedative state, blood pressure and pulse rate checks put on temporary hold. However, additional blood work proved normal. Prostate check ditto...as well as no signs of testicular cancer..."

"Pros...I knew...I fucking *knew* it!" Jorgensen bellowed, hopping up from the chair and surging directly toward the projected image, "I knew my asshole was puckering for a reason! Son of a bitch ass-bandit!"

He stopped just short in attempting to "chest bump" the representation, resembling an enraged baseball manager going chin-to-chin with a wholly disinterested ump.

"Mister Jorgensen, I assure you...a check of the lower extremities is par for the course...that is, a normal part of a complete physical. I was...as professional as necessary and as *gentle* as possible. Now, I'm going to need you to provide a pulse rate and blood-pressure reading. Please walk over to the BP station and place your arm inside the padded, circ..."

Jorgensen bristled, baring gritted teeth.

"Tell ya what, Bud, how about you crawl out of hiding and make me. As for your professionalism, if we were standing toe to toe about now, I can't promise how *gentle* I'd be removing your fucking spleen."

"Mister Jorgensen, correct me if I'm wrong..." McClintock replied, cocking a brow while crossing his arms defiantly, "...but normally aren't such expert practitioners of the martial arts legendary for their anger control?"

His predatory growl slowly fading, Jorgensen's taut stance melted into a weary slump.

Turning away with his head bowed in apparent defeat, he stepped over to the rolling cabinet and stretched his elbows across its heavy glass surface.

"Your...agitation is...understandable. Perhaps it's the effects of the multiple sedations," McClintock continued in a noticeably softer tone. "I'm apt to confess a bit of edginess myself these past few days, what with the anticipation of the challenges ahe..."

"Tell Hanley I'll play by his rules, asshole," Jorgensen announced while backing off a step as if sizing up the cabinet, "whatever warped shit he has in mind. But while you're at it..." he paused, shifting his left leg back with heel levitating several inches above surface, "tell him I plan on running up quite the bill along the way."

The leg shot forward in a reddish blur, the bagginess of the surrounding pant doing little to mar its destructive force as the heel of the slipper penetrated the thick glass panel with ease. An additional kick and forceful, double-palmed shove sent the colossal cabinet crashing against the wall in an explosion of glass, wood paneling, and assorted medical instruments.

Scooping up the TV tray by its squared top, he reared back and hurled, effectively decapitating the digital scale's bulbous top, which rolled to the center of the room like a dismembered skull with blackish wires hanging free like severed vertebra. Jorgensen then stepped back to survey the damage before strutting calmly back to his chair, flipping it around and sitting with its high back facing him. Despite the sudden flurry of exertion, his breathing didn't appear the least bit labored. He regarded the doctor's flickering image with a sarcastic wink.

In turn, the good doctor leered in disgust before retraining his focus onto the palm device, on which he poked madly with an extended forefinger.

"You're just making it more difficult than it has to be, Mister Jorgensen. Believe me, in time you'll look back and wish you'd shown more...restraint during this relatively peaceful transition."

"Call me stubborn," Jorgensen shrugged, "and that isn't liable to change no matter the duration of this aggravated kidnapping."

"Your decision, of course, unwise as it may be."

McClintock crossed his arms yet again, both his posture and soured expression spelling out his displeasure.

"Needless, the equipment you've destroyed will be repaired and/or replaced for future checks. Since you've bypassed step one in the itinerary, I'm not at liberty to state exactly when these will occur. I will have to insist that upon the next self-exam, in which you will be provided a detailed checklist with which to follow, that a BP and pulse rate is included. That said, the door to your left will grant access in the next few moments, Mister Jorgensen. Please follow the path to the next in-processing brief, which was, as stated earlier, originally slated to be first."

Jorgensen bowed his head and blew out an exasperated sigh.

"You mean you woke me up just to tell me what fantastic shape I'm in? Shit, why not just ask? By the way, doc, just who the hell serves as tailor in his joint?"

"Tailor? I don't quite compre..."

Reaching in with a curled thumb, Jorgensen tugged at the sweat's crinkled collar in order to display a seven to eight inch chasm.

"Appears they confused me with a pachyderm or a sideshow fat lady. Any chance for a refitting the next time you fuckers see fit to gas me?"

"I have no further answers for you, Mister Jorgensen," came the reply as the image noticeably faded, "good luck until next we meet...you're surely going to need it."

Jorgensen lifted both hands and flashed a double-barreled gesture of the obscene type just as the good doctor vanished from sight.

"Up yours, Bud...and the malpractice suit that undoubtedly brought you here to play mob doc. Either that, or that prick Hanley must've excavated some serious dirt. Regardless, McClintock..." he bellowed the final refrain through cupped hands "...I get the feeling you're as royally screwed as I am!"

Kicking the chair into a far corner, Jorgensen knelt and fell silent while keeping an eye parked on the handle-less panel door located several yards away. Two minutes passed. When it popped open with a faint hissing sound, he openly flinched. Stepping over on the balls of his feet with his left arm positioned to ward off an impending blow, he peered into the dark tunnel leading from the well-lit space and paused as if contemplating the distinct possibility of staying put.

Eventually he stepped inside a few feet and allowed his vision to adjust to the murkiness, blocking the opening with his left foot.

"Where have you brought me, old man?" he whispered, staring down the lengthy, circular tunnel lit solely by well-spaced emergency lighting. A split-second following the removal of his foot, the panel door shut behind him with a low click.

"If this *is* hell," he concluded, forced to hunker down to avoid scraping the tip of his scalp against the hard stone ceiling, "I've got a real strong hunch who's toting the pitchfork."

~ * ~

LeAnn sat stoically before the projected image, her hands crossed at her lap. Fresh beads of sweat coated her forehead, cheeks and upper lip even as her breathing seemed to be stabilizing upon entry to the bell-shaped room with its boarded-up staircase at the center—a staircase that looked to have penetrated the room like a drill-bit from either above or below. She sat facing a makeshift stage, complete with a slickly waxed oak podium. In the background sat the type of pull-up projector screen normally associated with grade-school classrooms. The chair she'd been afforded, the lone such luxury within the rounded space, was a high grade brown leather recliner that, despite its abundance of space, she'd found a tad restrictive.

The image had appeared within minutes of her arrival, developing in fragmented segments like scattered puzzle-pieces until full fruition was achieved. Once a voice emerged from its pulsating host, LeAnn's face instantly brightened as if she found its very presence strangely soothing—the familiar chimes of an old friend.

"Miss Garner? Now that ya got an eyeful...allow me to properly intro myself...Gabe Maxwell at your service."

Though she was unsure if the holograph was, in effect, '"actual size," LeAnn struggled to fight off a budding smirk at the very sight. If the 3-D image were in fact displaying factual size, Gabe Maxwell was the textbook definition of *short and stocky*. Dressed in a sleeveless black and gold Oakland Raiders tee and matching ball cap, bright yellow spandex shorts and high-top tennis shoes, to approximate he stood over five-feet six inches tall would indeed be generous. A tar-black, v-shaped goatee took up space from his lower lip to the edge of his chin, though his round face was cleanly shaven otherwise. His arms and legs, the former riddled with tattoos of the tribal variety, were bulky to the extreme, puffed to such grotesque proportions to appear weirdly *faux*. The thick-framed glasses he donned magnified his eyes to comically bloated magnitudes; the pulled-down cap causing his ears to jut out in Vulcan-esque style.

In attempting to gauge his age, LeAnn settled on the late thirties to early forties range, though one could have easily added five to seven additional years in either direction.

"Um, y-yeah...nice to, um, make your acquaintance, Mister Maxwell," she replied, visibly pinching her own outer thigh, possibly to refrain from laughing aloud as a sudden image of, let's say Mario Brothers, filled her minds-eye.

"Same here, ma'am. Hope the tour wasn't too much of a strain. I figure it came as quite the shocker."

LeAnn shrugged, a single droplet of perspiration dangling from the edge of her nose like a translucent wart.

"Perhaps if it were anyone but the *boss*, yes. As it is, the shock value is quite minimal. Still, have to confess this whole set-up is pretty out there...even for him."

For a single blink, Maxwell's image appeared locked in freeze-frame, his left brow permanently arched in bewilderment. It then shook loose with a pulsating surge, having instantly repositioned his pose to that of "the thinker" with his chin balanced atop a clenched fist.

"Hoo-kay...um....anyhow, allow me to apologize for your staleness of the tour guide. Recorded well in advance, ya understand, without a sliver of input from yours truly. Truth be told, I'd rather sit through seventy-three straight hours of the Golf Channel than listen to that damn robotic monotone blather go through the motions."

"No sweat. Believe me, I was in *no* danger whatsoever of nodding off," she replied wearily, wiping her forehead with an open palm before transferring the buildup onto her thigh. "Can't say the same about my circulation," she continued with a pained scowl, "any chance I can get a change of wardrobe? Even my ears are starting to go numb in this junior-sized jumpsuit."

Breaking eye contact, Maxwell stared down at his own feet like a hem-hawing, ultra-embarrassed grade-schooler.

"Um, we'll...um, discuss that situation right soon. Um, anyhow, before we get to the main gist, that bein' why *exactly* we're here to begin with, I feel it only fair ya know a few things about me."

LeAnn nodded silently, appearing gleefully entranced by the muscular little man's numerous hand gestures—a frenzied, never-ending assortment of hand-clasps, fingertip taps and heart-shaped folds.

"Though I've served in many capacities over the years, job-wise I mean, currently I'm employed as, for want of a better job title, a personal trainer *slash* motivator. Through the years I served in the U.S. military...did some amateur boxing...professional wrestler...strip-club bouncer...all of which led me to your father's employ as a...well, *bone-cruncher* of sorts. Ain't that proud to confess to the latter, but hey, a man does what he has to do with a wife and kids to feed, right? Well, more like a wife, kids, and one *helluva* gambling Jones."

Clearly mesmerized by the crystal-clear clarity of the 3-D effect, LeAnn no doubt craved to reach out and snatch the man's stubby, constantly dancing fingers just to cease their incessant gyrating.

"In your particular case, it appears my trainin' methods are in for one humdinger of a test...but then, *mucho* more on that later. After all, we'll be spendin' a crap-load of time together and I'm sure you're just chompin' at the bit for details, am I right?"

"Wh-where are you from, Maxwell?" she heard herself mumble, "Not to be rude, but the boss rarely hires anybody from farther south than maybe *south* Boston. You sound...well, kinda rube-ish. Again, nothing personal, I just know the boss and his, well, standards."

"First off, Miss Garner," he answered, parking his hands atop his hips, "call me Gabe. Formalities just get in the way of plain talk, I always say. As for my origins, they saw first light in Tupelo, Mississippi. Oh, by the way...just so we're on the same page, who exactly is this...*boss* you keep referrin' to?"

"Oh, sorry...that'd be my father...um...*Mister* Hanley to you, I'm sure."

Maxwell nodded knowingly.

"Oh, yeah…okay…got'cha. In retrospect, that makes perfect sense."

She returned the nod.

"Yes indeed it does."

Folding his short, bulky arms across an equally buff chest, the Maxwell image stepped behind the podium and centered himself behind its squared torso as if prepping a speech to the masses.

"Goes without sayin' I'd bet you're a might curious as to the point of all this."

LeAnn merely rolled her eyes and nodded again.

"It was Mister…the boss's decision…um, opinion, that you needed a, well, intervention."

She remained mum, though cracking a tiny smile in apparent bemusement.

"The many previous rehabs…how many were there total again?"

"He didn't provide this information?" she asked with just a vague twinge of irritability.

Maxwell paused while reaching up to adjust his cap. Afterwards, his ears appeared less bent, less jutted.

"I think he mentioned three or maybe four occasions over the past several years."

LeAnn held up all but the thumb of her right hand.

"Four in the past six years, to be exact. You need details or did he at least provide crib notes?"

She was quickly waved off.

"Nope. Believe I can recall the gist. The first in upstate New Hamp for alcohol: a few years later for pain killers at Betty Ford: the third about a year later for a serious crack Jones at some prestigious Long Island clinic, and last but not least for a nose candy overdose…believe the facility was located somewhere near Dallas-Fort Worth."

Struggling to lean forward, LeAnn regarded the projection through narrow slits, her lower lip trembling slightly as she spoke.

"I knew it. Jesus wept. Fine...didn't exactly take a brain surgeon to figure out the who behind my sudden relocation. All that's left is the whys and wheres...I take it this is where the hired stooge portion of your duties come into play," she paused, seemingly for effect, devious grin fully intact, "sorry in advance, but I've always been a call 'em as I see 'em kinda gal."

Maxwell cleared his throat and adjusted the cap again.

"Um, call me Gabe. As for the wheres...full details are forthcomin'. The whys...well, this is kinda touchy...exactly why Mister Han....the bo...your father brought me in to, um, oversee things. Ya see, I've kinda semi-retired from breakin' knee-caps. This was your fa...the boss's way to repay my past service. A welcome career-change, I gotta confess. Beats the hell outta designin' concrete shoes, if ya grasp my meanin'."

His lame attempt at humor apparently falling flat, Maxwell cleared his throat and resumed.

"Miss Garner, you do realize your father's deep concerns for your welfare? For your...health?"

She squirmed with the chair's padded armrests so tight they appeared positively form-fitted.

"Yeah, he's a real softy where his little girl's involved," she answered, her words practically dripping sarcasm.

In turn, Maxwell's façade of politeness briefly lifted, perhaps revealing the pit-bullish enforcer within.

"I've heard 'im speak of you, sister. I read his tone easy enough. There was sorrow, sadness, sincere regret. Those other efforts to...see you healed failed for a reason, he figured—failed because of a lack of proper motivation."

LeAnn leaned up with great effort, her brow creased in a sudden curiosity.

"Well then, fair enough. So what's different this time around? Tell me, what's the big push to steer me in the right direction?"

"Why, the simplest in motivation techniques, really. Elementary in its stone-cold logic," he replied with a wink.

Following a short pause, LeAnn groaned while gesturing with open palms.

"Yes, well? What is it this time? What's the golden egg of grand prizes if I pass muster in his beady little eyes? What possibly can one girl do to impress the likes of such an all-powerful deity?"

"Like I said, sister, it's simplicity at its finest..." Maxwell shot back sternly, all previous good humor having melted away—replaced by the hard, cold stare of a confessed professional in the art of inflicting pain.

"...after all, ain't nothin' known to man can fuel the inner fire like the threat of, well, extinction."

"Extinc..." LeAnn blurted, the word choking off in light of an involuntary swallow, followed by a fit of wild cackling that quickly morphed into a hacking cough.

"Ya see, Missy, this here particular session of rehab don't include the option of failure. That there word's been permanently scratched off the checklist."

He side-stepped out from behind the podium, took a step directly toward her and knelt until they were perfectly eye level. To LeAnn, he no longer appeared the least bit comical. He was no longer Gabby Maxwell, muscle-bound clown for hire with the comically exaggerated southern drawl. He was pure predator. A merciless bone-cracker completely without conscience.

"Therein lies the simple part, Miss Garner, as in do *what* you're told to do on the schedule that's been mapped out. Do what you *need* to do...what you *have* to do...that is, to avoid, at *all* costs, that last remainin' option."

"Which is precisely?" LeAnn frowned, leaning forward aggressively, her voice cracking with emotion.

Bowing his head silently, Maxwell's drawn out pause might well have been solely dramatic effect—ditto the gradual rise of his eyes and overall effect of the concluding stare in true Kubrick-sneer fashion. If so, it served the desired effect, as

LeAnn openly flinched, temporarily forgetting the visual scare was being provided via transplanted image.

"Missy, being that we're speakin' of *your* father, ain't that a might obvious?"

"Is...is that..." she swallowed hard, "...is that a threat?"

Nary a crack having emerged in either his crouched pose or intimidating glare, Maxwell lifted a hand and exposed a bare palm.

"Not at all, fat girl...that be a promise."

Long after the Maxwell image had faded from sight without further comment or movement, LeAnn remained frozen in place, tucked into the chair's deep padding with a low clicking sound escaping the back of her throat.

~ * ~

He'd stepped into the glass elevator with obvious apprehension, standing at its gaped threshold for several moments as if hypnotized by the diamond-shaped light which pulsated in bright yellow from its tube-shaped interior. Glancing downward between splayed feet, Jorgensen took note of the crystal-clear shaft below, the front side of which scaled a spherical structure of unknown origin while the opposite end appeared within reaching distance of an equally orbicular red brick barrier running perpendicular.

"Just like one of those damn pneumatic tube carriers," he muttered grimly, forced to roll up the ultra-baggy sleeves of his assigned sweats for at least the tenth time since departing the medical briefing.

Descent must be initiated by verbal order, Mister Jorgensen...please descend to level one...your current location is level twenty-two.

Repeat: descent must be initiated by verbal order, Mister Jorgensen...please descend to level one...your current location is level twenty-two.

Repeat: descent must be ini...

In the end, he might well have heeded the request just to cease the droning voice, the redundancy of its mechanical, emotionless tone akin to an old vinyl disc cursed with a hopelessly stuck needle.

"Just *go* damn it...but keep it under the posted limit, understand?"

Back-peddling, Jorgenson planted his shoulder blades to the rear glass and fell into a slight crouch, as if prepping for bone-jarring G-forces associated with the sudden drop from a great height. Instead, he hardly felt the initial surge, sliding downward without even the slightest tilt, jar, or jerk—the lone clue of descent being the gradual passing of the cone-like structure outside its crystal-clear barrier.

Upon reaching open walkways for each separate level, the elevator would pause just long enough for a brief audio description of each. Scanning the flat glass ceiling, Jorgensen spotted the half-dollar sized speaker poised at its center.

Floor twenty-one, patient services, contains the medical lab and office.

Floor twenty contains security office—closed and no longer active.

Floor nineteen contains sleeping quarters...as does floor eighteen.

From there, the elevator picked up speed and ceased the sporadic pauses.

Floors seventeen through seven are closed off, unfurnished condos.

"Condos?" Jorgensen croaked aloud, "Condos for whom, for shit's sake? A race of mole-people?"

Floor six contains the kitchen and dining hall.

Floor five contains the gymnasium and pool.

Floor four contains the theater and lounge.

Floor three contains stored supplies.

Floors two and one are dedicated to the main generator and HVAC units, pumps and septic, respectively.

Point of order: these particular floors will be sealed off following scheduled tours, as residents will not be required to service or monitor the equipment found inside.

The elevator eased to a stop just long enough for Jorgenson to read a bolted metallic sign which read 'Maintenance Personnel Only' in dark black lettering over a shiny blue background.

Throwing his arms up in disgust, Jorgensen's lower jaw dropped in exaggerated shock.

"Service or mon...well...shit, Hanley...and I was so looking forward to playing janitor. Waitaminnit..." he paused, creasing his brow in genuine concern, "...what...other residents are we referring to?"

Moving on...the schedule allows for a brief walk-through of your living quarters on floor eighteen.

Point of order: in case of elevator malfunction, a spiral-design staircase has been constructed at the center of the cylinder.

The crate then ascended equally smoothly, though Jorgensen still felt compelled to err on the side of caution by striking a wide stance with his back pinned tightly to the glass.

"You're one obtuse ass-crack, Hanley. Just won't allow for a straight fucking answer. Well, since I got no choice but play along...play along I will."

Please exit, Mr. Jorgensen...your living quarters are straight ahead...

Pushing away from the back wall as the doors separated with a faint whirr, Jorgensen paused at the threshold to turn back, peer upward and address the tiny speaker as if it doubled as a spy-cam.

"If you have any nasty surprises for me in there, Hanley, I hope you at least have the balls to witness the outcome first-hand."

He took a timid first step, standing half-in, half-out, before freezing in mid-stride.

"Power-mad bastards just have to play their games, right? Put us peons in our proper place."

Practically hopping into the waiting tunnel, he whirled about, perhaps in anticipation of seeing the elevator doors closing behind him before shooting upward at warp speed. Instead, the doors stood agape and the boxy transport's position unchanged.

Jorgensen then trudged onward, forced again to crouch down slightly or risk a potential scalping from the circular tunnel's stony ceiling. Unlike the previous stroll within similar confines, the duration of this particular jaunt was mercifully short. Less than a dozen steps saw him exit into an empty, triangle-shaped foyer painted, peculiarly, in bright orange. Just ahead stood a red panel door with the word 'HIS' stenciled in tar-black lettering across the center of its otherwise smooth, featureless surface. So well-lit was the foyer in comparison to the adjoining tunnel that Jorgensen was forced into a series of rapid blinks in order to adjust.

Please approach the entrance, Mister Jorgensen ...entry is contingent upon its detection of our presence within two feet of the threshold.

Upon first hearing the familiar monotone blare out within such cramped quarters, Jorgensen openly flinched, briefly collapsing to one knee and assuming a blocking pose with his forearms crossed across his face.

"Oh you miserable fu..." he grunted while reassuming a standing position, "...hilarious....some real rib-cracking, knee-slapping shit, Hanley. Go on, get your jollies. No doubt you consider *whatever* hell I'm put through fully justified."

Regarding the door and its single word pronouncement, Jorgensen stood his ground with hands on hips and flaunted a toothy grin.

"So I take it there's a 'hers' represented nearby? Either way, here's hoping I'm not sacking out near a community toilet."

A single step more and the door slid noiselessly to the left.

"Uh-huh...I'm supposed to buy this as sincere? Not...a...chance. Just a cruel joke...another in a series of practical gags old man Hanley cooked up to drive me bat-shit," he announced a few moments later while standing at the center of the oval-shaped chamber, the back of his calves rubbing against a brown leather sectional couch that ran the length of the room. To his front hung an enormous flat-screen plasma that took up the majority of the front wall. Underneath to the left sat a twin-cabinet entertainment center complete with Force-brand stereo system (tall, slender and encased in crystal) and Sharp blu-ray player.

Mr. Jorgensen, you are provided a total of two-hundred-seventeen digital channels to choose from, to include thirty-seven movie channels, six separate twenty-four hour news channels, four twenty-four hour sports channels, and three channels geared toward mature adult themes.

"Sure, sure...cut the crap, Hanley...nice show but I'm not buy..." Jorgensen moaned, just as, as if on cue, the television screen ignited with a low blipping sound, soon to reveal the grim visage of a vaguely familiar newsman chattering on about the assorted tragedies of the day. The volume remained muted even as the channels began to flip in chronological order, remaining in place for only a few seconds before moving on in timed succession.

"Well, I'll be damned," he muttered, stepping up to run a forefinger across the stereo's glossy squared edges, "and I suppose this baby here comes with an infinite supply of tunes from whatever genre I so choose. Gimme a fucking bre..."

The stereo is equipped with unlimited access to XM radio.

Even as the TV faded abruptly to black, a silky Jazz tune filled the space, the clarity of the musical waves utterly flawless.

As for the computer, it is internet ready with an average connection speed of five-point-eight Mbps. There have, however, been certain adjustments to your user rights. Certain restrictions will apply, as in, yours will be of the 'read only' type usage, meaning no incoming or outgoing communication, emails or use of message boards. Log-in information will be provided at the conclusion of the in-processing phase.

Sure enough, in the far right corner of the room sat a mobile upright desk and mid-back mesh chair, the former adorned with a wide screen Dell monitor and connecting tower.

Side-stepping the couch, Jorgensen kneeled cautiously into the tar-black chair as if expecting it to reveal itself as nothing more than a cardboard cutout and fold beneath his weight.

"I don't...I just don't get...*any* of this shit," he whispered, reaching over and retrieving the keyboard from its pull-out stand beneath the monitor. The monitor instantly came to life in blue screen, providing separate spaces in the lower right for applicable log-in and password codes. "Why would he...why are you providing all these luxuries, Hanley?"

He leaned back and gestured with flailing arms toward the TV and stereo and back again to the computer set-up. "How does all *this* fit in to your dastardly plan?"

Please reenter the elevator, Mister Jorgensen. The final segment of your in-processing will soon commence on floor three.

Jorgensen peered upward as if to personally respond to the tiny metallic speaker wedged in the popcorn-textured ceiling almost directly overhead, his lips briefly parting before clamping shut yet again. Sighing wearily, he rose from the chair with a bone-weary sigh.

Upon re-entering the waiting transport, Jorgensen resumed his previous pose by leaning his back to the rear glass. As the smooth, gradual descend commenced, he rolled up the sleeves of the baggy sweats to just below the elbow for the umpteenth time.

Your destination, Mister Jorgenson, is the theater for final in-brief. This will be followed by a mid-day meal in the dining hall.

"Well, hot shit. A flick followed by grub in the compound, huh?" Jorgensen retorted with a wry smile. "Yes sir-ree, sounding more and more like forced incarceration. Guess I'm fortunate to still be in possession of both my kidneys."

Suddenly remembering the involuntary draw of blood from the second reawakening, he reached down and rolled the ill-fitting shirt to chest level, apparently not at all surprised but *relieved* nonetheless at the absence of a dressed wound in or around either side of his ribcage.

A renewed spring in his step, he practically danced from the elevator to stand before a set of knob-less double-doors with the word 'Theater' stenciled in black lettering on the right and 'Lounge' on the left.

Please step forward, Mister Jorgensen... entry is contingent upon its detection of our presence within two feet of the threshold.

"I get the idea already...*shit*," Jorgensen griped, walking forward and pausing to allow the doors to separate with a familiar whish.

A few steps into the dimly lit space, he paused upon visualizing the shadowy figure sitting motionless in a far corner.

~ * ~

"You may relax, Miss Garner, while I...to use the vernacular you Yanks find so amusing...divvy up the stats."

Plopping down onto the narrow chair, LeAnn peered down blandly at the gauze wrapped snugly around her inner-right elbow. Her eyes still drooped from the effects of the self-administered laughing gas, from which a hazy dream sequence had brought forth a shadowy figure perched over her inebriated frame—followed by a sharp stinging sensation, like the prolonged effects of a nasty cut or bug bite. She awoke sprawled atop a well-padded examination table with the aforementioned dressing in place, thus providing an answer to the mysterious sting. Soon after, she was introduced to Doctor McClintock and told to follow the instructions left on a nearby serving tray. Once up and mobile, she'd retrieved said list, a single sheet of laminated bond paper, and proceeded to the blood pressure *slash* pulse reader. From behind a squared partition, she'd been provided a small plastic cup with screw-on top to deposit a urine sample, which was then left, per checklist guidelines, atop a large glass cabinet stocked with assorted medical supplies. Lastly, she'd stepped up on a digital scale and held the required thirty-second pose for an accurate reading.

"So tell me the truth, doctor," she asked off-handedly, the forced lightness of her tone tinged with a healthy dose of sincere trepidation, "are the Marines really *this* hard up for recruits?"

"My apologies for the cloaking of information, Miss Garner," the doctor replied while still pecking diligently on some unseen electronic device cradled in his right palm, "I'm afraid divulging such information as to the whys and wherefores of the situation is simply out of my range of knowledge. In other words, my dear..." he paused, peeking over the top edges of the thick-framed glasses hanging from the edge of his nose, "...since I am deemed by my employer as not having a 'need to know,' I have little choice but feign ignorance."

Tilting her head quizzically to one side, LeAnn crinkled her own proboscis as if detecting a particularly sour odor.

"Or to simplify, you don't know squat, but even if you did, you aren't telling."

Back to stabbing the device with an extended forefinger, the doctor nodded.

"Precisely."

While LeAnn busied herself in attempting to loosen the shirt collar that had, no doubt, been perpetually strangling her, her hologram physician cleared his throat as if prepping for a lengthy speech.

"All right, Miss Garner, I have your chart sufficiently filled in with all the pertinent data. Allow me a few moments to educate."

With that, LeAnn regarded the pulsating image with a worrisome glance, gnawing her lower lip nervously.

"Not to worry," he consoled through a tight smile she secretly found as unnerving as the Brit accent that seemed to fade in and out depending on the syllable, "this is hardly testable material. It's more for future reference."

"Fine, I...guess," she replied calmly enough, her round face shiny with a fresh coating of perspiration.

"I'm afraid it's news of mostly the negative type, Miss Garner. As concerns go, first off there is the frightening issue of your blood pressure."

"Subtracting the obvious stress factor..."

"It's still quite horrendous..."

"Even coming off sedation?"

"Normally this would *lower* the readings, Miss Garner..."

"Oh yeah. Not so in my case, huh?"

"More than likely, yes...wherein the frightening part emerges."

McClintock's image paced a tight circle while focusing solely on the tiny, black-shelled device, straggling from its set path only once, wherein a large portion of his left side was briefly swallowed by a section of wall.

"Of the two readings taken, roughly two minutes apart, the second was slightly more encouraging, though I must emphasize *only slightly*, as in...initial read: one-ninety over one-twenty, second...one-eighty-five over one-hundred. As for the blood work, I'm afraid the results are equally...discouraging."

Her eyes darting wildly, LeAnn's ritual of frenzied fidgeting continued with the incessant drumming of fingertips atop the chair arms and the spastic jig executed by each slipper-covered foot.

"Your cholesterol reading is, to put it mildly, bending the needle toward impending catastrophe. I...truly, Miss Garner, I'd define your very presence, upright, breathing and relatively active, as nothing short of a medical miracle. Obviously your relatively young age plays a part. Still, I'd say there is already a great risk of early stage heart disease and, at the very least, the potential onset of diabetes."

He paused, temporarily placing both hands at the small of his back and thus tucking away the device as well.

"Well, don't hold back now," LeAnn spat disingenuously, "give it to me straight already...how long do I have?"

With that, he turned his back to her while repositioning his hands to the front. Briefly covering her mouth with a cupped palm, LeAnn seemed to take an amusing note of the man's bird-thin legs and bowlegged stance.

"Your sarcasm in the light of such news speaks loudly to your apparent disinterest in your own welfare, young lady."

"Hey," she replied flippantly with the casual wave of a hand, "you're the one doling out the death sentence diagnosis. Exactly how would you have me react? Perhaps a rebel-yell hoot while I cartwheel across the room?"

"Hardly, Miss Garner...at your current listed weight of..." he paused to study the device again, "...two-hundred eighty-seven pounds, you'd be risking serious injury...not to mention liability for potential property damage."

Obviously perplexed, LeAnn's forehead creased dramatically.

"Property dam...?"

The projection pointed to the ceramic flooring.

"Structural."

"Smart ass, Brit," she sneered, "the bo... did my father hire you specifically for your talent to ridicule?"

"Not quite. Now, back to your vitals..."

LeAnn shrugged, sinking as far into the cramped confines of the undersized seating as her bulk would allow.

"By all means…let the belittlement continue in earnest."

"This isn't about belittlement, Miss Garner. It's about knowing where one stands at the starting point of a great race."

"Say huh?"

"Fear not, you'll receive the full gist in the next and final in-processing step. Now, to continue." He shifted focus back to the device, the thick-framed glasses appearing on the very cusp of slipping off the tip of his nose. "Your height was measured at five-feet two and a half…weight the aforementioned two-hundred eighty-seven pounds. Just a note here: for a woman of your height, the desired weight falls between one-eighteen and one-twenty-six pounds. This is, of course, dependent on body type. Your BMI…that is, your Body Mass Index, currently stands at forty-nine point seven…far exceeding the desired average of twenty to thirty-two. Again, I must stress the risk involved, the stress to your heart and oth…"

"Hey! Jackass!" LeAnn roared, her voice instantly hoarse with the effort as she pushed herself upright from the chair's squared fold. "Why not spew forth some of that vernacular you find so amusing, huh?"

"I don't…under…" McClintock mumbled, his left brow appropriately cocked.

"Just call it as you truly see it, okay? No need for the medical tap dance."

"Miss Garner, if you'd just elaborate…"

"Forget all the stats, measurements and *desired this* and *desired that.*"

"I'm afraid I'm not comprehend…"

Standing with the toes of each foot pointing slightly inward, she used one extended forefinger to slap the other, as one would do while verbalizing a numbered countdown, or spelling out separate points with great fervor.

"No strain. Allow me to assist. In pointing out the long, short and humongous details of my sadly overdue bill of health, simply jot down the one you find more appropriate in describing yours truly: how about…gothopotamus? Obeast? Heifer? Chancita? Oinker? Gut-Zilla? House of Cheese? Believe you me, I've heard 'em all."

McClintock held up a hand, palms out as if to ward off a pending flurry of blows.

"Miss Garner, this isn't about insults, as you will soon discov…"

"…then there's the blubber twins, *gut* and *butt*. These of course, are close relatives to the bubble twins of the same surname. How about roly-poly? Or perhaps the ultra-crude but still popular moldy-oldie, hippo-pussy-mas? I myself favor the recent urban-slang additions…wanna test drive a few…*dozen*?"

"Enough, Miss Garner. As I've stated, this isn't about degradation. We are…I am here to register a beginning…a starting point. This will…I promise…make sense upon completing the final phase of in-processing. Now please, allow me to conclude my findings so you may move forward to said phase."

Simultaneously defeated and deflated, LeAnn's lips clamped shut as her hands fell to her sides.

"Fine then. Let's continue playing scold the fat chick. Nice to see father's penchant for ridicule and debasement remains fully intact."

"It's not merely the dangers of your obese condition, but the numerous substances detected from the blood draw. I…the lab ran came back with only slight traces, true, but it was the…varied assortment that raises eyebrows."

Retaking her seat within the chair's severely creased seat, LeAnn's bland expression and slumped posture screamed indifference.

"In no particular order, we have the following representatives both legal and otherwise: Hydrocodone, Oxycodone, Propoxyphene, Fentanyl, and to top it all off, pardon the vernacular yet again, but this does qualify as 'on oldie but a goodie' for you Yanks...a fairly high dose of cannabis. For good measure, pardon the pun, there also existed just a faint trace of alcohol."

Upon concluding, the physician's projection removed his glasses and nibbled the earpiece like an unlit stogie while regarding LeAnn with unbridled bemusement.

"I must say, Miss Garner, quite the *painkiller cocktail* you have swimming around in those puffy veins of yours."

"So? I have...had a *varied assortment* of pains. What of it?" she replied meekly, pausing briefly before leaning up wearing an angry scowl, her tone equally agitated and cranked up several decibels, "Waitaminnit...puffy veins? Listen, you uppity snot, just because you're on his slimy payroll doesn't give you the same mock and scorn rights as dear old dad, *got it*?"

Re-donning the bulky-framed specs, McClintock executed a slight bow.

"My apologies, my dear. Such baseless cruelty is indeed...beneath me."

"Wow..." LeAnn blurted disdainfully with a roll of the eyes, "...doctor, you really need to work on the technical aspects of saying I'm sorry. It's generally a good thing not to make it sound as if the victim owes *you* their regrets."

"Please, Miss Garner, back to the test results."

LeAnn shrugged, having attempted in vain to cross her legs but finding the skin-tight sweat pants far too constrictive.

"I like to party. That's no secret. Just ask the boss. Surely he filled you in on my past discretions."

"Yes, indeed he did, but I'd...he'd been told you'd...curtailed...those specific habits. In fact, he was under the impression your dramatic weight gain over the past year or so was due to a...scaling back on the ingestion of such harmful chemicals."

"Well, wasn't that just a tad short-sighted?" she asked with raised brows. "I mean, the boss should know better than anybody that one can easily manage to have their cake and eat it too, so to speak."

With that, McClintock cleared his throat and tucked the device into an interior pocket of his ivory smock.

"Regardless, Miss Garner, this sad finding is liable to make things...even more difficult than originally thought. Alas, only time will tell. I thank you for your cooperation. You may exit the panel to your immediate left upon my departure. I trust you will soon have any and all questions answered."

"I'll drink to that," LeAnn answered curtly just as McClintock's image began a gradual fade.

"Farewell for now, Miss Garner, and good luck," she heard the voice echo as the hologram mutated to a spattering of circular, electronic dots before vanishing altogether.

She sat in the deafening silence, staring unblinking into the utter blankness of the light-green shaded wall that had, moments before, served as background matte for an entity whose very existence she surely began to doubt almost immediately upon its absence.

"Colossally weird, Dad, even for you," she mumbled with a bent smile just as the aforementioned panel door popped open as if lightly shoved from the outside. "Thing is, I've got a sinking feeling I ain't seen nothing yet."

Three

Opposite Goals

Notes to the Boss (General Entry):
   "A fellow inmate, I presume?"
   "Safe bet. You don't...look familiar. That is, the face doesn't ring a bell."
   "Ditto. Should it?"
   "I guess not. The boss goes through hired hands like busboys at the Corner Bistro."
   "By the boss you mean...Hanley?"
   "Who else? You here for movie-time?"
   "Appears so. 'Bout damn time the old fucker explains himself, ugh, pardon the fractured French."
   "No strain. I'm familiar with the word."
   "Yeah, well, ugh, I guess you're the *her*?"
   "Yep, and you be the *his*. Bizarre little resort they have here, right?"

"That it is...but then, when a fuc...ugh, a guy like Hanley has unlimited funds, the sky's the limit."

"Or the cave, at least in this case."

The theater room's surprisingly roomy interior was fittingly dim, though illuminated just enough for the well-adjusted eye to properly survey its content. A new smell, like that of a recently purchased auto, permeated the cool air within. With a dozen high-back recliners to choose from, all broken down into four rows of three, LeAnn had gone front row to the extreme right, within touching distance of the nearby wall. Upon reaching a brief respite in their initial verbal volley, Jorgenson side-stepped between the third and fourth rows and anchored down in the middle chair.

"Wonder if we're it?" he finally blurted, clearly overdoing it and coming off woefully insincere in the process. Going by reputation, he could probably care less if a troupe of boy scouts waltzed in to fill the remaining ten spots, much less the reason behind the fat chick's presence.

"Hard to say. The boss is nothing if not unpredictable," she answered flatly, refocused on the dark, flowing curtain at the front of the room. A curtain that, hanging within the surrounding gloom, could've been either dark brown or velvet maroon.

Upon first glance, LeAnn might've naturally assumed the stranger unkempt and thuggish in appearance, though as moments passed and he'd taken his seat, several shades of murkiness had faded to offer a better visual. Facing front to better cloak her interest, she might even have decided a rugged handsomeness existed, even with the addition of the horrendously baggy sweats. She tugged at her own collar, a red outline already present at her neckline from the constant friction. Wincing from the persistent discomfort, one could safely assume she pondered if their intended wardrobes had been accidentally switched upon arrival.

"Some pad, huh?" she spat, possibly for no other reason than to pierce the maddening silence.

"Some wild shit all right..." he replied, pausing to clear his throat, "...like canned Spam shoved in a rabbit hole. Makes me wonder where we are, I mean, still U.S. soil or maybe some third world shithole a thousand miles from nowhere. Knowing Hanley, I kinda tilt toward the latter."

"You see the tunnel physician, that is, you get your physical and pre-brief yet?"

Scratching a build-up of stubble at the tip of his chin, Jorgenson snorted.

"Oh yeah, and how about that cast of characters? Beam me the fuck up, Scotty. Oh, you have the displeasure of jawing with Foghorn Leghorn?"

LeAnn giggled despite herself, pinching a knot in her outer right thigh in order to refrain from guffawing aloud, an action she possibly feared might trigger a laughing jag she might not be able to control if it got its head.

"A real charmer, that one. Hologram or not, little psycho gave me the willies."

"Yeah, well...I'd take him over ol' doc Mengele any day."

Another brief bout of awkward silence ensued, the low hum of flowing air through unseen vents providing the lone dent. His vision presumably well-adjusted to the gloom, Jorgenson appeared to take note of the woman's extreme girth and no doubt felt an instant twinge of disgust. For a man who made his living from staying so remarkably fit, it would be an understatement to assume this was the single pet peeve he not only couldn't comprehend but also not tolerate: that being the lazy, bloated masses that made up a large majority of modern society. No matter the excuse, be it health issues or the ever-popular 'inherited glandular condition,' men of Jorgensen's ilk simply could not understand how anyone could attain, much less *maintain*, such a pathetic condition. Simply put, they despised what he referred to as the slob majority—despised their laziness—despised their inability to push away from the table—despised their doughy looks, labored huffs and multiple chins. It took equal effort, he'd presumably rant and preach, in terms of sloth and gluttony, to stay *out* of shape as it did to transform one's body into a slim, trim specimen of physicality. Fatties were, in such men's considerably biased opinions, justifiable targets for ridicule and loathing. In the case of this new, morbidly obese acquaintance, it was obvious her unflattering, skin-tight wardrobe did little to alter the perception. Then again, he had to figure the scuba gear had been no less her idea than the circus tent he had been forced to don had been his.

"You, ugh, land here of your own free will or someone el…" he asked boldly only to be cut off by a dull humming as the curtain peeled gradually apart at the center to reveal a wide ivory screen.

Almost immediately upon its reveal, the screen flashed to life in nova-like fashion, initiating a series of rapid blinks from both temporarily blinded viewers.

"Wowza. Let there be light," LeAnn grumbled through a tight squint.

The man's face didn't as much fade into view as explode there, a colossal head and shoulders shot that that filled the eight by ten foot screen in 3D-like grandeur.

"Greetings Brian….LeAnn," his voice boomed, the words not quite matching the speaker's lips as if badly dubbed.

Reactions to both the speaker's appearance and identity were similar, though expressed by each respective witness in both verbal and non-verbal terms.

"Well hello there, you ugly fucker," Brian Jorgensen whispered harshly, reaching up to clamp the chair back in front of him in a twin vise.

As for LeAnn Garner, she merely rolled her eyes, nodding knowingly and chewed into her lower lip.

"I know...I know...you both feign shock as to why you've been...displaced so." The man paused, leaning in to the camera with the back of one hand tucked to the corner of his mouth, "Feign...that means *fake* to you, Brian. From here on out, I'll attempt to dumb-down the vocabulary for your sake. This particular project is over-budget enough without me having to hire a translator," he concluded, dropping the hand and leaning back.

"Eat shit, old man," Jorgensen grumbled, the knuckles of each hand snow-white from the pressure applied.

Decked out in his trademark black suit, popularly referred to by associates and rivals alike as *undertaker duds*, Peter Hanley's cleanly shaven face was chiseled in deep furrows, the most prominent of which ran the length of each jawline like a river path's viewed from afar. His thick, full hair was tinged in gray and combed back to reveal a forehead creased in similarly defined lifelines. Thin-lipped and of full jowl, he peered into the camera with deep-set, dark blue eyes and blackish brows two shades darker than his coif. If one were to guess his age from facial features alone, the range could have swung dramatically by a decade on either side of fifty.

"Ah, it's a real shame that, since this is a pre-recorded message, I'm unable to hear what is sure to be a typical Brian Jorgensen response...full of filth and bile. As for my little *party girl*, I'm of the belief she'll remain silent and introspective as my little speech commences. She never was big on feedback, no matter how I ranted or raved."

"Party girl?" Jorgensen whispered to himself, staring over at LeAnn with wide-eyed curiosity.

In turn, as predicted, she refrained from any obvious response—resting a tilted head against a propped fist as if already overcome with boredom.

"Now, down to brass tacks. At this point, you've both been processed and given the ten-cent tour. I gave the staff strict instructions not to divulge my reasons for bringing you here. By 'here,' you should know that the facility you now inhabit is, or *was*, a former government missile silo located in, well, let's just say it is located within the borders of the United States. It was originally purchased and rebuilt, four years-plus in the making, with an underground resort in mind. A resort for those financially fortunate individuals with the means to invest in a nuclear fallout shelter that would include individual condos, a full kitchen, a theater, well, you get the idea.

"An obvious point here, but it needs to be vocalized nonetheless—to attempt escape is pure folly. Though the odds are truly slim and none, even if you did manage to reach ground level, the lobby is encased in unbreakable glass, as Mister Jorgensen can fully attest to.

"Also, abandon all hopes of outside intervention, law enforcement related or otherwise. Sadly, the two of you being plucked from society won't cause even the tiniest of ripples. LeAnn, every so-called friend you have is, in truth, no more than an acquaintance. Disposable one and all. A few might question your absence from the party scene, but not nearly enough to kick-start any potential investigation. I would think such drunken or stoned individuals hardly blink a bleary, bloodshot eye when one of their kind vanishes."

Pausing to retrieve a glass of water, pulled from off-screen, Peter Hanley took a lengthy sip before motioning to some unseen entity.

"More ice, please, and pop the top on a fresh bottle, will you? Nothing worse than stale purified water," he said sternly before handing the glass back off-screen, "Now, where was I?"

"Yeah, same old horse's ass," Jorgensen snarled, finally releasing the chair-back with partially numb fingers.

"As far as Mister Jorgensen's missing status goes, I'm assured nary a single inquiry will arise, unless one of many jilted exes he's squired and screwed-over through the years, pardon the crudeness, questions his absence only because she cannot track him down in order to extract a measure of revenge. Not to fear, Brian old boy, your martial arts studio will be unexpectedly closed for several weeks, only to reopen with a new staff of instructors. Bad management, I believe they will claim, was your downfall as you'd packed up and departed the back room of the studio that had also served as your permanent residence. As I understand, you'd distanced yourself from family years ago. Tsk, tsk, the lonely life of a gigolo."

"Eat shit, you smarmy bastard," Jorgensen hissed in rebuttal, temporarily lowering his eyes to the carpeted floor.

Hanley reached off-camera and nodded before retrieving a frosty mug. He enjoyed a lengthy sip before resuming.

"Now, just to generate a broader picture of what I humorously refer to as The Purgatory Inn to all potential clients, you entered through what was originally the control room. An eighteen foot tunnel led you to the missile room, where of course the Titan or Minuteman has been replaced by a full kitchen and dining hall, medical facility, one-bedroom condos with full bath, a full gym with indoor pool, and of course the generator and septic floor. The blueprint is, as seen..."

Hanley appeared to lean back just as a detailed blueprint filled the screen, clearly outlining the facility in shades of bright blue, yellow and green, with each floor individually labeled in black lettering.

"As you can imagine," he narrated dryly, "this was no simple undertaking, nor did the finished product come cheap. I do, in the near future, hope to make up the difference in condo rentals. With the constant political unrest sweeping the globe, I foresee no problem in terms of profit outweighing investment. If nothing else, I do have the peace of mind in knowing that several of the condos are reserved for immediate family."

To that, LeAnn snorted indifferently, though when Jorgensen had turned to gauge her expression, he'd likely been both surprised and disappointed to find it completely unchanged.

"I had originally intended to record separate briefings," Hanley continued, his stony visage having returned to dominate the screen, "but then, why bother? It isn't as if the lone two inmates within a cell block, albeit a very large cell block, aren't going to share some secrets, yes? So, with that in mind, I'll begin with the individual whose fate I admittedly care the least about. Oh, that's Mister Brian Jorgensen to you, Miss Garner."

Again, Jorgensen glanced LeAnn's way, but the favor was not returned. Her head was still tilted in his direction and her face cloaked in a blanket of dark, flowing hair. Shifting back to Hanley, he scowled as if dumbstruck by her bland, emotionless pose in the face of their abductor.

"Knowing your taste in men is...has been somewhat erratic over the years, I'm not really sure how you'll find Brian. You may, initially at least, find his macho manliness a plus, though I doubt his innate crudeness will pass muster. He is, and loves to proclaim *ad nauseam*, a fourth degree black belt in the Korean martial art Tae Kwon Do. Legendary on the Southside as the...now let me say this correctly as not to shatter his brittle ego...the 'instructor to the mob.' Over the past five or six years, his tiny school grew infamous as the place to go to add a martial arts flavor to everyday organized crime muscle. Always a big believer in boxing myself, just an old school pugilist at heart, I'm afraid. But then, I can alter my thinking with the times. When a few of my subordinates insisted on learning the ancient art, I was told there was no better teacher than Brian Jorgensen. Things went swimmingly, for a time. That is, until a...treasured member of my immediate family decided to partake in some, well, personal lessons."

Peter Hanley paused, his jaw muscles flexing and a thick vein at the left side of his neck growing increasingly prominent. He appeared, ever so briefly, to focus his steely stare direction Jorgensen's way.

"Know this, Miss Garner: the man my dear Cynthia referred to so lovingly as 'Jorgy' on countless text messages is renowned as quite the ladies' man. Yes indeed, just ask his two past wives or the countless mistresses he's managed to accumulate in a relatively short lifespan. Just ask my Cindy, who, as it turns out, was less interested in pursuing arts as martial *debauchery*. From what I understand, she earned multiple black belts in the ancient art of adultery. Of course, Brain would be a better judge of her, ahem, performance. Shame on me for thinking a woman twenty years my junior wouldn't yearn to stray now and again with one closer to her own age...and equal *lack* of morals. Regardless, it's merely water under the proverbial bridge. Cynthia has since been...expunged from the family. As for Brian here, well, there is a matter of blatant disrespect for another man's possessions."

Pulling a slim cigar from his suit's front pocket, Hanley tucked it between gritted teeth and lit the end with a match struck on a nearby paperweight that appeared carved from granite.

"I laid that out to say this: the die is now cast. In thinking up a suitable punishment for Brian Jorgensen, he of the multiple black belts and bloated ego, he of the chilled, reptilian blood who openly bragged of his many female conquests to include those possessing wedding rings, well, let's just say it wasn't overtly difficult in figuring what exactly would, let's just say, *hit* such a man where he lives. You see, Brian, men such as you are all about vanity, a self-loving man-crush that is most severely damaged when their manner of living is altered—their self-indulgent habits halted in their tracks. From what I gather, you had taken up temporary residence in the back of a combination saloon/billiard hall in order to avoid my reach. Tsk tsk, really? The legendary *man with the lightning fists*? A man who, I'd been told, feared no one? Ahh, say it ain't so, *Jorgy*."

Sucking greedily from the cigar's moistened end, Hanley paused to exhale a trio of perfectly circular smoke rings. His bright blue eyes practically sparkled with glee.

"As you've been informed, the Purgatory possesses an entire floor dedicated to physical fitness, thus there is indeed the opportunity for Brian to freely indulge in the first of his most treasured passions—his perfect, precious physique. For reasons I will soon spell out, however, I'd advise he prepare to fight said indulgence with every fiber of his rotted soul.

"As for that other vice..." he grinned devilishly, a fresh cloud of cigar smoke briefly forming a blackish halo over his wavy do, "...well, there's always LeAnn to woo, though I highly doubt you're her, um, type. In fact, I predict a *severe* personality conflict, not to mention drastically different goals, will derail any potential romance."

Hanley shrugged, the miniature stogie protruding from the left corner of his mouth like a leafy tentacle.

"Just an opinion, you understand. I could be wrong."

LeAnn's unexpected reply came via a loud, piggish snort. She then turned briefly toward Jorgensen, who openly strained to make out her expression amid the surrounding shadows consistently bathing the majority of her face.

"A born instigator is dear old Dad," he thought he heard her mumble, though the final few words were relegated to barely audible gibberish as Hanley had commenced his pre-recorded spiel.

"Da-...dad?" he muttered, alternating a series of comically befuddled glances from the screen to LeAnn, who had already turned to face front and thus completely cloaked her visage in dimness again.

Meanwhile, Peter Hanley paused to peer off-screen as thin tendrils of smoke leaked from both nostrils. Once his gaze refocused on the camera eye, the earlier sparkle had been replaced by a steely dullness. His tone had noticeably altered as well, from gleefully sarcastic to balefully grim.

"As for my sweet, dear LeAnn, always the blackest of sheep—no small feat considering stiff competition within the family, the constant stream of self-inflicted ills were, I'll confess, due to my own woeful lack of parenting. Well, Judy and myself, actually. I'm not about to shoulder all the blame. The alcohol and drug abuse from your early teens, the petty thefts that were little more than an embarrassment at the time, mere 'B' crimes birthed from boredom. A false sense of entitlement. Oldest cliché in the book, really. Bored rich kid with too much time on her hands and no real friends, at least, none other than those that kept you company as long as you were providing the party favors."

Perched on the very edge of the well-padded seat with both arms hanging loosely over the chair back, Jorgensen listened intently to Hanley's rambling tale while visibly focusing on the woman he'd clearly hinted was his own flesh and blood.

"How many jobs, LeAnn? How many opportunities were you handed and in turn tossed away with your carelessness and indifference? Try as I might, I'm unable to successfully tally the total or accompanying reasons for failure. By the time Judith and I divorced, you'd been enrolled in at least four colleges, the duration of stay on said campuses shorter with each subsequent enrollment. Truly, if they awarded degrees in inebriant behavior, you'd surely have earned multiple PhD's by now."

At this point, as Hanley paused for a lengthy draw from the cigar, eventually spewing forth the trapped cargo from both nostrils which temporarily cloaked the majority of his face in a blackish fog, LeAnn had taken the opportunity to talk back to the screen.

"What'd you expect, Father? Like you ever...really...cared other than how my...behavior marred your precious reputation," she barked sarcastically, her entire frame slumped into the seat as if gradually mutating into its cushiony folds to eventually meld together as a single flesh and cloth entity, "it was more about shipping me off every other month just to be rid of me."

Hanley's dialogue had resumed, his voice growing increasingly weary, as if he'd covered the same ground countless times—a one-hit wonder's nightmare of being doomed to bark out the same tune for all of eternity.

"The job history, if I may be so foolish to refer to it, well, there was no keeping up with the failed attempts save a bi-monthly checklist or spreadsheet. Perhaps I'd have been wise to employ some kind of troubleshooting specialist. Perhaps a team of such, utilizing pie-charts and psychological theory to determine a cause, and miracle of miracles, produce a cure. Perhaps a pill could've been developed ...a 'work ethic' pill ingested once or twice daily."

He sighed heavily, mashing the remains of the stogie in a glass ashtray, the top edge of which could just be seen taking up space to his left.

"It's sad how, at the end, I was so hesitant to force your services onto long-time trusted subordinates, especially once your...unreliability had become something of legend. I still recall the condescending tone of the human resources people as they swallowed their pride, one after the other, stating how happy they were to take you on....how privileged...how *honored* they were to have the opportunity to work side by side with the daughter of the Chairman of the Board. There was tardiness, various episodes of dereliction and insubordination, and of course the many reports of on-the-job drunkenness, or drug-induced hazes.

"Time after time, position after position, most of which you were sadly under-qualified to hold, you never failed to embarrass my good name, or to be completely fair, your mother's as well."

Jorgensen kept his eyes peeled on LeAnn, whose entire frame appeared to be trembling with either a building anger or crippling sadness.

"You...I was never given a fair chance at any of those places," he heard her sob, "and...and they were all...afraid of challenging me in fear of possible retribution."

"....was the last straw..." Hanley rambled on, jabbing each temple with the tips of a forefinger as if attempting to massage away a growing migraine, "...when I found out...my own...when the embezzlement charges came to light, I held out faint hopes it was just some...an honest mistake...a bookkeeping error. That is, until you seemingly vanished from the face of the earth with over one hundred sixteen thousand dollars of the company's money. There was no defending this disappearing act as anything but proof of guilt. Still, I did my fatherly duty, egged on by your mother's grave concern for your welfare. We'd both noted your pale looks and sudden weight gain just before your disappearance. Judith...she feared some underlying physical ailment had spurred your behavior and subsequent runaway. She had me hire a team of private eyes, all with past law enforcement ties and thus unlimited resources, to track you down and see you safely returned to the family bosom. Well..." he sighed deeply again, staring into the camera eye with a look that defined haggard—as if literally aging a decade in the ten-plus minutes since first appearing onscreen, "...so here we sit some eight months later, give or take a day or two since I've recorded this. From what I gather, the stolen money's long spent and you've packed on an extra layer or two, obviously of your own volition.

"Imagine my surprise to be told you'd been discovered passed out not in some halfway house for crack addicts but one of the East Coast family abodes."

To this, LeAnn did not openly reply, having sunk so low in her seat that her face was completely hidden from Jorgensen, who was practically leaning over into the row facing him.

"You must realize this isn't about the money, Lee," Hanley continued grimly, staring down at the backs of his own hands, "it's about a new type of intervention. Admittedly, an intervention of extremes, but one both myself and your mother deemed necessary. Please keep that firmly in mind. Your mother...Judith did, albeit begrudgingly, approve of these measures."

Once Hanley paused, apparently struggling to resume while watching the fingers of both his hands dance and fidget about the tabletop as if controlled by some unseen marionette, Jorgensen leapt from his seat with a shaking fist raised to the screen.

"Spit 'em out already, you fucking blowhard!"

Sneaking a glance LeAnn's way, he noted no change in her wilted pose.

"Son of bitch just adores the sound of his own pipes!"

Stepping out from between the rows onto the narrow walkway to his left, Jorgensen leaned a shoulder against the slick drywall and spat angrily onto the carpeted floor just as Hanley regained his voice.

"For you, LeAnn, the bar for success has been set quite high, and purposely so, as I,...as *we* deemed it no less than a life or death scenario. The choice to succeed or fail is, as is always the case when the issuance of such a...personal challenge, lies exclusively within yourself. The ground rules are as follows..."

Jorgensen temporarily dropped his veil of rage upon detecting movement from his right, where he saw the woman lean her considerable bulk forward, the fingertips of her left hand poised at her lips as she began to chew and gnaw.

Meanwhile, the man pegged within his own lengthy chat as her father seemed to actually stare her down directly, as if magically knowing both which side of the room and exact seat his offspring had chosen.

"...I've...I was informed that during the medical examination phase your weight was measured at exactly two-hundred eighty-seven pounds. Being that the last time I...the last time we saw you and my...our concerns for your weight had first seriously bloomed, I doubt the scales read more than two-hundred. I...the health implications are such that I...that we..."

Hanley paused yet again, his bottom lip trembling. He stared down at his hands before resuming with a combination sneer/snarl, his voice crackling with a hybrid mix of anger and desperation.

"....despite a myriad of personal issues, to include the aforementioned addictions to pain killers and alcohol, it appears obvious your main vice is now...over consumption. Thus to you, my dear Lee, an ultimatum: tip the scales at exactly one hundred twenty-four pounds, the desired weight for a female of your height, body type and age, within the next one hundred eighty days. Before you attempt the math, not your strong point if I recall, that is a drop of exactly one hundred sixty-three pounds."

Jorgensen's own, reasonably loud snort was easily drowned out by a trio of raucous belly-laughs which reverberated from the opposite side of the room.

"One hun....why not just have your hired medical man saw me off at the thighs?" he heard LeAnn whimper hysterically, her arms flailing about as if warding off a pesky gathering of flies.

Yet again, Hanley had briefly paused his own preaching to allow for hers. Once his latest reboot ensued, it was delivered in a more atypical monotone almost completely void of emotion.

"You will be far from alone in this quest, from personal trainer to hired chief, every available opportunity has, once again, been afforded to allow for your success. As for your motivation, the eventual loss of your own life long before the age of, let's just throw out the ballpark figure of forty, would surely be motivation enough. Alas, blind as you've been to this point of the potential dangers, there is this then..."

He raised a loosely clenched fist, the ring finger showcasing a thick-banded gold ring, the fingers of which were extended one at a time to coincide with the individual points made.

"One: the...your old monthly allowance...a rather modest sum your mother and I had hoped would force you to successfully hold down at least a part-time position, will triple. Call it a cost of...*living* raise."

The man flashed a shaky, pathetic smile.

"Two: stock in several companies will be issued in your name. Stocks that will safely ensure your financial future.

"Three, and in my admittedly prejudiced point of view, easily the most vital: you will be re-embraced by your family, both immediate and extended, without question and with the past effectively deleted, much like a pesky computer virus."

"And if she can't hack it, asshole?" Jorgensen shouted to the screen, oblivious to the stern, angry stare directed his way from across the room. "What's the alternative, a head shot, execution style? They gonna find her floating in a river with shattered kneecaps? I mean, those are your *preferred* methods in dealing with what you perceive as failure, right?"

Again, Hanley's slight pause seemed purposeful as to allow such an outburst. As for LeAnn, she managed to remain mute, biting her lower lip while refocusing on her father's dour visage.

"If you are not successful in this quest, Lee, if you are even a mere ounce over the desired weight...you will be...essentially expunged from the family. There will be no contact allowed even within the extended family. There will be protective orders drawn up if need be. You will be left penniless and on your own to deal... with those aforementioned demons."

Hanley's pained grimace transformed his already well-grooved expression into a virtual roadmap of fleshy crinkles.

"And yes, since I know what you're probably thinking, your mother did indeed sign off on this part of the deal also. For the record, there was great trepidation involved. There was anger, there was indecisiveness, but finally there was the cold hard truth that it *had* to be done."

"Expunge...but I was told...it was hinted very strongly by Max...y-your own employee that the...punishment for f-failure w-would..." LeAnn stuttered, standing with arms out and palms up.

Before she could ramble to a conclusion, her father seemingly read her mind.

"As for the rather vicious rumor of a more...fatal sentence, I will admit with no *small* amount of guilt, it was briefly...considered. Let's just say your dear, sweet mother vetoed the...such an abominable idea quickly and with extreme prejudice I too realized, over time, how...blatantly cruel the mere consideration and it...shames me deeply to confess it was ever on the board to begin with."

LeAnn's lone response, as Hanley brought a clenched fist to his lips and cleared his throat noisily, was a single, whispered moan that trailed off into an even softer, barely audible sob. She'd collapsed back into the chair, her enormous arms hanging loosely over the sides.

"As for Mr. Jorgensen..." Hanley resumed with a mischievous sneer, staring directly into the camera through narrow slits, "...the required goal is of the polar opposite variety. It took but a brief mulling over and the jotting down of the details involved. After all, your...kind and complexities rarely mix."

"Sanctimonious prick," Jorgensen grumbled, lifting his hands and regarding the colossal image with twin middle fingers.

"Knowing the infinite heights of such vanity, such a bloated ego, the possibilities were, I must confess, quite enjoyable to consider.

At the reported one hundred eighty-one pounds of chiseled perfection, it came to me that doubling that total would make for quite the challenge..."

Jorgensen threw his head back and howled, "...oh, dream right the fuck on, Jerk-off..."

Stone-faced, Hanley concluded.

"...So, let's make it official then. Mister Brian Jorgensen, you have exactly six months, starting yesterday, to increase your body weight to three-hundred sixty-two pounds." As had become the norm, Hanley fell conveniently silent, appearing to lean back as to allow the expected rant.

"The fuck you say, " Jorgensen blurted, striding purposely toward the screen with his arms crossed defiantly, "well, I got a few stats for you, pal, knowing damn well you can hear me barking back at your sadistic ass! Number *one*: even if I had the crazed inclination to go along with this sicker-than-fuck head game, it is not...is *NOT*, Sherlock, even remotely possible to double one's body weight in such a short span of time, not without blowing an artery, clogging same beyond repair or coughing up chunks of liver. Number *two*: you got a better chance of chocolate-covered gerbils flying outta your asshole than forcing *me* to gain a single ounce.

"Leading me to this third and final point: you might as well quit wasting your time and mine and send in the clowns with the heavy artillery, old man, 'cause neither of those first two stand a snowball's chance of transpiring."

"Failure, Mister Jorgensen..." Hanley retorted almost immediately upon the completion of Jorgensen's anger-driven rave, "...is *not* an option in your case. There is not, as opposed to my daughter, an *out* clause in place. Men who choose to sleep with another man's wife do not qualify for mercy... nor pity. Call me...stubborn that way. I can forgive many things in men... weakness, cowardice, dependency."

Sporting a deep frown, Hanley's gruff tone eased somewhat, whether by choice or simple fatigue.

"What I refuse to forgive or refuse to tolerate, is a man who willfully seduces another man's wife, knowing full well the potential consequences but who, in essence, seems to actually enjoy or thrive on ignoring same. From what I gather of your own failed marriages, failed due to your own blatant adultery, this is far from unusual behavior on your part. On the contrary, you seemed to have adopted the practice of fornicating with promised women as somewhat of a sick hobby.

"Lord, I do tend to ramble so before passing a sentence."

To that, Jorgensen muttered sourly, "First ounce of truth from that lying pie-hole yet."

"It's elementary really: reach the set goal in the set time allowed and you walk...well...*waddle* away from your stay at the Purgatory a heck of a lot stouter but with a working pulse. You will then be awarded travel fare to the destination of your choice and a small amount of cash. Fail to meet said goal and you will never again enjoy the light of day. See there?" Hanley concluded with a playful shrug of his rounded shoulders, "simplicity at its finest."

Crouching to one knee, Jorgensen parked his chin atop a clenched fist and viewed his adversary with a surprisingly wistful expression.

"Remarkable. It seems sweet Sandy wasn't just yanking my chain about you after all, Hanley," he exclaimed gleefully, "you do somehow manage to mix evil *and* boring."

"So then," Hanley resumed with a toothy grin and sharp slap of bare palms, "that just about covers it. I apologize if I got a bit long-winded. I've been told it's one of my least-appealing traits. As I've previously stated, the staff is at your beck and call. Though you will never meet them face-to-face, the services they've been hired to provide are more than adequate in aiding you both in meeting your goals...if you so wish. If either of you does decide to resign from participation, well, such regrettable judgment will not serve to alter your sentence here at the Purgatory. You'll do your time regardless, so why not choose to spend said time wisely? As in...going for the gold, or 'goal' might be more appropriate.

"To you, Lee, child of my loins, I wish only the best of luck. I am..." he paused, displaying crossed fingers on both upturned hands, "...sincerely in your corner ...rooting so, so damned hard for you, as I *always* have.

"It may seem hard to fathom now, but I...your mother and I truly saw no other way. As for Mister Jorgensen, well, I could lie, but why bother?"

Hanley twisted his head about just a few notches from right to left, as to pinpoint Jorgensen's position through a searing, unblinking gaze of unbridled disdain. The featured grin was nothing short of predatory.

"I truly couldn't care less if you give in, give up or *give it all you've got* in reaching the set goal. Given your rather seedy reputation and penchant for breaking rules, I'd be less than shocked than to enter the Silo six months from yesterday to find you'd gained nary a pound, having remained in tip-top fighting shape merely out of spite. I am, however, admittedly curious to see which trail on which you choose to tread. Men with your level of vanity do, after all, love thyself above all else. Question is, does such blatant self-adoration include a healthy dose of self-preservation...and at what price? As I confessed..." he concluded with a dramatic ringing of the hands, "...I cannot help but ponder, with grand trepidation, the eventual outcome."

Standing directly beneath and centering the wide screen, Jorgensen raised both hands in a 'come hither' gesture.

"Did I hear you say you're gonna personally check our status on day one-eight-one, chump? Well, I'll just have to buck up and tough it out then, won't I? 'cause I'm not about to miss out on *that* potential face-to-face."

Just as Hanley appeared prepped for his concluding statement, Jorgensen turned from the screen and fired a final volley.

"Old man, you don't have the balls...not without a roomful of well-strapped muscle covering your ass at every angle."

Hanley's own parting shot, his expression having regressed back to full Golem mode...stoic, stone-faced, emotionally void, was equally cold and mechanical, as if legally contracted to recite the words.

"Again, LeAnn my dear, you have my heartfelt prayers. Mister Jorgensen, though I hold you in utter contempt, I am of the belief that all men, lowlife scum included, do indeed deserve a second chance."

The screen did not fade slowly, but instead blackened as if the victim of a sudden power outage, the waking silence pierced by two distinct sounds, that of a subtle female sob and the Neanderthal-like grunts of the represented male.

Moments later, prompted by a stale, robotic voice that was becoming all-too-familiar, both the male and female were herded from the theater room to a waiting elevator.

Their first stop was floor twenty for an official introduction to the facility dining hall, as well as the final member of the staff.

Miss Jeannie has prepared separate meals for each of you, the voice retorted blandly, a low static accompanying each word, *it is, of course, up to you to adhere to the specialized diets she offers.*

As they exited onto the stone walkway and edged forward toward a single, glass-stained entrance marked at the center with the word 'EATS' in black lettering, it was easy to imagine LeAnn Garner and Brian Jorgensen secretly sharing a similarly chilling vibe—the gist of which could be summed up in two simple words that neither might claim as having experienced in vast qualities throughout their still relatively young, stress-free lives....*dread* and *fear*.

Four

Rituals

Part One: *Notes to the Boss, (reported verbatim)*
Narrator: *Doctor Darwin McClintock*

Initially, I must confess to finding Brian Jorgensen to be nothing short of the walking cliché Peter Hanley had so eloquently described as an egotistical cad whose bloated sense of self-worth saw no limits. His attitude and actions those first few weeks provided no reason to alter the impression. He was equal parts sour, mean-spirited and totally uncooperative, not to mention destructive...look no further than a roomful of damaged medical equipment.

No doubt out of spite, he barely nibbled at the vast offering of ultra-fattening dishes served via Miss Jeannie's magical hands, seemingly going to great lengths to avoid cleaning a single plate other than a salad bowl or a glass filled with anything save chilled ice-water. He visited the gymnasium floor twice daily; early morning weight and cardiovascular training usually lasting around two hours and an hour-plus in the afternoon completing countless laps around the indoor pool. Many was the night he'd conclude his trifecta of insubordination-fueled workouts with an Olympian-like display of speed push-ups, followed by a half-hour or more of assorted marital arts kicks and jabs.

In yet another example of insolence, he'd apparently decided to forego bathing or personal hygiene in general, normally sitting up to all hours staring at the big screen or surfing the internet, the latter normally resulting in masturbation via whatever porn site caught his fancy.

It wasn't until a week had passed, his building body odor apparently self-offending to the extreme that he began to shower again at least semi-regularly. Either that or he eventually came to the realization that holographic images had no sense of smell to offend.

There was a time, around day fourteen or so of witnessing this daily ritual of self-grandiose, that I'd written him off as a suicidal twit unwilling to part ways with his colossal ego in order to save his own skin. He was, of course, lectured daily by all members of the staff in the foolishness of his ways. He was advised, as days melted so randomly away, that he needed to buckle down and get with the program pronto, as it would take weeks or maybe even months for both his body and mind to accept the Spanish Inquisition-type torture such a dramatic change in diet and lifestyle could incur. To this he either scoffed, cursed, or utterly ignored. As far as contact with his fellow inmate, he appeared to make a point of avoiding her company. Stat: in just over a two week span, that's roughly three hundred thirty-six hours of sharing space, albeit a rather large, sectioned off space, LeAnn and Brian were spotted together a mere trio of times, the longest stretch being an awkward fourteen and a half minutes inside the gymnasium as he'd been finishing up his cardio workout and she'd hopped atop one of two available treadmills to begin her own. As with the other two meetings, both of those within the dining hall, the two had done little but nod in passing, the lone spoken word a mumbled '*hey*' courtesy of LeAnn as she'd finished up a dinner meal consisting of a small salad (romaine lettuce, carrots, spinach leaves), half a red delicious apple and two bottles of water, rising to depart just as Brian had entered for a cup of coffee.

Our first few sessions in the newly re-equipped med lab were predictably testy. He went through the motions uneventfully enough, but became purposely obtuse upon being questioned on a slight but continual pattern of weight loss since his arrival. Although he refrained from cursing me or taking out his frustration on inanimate objects, his perpetual sneer and occasional glare spoke volumes.

It was around day fifteen that the transformation began—not a gradual, slow-burn change but staggeringly abrupt, as in alien-abduction-like. Brian had just concluded his afternoon swim, the last few laps noticeably sluggish when compared to his usual all-out blitz of a performance. There, hunched at the side of the pool with his feet and calves still submerged, Brian appeared dazed, slack-jawed and staring blankly into the swaying waters. Following several moments of utter stillness, in which he hardly appeared to breathe, his upper body visibly tensed. He sighed once, twice, a third time just before his face collapsed into splayed fingers.

At the time of this unexpected clutching, I shrugged it off to fatigue...perhaps a wave of exhaustion born from building stress. It wasn't until the man's upper back and arms began to shake and convulse, faint and barely noticeable at first but with increased fervor, that I realized a complete breakdown had ensued. As far as duration of said event, perhaps no more than a full minute...in terms of shock value it may as well have lasted hours.

Shoving himself upright, Brian hopped from the pool's edge as if escaping shark-infested waters. He then stood with his hands on his hips, his shapely frame so chiseled as to bring to mind statues of the ancient Roman Olympians. The pose remained unchanged, as if he were mentally debating his next move, though I'd have to confess that upon viewing first-hand his eventual answer to said enigma, one couldn't help but ponder the alternatives being considered. Both hands shot toward his face in a blur even as his stance widened. I cannot provide an accurate count of just how many blows connected. Suffice to say Brian Jorgensen's slap-happy self-mutilation must've had the desired effect in his own mind, as it was followed by a casual walk-away that was as serenely executed as its prelude had been brutal, a barrage of open-palmed chops that had seen his head whipped violently from side to side in a continuous motion.

In the aftermath, as he'd exited the pool room with a noticeably wobbly gait, his cheeks were visibly swollen and glowed red. Still, for however warped such self-abuse might seem to all but himself, Brian Jorgensen had apparently experienced an epiphany of major proportions, as starting that very afternoon in the dining hall, the change at hand was equally dramatic.

~ * ~

In stark contrast, LeAnn Garner had embraced the challenge almost from minute one, her theater-room tantrum serving as the lone spark of dissention. It seemed she'd extracted all the demons of denial and rage and almost immediately set her mind to the task at hand. For someone reputed for terminal laziness and addiction, this early display of determination was, at the very least, admirable. I'd heard many a tale concerning the colossal divide between father and daughter—the classic confrontation between immoveable force and the irresistible object—a lifelong dispute wherein father's iron fist was repeatedly deflected by the offspring's shield of stubbornness and rebellion. All things considered, it was hardly a reach to believe LeAnn's staunch dedication was more directly related to 'showing up the old man' than the potential financial rewards. Regardless, the grit she displayed right out of the gate was nothing short of awe-inspiring. Proof of her dedication was short in coming, clearly substantiated upon that first session in the med lab, wherein in five days' time she'd dropped nine and three-quarter pounds. At that point, I'd felt it my duty to temper her enthusiasm over the accomplishment with hard, cold fact. Water weight, I preached, was the easiest to lose and thus fell away rapidly. The more difficult cycle would soon begin, and would test her will and inner toughness like never before. The weight could return, I reminded, as effortlessly as it had been voided. Still, despite my stern warnings, she remained visibly upbeat, actually clapping her hands at several intervals while hopping on and off the digital scale like an over-caffeinated hare. Her skin tight sweats still emphasized every flabby roll, particularly at her midsection and lower back, her entire frame jiggling and gyrating in tubby waves of past overindulgences as she danced about.

As for the source of that initial loss, it was hardly mysterious. LeAnn would begin each day at precisely 5 a.m. with a trek to the dining hall for a bowl of freshly cut fruit (she seemed to favor honeydew melons, kiwi and Gala apples) and a steaming cup of green tea. Next stop, with energy bar and two bottles of purified water in hand, came the gymnasium. Though comically feeble at first, her workouts gained in intensity by the day, from less than fifteen minutes spent on the treadmill per session to a full hour and a half on the eve of week three; from huffing and puffing as if on the verge of a massive coronary from mere minutes of exertion to multi-hour workouts from which she hardly seemed winded. Amazing how quickly the human body can adapt, as if once awakened, long-dormant muscles, tendons and bone cherish the opportunity for rejuvenation.

Once the initial expected soreness had passed, aided by long soaks in the hot tub, LeAnn's production increased by leaps and bounds as days progressed. Meals were sparse in amount but high in protein: steamed brown rice, baked chicken, lean ground beef, wheat pasta and an assortment of frozen and fresh vegetables, all served with her lone drink of choice other than morning tea...chilled, bottled water, which she drank at the rate of six to eight sixteen ounce bottles a day. Night activities were limited to TV viewing and the occasional trek to the worldwide web, though around mid-week of week two she discovered the facility library and from there, a new love emerged. All this, and she never made the first move toward the theater floor—in particular the adjoining lounge across from said film room, where full cantors of whiskey, gin, tequila and vodka sat in murkiness, awaiting a thirsty suitor from which she had easily been the most obvious prospect between the two facility inhabitants. From what I'd been told of her past addictions, the odds of such granite-hard willpower maintaining such a stance were, despite the encouraging beginning, on the lower end of the scale.

On day fifteen at just past six a.m., LeAnn had strolled into the dining hall expecting the usual dimly lit space with her previous day's meal request tagged and sitting in one of two refrigerators, specifically the one marked 'HERS' in stenciled black lettering across its light brown door. To her utter shock, though her facial features bore no obvious signs, the globe shaped room was brightly lit and occupied. This was where, as Yanks are apt to say, the worm officially began to turn.

~ * ~

Part Two: *Breaking Bread*

"Morning, fellow inmate...coffee?" Jorgensen inquired while refilling his own cup from a steaming black pot. His baggy sweatpants were rolled to the knee, while the shirt hung from his shoulders like soggy tent flaps. He glanced at her briefly before reaching to remove a clean cup from a nearby pantry.

"Um, I...well...yeah, sure. Black...please..."

"Black as tar, coming your way," he replied cheerily, suppressing a yawn as he poured.

He side-stepped over and handed her the offering, which she clasped tightly between the flat of each palm. Taking her usual seat at one of a trio of tables, all of which held sufficient space for two diners, she turned about and sat facing the exit.

"You hit the chow line this early as a rule?" she heard him ask at her back between noisy sips.

By her bleak expression as she blew over the cup's steaming rim, she appeared less than thrilled by having to entertain.

"Pretty much, yeah. Never later than six-thirty anyway."

He slurped an additional sip just as LeAnn was tipping the cup toward barely parted lips.

"Yeah, well, I got in the bad habit of staying up all night. Usually didn't roll in here until noon or after."

LeAnn grimaced at the stoutness of the brew, her stiff body language and awkward movements emphasizing her discomfort at their chance meeting.

"It's...well, that's an easy trap to fall into, all right."

"Yeah, always have been a night owl."

She saw him take a seat at the table directly across, a large serving tray already in place. Her nostrils flared at the scent of freshly cooked, or at least freshly *reheated* bacon. Seeing that he had busied himself tucking a napkin into the baggy collar of his sweats, she turned briefly to survey the tray. Bacon was indeed present, what appeared to be a dozen or more slabs, along with a tall stack of scrambled eggs, four squared, fluffy country-style biscuits and a tall glass of orange juice.

Refocusing on the entrance as she sipped anew, the longing in her eyes reflected base, primal hunger.

"Yeah, even when I was running my studio, I'd work 'til well past nine some nights and then hit the town. Stay up all fuc-...all night, come home just long enough to shower, change clothes and head back to work. Must've slept-walked through thousands of classes, but hey, never heard complaint one, so I guess no one was the wiser."

"I've been known to greet the dawn a few times myself without benefit of shuteye," she responded wearily, her nostrils still flaring wildly at the delicious fumes permeating the air.

"Oh, sorry about all this, uh, the spread here," Jorgensen stammered, a forkful of eggs balanced mere inches from his mouth, "I didn't figure on us sharing breakfast. Truth was, I was so damn hungry I couldn't sleep a wink. Haven't eaten enough to keep a hummingbird alive since the warden's intro speech."

LeAnn shrugged in between puffs over the smoking rim.

"Hey, it's a free kitchen. I'll live."

When next he spoke, it was through a mouthful of biscuit smothered in butter and dripping honey from its rounded edges.

"Damn, this is great chow. How come no host? I was thinking it mandatory she pops up once we park our asses onto these chairs. Think she overslept?"

"Do holograms oversleep?"

Jorgensen giggled between chews.

"Good point. I'm still trying to figure out what's creepier...when they don't show up or when they do..."

As if beamed in on cue, the figure took gradual shape behind them, standing half-in and half-out of the kitchen's swinging double-door entrance at the rear of the room.

"Well, good morning, children. Soooo good to see you two dining together."

"Good morning, Miss J., or whatever time zone you're being beamed in from," LeAnn replied with a sheepish grin.

The hologram performed a mini-curtsy, no doubt limited by her imposing bulk. As nearly as wide as she was tall, middle-aged African-American with short-cropped hair streaked in gray, Miss Jeannine had introduced herself as *The Iron Chef of the Projects*, having been born and raised in Hawthorne, California public housing until the age of nineteen, where she'd eloped with a U. S. Navy short-order cook. For over twenty years, until his retirement, she said they'd traveled the globe and, along the way, developed her husband's interest in cuisine. From Bangkok to Manila, Dusseldorf to Glasgow, she'd picked up preparation tidbits from a half-dozen or more varied cultures, culinary experiences and hands-on teachings that she claimed proudly, had served her well through the decades.

"Good for you, Miss Butterworth," Jorgensen cracked, sticking to the nickname he'd pegged since their initial meeting. "Hell of a gig, all right—cooking meals for the condemned. Hell, why not apply for head burger flipper on death row?"

"Aw, come now, Mister Jorgensen," she'd cooed warmly, doughy hands folded across a massive bosom, "no need for the nastiness at this early hour. I'm here to support you and Miss Garner. We all want to see you two succeed, you know."

From that point on, Jorgensen retreated from further attempts at baiting, the sparkle of sincere warmth in the large woman's dark brown eyes instantly draining all motivation.

On this particular day, said warmth was on display two-fold, and Jorgensen appeared more concerned with filling his face than challenging her overt, downhome cheeriness.

"Now, how you finding the meal this morning, Mister Brian? You sure you got enough? There is a second helping in the ice box if you still got space."

"This'll do for now. You got my lunch order, right?" he mumbled through a mouthful of eggs.

Stepping between the two in a flowery, ankle-low dress, she practically beamed, her hands gesturing in time with her words.

"Yes sir...triple cheeseburger, meat sizzled to the edge of burnt, with double-order of steak fries, apple pie and French vanilla ice cream along with a two-liter Mountain Dew chilled to perfection. Glad you finally saw fit to place your order online. Man can't go but so long on peanut butter and crackers. As for Miss LeAnn here, she's the organized kind for sure," she laughed, her bosom and midsection jiggling wildly. "Got her orders placed in advance for the next month. 'Course, a week's chowin' down on that particular menu don't rate a single calorie compared to Mister Brian's upcoming lunch meal."

"Well, we are definitely riding on opposite sides of the food nutrition highway then, aren't we?" LeAnn exclaimed with a slight grimace following a loud sip of Java. "Got to admit, his choice does sound quite tempting. Time was I might have gone back for seconds even. Time...was...not that far back, as anyone with eyes can obviously deduce."

Chewing a fresh mouthful of bacon with buttered biscuits serving as chaser, Jorgensen shot her a glance and nodded as if to second the motion.

"You got lots of work to do, child," Jeannine replied with a smile, her ultra-ivory teeth flashing like tiny incandescent bulbs when compared to the dark ebony shading of her flesh.

"But I'm here to say you possess the vim and vigor to pull this off. I've seen enough to convince me. You just gotta stay on track. If you start feeling the hand of the devil tugging at your ankles trying to pull you down, you just kick that horn-headed buzzard right in the sweet meats."

Twisting about with a divine grace that belied her considerable bulk, Jeannine regarded Jorgensen with a similar smile, though her eyes squinted with a renewed intensity.

"Same goes for you, Brian. Ain't my job to find out why you've suddenly switched gears...ain't my business neither. I'm just...we're all just glad to see you on board."

Following a short pause, during which he'd washed down the last of the bacon strips with a full glass of juice, Jorgensen twisted about in his high-back chair and belched loudly.

"Yeah, I hear you, sister. Halla-fucking-luyah. Bet your boss is wackin' off at the news of my...switching gears. Let's just say I got my reasons and they don't have Jack-Shit to do with his little eye-tinerary."

Waddling over to him like an overstuffed penguin, Jeannine raised a hand airborne and began wriggling a chubby, extended forefinger to and fro.

"Ohhhh I should've mixed in a bar of soap in those eggs just to wash out that filthy mouth."

"I call 'em as I see 'em, Aunt Jemima. Not about to apologize to anyone, much less a fat fucking pile of airborne molecules masquerading as flesh and bone."

Throwing up her arms in apparent surrender, Jeanine turned away and headed back toward the murkiness of the kitchen area.

"I get it...I get...*anything* to maintain that macho image. Pat, my dear departed, was the same way. 'Fessed up to me once that the only reason he smoked was 'cause it made him look tough. Damn things ended up killing him. Anyhow, I have to get started on those meal orders. You two have a blessed day."

The image gradually disintegrated, leaving a vapor trail of sparks, much like the pulsating glow of scattered fireflies, in its glittering wake.

Gulping the last of her coffee, LeAnn arose, her chair squeaking loudly against the linoleum floor, and strolled back to her assigned fridge, where she removed a breakfast meal consisting of a chilled fruit-bowl (thinly sliced peaches, pears, cherries and grapefruit) and an equally frosty half-glass of soymilk. At her back she heard Jorgensen belch again, a hollow, echoing blast that caused her to flinch involuntarily, almost dropping the fruit bowl in the process.

By the time she returned to her seat, he was leaning back with one hand massaging his midsection and the other tucked behind his neck. A toothpick hung loosely from bared, gritted teeth; his eyes sparkled with mischief.

"I see you're down with the program. Not enough calories there to keep a maggot alive."

LeAnn retook her seat while stifling a yawn. She replied only after a quick sip of milk.

"Could say the same thing about you, sport, considering the cholesterol bath you just awarded your liver."

He stood, facing her with his arms crossed, the ill-fitting sweats hanging from each sleeve like blue-tinted ruffles.

"Yeah, well, we each got our own reasons. Polar opposite as they may seem to the ill-informed eye...there are similarities."

Forking up a dripping helping, LeAnn eyed him curiously.

"No argument here. Why, you taking wagers on who reaches the finish line first?"

"Nah...sucker's bet," he replied, sauntering casually from the room. "I do believe what binds us as birds of a feather is our talent for swallowing self-pride as casual as say...a saucer-full of scrambled eggs or...a bowl of fruit. See you around."

LeAnn did not reply and waited until she'd heard the outer elevator's familiar hum to resume consumption of her morning meal. Probably assuming Jorgensen had headed straight for the gym, she opted to return to her living quarters in lieu of beginning her own daily workout.

As for Jorgensen, he'd actually bypassed the gymnasium for the lounge, taking a center seat at the winding oak bar with a fifth of JB Scotch, a bucket of ice and a shot glass as his lone companions. Between shots, his face would contort in rage and he would curse aloud before refilling for yet another round. By the time the bottle lay on its side with but a thin layer of content remaining, he'd retreated to a nearby booth and passed out with his baggy sweat pants spattered in his own vomit.

Upon awakening, he'd stumbled back to the bar with a fresh bottle in hand and a string of familiar profanities passing his booze-chapped lips. Eight and a half hours from the time he'd strolled stone-cold sober into the facility watering hole, he wobbled out half-lit and layered in his own extracted bodily fluids. Following a change of sweats and an ice-cold shower, he'd proceeded to the kitchen, where he'd consumed, quite greedily, both his saved lunch and dinner meals simultaneously. The next day, a similar ritual was followed almost to a T, minus the up-chunking. Within a week, a hefty tolerance level had been achieved, wherein Brian Jorgensen spent each day sucking down the lounge's generous inventory of booze, sleeping off the after effects, and consuming multiple platefuls of pre-cooked meals that naturally induced additional downtime. In essence, the transformation to his evil twin, a kind of 'alternate universe' clone, was gradually becoming a reality. Tucked within his daily booze-fueled rants and curse-riddled raves, Brian Jorgensen's personal *doppelganger* avoided self-pity, but instead centered his rage on the man responsible for his birthing. The man Brian Jorgensen's evil twin began to think of as a father-figure of sorts—a father-figure who specialized in abuse...in humiliation...in belittlement. A father-figure that, in less than a year's time, would be introduced to the bastard son Brian Jorgensen had spewed forth from a poisonous womb of unbridled fury.

~ * ~

Part Three: *Notes to the Boss*
Narrator: *Gabriel Maxwell, personal trainer*

It was day twenty-two when Jorgensen came to me with his plan. Being that I hadn't heard from 'im at all since day one of initial processing, the request for a pow-wow came right outta the blue. That mornin', hours before I'd beamed into the gym for our meeting, the curiosity was killin' me. Truth is, I hadn't figured on hearin' from him at all, being his particular goal didn't exactly call for training in a physical sense. In fact, if asked, my professional advice to him would've been to limit any and all exertion to hoofin' it back and forth to the fridge, and at a turtle's pace at that. 'Bout noontime that particular day, I was informed that my client list had doubled by exactly one. Brian Jorgensen, black belt martial arts instructor, who'd arrived on site as cut and buffed a physical specimen as I'd ever seen for a man of medium size, had scribbled out a blueprinted regimen that would transform him into a specimen of a different kind while also servin' to help 'im reach the mandatory goal.

My participation would be as advisor, though Jorgensen was quick to point out it was hardly necessary. Said he was just makin' sure he involved the staff in every aspect to make *damn sure we earned our keep*. As with our first face-to-face, I found 'im the same cocky asshole, though the change in his overall appearance since in-processing was surely an eye-popper. First off, his mug hadn't seen the sharp edge of a razor in a spell, as he was cultivating a scraggly looking beard that gave 'im a serial killer *slash* Uni-bomber look. Speakin' of cultivating, it had taken 'im a little more than three weeks to lose the majority of his muscle-tone and, in studying his midsection, get himself knocked up. Hard to believe a man could drop off in such a brief span, from rock-hard abs to the beginnings of a lifelong beer-guzzler's gut, from arms of steel to toneless flab. Truly, I'm never seen such a...well, damn near perfect specimen deteriorate so rapidly. To top it off, he gave the impression of being perpetually hung over, which would explain a lot concernin' such a colossal drop-off.

That in mind, that day his gait was noticeably wobbly, like he was just comin' down from one hell of stupor. No doubt if a holographic image was allowed a sense of smell, the room would've reeked of rot gut whiskey. Sure goes a long way in explainin' the mysterious stains on his sweat shirt and pants...no doubt booze-barf related.

Anyhow, stew-bum appearance and all, Jorgensen came across crystal clear in what he wanted to accomplish...hell, fiery even. There was a gleam in the man's bloodshot eyes that told me all I needed to know in terms of his sincerity. He was deadly serious.

"The weight gain can work...and it don't have to kill me," he said with an upturned brow, "that's what Han...that's what your boss wants, for me to keel right the fuck over, choking on a chicken-bone or from an overdose of Twinkies. He wants my arties to harden and my kidneys to shut down from gluttony. Not a fucking chance, pal. But…" he raised a finger airborne, "…if over the half the weight gained is muscle…pure *bulk*, I can still maintain a semi-healthy frame, not to mention heart. I mean, shit, it's not exactly a stretch. Look at the NFL. All the interior linemen tip the scales at three-hundred or better but can still motor like greased lighting."

"You do realize you're startin' the program twenty-two days in, chief," I'd replied, attempting to apply a smidgen of reality.

Jorgensen bulled ahead and bowed up like he wanted to take a poke at me.

"So?"

"Soooo…means you need to gain a little more than a pound a day for the next one-fifty-eight. Bud, that's some serious gorgin'."

Backing away, Jorgensen shrugged.

"Be honest with you, Goober, what else a guy got to do in this suppository-shaped burg than eat and work out? No chicks to hump. None to my standards, anyhow. Can't cop a joint. No sparring opportunities unless I pick a fight with Hanley's lard-ass daughter, and as for the lounge and its unlimited supply of hooch, let's just say I've had my fill. Might go ahead and say the same about the self-pity I've been carrying around like a second skin. Time to do some seasonal *shedding*, you might say."

There's no denying I saw a high level of determination in the man's eyes, along with no small portion of insanity. Yep, I'd seen the look before—far too often if truth be told, more than once in a mirror's reflection. But then, logic dictates a sane man would never even attempt the plan Jorgensen laid out for himself. Throwin' caution to the wind don't require saneness, but a heapin' dose of someone gone just a mite bat-shit. For that reason only, I had to give the bastard a fightin' chance.

"So what do you need me for, chief? Surely not fitness advice."

He started pacin' the room from section to section, starting at the bow-flex equipment and then to the treadmills, tread-climbers and Gazelle riders, finally stopping to size up the vast array of free weights and the trio of benches accompanying them.

"Well, yes and no," he finally said with a boot propped on the incline bench. "You see, I need no instruction whatsoever on cardio or light toning, but these bad boys here..." he motioned toward the three-tiered free-weight rack, "...I'd made a living out of avoiding. Bulk and agility rarely mix, and in my business I could never afford to get too pumped."

He turned back toward my image and grinned wide, nice and toothy, the choppers in question a bright shade of yellow, lookin' very bit the severely cracked egg.

"That's where you come in, Goober. I'm gonna need training tips on how to plump up while I'm pumping up, get it?"

I nodded agreeably.

"No sweat. You talkin' daily workouts or every other? Some like to rest torn muscles a day before tearin' back down."

"You tell me, Maxwell," he said with a wink, his baggy sweats hangin' like shredded curtains, "I'm here to learn."

"When do we start?" I asked with a twinge of sincere apprehension. Despite bein' safely out of harm's way, the man nonetheless still scared the bejesus outta me.

"No better time than right...fucking...now, Teach," he replied, peeling off the sweat shirt and discarding it with the flip of a wrist before walkin' over to the weight rack and eyein' it like a starved man would a freshly heated roast.

That first workout, nearly four hours in duration, told me all I needed in verifyin' my fears concerning the man's mental state.

Three words: *Bat...shit...crazy.*

Things got substantially weirder around hour three of said marathon, once the other inmate joined the party. Actually, the correct term is rejoined the party, as we'd already completed her daily session early that morning. Seems she'd gotten bored surfing channels and opted for a two-a-day, ignorant of the fact that the Kung-Fu Master was off the wagon and rarin' to turn over a new leaf. As for that earlier workout with the woman I'd secretly nicknamed *My Lady of Repetition...*

~ * ~

Always the slap-happy jokester, Garner had entered the gym that morning wearin' her usual game-face. Translation: severe constipation. Over the years I'd worked with many folks similarly blinded by their own tunnel-vision. Don't get me wrong...determination, devotion and good old-fashioned moxie are damn fine traits, and pretty much mandatory when attemptin' to reach a goal most would instantly wave off as damn near impossible. All that said, when your sole focus is that singular goal, there lies the prospect for potential burnout. In other words, you gotta find a distraction to cut the inner tension, a hobby, a pastime, something to occupy your mind other than the big G.

The three weeks I'd worked with LeAnn Garner, her focus was, if anything, growin' more constricted. When asked that first week how she was spendin' her time, she'd shrug and mention a particular TV show she'd watched or a book she'd been readin'. As days passed, she grew grimmer and gloomier, not even botherin' to trade banter. I could guess she figured any attempt at small talk with the hired help was considered wasted energy. As far as she was concerned, I was there to count her reps and correct any bad positioning or posture, period. I wasn't there to shoot the breeze. Only thing is, I could tell even as her workouts grew longer in duration and more intense with every set, there was gonna be a price to pay down the line.

One particular day, around the middle of week two, she came in huffin' and puffin' and frownin' like Miss J had left a fresh turd in her mornin' fruit bowl.

"Mornin', Sunshine," was my greeting of choice, the response a silent scowl as she adjusted her sweat pants across a midsection that, colossal as it still was, had obviously started to birth tiny folds in its previously skintight covering. Her face, though still overly jowly with double-chin intact, had also noticeably deflated a layer or so. It wasn't 'til she openly cursed me for losin' count on her fifth set of crunches that the fog started to lift on exactly what had crawled up her poop-shoot to make her so damn ornery.

The chick was in chemical withdrawal on several counts, and it was kickin' her hefty ass. From what I'd been briefed about her, alcohol and pain meds were a double-whammy start. Toss in a fondness for the whacky weed and, last but for damn certain not least, there was the matter of a radically altered diet, as in from the seafood (*see food*) to a menu more suitable for bunnies or gerbils. I can only imagine how hard it is to go from five-thousand-plus calories a day to seven-fifty, especially considerin' the fuel consumed durin' her daily marathon workouts.

Now, when I say marathon, I ain't talkin' *sweatin' to the oldies*. I'm talkin' a non-stop four to five hour session to make an Iron Man decathlete proud. She'd normally start with fifteen, twenty minutes of stretching before hoppin' on the treadmill, where a causal stroll would conclude ninety minutes later in a full-bore, uphill sprint.

From there she'd mount the tread-climber for thirty to forty minutes, this usually without even takin' a blessed water break in-between.

Before tackling the Gazelle-rider, she'd hit the canvas for three or four sets of crunches, usually twenty-five or thirty reps each.

The rider would eat up another half hour to forty-five before she'd normally take her first water break, those tight sweats soaked through and stickin' to her like soggy flesh. From there it was off to the pool, where she'd lap for an hour or so before draggin' herself to the shower, limpin' along like a weathered ol' zombie. 'Course, this was the broke-in model of my *Lady of*

Repetition. Those first few weeks had been as laughable as they were pathetic, though not at all surprising. I mean, the first time she'd climbed aboard that treadmill, she'd practically crawled off ten minutes later, pasty-faced and on the verge of blowin' chunks—this at one of the lowest settings...a walk on spongy park grass on a flat surface compared to the blazin' path of later days. Watchin' her attempt a crunch, only after a good ten minutes of tutoring on how *not* to perform said exercise without snappin' one's neck, was a comic disaster. Truly, it was a beached whale scenario come true. Sadly amusin' as that was, and I'd have wagered a stack of dead presidents there would be no day two, she didn't let a little fatigue and soreness derail the process. Day two saw her double her time on both the treadmill and tread-climber. Yeah, she limped plenty and looked pastier than a soggy bowl of pasta, but that didn't stop her from showin' up bright and early for day three.

By the end of week two, week *two* I say, she had built up an impressive tolerance, more than I would've ever thought for such a hefty chick.

By the end of week three, I'm confident enough to say of her progress that LeAnn Garner, all two-hundred fifty-plus pounds of 'er, could've finished a mini-Iron-Man. She had the leg and lung strength for the ground pound, ditto the bike ride, and as for the half-mile swim, I'd seen her lap the pool non-stop for twice that length. All physical qualifications aside though, what allows a man or woman to compete in such torturous events is will-power—the ability to shut off the pain valve runnin' to the brain. To that, I'll just say my *Lady of Repetition* ruled. Tunnel-vision, baby...pure and primal...she shut it all down for a single purpose. As I saw it, only one thing could derail the locomotive...that being the haunts of her former vices. Bein' as the only habit I'd ever kicked in all my years was a pot-and-a-half coffee Jones I'd developed in my late twenties and early thirties...oh, and there was that little gambling thing...I couldn't imagine how tough it would be to conquer the three-headed beast she was holdin' in check.

All that preached, it was on that mornin' of day two-two that the severest of the trio reared its ugly mug...and then some.

A simple question, asked exclusively out of boredom. After all, my attendance was little more than a technicality, a diversion from the self-inflicted agony. As she stepped off the treadmill with a loud groan, I'd casually checked my watch to see barely a half-hour had passed—her normal ending time of one hour-plus dramatically undercut. Her face was set in permanent scowl mode, her eyes squintin' and un-squintin', her jaws set tight and her teeth clinched. I saw her caress her midsection and made an assumption. Innocent enough assumption I figured at the time. Problem was, it was an assumption I should've known to keep to my damn self and not, I repeat NOT, relay verbally.

"That time of the month?"

"Say...what?" she'd growled, turnin' on me like a rabid feline, though still rubbing her midsection like she was in the midst of some fierce crampin'.

"Well, I...just...looked like you're in the kind of pain that originates from the nether regions..."

If anything, her grimace grew, well, grima-cier.

"Nether...regions?"

"Uh, yeah, you know, female problems. Curse of the weaker sex and all that..."

At this particular juncture, she appeared on the verge of chargin' me like a ragin' bull.

"Curse of...*weaker* sex?"

For want of anything else to do, I actually bowed and stepped back defensively. In retrospect it seems damn foolish, I know. Ain't like she could actually get at me, but at the time, I guess instinct was kickin' logic's ass like a rented mule.

"Um, sorry ma'am, um, Miss Garner. My bad..."

"Let me...explain something to you, Maxwell...," she sighed, the tension draining away in a blink, replaced by a look of complete exhaustion. She continued only after leaning against the tread-climber's solid-steel frame with a perched elbow.

"No form of leakage accounts for my...present lack of enthusiasm or...energy. It's...all...about lack of consumption. You want the truth....unvarnished and as plain as the noonday sun?"

So it began. Swear to God, the woman's formerly snow-white cheeks turned every color of the rainbow in that four to five minute rant. But then, what's a dramatic transformation without a little strip tease? She started with the shoes...pair of second-rate Reeboks that she unlaced and kicked free into a far corner.

"I don't know...how much longer I can keep...keep up this pace or this...routine. I would say charade but...I've been doing it for real...full-steam ahead since day two. There's no...faking this kind of...pain...or anguish."

Naturally, the socks came next...rolled up into a single bundle and tossed casually over one shoulder.

"A big part of me...about the size of my butt-cheeks big, wants nothing more than to...throw in the towel. That part, what I like to call my inner food processor, dreams...yearns to instruct Miss Jeannine to prepare a daily feast...a buffet table for one. Food enough for ten men. Not just any ten men, but let's say...ten professional wrestlers who've been living on stale saltines for a week. Afterwards, a quick ride down to the lounge for a belt of....well, *whatever* as long as the alcohol content reads at least eighty-proof..."

The sweatshirt was next in line, so scuba-gear snug she'd had to pause a full half-minute just to peel 'er off.

"...so you see, Maxwell, my former identity...the lard-ass, pill-popping rum guzzler whose untimely demise came a scant twenty-two days ago, would sell her putrid soul to spend her days gorging, swigging and snoozing. If my father had just seen fit to add a pharmacy floor to this place, the only salad I'd scarf would be topped with oxycodone."

So, just for kicks, let's take a quick inventory on what remained of Garner's wardrobe at this point in time. Hint: The list ain't exactly lengthy. As in: bra, sweat pants. The latter was discarded after a similar scuba-suit scenario as its twin top. This left the aforementioned boob-sling and a bright blue, extra, extra-large pair of what my dear old grandma used to refer to as *wide-load bloomers.*

"So far, three weeks and counting, I've been able to...keep the varied hungers at bay. You see, I had a secret weapon to ward off all those demons..." she whispered the last, leanin' forward and shootin' me a wink.

"R.a.g.e. I found a never-before discovered range of anger and hatred, the target of which should be fairly obvious. Poppa Hanley is the catalyst...for placing me in this position...and having the unmitigated gall only he possesses with this...*his* ludicrous proposal. I'm finding....finding out as days pass...that driving anger weakens. No matter how I try to maintain....dipping into the same old well does tend to have that effect."

When I saw her reach back with both hands, I really should've turned away. I mean, it would've been the gentlemanly thing to do. But, in my defense, it was what I call the *crash effect* that kept the eyeballs pasted firmly in focus as that double-barreled, double-D sized slingshot sprang loose, as in a really gruesome car wreck you're helpless to look away from.

"Worse thing is, as the motivational anger slowly fades, I'm finding the same old cravings calling to me louder than ever. I'm being pulled in about five separate directions, tugged and jerked 'til I feel like I'm being slowly...dismembered...a single limb at a time—drawn and quartered from the inside out. The inner defenses...the inner force-fields are weakening...big time."

And yep, the panties came next. This time, I did manage to turn away, starin' down at my own shoes and scanning the surroundin' floor space like I was tryin' to avoid fallin' in a hole. If I'd held the power to shut off the replicator, that most certainly would've been the time.

"My sleep grows more fitful by the night...from seven hours to six, then five and four...last night was more like two and a half. The pains...the *pangs* really come a'thumpin' at night. The wolf...*wolves* are at the door...and it's...it's getting harder and harder not to reach for that shining silver knob. Over the last...several days...a cold truth has come to light. This...body...this bloated *shell* I occupy. My father wasn't the creator of this...he's not to blame. I built it...constructed it over decades with my indulgences. So...the bottom line is...who's really to blame? You...have a mirror handy I can stare into and *Shazam*! I have my answer. The weak of mind can usually be counted on to go to pot physically, and accept the dilapidated results without undo fret. It's just...what *my* kind does..."

Avoiding a full-frontal view, my peripheral caught her substantial shadow roamin' about to my left. At this juncture, I figured a verbal intervention was in order. Couldn't hurt. After all, part of a personal trainer's job is to counsel the weak of mind—to motivate—to have memorized dozens of Knute Rockne-type dialogues, sliced bologna they might be, to inspire.

"Miss Garner, I can only imagine the struggles you're facin', but I have had clients who had similar...weaknesses. I watched 'em all fight the demons you spoke of. I ain't gonna fib. Not all of 'em succeeded, and their situations can't even begin to compare to thi...to yours. I say all that to say this..." I paused, lookin' in her general direction but staring just over her head to the far wall. From what I could see of 'er, thank the lord it wasn't the full monty, she stood with hands on hips, her tree-trunk thighs spread shoulder-length, "...I've seen enough of you to know you got the intestinal fortitude to do this. I can spot a quitter a mile away, ma'am—sniff 'em out like a bloodhound on a coon's trail. You can beat this. You can beat...*him.* Just look into your mind's eye and envision the future. A future where you face 'im down and prove 'im wrong. Focus on just how sweet the moment when he eats crow...and is forced...*forced,* mind you...to admit he was wrong. Wrong about doubting his little girl's iron will."

Yeah, I was tap-dancin', spewin' forth a pep-talk pulled from the archives, but hey, as doused in cliché as it was, it wasn't altogether BS. Daring to peek downward, I saw her gatherin' up her discarded duds, drapin' 'em over one arm. I could tell she was still mighty flustered. Wasn't even sure she'd heard my rah-rah ramble 'til she finally blurted a response.

"Words do not halt the constant grumbling of my midsection or the nightly throbbing at the back of my skull. Nor do they quench the parched throat that craves the smooth burn of fine scotch. Using words to sway, intimidate and overpower is my father's specialty. So as the old saying goes," she paused, huggin' her boobs with the crinkled clothing, "don't bullshit a bull-shitter. All the flowery words and inspirational speeches are just static. I learned to zone out the old man years ago. Nothing personal, but you're a rank amateur by comparison."

Undaunted, I proceeded to stick the other boot straight into my own kisser.

"Understood, Miss, but *you* have to understand I'd feel like I wasn't doin' my job if I didn't at least try. 'Sides, it ain't all bunk. I meant those things. And if you need me t..."

She whirled about, stormin' off toward the exit.

"It's up to me and me alone to not trip up on my own frailties. I know now it's not just a switch you can click off and never fret about powering up again. I'll be back when I'm back...*if* I'm back at all."

She was back, less than five hours later, leadin' to what was no doubt the first meaningful rap session between the silo inmates.

~ * ~

"A...little help...here," Jorgensen grunted, the thick steel bar pinned at his breastbone and occasionally leaning to one side or the other.

"Um...l-lady...y-you m-mind?"

He released a strained groan in attempting a final push that resulted in a brief separation, the space between bar and chest a scant two to three inches before rapid descent with a low thud.

"Son-o-fa-bit-..." he bellowed just as a pair of chubby hands curled around the bar on either side, just outside his own.

Once the bar had ceased shimmying atop the bench, Jorgensen leaned up with a loud sigh before turning to his savior and executing a weak salute.

"Appreciate...the aid...I was about three seconds away from...giving birth to twin hernias."

"You attempt suicide by weight bar very often? Good thing I *was* here."

Not waiting for a reply, she walked briskly back to the tread-climber and resumed the set that had been so rudely interrupted.

Jorgensen sat on the edge of the bench, his breathing still labored. His bare, hairless chest held a fresh coat of moisture, the baggy sweat's elongated sleeves tied snugly about his waist.

"My apologies. Guess I got a little cocky. Haven't benched the big three-oh since...well, never. Shit, barely two hours in and the limbs are rubber."

He stood, reaching up with both hands for a vigorous neck massage. Strolling casually toward the tread-climber, he kept his eyes peeled on the woman's sweat-soaked tee and the perfectly symmetrical rolls beneath. Rolls that appeared less bulky by far than upon their initial meeting.

"Riddle me this, my lady...what's the real reason for Pappa Hanley's hard-on for his own flesh and blood?"

Legs and arms pumping, her reply was a hoarse, barely audible whisper.

"Why, isn't that obvious?" she huffed, "baaah baah black-sheep."

Standing at parade rest, Jorgensen stared at her colossal rear end through a disgusted scowl.

"Yep, figured as much. The farther away he can bury you, the less embarrassment you cause. You're the one they all speak of in hushed whispers at the family reunion, am I right? But it's Hanley that receives all the pity at the sob party. As in…he's *done all he can but she's just a lost cause*, yeah?"

Her rhythm remained constant even as she blurted out a curt response.

"You're a genius. And here I'd always compared the intelligence level of you jocks to the average tree-stump. My turn to apologize."

Sliding forward and to the left, he leaned in and found his eyes instantly bypassing her frazzled doo and sweat-soaked cheeks, instead locking on the substantial breasts bounding wildly beneath an equally saturated tee.

"So why not use the Hanley name? Seems to be you're doing a little distancing yourself."

Her pace briefly slowed as she strained for an ample supply of air to reply.

"No big conspiracy, just decided to keep my married name."

"Got'cha. Distance yourself from the man, so to speak."

"Maybe subliminally. I'd say moreover I just grew accustomed to it and didn't want to go back to using a name I'd possessed previously. It's almost like… morphing back into that other person."

Jorgensen nodded, unable and/or unwilling to avert his eyes from her jiggling boobs.

"Ohhh-kay. Sounds reasonable enough. So how long were you hitched?"

Slowing her pace considerably, her dialogue was noticeably less labored.

"Year...year and a half. Dated for two years before tying the knot. The bliss ended almost immediately after we exchanged 'I dos.' Making it official was the kiss of death."

"Sooo, you've been single now for how long?"

"Oh, eight, nine years. Looking back, I find it hard to believe I ever even attempted the whole 'death do us part' thing. Just not my bag."

Nodding knowingly, Jorgensen's trance was shattered only when she hopped off the climber and began a series of leg, back and shoulder stretches on a nearby mat.

"I dig, lady, I dig," he replied with a wink. "Personally it's the monogamy angle that kicks my can. It just...isn't natural. Variety has always been the spice of this boy's life."

She paused in mid-deep-knee bend to regard him with a cocked brow.

"So I've heard."

Jorgensen shrugged before strolling to the opposite side of the room to hand several hard left jabs and a vicious right to a hanging hard-bag. Following several additional combinations, his hand speed increasing dramatically with each set, he reached out to halt the bag from its dramatic sway.

"So, you're really intent on sticking it to the old bastard, ain't ya?"

Having laid on her right side to begin a series of leg raises, Garner hoisted an arm and pointed an open palm his way.

"Hang on, hang on...I'm starting to catch an interrogation vibe here. How about I toss a few queries your way for a change?"

"Go for it. Gotta warn you, though," Jorgensen sneered seductively, "I'm one fascinating subject."

With no small amount of strain, Garner then assumed the nearest to a lotus position her ample bulk could manage.

"Uh-huh, thanks for the warning. I'll do my best not to swoon."

Jorgensen's smile appeared to hold just a tint of malice. He retrieved a towel from a nearby rack and began wiping his bare, sweat-coated chest.

"Easier said than done, sweet cheeks. Fire away."

"First off, what's with the Mister Olympian routine? I thought the whole idea was to avoid exercise at all costs as to...properly plump-up. I mean, if you need advice on how to pack on the pounds, you're obviously in the presence of an expert."

"Nope, not my style, lady. No way I could just lay around gorging and watching myself bloat. The trim, taunt physique you see before you..." he paused, tossing the towel away before striking several flexing poses, "...this took a lifetime to build and maintain, and going completely to pot just wasn't gonna happen. I did consider it for about two winks—long enough to know I'd prefer having Miss J brew me up a warm, bubbly batch of oleander soup. Then, right out of the clear blue sky, it came to me. So damn simple I temporarily doubted the logic."

"Oh, I get it," she replied with a sluggish nod, "you're going to over-bloat your biceps instead."

"You got it, sister. I trained some serious muscle-heads in my time, some of 'em with arms thicker than my waist. Pot guts, soggy butts, but still quick as cats by the time I got through with 'em. Some of those dudes went upward of three, three-hundred fifty pounds. If it worked for them, well, it beats the hell out of treading the glutton path and listening to my arteries harden. From a psychological standpoint it's still gonna be damn difficult. Then again, what's the alternative, right? Hell, even if I did make the weight by D-day doing the fat-boy regime, my first step to freedom would probably be into a waiting hearse—croak right the fuck out with a drumstick in one hand and a gallon of Rocky Road in the other. Nope...not this boy...no sir."

He took a few lazy jabs at the hard bag, interrupting Garner's impending reply even before it commenced.

"Who knows? Maybe I'll even decide to maintain the bulk once all is said and done. Go into pro wrestling. Chicks dig the grapplers, I've heard."

"Ugh-huh," Garner said with an intentional roll of the eyes. She stood a bit wobbly and stepped over to the rowing machine, her copious backside essentially cloaking its narrow seat.

"So it appears we'll be competing for gym space."

Jorgensen released something akin to a giggle before delivering a wicked right-jab-left hook-right uppercut combo that sent the fifty-pound bag sailing forward. Upon its return, he twisted in a three-hundred-sixty-five degree blur and hooked it dead-center with the heel of his left foot.

"Yeah, it does appear so. Truth is, lady, I'm counting on it."

She halted in mid-row, her brow severely creased as she stared him down.

"Really? Why exactly would that be? Got to say, you've done a pretty sufficient job in avoiding me thus far."

"Well, might sound a shade on the selfish side," he replied, shrugging shyly, "but I just might need you to save my ass on a regular basis."

"Save?"

Jorgensen flashed a roguish grin while motioning towards the weight bench with an extended thumb.

"Hey, if not for you I'd probably still be laying there wearing that bar across my ribcage. Soooo, I sure would appreciate the occasional spot."

Garner sighed heavily and remained silent as if contemplating the proper rebuff, but was unable to fight off a tiny smile as Jorgensen alternated flexes between his pecs and biceps, the effect of which was a spastic dance of sorts, a muscle-spasm boogie.

"Fine…" she conceded, turning her focus back to the rowing, "…but the oh-cassional spot does not a romance make, big guy."

His eyes again found her bouncing she-mounds as the sly smile widened ever further.

"Got'cha. No strings attached whatsoever."

From that day forward, an innocent-enough daily ritual was set in motion. As days and weeks would progress within the cylinder-shaped habitat, it would be far from the last.

~ * ~

Part Four: *Notes to the Boss*
Narrator: *Miss Jeannine, facility cook*

Lord almighty, how that white boy could eat! A decade's experience whippin' up meals for the likes of men twice his size, I never saw such an appetite. More amazing was the way he was gulping down my fixings. False modesty aside, I've long ago accepted my special talents to satisfy hunger. Bottom line, this girl has seen her dishes turn frowns upside down from scent alone, but I ain't never, ever witnessed such a *joyous* eater as Mister Brian Jorgensen, not to mention such a reversal of attitude. From foul-mouthed sourpuss to whistling, humming, and grinning like he'd woke up each day with a winning lotto ticket tucked in his palm. Probably no coincidence these changes seemed to coincide exactly with his sudden switch in diet. The boy went from nibblin' the outer edges of his meals, bland selections he'd obviously not spent much time contemplating to scarfin' everything he'd requested and more.

Once he'd let me in on his plan to muscle-up as much as fatten-up, I put 'im on the path to success by providing the nutritional keys to do so. Four simple words separated by two commas: fish, lean meats, carbohydrates, emphasizin' the big C. Brian became a carb maniac, shovelin' in and packin' down pasta by the pot-load, baked potatoes by the half-dozen and baked fish, lean beef and yard-bird by the mess, head and flock. Nothing to scrape off the plates but well-chewed bones. Up until that third week, I'd say he was averaging two, maybe two-thousand five hundred calories a day...about average for a man his size. Piss-poor effort for someone trying to double his body-weight, pardon the crudeness. Since, he's doubled that total on a daily basis, some days sweeping past the five-thousand mark and closer to six, all without sweets or saturated fats. Now that is quite the accomplishment. Easy enough to pack on the cottage cheese if one turns to the dessert tray or spends hours on end starin' at the boob tube with their hands submerged in a potato chip bag. The way Brian was goin' about it was textbook for his cause. Damn smart for a man bent on athletics. Nothin' personal...I've seen 'em...I've fed 'em. I've watched 'em bloat like Macy's day floats. Mister Jorgensen had a plan and from what Miss Garner spilled to me 'bout his gym habits, the boy was surely goin' for the gold. Problem was, he started twenty-some days late on the quest. I figured it was gonna go down to the wire to see who triumphed 'tween him and that weight scale.

As for Miss G, she was locked onto the target from day one, focused on the prize, yeeeess ma'am. I'd seen tubbier for sure, but once briefed on her numerous other...weaknesses, I didn't hold out much hope for her stayin' on course. Easy enough to jump from the gate all fired up...all it takes is a heapin' helpin' dose of anger or resentment. Once that initial surge starts to fade and the inner hunger starts to howl, that's normally when reality hops up and takes a big ol' chew of rear end and those weaknesses seep back in and retake a firm hold. I'll go as far as to say she surpassed whatever expectations I'd had by reaching the thirty-day mark without regressin'. Apparently she'd just come from jawin' with the doc and had received some mighty positive news in the digital scale department. Grinning from ear to ear, she began to wolf down her lunch order of a turkey sandwich on wheat, her fingers and toes rappin' and tappin' to some inner tune only she was privy to.

Her and I had just started jabberin' about her good fortune when Mister J stomped in lookin' like somebody had stowed a steamin' pile of dog doo into his joggin' shoes. I stuck around for no other reason than just plain nosiness. Hey, even an old pot-slinger like myself has the occasional tug of curiosity.

~ * ~

"Pompous jerk-wad," Mister J came in bellowin', the muscles of his arms and shoulders all bulgin' and hunched up, lookin' like a snarlin' junk-yard dog in search of a good scrap. It took me a jiff or two to put my finger on it, but it wasn't 'til I focused more on his appearance than his tirade that I took note he'd razored off all his hair and jaw-whiskers. Bald as a honeydew melon and slick with sweat, it was damn near blinding. Doggone but how a severe overdosin' of carbs can alter a person in a lickety-split. Oh, the boy was muscle-bound as always, even puffier than usual in the arms and chest. Thing was, so was the paddin' around his gut. Those washboard abdominals were slowly bein' swallowed up by an outer layer of flab. Can't lie—my own breasts burst out in pride in knowin' I was responsible. Well, drooping down, but still pokin' out.

"What the hell does he know anyhow? Goddamn snooty Brit with a wall full of diplomas but not a lick of common sense!"

Marchin' past Miss G as if he were talking solely to hisself, he snagged a chair-back and slung it back like he aimed to toss it against the nearest wall. In the end, he sat down with a huff, his lips all puffed out like a scolded young 'un. 'Neath the bright lights of the dining hall, he resembled one of them hateful, constantly scowlin' skinheads we used to see prowlin' the outskirts of the projects.

"Well hello to you too, Mister Happy. Forget to put on your hair this morning?" Miss G asked with a giggle, spittin' out a few flecks of wheat bread in the process.

He ignored her easy enough, drummin' his fingers across that tabletop like he was tappin' the keys of an invisible organ.

"Smart-ass pill-pusher talks like I've got five *years* to pack on that weight instead of five months! Tells me if I keep up present daily calorie intake, I'm liable to seize up with either a heart attack or major stroke. So I say, gimme an alternative, shit-for-brains! Tell me how I'm supposed to seal the deal, a fucking *impossibility* as it is…by nibbling on carrot sticks and romaine lettuce! To that, the peanut gallery had no answer except to say I need to add an assorted veggie or slice of fruit to the diet. Soooo, I figure six to eight bananas smeared in peanut butter between meals oughta turn the trick. What say you, Miss *Wheezie*? Sound like a plan or what? As of right now, add a tree load of Chiquita bananas to the mix!"

Always with the baitin', but I was not about to cooperate by returning the spite.

"Oh, Mister J, you are a bird in this world, you are! Consider the banana order placed…in *bunches*."

"Okay…correct me if I'm wrong…perhaps hopping out to the very edge of a very shaky limb," Miss G chided, having more fun than I'd ever seen her allow herself, "but I'm catching a vibe…vague as it may be…that you and the kindly physician on staff are not seeing eye-to-eye on a diet strategy?"

Leaning back in his chair 'til I thought he was gonna topple over onto his bald noggin, Mister J's scornful expression made it obvious he was not seein' the humor.

"Clam up and eat your raisins, lady."

When he leaned back forward, I swear I detected just the tiniest of smiles cross that rugged face.

"Meantime, I got three pounds of lasagna and a dozen slices of garlic bread to stow away."

Taking a last sip of water, Miss G stood stiffly and yawned, spreadin' her arms like a bird about to take flight. Though those ugly-as-sin tights were still huggin' her snug, I could see a definite loosening around the midsection, hips and thighs.

"Don't forget the dozen bananas smothered in Jif. Later, alligator. See you at the gym first thing a.m.?"

"Hey, the hell else I got to do, lady?" he shot back gruffly, though the hard-ass jig was up and they both knew it. "Better bring the A-game, sister, 'cause this boy don't share gym-time with slackers."

Yep, they were slowly, ever-so-gradually, becomin' birds of a feather—birds with opposite but similar goals—birds holdin' a similar grudge against the same foe—birds that might find, over time, they just might have more in common than first meets the eye. Yessum...much, much more.

Five

Nailed into a Groove

Part One: *Notes to the Boss*
Narrator*: Doctor Darwin McClintock*

There is but a single word that so effectively describes the transformation of Brian Jorgensen at the dawn of day sixty of this one-hundred-eighty day gauntlet. Shocking. If able to stand with his former self, day one's version, back to back with this new incarnation, the resemblance would be vague at best, other than say, the facial features. I'd observed this metamorphosis in weekly fragments at his regular weigh-in and blood-work session. If framed in still frames like a grainy, black and white slideshow, the changes would be breathtaking, akin to some freakish mutation filmed exclusively for a B-grade sci-fi film. The weigh-in from the previous week alone was enough to initiate a double-take of disbelief on my part and subsequently, a knowing nod and devilish grin from the source of my befuddlement.

"What's the problem, Doc? Doubting what the spectacles are reflecting? Well, don't pop a pupil, bud. What you see is what you get," he'd gushed, stepping back and flexing like an enraged bull-ape.

"Indeed," I'd mumbled, pecking furiously at the I-chart filling my left palm. In a single week, seven days, one-hundred sixty-eight hours, Brian Jorgensen had added an additional ten and three-quarter pounds to his ever-expanding frame. This relegated last's week's number, a then-astonishing eight and a half, to pale secondary status. All told, the accumulative total now stood at forty-two and a quarter. Considering his present regimen had not even begun until the three week point, such gains were as frightening as they were miraculous. Forty-two-plus pounds in thirty-eight days. If then, he'd initiated said program at the outset, I quickly deduced a possible gain of seventy-four pounds. Elated as Jorgensen had been, and not to *burst his bubble* as is the popular refrain, I felt it my duty to spell out the potential hazards of such a dramatic alternation to one's physical makeup.

"I take it you've shaken off the effects of the sedative then," I began, tapping on the I-chart's miniscule keyboard in order to bring up the blood-work results.

"Like wow! Those laughing-gas power naps do wonders for my bloated old soul, Doc. I do believe there's a six-hour workout in my immediate future."

"Of that I have no doubt, Mister Jorgensen," I replied honestly, taken aback by the man's sudden jubilation, being as I'd grown quite accustomed to his...less amiable side.

"As far as your numbers go...I've got some, well, positive news to impart."

He clapped his hands spastically and I involuntarily flinched.

"Well, by all means spill the beans, Doctor Doolittle. Damn, this is turning out to be the finest day I've spent inside this concrete suppository."

"I'm...well, glad to hear it, Mister Jorgensen. Now, about my readings..."

"No bullshit, Doc, whattaya think? I mean, am I the *shit* or what?" he beamed, stepping back and striking a classic bodybuilder's pose with arms raised, clenched fists turned inward, biceps pumped and bare chest expanded. Indeed, it was a breathtaking transfiguration.

"You know, I'm beginning to think I pegged this all wrong from the get-go. Chicks always dig muscle-men, right?"

"Well, um, I'm no expert...that is, I can't really say what best stimulates the female libido..."

No longer flexing, he kneeled before my image with his elbows propped atop bent knees. His expression held a unique curiosity, as if for the very first time, he actually deemed my opinion vital to his own way of thinking.

"Think about it, man. I got three, four more layers of slab to lay before that final bell chimes. I'll be a real life Hulk, sans the jade shade, only with charm...charisma...cock-strong and stout as a 'dozer. How can your average Jane hope to fight off the urge to jump my bulky bones? Yep, it's all clear to me now, Doc...this is my second phase...my *blooming* as you Brits might say. I'm slowly shedding the skin of that initial phase...well, more like blowing it up 'til it snaps off like strips of elastic. Either way, I'm learning...no, I've *learned* to embrace the metamer...metamac...meta..."

"Metamorphosis," I interrupted, focusing intently on the I-chart in order to avoid his warped, rather disturbing smile.

"That's it! Sooo, about those stats you were so eager to share..."

Though not comprehending quite why, I suddenly dreaded the act of providing his bloated ego, pardon the pun, additional ammunition. Still, it was my job after all, and blatant dishonesty is most definitely not a part of the physician's oath.

"Yes, well...they are...encouraging, especially in considering the horrid totals of the past few weeks. Despite the remarkable weight increase that seems to be...picking up steam in lieu of slowing, your blood sugar has stabilized, as has your cholesterol. Cell count normal, as are liver functions. Blood pressure only slightly elevated at one-thirty-five over eighty-five. As for the weight itself, I wonder..."

At that juncture, I paused, peeking up from the chart to Mister Jorgensen with a cocked brow, an expression that was met with raised palms.

"Nary a steroid injection or HGH supplement has this boy induced...Scout's honor. Seriously, bud, where exactly would I procure such a stash?"

To conclude, and as to officially seal the deal, he flashed the Scout's three-pronged salute of honesty.

"There is no questioning the legitimacy of your...performance, as access to such chemical enhancers is, as you stated, not remotely possible."

Scowling, his hands dropped while his shoulders simultaneously slumped in comic despair.

"I was jerking your stethoscope, Doc. Numbers don't lie. It's a lethal mix...splitting the day into three distinct activities: diet, weights, and slumber, usually doled out in hourly increments of four, five, and at ten a day, emphasis on the slumber. Can't make the gains without the pain...can't take the pain without proper nourishment...and can't digest the nutrients or heal the tissue without plenty of shuteye."

"You make it sound so...well, simple."

He nodded agreeably, his squared, cleanly-shaven chin resting atop a clenched fist. In such a pose, he resembled an overly puffed version of the Thinker statue.

"Well, it also helps to abstain from nasty little habits that tend to stunt the growth potential. Lack of sleep from an overabundance of boob-tube or 'net surfing, the latter usually leading to countless sessions of yankin' the pud."

"I don't...yanking the pub?"

He smiled rather...mischievously.

"You know, Doc...choking the rooster."

Utterly clueless, I shrugged helplessly.

"Strokin' the monkey."

"I...um...well..."

"Mas-tur-ba-tion."

"Ohhh, yes, of course."

"Weakens the mind and body...drains a man's will. Abstinence from groping my privates has been, other than an almost unbearable yearning for the occasional beer while watching sporting events, the biggest challenge by far."

"May I ask...," I began, hesitant to continue in fear of spoiling the rare upbeat mood of my patient.

"Shoot."

"Well, it's just that...your file describes one of your more...notable personality traits as being that of a...well, a romantic rogue of sorts."

Bowing slightly, Jorgensen rebounded with a grin of pure, unbridled pride that instantly enhanced even further my natural dislike of the man.

"Yeah, well...my rep precedes me," he chortled, "actually, it's the main reason I found myself checked into this wacky hotel. Sticking my tool where it didn't belong never has worked out, but it was always a craving...a deep-down itch that begged to be scratched, if you know where I'm coming from. Bet you've had a few carnal knowledge couch sessions yourself over the years, right, Doc?" he concluded with a wink.

"Well, um, my point is...there is, obviously, an unattached female on the premises, correct?"

From his wild, comically wide-eyed expression, one would think I'd suggested a tryst between himself and a water buffalo.

"Say wha…? Ugh, you injecting your own goods, Doc? Inhale a few whiffs of laughing gas, did we? Shiiit, me and Hanley's daughter an item? Brother, not if she were the last chicky-pie on the planet…um, well," he sputtered, gesturing spastically with both hands as if to ward off evil spirits, "that didn't sound…I mean, technically she is the *last* chick… anyway… enough nonsensical horseshit, McClintock…let's snap back to reality, what say?"

Abruptly, his entire deportment altered from relaxed and casual to edgy and tense, his face glowing beet red. I decided, wisely I'm sure, not to press the issue despite a nagging curiosity.

"Y-yes…fine. Back to business then. As I've stated, your current readings are indeed a pleasant surprise. Sticking to the new, improved diet I suggested?"

"Carbs, carbs and more carbs, my man, with the occasional sea of baked fish or flock of chicken tossed in for good measure. Oh, and baked potatoes by the half-dozen."

"And breakfast usually consists of?"

"Ahhh, the most important meal of the day…well, lately it's either been a pitcher full of raw eggs mixed with handfuls of wheat germ, or heaping bowls of baked liver washed down with a jug of two-percent cow's milk. Stomach starting to growl yet, Doc?"

"Truly tempting, yes…think I'll pass for the time. I can only advise you, well, keep it up then. No cardio still?"

Jorgensen nodded vehemently before concluding this particular rant with a nasty sneer.

"You kidding? Pure sacrilege, brother. Rules are simple: walk instead of run; sit, don't stand; lay, don't sit when you can lie down. Burning calories is limited to weight pumping only. Even gave up the daily battering of the hard bag. No small feat that. Old habits, you know? "

"Yes, well, um…"

It would've been simple to merely humor the man in order to maintain what had been by far our most civilized exchange since initial intros. It was hardly my intent to rain on the man's parade in wake of such an unusually cheery mood. But then, there is always the matter of professional ethics to entertain—indeed a curse at such times when it threatens to further damage an already shaky physician/patient relationship.

"Ahhh hell, here we go," he moaned, leaning back with a dramatic roll of the eyes. "I had a feeling we wouldn't reach the finish line without at least a cameo appearance from good ol' Doctor Death."

As had become habit, I ignored the gnawing sarcasm and pressed on. Jorgensen arose and began to pace with his head hung low. I felt at least fortunate of being incapable of enduring the sour stench of stale perspiration no doubt swirling about his hulking frame like a misty vapor trail.

"Despite this present dose of admittedly positive news, it is my obligation as on-site physician to warn you of some, well, potential roadblocks lying in wait..."

Falling to one knee, he flung his massive arms around like twin windmills before pointing to the stone ceiling with extended forefingers.

"Yep...here come the storm clouds...dark as a coal-miner's bunghole to swallow the sun."

"Mr. Jorgensen, I assure you I am not playing alarmist. The risk is very real for someone in the throngs of such a, unique alteration of the physical shell. Perhaps, by setting a few simple ground rules, we can better the odds of tiptoeing through the minefield ahead without losing a single toe."

"Minefi....losing a toe?" Jorgensen howled gleefully while whipping his head back like a baying coyote, "shit, Doc, then by all means you gotta give it to me straight."

He paused, the maniacal grin now more akin to a wolfish scowl. Cracks in the façade, no doubt. Not surprising, considering the immense pressure.

"How long do I have?"

"I'm assuming the answer you seek is somewhere in the one-hundred twenty day range."

"One-twenty-one, to be exact. Just want to hang on long enough to spit in the eye of a certain mob dictator before swallowing a sizeable load of lead."

"I won't and cannot make promises concerning your mortality, Mr. Jorgenson. However, what I can promise..." I paused, tucking the chart to my lower abdomen and striding within a tiny circle in and around where my bulky patient crouched.

"...that despite such valiant efforts on your part to maintain a semi-healthy diet, the human body is not designed to add a pound of weight per day...every day. Not without...probable consequences."

"Such as cultivating a six to seven time a day crap habit? Done."

"Such would have to be considered normal bowel movements in light of the daily consumption involved. The more alarming symptoms..."

His interruption came without passion; throwaway dialogue meant only to annoy.

"Noticed a shortage of breath the last week or so. Forcing me to wait longer between sets of bench... squats.... leg lifts. Cutting down on reps has helped."

I broke in only when his labored sighs allowed.

"Perhaps nothing more than exercise-induced asthma. No, Mister Jorgensen, I'm speaking more of...internal dangers."

"Like what, Doc? A ruptured spleen? Shriveled liver? A dislodged gonad, perhaps?"

"More like clogged arteries leading to a sudden stroke or failing kidneys. I'm speaking of the outset of diabetes, Mr. Jorgensen. Such extremes in diet could serve as not only the igniter, the lit fuse if you will, but trigger an acceleration through the stages of said condition at warp speed."

A true rarity, I read true concern on the man's normally stoic guise—a squinting of the eyes and crinkling of the forehead.

"Soooo Doctor Giggles, since I have little choice but to keep on truckin' with the status quo, what do you suggest as a...well, a buffer to avoid such a...fatal pitfall?"

Utterly ridiculous as it sounds, such sincere concern within myself brought forth a brief rush of excitement.

"You're...willing to listen? I mean, seriously listen?"

"Listen, Doc," he replied, rising to stand with hands on hips, his expression stony; so deadpan to appear almost comical, "I'm willing to learn whatever I need to learn to reach the goal. You think I'd have gone through the early stages of this shit otherwise? Dude, I've already taken a moon-sized wrecking ball to the cathedral that was my former physique—a physique I'd created and then maintained through decades of self-control. Blew that shapely, chiseled motherfucker up in a matter of weeks. Yeah, I'm dead serious. Talk to me."

For the next twenty-six uninterrupted minutes, I did just that.

~ * ~

Part Two: *Notes to the Boss*
Narrator: *Personal trainer Gabriel Maxwell*

Two months in and LeAnn Garner has come leaps and bounds from the emotionally deflated, rolled mass of lard with worm-dirt level self-esteem that that been hauled feet-first into the silo's ground level entrance like a soggy slab of beef. Earlier that morning at her bi-weekly weigh-in, ol' doc prissy-britches had confirmed what these twenty-twenty baby-blues could plainly decipher without benefit of digital scales: she was right on schedule to grasp the brass ring four months down the road. The six or seven sizes too small jumpsuit she'd been squeezed into like a medicine ball into a peanut shell was beginning to hang in places, most obviously at the midsection and buttocks. Her jowls, before so puffy they resembled a gluttony squirrel collectin' enough nuts for multiple winters, appeared noticeably deflated. Similar shrinkage was occurring at a rapid pace just below the feedin' hole, where the triple-chin from in-processing day had vanished by exactly half. Strange, that in the face of all this positivity, the girl's dogged expression and dumpy, energy-less posture was the exact opposite from what I'd expected. With a resounding grunt, she sat at the center of the warm-up mat and sighed, scowlin' like she'd just taken a big ol' heapin' chew from a dog-turd sub. Though not exactly rare for the female type to exhibit such behavior, I was beginning to see a pattern in her grouchiness—a pattern that had little to do with menstruation-type issues unless her bleeding cycle was striking bi-weekly.

"Well, top of the mid-mornin' to you, sunshine. Decide to sleep in, did we?" I asked with as much mock cheer as could be drudged up. After a short pause, wherein I actually thought she nodded off with chin atop chest, her head slowly arose as if being gradually lifted via invisible marionette strings. Dark shading underlined each eye, resemblin' ballplayers from a lost era. Toss in the disheveled, birds-nest doo, ashen-colored cheeks and chapped, chalky-pale lips and the undead look was complete, as if she'd just walked off the set of some z-grade zombie flick.

"Can't claim the act of actual sleep had anything to do with it, no, but it isn't as if I didn't give it the old college try."

"You...sure you're up to this, Miss Garner?" I asked timidly, actually taking a step back as if physical retribution were possible, "I mean, you're...you appear a little under the weather, if you don't mind me sayin'."

Not surprisingly considering her appearance, her response was weak, drained. If I didn't know better, I'd say the woman was sporting the King Kong of hangovers. But then, even the non-brain surgeon such as myself could figure out the source, make that *sources*, of her ills.

"How about a streamlined version of the usual torture session? As in, maybe half the usual? Figure I can hack my way through at least that much without a coronary interrupting."

Though not at all necessary, I felt the need to sate my curiosity.

"Diet's still getting to you, big time. The limits of said menu, I mean."

"Miss Jeannine is a master, but...yeah, my kingdom for a sixteen ounce sirloin smothered in onions."

"Lack of protein. Ever consider splurging now and then? I mean, a couple'a cheeseburgers ain't gonna derail the whole train, right? Maybe just the caboose..."

She shook her head weakly from side to side, though not before licking her lips at the mere notion. Damn if I didn't feel a twinge of pity at the sight.

"Negative. I know my limitations and especially my weaknesses...assorted they may be. I go down that road once, I might never reclaim the same level of self-control."

She sighed heavily, holding up her pasty right hand and watching it twitch and shake like a wino in the throngs of a forced detox.

"Besides, it's not just...it's more than that."

"Still with the chemical withdrawal?"

The smile she flashed was just about the saddest I'd ever witnessed. She shot me a wink.

"You got it, Ace. Thought I'd shaken such urges after the first month. Obviously not. Maybe the lack of sleep gave 'em an opening to restart. Immune system is in tatters...only makes sense, I guess."

"Personal ignorance aside, I'd say yeah," I nodded in sincere agreement, "I take it a sleeping pill's outta the question?"

"You think?" came the sardonic reply I'd secretly hoped to hear in order to rebirth a spark from her lifeless husk.

"Oh yeah...guess not."

"McClintock said my blood-work was borderline anemic. He suggested Jeannine toss in some baked fish and maybe a tuna salad just to get the oil levels up."

She stood and began a half-hearted set of side-stretches.

"I still say toss in a slab of bovine every few days, maybe a six-ouncer with a baked 'tater. You'll burn it off the next morning. Hell, I'll see to it you do. Otherwise, you sink any lower I'll have to hook up a set of pulleys just to get ya movin'. As for that...other thing, 'fraid those are demons nobody can exorcise but you."

She halted in mid-hand-to-toe touch and stink-eyed me like I'd just called her mama a crack-whore.

"Playing counselor again, Maxwell? What say we get through this without further skull-massaging, huh? I just want to get back upstairs and attempt to get comatose."

Sufficiently fired up, she waltzed over to the Gazelle-rider and hopped aboard with renewed vigor. Hours later and having actually completed the full workout, she limped silently away with only a weak wave my way serving as the day's farewell. The chick was tough, I'll give her that. The shit was, as nail-stout as her psyche might be, there were harsher times ahead. Mucho harsher indeed.

One-hundred and twenty days and a wakeup away from sweet deliverance, she'd barely tipped the ice-burg. If I were a...still a betting man, well, sad to say if the choice were her or the field...I'd still have had to lay all chips on the field...but only by a whisker.

~ * ~

The corners of his mouth dripped butter as he'd turned in greetings, manning the middle of three seats that made up the theater room's front row. The lights dimmed only partially, Garner could plainly make the oily sheen coating the fingers of Jorgensen's left hand, extended high in animated salutation. On the wide, brightly illuminated screen, a bearded, badge-wearing

Chuck Norris was taking on a bar full of beer-gutted buffoons, most of which chose foolishly a one-on-one assault in lieu of a group effort, and was kicking some serious butt.

"Well, hello there, lady-slim…" Jorgenson cracked between noisy smacks, the screen lighting reflecting off his bald dome like a vintage strobe, "…popcorn? Looks like you could use an extra-large tub."

Before taking a seat in the back row, she displayed a bare palm his way.

"I'll pass, thanks. So, like a little corn with your butter there, chubs?"

Jorgenson tossed in a mouthful and chewed greedily, a few puffy kernels popping free from between his butter-slick lips.

"Oh, so that's how it's gonna be now? Fat jokes? Strange, I sure as hell didn't hear any complaints last night, at least not about a certain *bulkiness* south of the border."

Wide-eyed, Garner pursed her lips and waved frantically with both hands, as if to whisk away a nasty stench.

"Shhhh, stow that kind of dialogue, mister," she whispered, scanning the room from side to side. "Who's to say who might be eavesdropping?"

Jorgensen's curt response, delivered with a toothy, Cheshire-cat grin, was drowned out by the film's booming audio.

Each temporarily turned their attention to the screen just as Chuck drop-kicked a shirtless biker through a saloon's glass window.

"You want I should rewind? Its only about halfway through, I think," Jorgensen bellowed between sips from a tall plastic cup, the faint sound of rattling ice heard upon its descent back towards his lap. "*Code of Silence*…one of the Chuck-ster's best."

"Not necessary," she retorted unnecessarily loudly between cupped hands, "pretty sure I can guess the ending. I surmise from this particular choice you've had your *rom-com* fill."

Shoving in yet another handful, his head reared back like a feeding buzzard, Jorgensen's only reply was a slight shrug of his massive shoulders.

Comically underdressed as usual for their thrice-weekly 'movie night' in only a food-stain-spattered white tee and faded sweats—sweats that once hung like circus netting now semi-snug against each thigh, Jorgensen stood just as the fight scene concluded to effectively mimic the lead actor's martial arts moves almost to the tee despite the recently added bulk.

At the conclusion of said exhibition, a reverse-roundhouse delivered with a resounding warrior's yelp, Jorgensen practically collapsed back into his chair just as the lone spectator stood to deliver a raucous round of applause.

"Bravo! Encore! *Author!*" she blurted between claps, the noise level of her efforts doubled due to the sudden silence of the movie, which had fallen silent for a scene change.

Madly panting, Jorgensen was only able to toss her a quick salute.

A half-hour later, they sat in blissful silence, the screen faded to black and the lights dimmed to almost complete blackness.

"So how's about a nightcap, Slim?"

"My god but you're an insatiable scamp, aren't you? And here I'd always heard fat guys were without passion."

"What can I say? High T runs in the family."

There was a pause, followed by a weary sigh.

"Give me a rain-check, lover-boy. Energy level's at an all-time low. Afraid tonight the Sandman has my heart."

"Good luck with that, sweetheart. From what you've told me, *that* lying prick ain't nothing but a tease, unlike yours truly, who *always* delivers the goods."

"There's some truth in what you say..." she replied wearily, pausing to stifle a yawn, "...he most certainly does tease."

Their smiles originated in perfect unison, as were the matching, playful winks, followed by a brief but comfortable silence.

"So tell me true, Slim. You think old man Hanley wi-...would take issue with our couplings? I mean, if he was to find out?"

"It's no game-changer. We're all over twenty-one here. I mean, he tossed us in here together like breeding pandas, right?"

Laughter, deep and hearty.

"Breeding Pan...? Wow...that's hot."

Garner giggled, a girlish cut off in mid-cackle by a pressed palm.

"Pray tell, is there anything that's a turnoff in that sick little mind, Romeo? Hairy toes? Wart-infested Cankles? Smelly armpits, perhaps?"

"Keep going..." he chided, reaching over to jab her shoulder with an extended forefinger, "...so far, no dice."

"But seriously, the man can't be too thrilled with the prospect. I mean, the same guy humpin' both his wife and daughter? Could be some serious fireworks on homecoming day, ya think?"

"Humpin' both his....wow. What a sweet talker you are, muscles. No wonder alllll the women swoon."

Jorgensen leaned in, his voice dropping an additional few decibels.

"Serious, Slim. You've got to figure his team of spies have...caught wind of our little non-secret and are under obligation to share with the man signing their checks, right?"

"Probabilities are high, yes," she agreed without pause, "that is, if all the hidden cameras haven't given up the ghost long ago."

Playing dense, Jorgensen nodded while scanning the surrounding gloom.

"You got that straight. Regardless of how he finds out, you think they'll be a price to pay once this train rolls into the home station?"

"Are you asking me whether or not I think my father is capable of pulling a double-cross?"

Jorgensen cocked a brow and flashed a thumbs up.

"Bingo. Let's say we both meet the set goal upon the sun's rising on D-Day but your pop's anger over our...coupling gets the best of 'im..."

"My father is a lot of things," she spat without hesitation, her lips pursed tight and her eyes slightly squinted, "but a liar isn't one of them. Ludicrous as that sounds when taking into consideration his...business interests, it's a...Hanley trademark. Honest as he is vindictive, I've heard it said."

The big man sighed in either exasperation or relief, Garner's cupped hand gently rubbing his massive left forearm, both her curt tone and strained expression instantly easing.

"If we beat him, we beat him. They'll be no surprise retribution over our...humping sessions, okay?"

Before departing the space's tranquil, murky confines, Jorgensen leaned in and delivered a peck on Garner's exposed left cheek, a passionless smooch more suited for brother and sister.

"Hey, you need a shoulder...or anything else for that matter, you know..."

"Where to find you," she concluded morosely, "not to fear, lover-boy, a handful of vitamins and an egg-white omelet and I'll be good as new."

As they stepped into the waiting elevator, she leaned on him for support.

"Don't fret, Slim," he whispered near her exposed left ear, her head tilted sharply onto his shoulder, "or lose any sleep over us. It ain't love, after all."

"Far from it, Chubs," she replied with similar aplomb, "so far from it that, by comparison, liberation seems only a hop, skip and weigh-in away."

Jorgensen snickered, nudging her head gently.

"Damn. You sure know how to hurt a guy."

Six

Of Milestones and Miseries

Part One*: Notes to the Boss*
Narrator*: Miss Jeannine, facility cook*

Reaching day one-hundred should've been reason to celebrate. Not only had they survived the first three-months plus, but in terms of reachin' their goals, thrived even. Just as I'd figured, though it had taken longer than foretold, a bond had formed 'tween 'em—that special man-woman bond that god created just for us to help maintain sanity. Tangible proof withstandin', I had an inklin' the bond in question had snagged a might, leading directly to the odd behavior on exhibit the mornin' of that milestone day. They'd been many a hint of things being askew, none of which were concrete enough to donate fact, but stout as steel nonetheless for these bleary old eyes.

First off, for the first time in weeks, they'd shown up separately for breakfast. Secondly, upon arrival, both had worn similar masks of sourness. Third and lastly was the eatin' habits themselves. As my dear departed lesser half was apt to say about such peculiarities, they was strictly *ass-backwards*.

Miss G had appeared first, just past six, her slumped posture and wobblin' gait a perfect match for the gloomy sneer pasted across a mug that was fast becomin' unrecognizable from earlier days. Bein' that she hadn't outlined a menu for that morning's feedin', a first since waaaay back in week one, I'd had little choice but to leave behind the default, that bein' a fruit salad and pre-brewed green tea. Well, it was clear as crystal within a few ticks she was less than thrilled at the spread.

"Miss Jeannine," she whispered softly, her eyes never leaving the bowl parked 'tween her spread forearms, "I'm going to need something a bit...more...no, a *ton* more substantial."

"Fine," I replied as she'd pushed the bowl aside and laid her face flush atop the marble table, "of course, you'll have to submit any amendment as a lunch reque..."

"*BULLSHIT!*" she hollered, a boomin' screech I was surprised didn't shatter the tea cup.

"Miss G, you know I can't prep..."

Though the noise level had dropped back down to normal, the tone was a damn mite scarier than any scream. It's like I was talkin' to a total stranger. Raised under a cloud of ancient superstition as a child, I'd oft been told of demon possessions. Until that very moment, I'd never bore witness to anything resemblin' such. Swear to the good book, every wild hair I owned stood straight out like a porcupine quill.

"Not today, da-damn it...no rabbit servings this day," she sobbed, her shoulders shakin' and her lips quiverin' like worms on a hook, "We...I need...real food."

She looked up at me then, Miss G...her expression nothing short of haunting—eyes brimmin' with tears. If physically possible, I would've surely walked over and wrapped these big, blubbery arms around that woman and provided my best comfort squeeze.

"Y-you need...you have to help me, Jeannine. W-we have to...work out a...new menu."

"Surely, Miss LeAnn. Surely. Whatever you need, hon."

Once she'd wiped the moistness from her eyes with a table napkin and blown her nose into same, she'd spewed out one final, exasperated sob and stared up at me with a renewed fierceness—a mask of fiery resolve that spoke volumes for the courage of the woman, especially considering the moon-sized secret she was soon to reveal.

"I...require...need meals that are protein-high while, if possible, remaining as low in calories as possible. I need to know if...it's even possible to..."

Another pause as she pawed another napkin and commenced to re-wipe her nose. With this brief respite, I couldn't help but ponder the origin of the darkness that was drivin' Miss G to such a state. At first I figured an argument between herself and Mister J might've turned ugly, but saw no proof of such a skirmish. It was no secret the two had become an item, so a lover's quarrel or two is just natural progression as the relationship gradually builds and finds its natural groove. Takin' into consideration the differences in the two's personalities, there was gonna be battles to overcome, no doubt. As it was, though, I'd been a tad off-base with such thinkin', at least I was tooling around in the right neighborhood.

"What, child? So far, I ain't heard nothin' I can't handle."

In cupping her hands at her bosom, it appeared as the poor child was preppin' to pray and beg at the same time.

"I mean, what it is...I don't want to give up...and revert back to old weaknesses. I've...come so far and to...throw it all away with...the finish line just...over the horizon."

Figuring she was teeterin' on the edge of confession, I couldn't help but provide a slight nudge.

"What's this all about, dear? I don't mean to pry, you understand, but I can help you best if I know the whys and wherefores."

Didn't know how she'd react to such boldness. Wouldn't have been a shock if she'd kicked the table over and stormed out like a rabid 'coon. Instead, she sucked in a fresh lungful, folded both arms around her chest and let me have it with both barrels.

"Well, why not? According to the good doctor, I am now eating for *two*."

Despite my best efforts in blocking such a knee-jerk reaction, I gasped aloud.

"You're...with child?"

"Apparently. *Two* pregnancy tests can't be faulty, right?"

"Did the doctor confirm?"

"Blood test did just that last yesterday afternoon."

Not often in her lifetime has this woman lost the power of speech, a fact my dear departed would gladly verify if he could, but those next few moments were spent attemptin' to string together a suitable reply. In the end, after what seemed like a half-hour but was probably no more than forty, forty-five ticks, I could only manage this: "Well, you just know I'm here for you, LeAnn. You and your...that little miracle you're carryin' will be fed the best and healthiest my kitchen as to offer, you hear? Miss Jeannine's *mental* cookbook is just chock full of meals meant to keep mama and offspring healthy and trim," I blurted, probably a bit too enthusiastically and hoping it didn't come off that way.

Her reply, indifferent or otherwise, was cut off with the less-than-tranquil arrival of her better half, who came stompin' in like a pissed off bull-moose.

"Holy shi....just what the fuck were you thinking? Jesus, why is it that females are totally incapable of keeping their lips from flapping free like loose sails in a stiff breeze?"

Miss G just rolled her eyes and snarled, not even botherin' to acknowledge his presence otherwise. I should say his *massive* presence. Dramatics aside, the man was gradually evolvin' into a frightening sight to behold. All swollen and bloated like a blow fish 'til he was almost unrecognizable from the man of one-hundred days previous. Swear on the good book it was like he'd grown a suit of blubber over another of pure muscle and the two had blended or mated 'neath the skin. Sounds gruesome I know, but it's the best descript I can give.

"Ahh, clam up, asshole...like it's a big secret. I'm of the belief my father knew of the pregnancy mere moments past conception."

"Well, if he didn't before he sure as *hell* does now, right?"

"I need to eat. Either sit down and join me or please skedaddle away like the half-man, half-roach you are."

There was no anger in her voice or gestures, just a weak-kneed weariness, like she'd built up some kind of inner immunity to further pain, physical or mental.

Cursin' under his breath, Brian Jorgensen waddled around to the other side of the table and took a seat. Huffin' and puffin' like a scolded preschooler, he struggled mightily for just the right comeback. Guilt or no, I have to say this amused me to no small degree.

Finally, he managed, bowing his head and mumblin' into the tabletop while rubbin' that bald head with both palms. I hadn't noticed the thickness of his neck and shoulders 'til that time. It was like he had slipped on a pale, puffy necklace...an inner-tube sewed of muscle and flesh. Lordy, it was like I was bearing witness to a gradual body-swap 'tween the two of 'em. It was downright *queer*.

"Hey, we have to talk about this, you know? I mean a serious discussion, not like that parody that barely passed for one last night. I'm damn near hoarse from that particular rant...not to mention the pain in my heels from pacing the floor at warp speed."

"I'm not in the mood. I need...to eat," Miss G countered, finally lookin' up and firin' twin-beams of anger his way.

"Speaking of which, what was your breakfast order?"

His eyes were saucers, his maw swingin' open like a busted shutter. She might as well have asked him if she could borrow a testicle for soup preparation.

"Say wha?"

"I need a meal. Substantial filler. What'cha got in the fridge for soggy-bottoms over here, Miss Jeannine?"

So distracted by the developments, I had to mull that over for several ticks before recallin' the previous night's preparations.

"Um, that'd be thick-cut ham slices, half a dozen in all, four eggs scrambled with cheddar cheese topping, steamed rice with peas and carrots and a bowl of Cheerios with sliced strawberries—all washed down with the daily quart of chocolate milk."

Swallowing hard, Miss G's face was pale as a virgin snowfall, like the mere mention of such a feast was twistin' her gut into a knot.

"Fine. The rice and veggies and maybe the bowl of cereal for now. N-not sure I could hold down much more at this juncture, being that the last three months-plus of nibbling like an anorexic gerbil has shrunk my stomach to the size of a coin purse."

Pathetic as it was, I felt the need to console as best I could.

"Miss G, don't you fret. I can whip up a cookbook's worth of special dishes guaranteed to both keep you on track for the required weight loss and maintain a normal progression of your unborn's health. It surely won't be the first time, believe you me. Fact is, you'd be surprised at the variety of choices."

Raising his hand like a young'un clamoring for a pee-break, Mister J's tone had softened several degrees since the boisterous entry. As we spoke, his eyes never left LeAnn, who seemed unwilling to match the gesture.

"I'll...I emailed both lunch and dinner...mostly beef, turkey and several tons of buttered pasta. Just don't wanna be forgotten here amongst all the drama."

With that, Miss G did react, slamming her palms on the tabletop and no doubt secretly reveling in Mister J's spastic, wide-eyed reaction.

"God, but what an A-one prince you are, Jorgenson," she snarled, baring her teeth like a cornered canine, "you really want to hop aboard that particular train again this early in the a.m.?"

"Hey, just a friendly reminder to Misses Butterworth that I've still got a dog in this race."

Hoping to provide a buffer 'tween 'm, I waddled over and took up a stance just a reach away from the table they shared.

"No worries, Mister J...I'll keep stewin', bakin' and fryin' up 'em as fast as you can gulp 'em down. Workin' on whippin' up those orders as we speak. Miss G's...special needs won't interfere with my plumpin' you up. Not in the least. I welcome the challenge, on both fronts."

He waved me off, continuing to stare LeAnn down with a pained scowl of his own.

"Yeah, whatever, *Wheezie*. Just see that you do. That *is* what you're being paid for, right? So what say you teleport your fat ass into the kitchen and get to it. I'd like to speak to my fellow inmate without the boss's hired help hovering overhead."

With that, Miss G turned to me and extended a finger that would've surely poked my left breast if physical contact were an option.

"You stay right *here*, Jeannine. I want you to hear this, and if necessary, record every word for future reference. Fact is, I'd even like an opinion. That is, if my father allows such verbal boldness from the hired help."

"Tell you the truth, Miss G, I'm not really in the position to give advi..."

"Just...do me a favor and stay," she cut in, peerin' up at me through desperate eyes, "I need a woman's perspective at the very least."

Backing away a step with my arms folded at my back, I stayed. With that, Mister J slid back in his chair with a loud squeak, scowlin' like a man suffering from permanent bowel blockage.

"Fucking-A then. Bring it on. Sure as hell won't be this boy's first *ménage a trois*. The female of the species have been teaming up on this dude for as long as memory serves," he paused, briefly breakin' character to wink, "one way or another, that is."

"Seriously, man? Sex jokes?" Miss G frowned, her pinched lips glowin' as ghostly pale as the rest. "Your kind possesses no shame."

Standing to swing the chair around, he then straddled it with those puffed-up arms hangin' over the seatback.

"Listen, Slim, if you're waiting for an apology, you'd better have the patience of Job. I said what I said and stand by it. Like I told you last night, it's nothing personal. I just require...verification."

"I've got a nine a.m. with McClintock this morning to inquire of your request."

Jorgensen shrugged, a brow still cocked in suspicion.

"Hey, that's all I ask. Now, I'd be more than happy to share my morning meal."

Pushing his bulk upright with a grunt, the grin he manufactured was as artificial as the static-shadow flowing at my backside.

"So riddle me this, Brian," Miss G asked with a clinched, pasty fist parked 'neath her chin, squinting through eyes slit pencil-thin, "once the DNA test comes back to reveal the only possible result, what's your plan?"

He stomped off toward the kitchen without reply, leavin' Miss G to drop her head and slump her shoulders. She soon regarded me with what had to be one of the sadder smiles I'd ever witnessed.

"He...his negative thinking is two-fold. To him, I was knocked-up upon arrival and in him have found the perfect scapegoat, or I purposely seduced him in order to entice our liaisons, thus leading to my present condition. Either way, I garner a free pass, pardon the pun, with the old man and, even if he does meet his goal, he's trapped as *mob baby-daddy* upon our liberation."

Strange, but the words came easy to me. Always is easier to speak the truth than manufacture a wheel-barrow packed with manure.

"I know I'm just one of many outsiders lookin' in, but I'd have to think a man like Mister J ain't exactly the type to own up to anything that don't suit 'im. Then again, if...if the child does prove to be of his makin', he just might surprise you in terms of takin' responsibility."

She laughed...no, giggled actually—a schoolgirl's cackle, rollin' those hazel-green beauties as if I'd just suggested her unborn might well be of the immaculate conception sort.

"Taking respon...you think I *want* that horse's ass involved in whatever comes to pass? As in...the two of us set up shop in some beach house, white-picket fences and the pitter-patter of little feet? Jeannine, you'll as soon be serving up popsicles on the banks of hell's hottest pit."

Rising stiffly, she gently tapped her midsection with both hands and sucked in a deep breath before inhaling with a low, drawn-out whistle 'tween gritted teeth. No doubt LeAnn Garner had played the role of strong, stalwart female most of her relatively young life. Regardless of the outer shell, I glimpsed the mask beneath. A mask sewn of apprehension and fear. A mask slowly splitting—unraveling at its brittle seams. It was, sad to say, a disguise I'd worn myself from time to time during spells of massive strife.

"All I want...from him...," she waved a hand toward the kitchen, where the sound of clanging pans emerged, "...and from my father, is to do the right thing...the *fair* thing. Not exactly reaching for the stars, right?"

Finding no suitable reply, I could only nod in agreement.

"Right. Then again, it may well be one hell of a reach at that."

~ * ~

Part Two: *Notes to the Boss*
Narrator: *Doctor Darwin McClintock*

I wouldn't have thought such a proclamation possible, and although it means less than nothing within the grand scheme, I truly didn't think my opinion regarding Brian Jorgensen's character could've possibly rated any lower than from our previous encounters. All that said, the check-up of morning one-hundred brought forth new, increasingly disturbing flaws in a shady deportment I'd long-since labeled Swiss cheese at best.

"I provide facts, Brian—facts which render such wild speculation on your part...well, utterly meaningless."

If ever a time he might've reached over and throttled me with those tree-trunk-sized arms, that most certainly would have been the moment. As it was, he could only fire laser-beams of fiery malice my way—not exactly a first.

"Well, moot or not, smartass, the chick didn't exactly waltz in here a virgin, right? So what the hell's so *wild* about it? Just spit out the gist as plainly as possible, Doc, omitting all the unnecessary vowels. Painful request I know, understanding how ego-maniacal types with built-in God complexes simply *adore* the sound of their own voices."

By this time I had grown quite accustomed to the man's constant baiting, thus maintaining a normal level of composure was less than strenuous.

"The gist is, Brian, is that the possibility that LeAnn Garner is three-months pregnant is absolutely, categorically nil. Oppositely, the pregnancy tests, that is plural, administered are ninety-nine percent effective within twenty-four hours of conception."

Tugging at the collar of his sweats, the fit of which grew snugger by the day, Brian appeared less exasperated at my verifying his fear than strangely...dare I say it...reassured.

"So the odds of my knocking her up are within the same general percentile as those aforementioned pregnancy tests."

"As you Yanks are apt to say...bingo."

With surprising grace considering his considerable bulk, Brian then hopped from the exam table and executed a single sharp clapping of his hands.

"Wonderful. No more mystery. Just needed to know, officially, where I stand. On to other issues, as in, how are the stats looking?"

Amazing the transition. Of course, perhaps those warped psyches—those void of conscience, are programmed with an internal diversion switch of sorts that allows for such effortless shifts in priority.

"Well," I complied, scanning the palm-pad chart though I'd already memorized the results, "at day one-oh-oh, the numbers, as usual, harbor a hybrid of both good and bad omens."

"You trying to say mixed bag, Shakespeare?"

"Indeed I di...am."

"Expected nothing less. So spill the beans already and..." he paused with a frown, folding massive arms over an equally bloated chest—a chest that, according to digital measurements, had expanded an astonishing six and a half inches in just over three months, "...could you spare all the big words this time around? Just...not in the mood."

For that single moment, recklessness overcame logic. In laymen's terms: I simply could...not...help...myself.

"Yes, I would imagine discovering one's impending fatherhood has the tendency to induce psychological traumas."

Shockingly, Jorgensen displayed the briefest of smiles before silently gesturing for me to continue.

"Weight is presently two-sixty-one point six."

Jorgensen shrugged, not at all fazed...at least outwardly.

"Understood. Just have to buckle down. Cut down on the cardio and double-up on the carbs."

Again, the casual wave of a hand as if to underscore an inner calmness.

"I'd lay off the red meats. Cholesterol levels are skyrocketing since last ch…"

"Fuck that heart-healthy mess, doc. I'm way past the point of no return."

In taking in the whole of the man: rounded midriff, puffy cheeks, pasty complexion, the faint but unmistakable formation of a double-chin, there was little point in arguing. Still, dishonesty in matters of medicine hardly comes easy in light of the cursed oath.

"Fervently *disagree*, Mister Jorgensen, but I digress in light of your apparent disinterest in your own mortality. I take it you require nothing further save a daily calorie intake gauge."

A double-thumbs up provided the obvious answer.

"To add the aforementioned poundage in the remaining time would require an intake of approximately… eight-thousand, six-hundred per twenty-four hour span. This is, of course, taking into effect that the daily burn does not exceed one-thousand, two-hundred."

"Geez, sounds like I'm even gonna have to slow my pee stream."

He sighed in apparent exasperation while picking at the gauze taped to the inside of his left elbow.

I took the moment to sneak in a word of advice. Again, the cursed oath raises its ever-persistent head.

"I'm aware of the temptation, but watch the sugar and sodium intake. Meeting the goal only to end up on a concrete slab in the immediate aftermath kind of…defeats the purpose…yes?"

"Yes, mother," he groaned, heading to the exit with a slight limp, the man's formerly taut backside resembling a pair of gradually inflating beach balls.

"Stick with the pasta, lean meat and fruits!" I continued as he nodded and waived me off like a pesky fly circling his noggin, "take your vitamins and cut down on the peanut butter or it'll pack your arteries like...like fix-a-flat!"

I was unable to refrain from smiling in wake of his final, barely audible response.

"Nag...nag...nag."

Despite Jorgensen's many and varied character flaws, there was undoubtedly a roguish charm there. As to whether or not he made it upright to that mystical finish line in eighty days, it was a veritable tossup. With what seemed a mountain of stress perched atop his ever-expanding shoulders, I figured it could go either way. Men like Jorgensen, lacking conscience and morals, often thrived when faced with such outlandish odds. They could also wilt faster than most if the steely outer shell suffered even the tiniest crack. Though sworn to indifference one way or another, I could not deny that the stretch run was going to be fascinating to watch...on both counts.

~ * ~

Part Three: *Notes to the Boss*
Narrator: *Personal trainer Gabriel Maxwell*

"Not sure what you want me to say, boss. Being that I've never worn the shoes you're presently wearin', I'm hardly qualified to spout advice."

"Crock of shit, Foghorn. You're just afraid old man Hanley will clip your pee-pee for speaking out."

Oh, Karate Charlie was in fine form this day, much to my misery. Chatterin' and yappin' like a toy poodle with a gut-load of espresso. But, in all fairness, he did have an issue or two to mull over, and folks like him are apt to do so by blarin' out everything in their mind to the nearest ear willin' to listen. In my case, there was no choice but let 'em bend.

"Nope, not even close. Truth is, I don't know the man near well enough to say what he'll do. Hell, not sure anybody does. First off, he ain't exactly Mister Predictability. Second, the issues on the table are not quite what one would consider, well, the ordinary type. Got a script right outta one of them nighttime soaps my ma was so fond of back in the day."

I stood over 'im as he pumped his third set of flat bench reps that mid-morning, increasin' the weight by fifty with each 'til he'd reached three-hundred-fifty even. In just over three months, I'd seen him go from a beginning weight of two-ten to past the big-three-oh and beyond. Damned impressive, considering the utter lack of chemical enhancement. Smart-mouthed bunghole that he was, I gotta give credit where credit was due. Layin' on layers of fat at a record clip hadn't done a thing to douse his determination.

"Yeah, yeah, and I'm sure you and the rest of Hanley's hired boot-lickers are enjoying every twist and turn."

No way I was letting him bait me into an argument as pointless as my phantom spotting.

"Whatever you say, boss. Change up..."

Pulling himself upright, he blew out a lungful and trudged over to the squat rack.

"Make no mistake, Goober. Despite the gradual movements and widening ass, the old IQ hasn't suffered an iota. On the morning of D-Day, Hanley's either gonna be forced to accept me into the family or sacrifice his own flesh and blood...times two, or he's gonna have me eradicated on site. For the life of me, I can't decide which. I'm guessing LeAnn's gonna have a say in deciding daddy's actions. Therein lies the main conundrum amongst a boatload of smaller ones."

Watched 'im secure his shoulders 'neath the racks pads without bothering to reply. Why bother? It ain't like he wasn't gonna keep flappin' his gums. He was on a roll and the way I saw it, I could just have well been a slab of sheetrock for all he cared.

"Have to say I laid into Slim... LeAnn... pretty damned good once she broke the news. Openly accused her of plotting to get knocked up just to garner...wow...pardon the pun...just to *gain* sympathy from the old man. I mean, no way he shuns her with a future grandchild baking in the oven, right? Gives her an instant pass on meeting the set goal too, I'd imagine."

As he paused to complete a set of three at two-twenty-five, huffin', puffin' and groanin' in the aftermath as I circled the machine, finally blurtin' out what I figured was a safe enough comeback.

"Tryin' to figure out how to apologize, chief?"

Once he didn't reply, I dared take it a step further.

"Collecting brownie points isn't exactly your bag, I'd wager."

He pounded out another three, his left knee poppin' like a snapped branch on the last.

Slipping free, he stepped into my path and I damned near passed right through 'im.

"Bet the farm, Goober. My balls are in the proverbial vise. It isn't like I completely trust that she *didn't* plan it, but.....hey, it isn't like anybody forced me to commence screwing."

Though it wasn't at all necessary, I side-stepped 'im. Old habits die hard. Easy enough. The hard part was fakin' sympathy to his plight.

"You're only human, bud."

"Funny, I'd never been attracted to the chunky types," he confessed while scoopin' up a nearby curl bar with fifty-pound plates attached to each end, "shit. There's the understatement of the millennium. Actually they sicken me no end. Lazy, plump-cheeked dimple-butts who usually reek from lack of hygiene. Had...*got* no tolerance for their kind, male or female. Trick is, I've grown fond of the girl. She's got moxie...and damned if she doesn't make me laugh. Sincerely, how the hell did this happen?"

I shrugged for want of anything else.

While completing a set of five, he finished the thought between inhales and exhales.

"Ironic, huh? Forced...to...become what I...despise the...most. Hanley must be loving every minute...of this shit. Probably whacking...off...with every new...layer of flab I add."

Droppin' the bar, he sauntered over to the free-weight rack and snared a couple of forty pounders before taking up position directly in front of the wall mirror and pumping out a set of lightnin'-quick shoulder presses. Big lug was sailin' through the workout like he had an appointment to get to.

"What's the hurry, boss? Got a load of laundry that just can't wait?"

He hauled a couple of fifties to the nearest bench and commenced a series of upright rows, right arm first. Added paunch aside, the man's triceps and biceps had pretty near doubled in girth from two months back, while his thighs and calves were both creeping up on tree-trunk status.

"Nope...just cutting down on...the duration. It's...a...calorie saving...technique. Gotta...save...and store...as many precious fat cells...as possible. They're like...little gold nuggets of s-salvation."

"Got'cha. It's the old don't run when you can walk...don't walk when you can sit...don't sit when you can lie down method."

Tossing the weights aside, he bent down with bare palms cupping his knee caps and blew wind like a monsoon—packed full of hot air with the occasional nugget of truth thrown in just to keep one off-track.

"Precisely. Simple logic I would've thought a *professional* trainer might've advised weeks prior. You're a piss-poor excuse, Goober."

With that, he lumbered away, wearin' the sourpuss scowl I'd grown so accustomed to, but hardly grown fond of. Unlike his incarcerated counterpart, Brian Jorgensen was a hard man to root for. Problem was, I was gonna have to start thinkin' of 'em as a team, and if rootin' for one meant rootin' for the other, so be it.

Moot point for the time being anyhow, as the script was about to flip...big time.

~ * ~

LeAnn gnawed at her left thumbnail while watching the closing credits flow gradually upward. Having apparently been in no mood for the usual dose of either romantic fantasy or comedic rom-com, she'd decided to match her present mood by choosing a particularly grisly horror flick. Such films had been referred to as torture porn—a mercifully short-lived subgenre that seemed to take great pride in excess gore through human cruelty, directed mostly toward women. Fifteen minutes into the movie, a brutal blood-fest entitled *Hostel*, she'd been forced to turn away from the screen's grimy glow before full-fledged entrancement set in— entrancement akin to viewing a particularly gruesome car crash. One hour and twenty minutes, a dislodged eyeball via rusty pliers and several severed fingers later, she'd no doubt been left to ponder the impossibilities of sleep once the time arose.

Once she'd powered down and departed the darkened chamber, the thumbnail replaced by an equally jagged twin from the same hand's forefinger, the abrupt, eerie silence seemed to engulf her. That is, until the faint echoes of a familiar pop tune reverberated from across the dimly lighted hall.

She paused roughly halfway between the theater and lounge, the toes of her bare feet gripping the deep shag carpet. Tip-toeing toward the entrance with cat-like stealth, she eventually posed with her back against the double-doors, careful not to exude enough weight to swing them inward. Just as the tune muted between piano and vocal riffs came the unmistakable sound of glasses striking together, as if a toast had been proposed. Soon to follow was the obviously drunken warbling of the mystery toaster, their comically off-key rendering easily drowning out the singer being mimicked.

Openly hesitant, LeAnn initially took a step back in the direction of the waiting elevator. Instead, she swung around and charged forward, shoving forcefully through the swinging doors and taking a full three strides inside.

Sitting atop the glimmering, slickly waxed bar top with his sandaled feet balanced loosely on a rounded stool, Jorgensen's eyes briefly widened in shock before a gradual recognition allowed for a softer reaction. The grin that ensued was as laughably warped as he raised a clear glass to eye-level, spilling a bit of content and several cubes of ice in the process.

"Well...hiya, Slim. Wet the whistle?"

"Think I'll pass, thanks."

She took a seat three barstools down just as the final chorus of Elton John's *"Rocket-Man"* faded to closure. Draining his glass with two long swallows, Jorgensen then slid it down the bar until it slapped against an empty bottle of JB Scotch, which had been turned onto its side.

"Ye-yeah...figured as much. Not to worry. I'm bel-beltin' down enough for the both of us."

His sweatshirt sat crooked on his upper torso, as if he'd recently attempted to strip it free but had halted in mid-tug. He'd removed his tennis shoes and was missing the sock from his left foot. As if pulled upon by opposite gravitational forces, the pointed tip of his mustache pointed upward from the left side and down from the right.

"So it appears," she replied, stone-faced despite the many humorous overtones of his inebriated appearance, "I didn't intend on interrupting or halting whatever it is you're...celebrating."

Jorgensen immediately hopped from the bar, landing somewhat awkwardly and reaching back to grip the bar's rounded edges in order to avoid toppling over a nearby table.

"Well....well, maybe I am at that. Didn't start out that way, I must conflesh...confess. Three and a half weeks since my last belt, I figured it might be a mistake to break that first label. But you...you see, Slim, I was feeling a bit of pressure that no amount of pounding weights or my pud was gonna alleviate."

LeAnn cracked a smile despite herself.

"Such a way with words, Romeo."

"Series-ly...seriously, Slim. You have...n-need...I need you to try to understand where I'm coming from here."

Lightly belching, he stumbled toward her and struck a beggar's pose, dropping to a knee with bare palms raised.

This time, it was LeAnn's eyes that widened.

"Lord G-God...please tell me this isn't a proposal..."

"N-no...not to worry. I would never in-insult you to the...that decree...degree. No, I just...this isn't easy for a horse's ass like me...to admit."

He paused as if attempting to form the desired dialogue, while no doubt struggling to form said words in the correct sequence.

"When...you told me about...when you revealed the...pregnancy, I have never...ever in my days been so damn shaken. I mean ever...not in competition or fighting for my very life. No lie, Slim. I...guess my...natural reaction...my way of rea- ...rationalizing was to strike out...and accuse. I...that shit just...wasn't right. I humbly and sincerely...apologize."

Staring down at the bowing drunkard with her arms crossed at her breasts, LeAnn's lips trembled and she was briefly forced to break eye contact. In the interim, Jorgensen resumed, an occasional normalizing of his voice breaking through the slur.

"Thick as a brick as I may be...I finally had an apiff...apaf...it came to me like a bolt outta the blue. We...we're in this shit together, Slim. I know...I realize that now. Whatever happens, we're peas in a pod. I...don't really think I can handle it...this alone. Believe you me, that's a first in itself. I've cursed your old man to hell and back for dumping you in here with me. But now...I kind of understand the mad...the method to his madness. He figured you'd use my failure as inspiration. He wanted you to see me fail...to not even try...and gain some inner strength from it. I...there's no fucking way he figured we'd form a team...or a...the bond we have, right? See where I'm going? Sorry if I'm rambling....but I've had two days and nights to dwell this over. As for...well..." he glanced her midsection, stopping just short of pointing, "...sounds cornball I know, especially considering the source...but I mean this... you can....count on me."

At the sight and sound of LeAnn rolling her eyes and sighing, respectively, Jorgensen raised both hands in surrender.

Their eyes reunited—his bloodshot and slightly moist, hers squinting and intense.

"I know...I know...taking into consideration my rep...well-earned I must confess...this is not bullshit, LeAnn...I'm speaking from the gut."

"Moreover, from the bottle," she added.

"Nope, not this boy," he protested, sliding over and gripping the empty scotch bottle before cradling it to his beefy chest with a drunken sneer. "This shit might serve to loosen the tongue a degree, but not the old noodle. I'm completely shin...sincere, my dear."

"So, ready to be a daddy, are we?" she chided, pushing away from the barstool to begin a gradual pace around the nearest table. "Just like that? A master of transformation...both physically and mentally."

Jorgensen shrugged meekly.

"Well, I don't...I mean, I'm not claim..."

"In terms of the physical, from the near-perfect physique, so meticulously chiseled to appear right at home if rendered in a superhero comic panel to the present version: a cumbersome, hybrid mass of blubber and bloated muscle."

Scowling, Jorgensen leaned back and slapped bare palms against his considerable yet still tightly packed midsection.

"What was...? Blubbersome thyroid? Hey, I resemble that rem..."

"Even more astounding by far is the mental metamorphosis."

"Slim, all that time you been spending in the library must be paying off, 'cause I'll be damned if I can tell if you're insulting or complimenting m..."

Now pacing to a far wall and back while zigzagging gracefully between tables, LeAnn paid no attention. Staring into the hardwood flooring, she'd tucked both hands tightly at the pit of her back.

"From conscienceless, egotistical, one-track-mind Lothario to caring father-to-be...all the matter of forty-eight short hours."

Twisting about like a stalking feline, her icy stare bore into him.

"Tell me something, Tubby...that is, while we're being so...heartfelt..."

Alcohol-boosted courage aside, Jorgensen unconsciously backed away a step until the middle of his back struck the bar's rounded edge.

"Y-yeah, Slim...sure...fire away."

Her voice hitched faintly at her throat as she seemed to levitate toward him without benefit of taking any actual steps forward.

"If I hadn't lost those first eighty or so pounds, would you ever have started fucking me?"

This time, it was Jorgensen's voice that hitched.

"W-wha....well, I...um...what the *hell* kind of ques...?"

"C'mon, Romeo...talk to me...think you could've ever got it up without me dropping a dozen rolls? Ever consider rolling me in flour to find the wet spot? I'm thinking you didn't feel the first twinge of horniness 'til about...oh..." sticking a forefinger to her left temple, she tilted her head as if in deep thought, "...week nine or so. If I recall correctly, that was about the time my ass cheeks had reappeared amid a drastic melting away of cottage cheese."

Hands parked atop hips, Jorgensen's expression fluctuated from slack-jawed shock to jaw-clinching rage.

"Y-yeah, okay...sure...fine and d-damned dandy. Go ahead and vent. Guess I had it coming after my jackass behavior the other night...but you gotta understand...this isn't easy..."

Fangs bared, she lunged forward, prompting an involuntary and woefully delayed flinch from the target of her rage.

"Not...easy? *NOT EASY*?! Oh, my heart bleeds, asshole!"

Backing away, she refolded her arms at her lower back while simultaneously reeling in the incisors. Still visibly shaken, Jorgensen fumbled for a reply—managing only a barely audible series of grunts before being unceremoniously cut off by a fresh salvo.

"So, you done waxing poetic? If not, by all means continue to declare your newfound dedication to our love-child."

With that, he stumbled forward with a wobbly forefinger raised airborne.

"Now wait ju-just a damn minute, wom..."

Ignoring his slurred objection, she barged ahead at full volume while resuming the circular pace from minutes earlier.

"Out...standing. Then it's officially my turn."

"First off, I will and...cannot forget nor remotely *forgive* your behavior when given the news of our...shared dilemma. I'm inclined to believe that little tirade revealed your true colors—colors long-since trademarked through years of self-serving acts from which that well-earned reputation was built. In other words, as much hurt as it did cause at the time, hindsight has shown it should have come as no surprise whatsoever. Once a selfish prick, always a selfish prick, I surmise."

"Hey, I said I was sor..."

Facing the lounge entrance, she twisted about to face him while shrugging casually.

"Not to be hypocritical, mind you. It isn't as if any divine entity's seeking this girl out to pass out angel wings. Slough-riddled junkies have little room to judge."

The sudden, seemingly sincere admission appeared to calm Jorgensen, whose lips clamped shut without benefit of a reply. Visibly wobbly, even posed with feet wide apart and hands on hips, he leaned gently back until the bar provided sufficient support.

"I'm no giddy school girl, fat stuff. Jackass behavior aside, your little rant and rave the other night did not serve to shatter a fragile heart. In other words, I didn't for a minute consider you my Prince Charming, nor did I register anything other than base lust in those baby-blues of yours as the mating season commenced. The wooing was mutual, buddy-boy, despite what your ego might claim. We used each other, plain and simple. It ain't love, remember?"

Wearing a thin, knowing smile, Jorgensen bowed his head in lieu of attempting an upper torso bow.

"Touché, Slim...touché. Basic human needs. Guess my...withdrawal skills were...a bit overrated after all. I just thou...figured twenty-some-odd years of practice made perfect. Guess one of those sneaky sac...suckers paddled upstream without our consent, as they are apt to do."

LeAnn turned away, pushing the doors open just enough to take an initial step out onto the walkway.

"Just so you know...I haven't decided on whether or not to...terminate the pregnancy. Talked it over with McClin...the doc. He has several alternatives at the ready. I told him I...need some time. Lots...angles to consider...obviously."

Lunging forth as if to depart just as Jorgensen pushed from the bar with his lips parting to respond, LeAnn froze in mid-stride.

"And no, you *don't* have a say. Decision's mine and mine alone. We...I think we should avoid each other's company for the time being, agreed?"

He sighed deeply, crossing his massive arms.

"Whatever you...say, Slim."

Just moments after the doors had shut quietly behind her and Jorgensen had staggered back to the bar to seek out a fresh source of liquid pain-killer, everything went as black as freshly lain tar.

Seven

Canned

Part One: Scaling the Nest

The first several moments of his reawakening saw Brian Jorgensen crawl about the carpeted floor like a skittering bug madly attempting to avoid the light. Rising to his knees, the lone noise piercing the deathly silence were his own strained huffs and the squeaky, drawn-out whistle of a fart he'd been hapless to contain.

"Wha-...where the...? Wh-hat the h-hell?" he muttered, reaching up to wave the back of one hand back and fro mere inches from the tip of his nose. Following several apprehensive moments, a faint blur was detected. With his vision sufficiently adjusted to recognize the closer objects, he stood upon loudly creaking knees and lumbered forward with arms extended, resembling a recently reincarnated mummy on the prowl.

"Wh-who turned out the li..." he'd whispered, just as a door flung open to his left, bathing the space in light that, compared with the interior's woeful lack of same, was akin to a supernova giving birth.

"Glad to see you back among the living, Tubs. How's the head?"

Shrieking and squinting as if to ward off the blazing rays of a noonday sun, Jorgensen nonetheless regarded LeAnn with a grin of pure, unbridled relief.

"Like a split melon, but feeling better by the tick."

Stumbling forth, he appeared to briefly consider delivering a bear hug to her ever-shrinking frame but wisely refrained, considering the two previous encounters.

"Wh-what happened, Slim? I pass out or..." he continued, wiping the sparse hair atop his rugged scalp with the bare palms of each hand, "...last thing I remember is you...stomping out in a huff talking about....talking of an abortion."

What he'd initially thought to be a great influx of bright light was promptly identified as a fraud, as LeAnn faced him while bathed in shadow, her cloaked expression a mystery.

"Sounds about right," she replied blandly, standing with hands on hips as the theater doors swung gently at her back, "just as dusk fell like a black cape."

Releasing a low belch reeking of stale booze, Jorgensen's face creased like crumpled tin foil.

"The English-language version is preferred, professor."

Though he was unable to visualize through the murk, Jorgensen was fairly certain a sour smirk accompanied the impending response.

"Somebody tripped the main, genius. Either that, or somebody's woefully behind on the power bill."

"*Jesus.* Then, why are we...are we able to..."

"Emergency lights. Three fixtures along the walkway—one about every ten feet of walking space. Probably the same set up on every floor. Strange they didn't mount at least one for the interiors."

Through a flutter of incessant blinking, Jorgensen reached out and clutched the tops of two nearby chairs for support.

"Why waste the hardware for a room known mainly for its darkness?" he countered, twisting his head around while keeping a firm grip on the chair-backs and locking in on the faint ivory aura of the mammoth movie screen.

"Waitamin...how'd I get in here? Shit-faced or no, I clearly recall my last well-lit moment being spent pawing around for fresh booze."

"Feel your forehead."

He did so, wincing upon discovery of a quarter-sized welt just above his left eyebrow.

"Damn, but that smarts. Must've taken a header into the bar. But how di..."

"The emergency lights had barely kicked on when I saw you waddling toward the railing with one hand parked on your head and the other stuck out like a roach feeler. Fairly certain you would've taken a dive if I hadn't pulled you back by the collar."

Gently rubbing the outer perimeter of the knot with a forefinger, Jorgensen snickered.

"And I sincerely thank you for fighting off what had to be a mighty temptation, Slim."

Her tone, much like her stance, remained remarkably unemotional, staid, "Basic human kindness...nothing more. Perhaps even a twinge of pity. By the time I led you here, you already had one eyelid closed."

"Well, that's not embarrassing. Sooooo, how long have I been out?"

"Two...two and a half hours. Wish I could confess to using that time wisely, but apparently bellowing through cupped hands into the darkness provided little but the sound of my own echo."

Tentatively removing each hand one at a time from their death grip on the chair backs, he appeared to test his balance by stepping back into a wide stance.

"Quiet as a tomb in here without the familiar hum of the generator."

She grunted in apparent agreement.

Jorgensen peered up into the murk and twisted about as if scanning for a falling star.

"Damned suppository-shaped mausoleum. Got a theory, Slim?"

"Theory?"

"Yeah, as in, you know, the hows and whys..."

"The...what?"

"How or why this blackout happened, or was...*allowed* to happen," he continued snappishly, seemingly fed up with her continued obtuseness.

"*Allowed* to happen?"

"Oh come now, Slim. You don't think this whole thing might just be another Hanley concoction? Yet another scripted chapter to put us through as much hell as possible?"

Crouching in the dimness, LeAnn sighed.

"Really, Tubby? Yet *another* conspiracy theory? Couldn't just be a power outage due to faulty wiring? A blown fuse? A frazzled plug?"

"Sure, sure. All logical enough conclusions," he conceded blandly, "but why so mundane, sister? Hell, think *big*. Think zombie apocalypse, or underground cannibalistic cave-dwellers. Think spectral entities. Think mutated rats gnawing their way through the concrete just for a warm sampling of our, well, my ample butt-cheeks anyhow. Imagination, woman. Show me some imagination!"

With no reply apparently forthcoming despite the obvious baiting that begged for same, Jorgensen concluded the sarcastic rant with a shaking, raised fist.

"Nothing your father does is a fucking *accident*, lady. Surely you know this better than most."

"You give the non-relationship between him and me far too much credit," she spat indifferently while taking a seat in the back row.

"So you think dear ol' dad is beyond pulling this shit?"

"Cannot honestly say."

Jut-jawed and wild-eyed, Jorgensen's massive chest expanded like an overfilled inner-tube.

"Well then, sister, allow me to spell out the painfully simplistic. Hanley, having no doubt received thrice-daily updates on our respective weigh-ins and medical results, figured it might well be primetime for a little roadblock. Man like him doesn't make deals without a few well-plotted fail-safes in place."

When LeAnn remained mute, he resumed while pacing up and down the narrow row, his gait noticeably robotic as to perhaps avoid bumping a knee or stubbing a toe.

"He pulls the plug and we go off the rails. After all, what we're trying to accomplish here is all about routine, right? Eat a ton—work out a ton—sleep a ton. Kick us off the routine and the great strides we've made not only start to slip, but depending on how long he keeps the joint unplugged, goes to complete hell in a matter of days. Don't know about you, Slim, but seventy-two to ninety-six hours lost in feeding the hernia and I'm toast."

Her timid response, a low whisper exclaiming something to the effect of 'but, that's not fa.... That...wouldn't be...right,' was first met with a raucous howl and then a screaming retort.

"Tell me you didn't start to say fair. Fair, Slim? You're pulling my chain, right? You think Han...your old man cares about *how* he wins? Damn, daddy's girl finally makes an appearance. I was beginning to think an all points might be in order."

"Go to hell," she spewed back, albeit a bit shakily.

Backing off, Jorgensen threw up his hands in mock surrender.

"As hangovers go, Slim, I'm already there. Hey, I sincerely hope I'm off-base here. If so, I'll be the first to retract said accusation once the place lights up...say in the next half-hour. Honesty though, this kid isn't about to make any wagers."

They sat shrouded in the eerie silence for perhaps three minutes; LeAnn slumped comfortably within a similar chair as one she'd been forced to squeeze into four months earlier, while Jorgensen continued to pace while occasionally mumbling under his breath.

"So, you up to a hike, or are we just gonna sit in here and wait for a double-feature of nocturnal-themed vampire flicks?" he finally inquired, his freakishly white teeth glowing like tiny, squared night-lights within the surrounding opaqueness.

LeAnn arose with a groan, following his sullen lead with a slumped pose and leaden feet.

"Where to first, then?"

"Where else?" she heard him reply morosely. "You may be used to tooling around for days on a handful of sunflower seeds and half-filled cups of apple juice, but I'm craving something a hell of a lot more substantial. For now I'd happily surrender my right nut for a handful of aspirin. Well, maybe not happily..."

Keeping her eyes fixated on his trunk-thick, V-shaped upper torso, LeAnn remained several steps behind as they rounded a slight curve and headed toward an unmarked exit located perhaps a dozen feet past the lounge doors.

"Here's hoping Aunt Jemima packed the fridge and cabinets before the fallout, buuuuut somehow I wouldn't be at all shocked to find nothing but cobwebs."

~ * ~

"Might look bleak past the first few meals, but I shit you *not*—this boy will not hesitate to chow down on pure rawness if need be."

Having flipped open every cabinet door, fourteen in all, to reveal a surprisingly limited inventory consisting mostly of boxed and bagged dry goods, Jorgensen leaned against a squared cabinet and sighed.

"Cardboard is edible, right?"

LeAnn replied without a hint of actual emotion. "Salt is the key, *Amigo*."

Upon entry into the dining hall's shadowy core, she'd pulled a chair to the center of the room and straddled it, resting her chin atop folded forearms.

Chugging greedily from a mostly voided milk jug, Jorgensen wiped his mouth with the inside of an elbow before releasing a gurgling belch.

"Yeah, well, it's a damn good thing we're not both on the same seafood diet, or this puny haul wouldn't last three days. Besides, I'm thinking a gold mine of munchies awaits on level two. Probably dig up a flashlight or two while we're at it."

They'd shared nary a word of dialogue during the short two-story trek up the winding stairwell to the dining hall floor, its slick, tube-like appearance made all the more foreboding by a noticeable lack of illumination. Though neither dared share the thought, each might have secretly described the experience as scaling the blackened intestines of some giant, metallic reptile.

~ * ~

Pulling a package of semi-frozen wings, its plastic coating already possessing a layer of moisture from a gradual melt, Jorgensen gave its square edges a cautious sniff.

"Obviously traditional cooking's out of the question, but an old-fashioned campfire is always an option if the assholes responsible refuse to wise up. Either way," he paused to toss the package back inside the fridge and secure the door, "I flat fucking refuse to drop a solitary pound of body mass. Swear, I'll start gnawing furniture if need be."

Resting her forehead on crossed wrists, LeAnn's lone reply was a low, noncommittal grunt.

"Hey," Jorgensen barked, his nostrils flaring wildly as he departed the kitchen for the dining room.

"Hey, you smell something? I mean, something other than our shared rankness?"

LeAnn stood stiffly and yawned, stretching her arms upward in an impromptu *touchdown* gesture. Facing the dining hall entrance, she strode forward with her head tilted back.

"Now that you mention it, yes I do."

"Smoke, as in...something smolders in the distance?"

Coolly indifferent, she nodded weakly.

"Usually how that works."

With a disgusted roll of the eyes, Jorgensen stomped back to the kitchen only to return moments later with a full gallon jug of milk, a loaf of bread, and a jumbo package of peanut butter in tow. He tossed them onto a nearby table, all the while taking in the ample, well-rounded buttocks of his lover *slash* rival, who remained posed with her back to him.

"After chow I had planned on a trip down to the generator floor. Guess priority one is to check out the mysterious stench, huh?"

"I'll trail the smoke," she replied dryly, "*you* check the generator."

He paused, brow cocked, holding a plastic knife loaded with peanut butter inches from its intended runway of sliced wheat.

"Um, I can't really advocate separating. That splitting up jazz is definitely overrated. Think of every lousy-ass B-movie you ever s..."

"Suit yourself, Chief," she interrupted with a forefinger pointed toward the ceiling, "descend away. I'm headed up top."

"Awwww shit, Slim. That's eleven floors...twenty-two separate cases. I'm liable to drop five, ten pounds. This...stench is probably just residual from the last meal Aunty J grilled up before the plug got pulled."

Practically drooling, he smeared an inch-thick topping onto the bread and folded it over.

"We can check the generator and stock up in two winks and if you're still worried, then I'll happily follow you up the snake's gut. Sound feasible?"

She turned to reply just as he was jamming roughly half of the folded sandwich into his waiting maw.

"Hmm, twenty-two cases, huh? Sounds like just what the doctor ordered," she spat sourly with crossed arms.

Jorgensen chewed several times before swallowing and then tipping the jug to his lips. Following a low belch, his reply was delivered in a guttural moan.

"B-but, what if we get halfway up and the emergency lights crap out? We gonna crawl back down on our bellies? We'll pick up a couple of flashlights just for backup."

"It's just a short hop and skip down to floor two, fat man. Like I said, I'm headed topside."

"Fine, Slim," he replied after gulping down a final, heaping mouthful with a three lengthy chugs and wiping whitish foam from a stubble-coated chin, "we'll do it your way."

Less than ten minutes later, empty-handed save a bottled water each, they did just that.

Part Two: *Where there's smoke...*

"What exactly you expect me to do, Slim? Pull an acetylene welder from between my ass-cheeks?" Jorgensen panted, bent over with his hands parked atop his knees and a fresh-stream of sweat trailing both reddened cheeks.

"Sorry, woman—fresh outta battering rams at the minute. Can I interest you in a well-worn but sturdy *erection* for which to peck through yon metal door?"

"Keep it in your pants, Romeo," LeAnn snorted, "despite the weight loss, I can hardly fit through a *pin-hole*."

Gripping his chest with clawed fingers, Jorgensen tossed his head back and grimaced in mock pain. "Ah, the scorpion's infamous sting—a di-rect hit to the ol' nut-sac. Funny, I wasn't hearing similar complaints 'tween the sheets, my dear."

Standing with her back against the knob-less exit to floor twenty-one, LeAnn Garner was, unlike her bulky cohort, unstrained of breath and practically perspiration-free despite the laborious trek. They'd found the winding well adequately lit and relatively fume-free.

"The burn's metallic for sure. Wiring maybe. Regardless, the scent is definitely weaker up here—seems to be originating from closer to ground level. "

His head dipping almost to the concrete floor, Jorgensen giggled briefly until a woeful lack of oxygen cut it short.

"Bastard father of yours is trying to smoke us out...or *in*, depending on one's outlook."

"Disagree. Can't see the logic. The timing just doesn't fit."

"The timing is picture perfect, Slim. We're winning, don't you see? The son of a bitch cannot stand losing."

"Let me ask you something, strictly *fat ass to fat ass*," LeAnn barked sourly, lunging over until the two stood almost toe-to-toe, "all hard feelings between my father and you aside...do you truly think premeditated torture and impending death was in his plans for not only his daughter, but a budding grandchild?"

"I put nothing past 'im," Jorgensen scoffed, "but then, you definitely know the evil rat-bastard better than I."

Without response, LeAnn took a final sip from her bottled water, tossed the empty into a dark corner, and practically jogged toward the stairwell exit.

Shoulders drooping, Jorgensen soon followed, sauntering toward the stairwell as if heading a funeral march.

Approximately half-way down, in-between floors twelve and eleven, the emergency lighting briefly flittered and blinked before resuming its steady glow.

During this single speck of time, no more than two ticks of the clock at best, originated two distinct sounds: a decidedly feminine gasp and equally masculine groan.

The source of the former spoke first—the shakiness of her tone obvious despite the effort to mask same with light banter.

"Ohhh boy. Let us hope and pray *that* was a one-time glitch."

The author of the latter cleared his throat noisily before responding, perhaps to cloak a pending uneasiness within his own voice.

"If that was your sire's idea of a joke, he's a sicker pup than I imagined."

"It might actually be a good sign," she countered weakly, "Ma-maybe the generator's coming back on line."

"Uh-huh. Yep. That's it. Thank you, Susie Sunshine."

As if to punctuate the fear woven into her earlier statement, LeAnn picked up the pace considerably, taking two steps at a time until she reached a new platform, then swinging gracefully about with each hand curled loosely on the guide rail and leaping forth yet again. Similarly affected, Jorgensen quickly ditched the sluggish pace he'd maintained since their reentry, easily tripling his own speed until he was practically riding his fellow inmate's coattails.

"Temp's dropping like a stone, Slim. You feel it?" he barked between huffs.

LeAnn's reply, though noticeable less labored, was delivered with obvious pauses between bone-jarring landings.

"Affirmative... fats, despite...the workout."

Driven by nothing more than base curiosity, Jorgensen attempted to enter one of the 'lockdown' floors but found the entrance door impenetrable—immune to either excessive knob-twisting or a firm bashing via a tucked shoulder.

"Chintzy butt-wipe probably has bundles of cash tucked neatly away on every floor. Pallets stacked upon pallets of blood-money just in time for the apocalypse, where the en-tire stash won't hold nearly the worth of a single roll of shit paper."

To this, LeAnn had refused to respond by either word or gesture, having gradually honed the talent to blissfully ignore.

A quick stop into the dining hall (wherein the mystery smoldering scent reappeared with a measure of gusto) saw a bottled water refill for her and a three-layered ham and cheese sandwich and fresh glass of milk for him before an even briefer jaunt to the generator room.

~ * ~

"Jackpot. Visualize the wafting vapor, Slim? And who was it that suggested we check out this particular space first? Damn. I must've burned a day's worth of fat cells on that little stairwell jog *you* suggested."

Her eyes practically gleamed within the surrounding murk.

"Oh, what a shame. On the *bright side*, hell's belles, so did I!"

Upon entry to the circular chasm housing a squared, fenced-off core, not even the now-familiar, strangely soothing shadows could hide the occasional thin tendril of smoke fluttering overhead like wandering cobwebs.

"Fine, smart-ass," Jorgensen retorted weakly, wiping a bare forearm over a sweat-coated forehead, "stand here cracking wise 'til the...horses trot home. I'm going in."

"Horses trot...?" LeAnn replied with equal feebleness, not quite leaning against the entrance but collapsing onto it with a teeth-rattling thump.

"I be...believe you meat...meant c-cows, genius."

She watched through rapidly blurring eyes as Jorgensen's bulky frame appeared to stumble clumsily toward the generator's double-gated entrance. As a series of gut-clenching cramps drove her to one knee, she watched him tumble face-first onto the slab, his arms and legs splayed as if he were attempting to form a snow-angel atop cool concrete.

"No...n-nope...no t-time for...a n-nap...not w-with th-the smike...smoke...a f-fire," she mumbled just moments before planting a kiss of her own on a similarly frigid patch of stone.

~ * ~

Coming to in segmented fragments, each a tad less fuzzy than the one before, Jorgensen eventually rolled onto his back and wiped a thick layer of semi-congealed drool from his left check and the tip of his stubbly chin.

"Ohhh, f-f-fiddle-knobs and b-broomsticks. Wha-what...a...hellacious be-bender. Happy fu-fudging New Year."

It was with Herculean effort that he eventually pushed himself upright and sat on the far end of the bed—his own bed of the previous four months, complete with a familiar feel and strangely comforting squeaks. The interior lighting pierced his vision like direct rays from a noonday sun.

Following a brief rubbing of the eyes to clear away at least a top layer of cobwebs, he stood on visibly trembling legs until the shakes subsided to hardly a tremor.

"Whooooaaaa, Nellie. Steady, b-big guy...s-steady as s-she goes."

His subsequent movements, first directed at the computer to his left and secondly to the flat-screen plasma to his right, were executed with comical, quasi-robotic deliberation.

What was discovered through these actions Jorgensen could've found either surprisingly reassuring or a degree suspicious, considering his most recent memories of what had come before. That was if recent memories were indeed factual and not the result of an alcohol binge of record proportions.

"Nope...no way, Jose. That shit was real. I can still..." he reached up with an extended pinky finger and probed his lower set of teeth, sucking noisily upon the digit's moistened departure, "...taste the ham and cheese. Plus which..." he squatted slightly, feeling the soreness at his calves and the backs of both thighs, "...that damn stairwell danced a jig on the old gams."

Discovery one: a live internet connection from which he quickly surfed a plethora of meaningless headlines from the *Yahoo* homepage.

Discovery two: a frenzied flipping through a preset list of boob-tube favorites, all of which flared fourth in crystal, high-definition clarity.

The present time, from each source, had read three-sixteen p.m.. Retaking his place among the crumbled sheets of the king-sized sleeper as CNN news blared in the background, Jorgensen couldn't recall which day, much less an approximate time from which his historic binge had either commenced or concluded.

"Stow that happy horse-crap, muscles. That was no dream—no Johnny Walker or Jim Beam-fueled stroll through your own personal Blunder-Land. You were there....Slim...she was there...in alllll her nagging glory."

Lying back, he appeared on the verge of dozing before rolling gracefully from the mattress to the floor, poised on all fours and inhaling deeply before executing a lightning-quick set of twenty marine-style push-ups.

"Ho-kay then...a quick shower and it's off to verify what I already know...or hope I know."

A thick wall of vapor soon filled the closed-off latrine, its still-bulky inhabitant standing statuesque beneath a blazing torrent—a torrent that might well have consisted of a concrete and mortar mix that had already transformed his motionless frame to stone.

~ * ~

Forking up a heaping helping of sliced peaches, chopped apples and thinly sliced pears, LeAnn leaned past her own plate with nostrils flaring.

"It's a killer, isn't it?" Jorgensen inquired, curling his bulky arms around the twin plates like a protective mother to her cubs, "Gotta admit, Slim, you do possess a truckload of will power. More than I could ever claim."

Relieving her utensil of roughly half its cargo, she chewed the cool fruit slowly as to savor each tangy bite. Before cleaning off the reminder, she paused to reply.

"Force of habit by now, chief. Though I adore the scent, more than two bites of that fattening swill would surely trigger a rapid regurgitation."

Balancing a large spoon overflowing with steaming eggs and sausage bits mere inches from parted lips, Jorgensen snorted indifferently.

"Uh-huh. Yep. I'd wager gulping down a plate-load of this...fattening swill is a damn site easier than swallowing the load of BS you're serving up, Slim."

They consumed in silence for several moments, each staring off into space while blissfully lost in separate thoughts. The return of power—of light specifically—had definitely brightened the mood, though likely a thin of panic still lay just below the surface, as if this newly reenergized world were just as temporary as the realm of blackness that had come before it.

Upon departing his own quarters, Jorgensen had trekked upward a single floor to discover LeAnn passed out on the carpeted floor to the right of her bed, a single, thin blanket wound around her midsection like a coiled python.

He'd gently nudged her to consciousness before providing a glass of tap water pulled from the bathroom sink.

Once she'd come to sufficiently to converse, he'd informed her of his own waking adventure, complete with updated calendar reading and current time data provided by both television and computer sources.

Eventually they'd traded queries on what Jorgensen had deemed 'the blackout' and come to the conclusion that it had indeed occurred and was not the result of some telepathically-shared dreamscape.

Jorgensen had waited patiently, flipping channels on the plasma without ever landing on a specific channel for more than full thirty seconds, while LeAnn had showered and dressed.

~ * ~

Upon departing the elevator, Jorgensen insisted he'd smelled the food's seductive aroma even before the glass doors had parted.

"Talk about crackerjack timing," LeAnn had said just as they'd entered the dining hall to the sight of their respective meals parked atop adjoining tables at the center of the room. For her: a fruit salad and steaming cup of Green Tea. For him: twin plates piled high with scrambled eggs, sausages, bacon, and buttermilk biscuits along with a frosty mug of chocolate milk, the former still emitting thick tendrils of smoke.

"No coincidence at all, Slim. Big brother sees all, hears all. Probably started whipping up this here brunch about the time you stepped into the shower stall and I was surfing the wasteland of satellite television. Admittedly, questions do abound, but the degree of difficulty in timing this little feedbag session is highly questionable without some serious forewarning."

LeAnn watched in apparent fascination as he shoveled in a colossal mouthful and barely chewed before swallowing it down.

"W-what happened down there? I mean, we...I was...I remember watching you walk...stumbling in the direction of the generator before the lights didn't just fade gradually. They just...shut off."

Following a ringing belch and two quick swallows of milk, Jorgensen nodded in apparent agreement.

"I recall taking a few steps forward when things got...fuzzy. Never even made it to the gate...or at least I don't think I did. Sure can't recall eyeing an actual generator."

"How did we...I mean, who hauled us back up to our rooms?"

Jorgensen shrugged while halving a biscuit and padding each slice with thick layers of butter.

"Same mystery savior that put out our lights down there. Same angel of mercy that conjured up this spread. Silo elves maybe?"

LeAnn twirled her spoon expertly between thumb and forefinger, her brow creased with newfound concern.

"Speaking of which, I've kinda been, well, putting off asking this in light of being regarded crazier than I actually am…"

"Not possible…shoot," he mumbled between chews.

"I've been…hearing things…late at night, I mean. Usually between two and three. Sometimes earlier but never before midnight."

Jorgensen nodded knowingly, pausing to swallow and subsequently wash down the intake.

"Rest easy, sister. You're not any loonier than yours truly. I've heard some rumblings myself. Random creaks and groans. Chalked it up to structure settling, that is 'til it came to me this burg is practically ancient and should be well past such shifting. That is, unless there's volcanic activity brewing."

"To me," LeAnn interjected through a tight squint, "at times anyway, it sounded like…just like echoed footsteps."

"You're creeping me out, Slim, sincerely," he grinned, revealing assorted chunks of food packed between otherwise perfectly squared teeth.

"You didn't truly think we were alone in here, did you? I mean, hologram staff aside, somebody has to do the grunt work. Place doesn't run itself. What better time than past the midnight hour?"

As if on cue, a familiar voice rang out from above.

Sipping noisily and jolted by the sudden intrusion, LeAnn's hand had jerked a bit upon its descent, sending the spoon spinning free to just clear Jorgensen's left shoulder.

"Oh, I do apologize, Miss G. I surely did not mean to startle."

The hologram figure materialized to their immediate right, greeted by a series of loud claps and a single, piercing catcall as Jorgensen flipped his chair around in its direction.

"Well, well, well, the prodigal chow-slinger returns! Let me be the first to say, welcome back, *Wheezie*! Your bloated old carcass is indeed a sight for these ravenous old eyes."

Jeannine had begun to bow but halted in mid-bend at the 'bloated old carcass' remark, arising with a nod and an extended forefinger waving to and fro.

"Now, now, Brian Jorgensen. Ain't no need for such vileness. I am indeed delighted to serve the cause yet again. Since you two have chosen to visit me right off, allow me to be the first to extend a heartfelt apology for the...difficulties of the past twenty-four hours or so."

In silent response, LeAnn nodded casually and commenced digging into her fruit bowl with a newly obtained spoon.

Scooping up a fresh forkful of eggs, Jorgensen feigned taking a bite before slinging it, utensil and all, at and through the computerized figure.

"Yeah, and since you're the first we choose to grace with our still slightly dazed presence, how 'bout you spill the beans on exactly what the fuck those difficulties were, sis-tah?"

Upon glancing over to LeAnn in hopes of a sign indicating moral support but finding a blank stare instead, Jeannine's eyes turned to the scattered bits of food at her feet. Despite the impossibility of stepping atop same, she carefully sidestepped the carnage while departing toward the kitchen.

"Well, I'm...not at liberty to tell what I don't rightly know for certain. You might wanna ask the rest of the staff when you see 'em. Being just a preparer of meals, I reckon it's assumed I just don't have a need to know."

"Whatever, Miss Butterworth," Jorgensen grumbled between muffled belches, "I'm taking it that same lack of knowledge wasn't a factor when it came to spiking the grub we scarfed down before heading to the generator room, yes?"

"I...ain't at liberty to s..." she began timidly before being cut off with a casual wave.

"Just take down my dinner order. That is, if I'm not *assuming* too much."

"Certainly, Mister J. Fire when ready..."

"Pancakes. Lots and lots of pancakes. Preferably of the blackberry variety and served with maple syrup. For an appetizer, I'm thinking eight, no, ten slices of turkey bacon and thr...no, four slices of wheat toast, buttered to the max of course."

With each additional item, Jeannine gave a slight nod, having crossed each arm over her ample bosom.

"Dessert?"

Forkless, Jorgensen had dipped his head toward the plate and licked up a large mouthful.

"Nothing fancy," he mumbled, the words comically garbled, "banana pudding maybe. Yeah, that's it. A quart of the stuff. Got all that, Maybelle?"

"Damn but you're a jerk," LeAnn chimed in, staring him down sourly.

Jeannine regarded her with a sad, tight-lipped smile.

"Never you mind, Miss G. Mister J has valid reason for this particular tantrum. You got something in mind for your own nourishment this here night?"

"Um, sure, um, how about a tuna salad on wheat and a spinach salad?"

While delivering said order, LeAnn had lunged toward the beefy cook as if to reach over and execute a light, consoling tap to the back of her hand.

"That you shall have, Miss G. Again, sorry for the...discomfort, and I'm sure the others can...will somehow will provide the answers you seek."

With that, she levitated from their presence like a wind-blown leaf, her head slightly bowed and her shoulders similarly slumped.

His plates literally licked clean, Jorgensen leaned back and patted his swollen gut with both hands. He studied his fellow inmate with a cocked brow amid the soothing hum of the overhead lights.

"A sandwich and a bowl-full of green leaves? Really? Damned blackout was a blessing in disguise for at least one of us, anyhow."

LeAnn remained mute while nibbling a final, overly plump grape.

"No wonder you're raggin' so. Bummed out that it didn't last another week or two, am I right?"

"Ragging? Ragging you say?" she retorted snappishly, pushing away from the table as the chair legs beneath her squalled their disapproval.

"In case you've forgotten, basic biology dictates that my being on the rag a scientific impossibility."

Instinctively tugging at his tee's crinkled collar, Jorgensen's cheeks instantly reddened.

"Oh, ugh, yeah. Bad choice of words."

"Gee whiz," she exclaimed with the casual wave of a hand, "that's certainly a first."

She exited without further comment, leaving Jorgensen to slurp and sip away the remainder of the milk jug. He waited to hear the elevator's familiar buzz before rising with a groan and ambling toward the dimly lit kitchen with all the energy of an overmedicated sloth.

The space was, predictably, deserted.

"Oh lawdy yes...get right on that, yes-sah, Master J. Get right the hell *on* that for yah," he mumbled in a comically butchered attempt at mimicking a southern dandy.

"Just who the hell *are* you people?"

On the way out, he flipped a table with little more than a flick of his left foot, sending his dishes and the empty milk jug sliding across the slick tile floor like waxed steel across an iced-over lakebed.

"Yep...fat as an ox but haven't lost a step."

~ * ~

"All I can divulge without overstepping the boundaries of my personal knowledge, Miss Garner, is that some technical

177

difficulties of some sort involving the main generator. Perhaps Max...um, your personal trainer can provide a clearer pic..."

"Whatever, Doctor. To be honest, it isn't the happening itself that worries me, but the possibility of further...technical difficulties. I can handle my own cooking well enough, but a future without working toilets is one I'd rather skip."

Cross-armed and pale faced, LeAnn's backend was propped at the far edge of the exam table.

"I have been assured the chances are miniscule at best. Apparently a specialist was...the problem was rectified by someone of great expertise."

LeAnn nodded indifferently, thumbing the small vial gripped loosely in her left hand while her right held firm a single piece of gauze just inside the crook of her left elbow.

"Good to hear. I...we were thinking Da...Father was...might simply be screwing with us."

"Retribution for what specifically, Miss Garner?"

Tossing the gauze into a nearby trash can, LeAnn gently patted her midsection and smiled wanly.

"Surely you jest, Doctor."

McClintock hugged a bright yellow manila folder to the snow-white smock covering his torso and stepped forward as if to better hear.

"You believe Mister Hanley would attempt to extract some form of revenge for his daughter's pregnancy? Certainly I cannot claim to know the man personally, but that would seem a far-fetched theo..."

"I've spent my entire life lowering his expectations," she countered grimly, reaching over to place the glass vial, filled to its narrow brim with her dark crimson life-source, onto a nearby metal tray.

"But this...latest bit of drama just might have topped 'em all. I could very easily see him reaching over to pull the plug with a level of anger and exasperation never before reached."

Peering down at his own shuffling feet, McClintock paused to clear his throat before flipping open the folder and rummaging inside its thin folds.

"Well, again, Miss Garner, All I was told was a techni..."

"Can I do this, Doctor?" she asked curtly, the volume of said query cranked up several octaves.

"Pardon?"

"With this...latest complication...can I do...*should* I do this?"

"You refer to the overall goal?"

"I'm still roughly sixty pounds from the finish line and somebody new just hopped aboard the bus. I mean, this...there are...is a moral obligation here, right?"

"Miss Garner, I'm not really qualified to...advise on matters other than the medical aspects."

She bit her lower lip, likely to prevent an acceleration of trembling.

"I know, I know...heard you the first time—straight from the textbook. Physically it can be done without harm to either the mom or fetus."

Avoiding eye contact, McClintock continued to finger pages, his stiff tone the definition of clinical."

"Correct. Diet is the key, along with a specialized program of light cardiovas..."

"Pardon me for stating the painfully obvious, Doc, but there isn't a licensed psychologist in sight, so I'm asking you straight up, from a medical standpoint then; is it...is this something you would...*normally* recommend for a newly diagnosed pregnancy?"

First closing and then tucking the folder beneath his right arm, McClintock finally conceding in locking eyes with his patient.

"No, I most certainly would *not*, Miss Garner. That is, under normal conditions. But then, this scenario is hardly normal, now is it?"

LeAnn shrugged—her tone a tad less irritable. "Goes without saying, Doctor."

"Miss Garner, with a closely monitored diet and exercise regime, your unborn child will indeed develop normally. Rest assured I will outline said specialty menu and pass this on to the facility cook, just as myself and your personal trainer will discuss a proper training program."

Turning on a heel, LeAnn faced a far wall with her arms crossed.

"I take it, then, you've made your decision," he chided timidly and saw her slumped shoulders instantly tense.

"Not by any means, no. Not yet," she replied without turning, "just weighing my options and collecting facts."

"Understood. Just know I am here to provide medical counseling. With that in mind," he paused, clearing his throat just as a newcomer bounded through the entrance door to take up a defiant stance between doctor and patient.

"Howdy doodie, Doc," the interloper spat in mock cheer while flashing choppers so ivory they appeared to have just undergone an extensive polishing, "how hangs the stethoscope?"

"Greetings, Mister Jorgensen. Um, if you don't mind, I was speaking privately with Miss Garner and we require a bit more priva..."

The big man lunged as if to deliver a head-butt to the physician's hologram image, the welcoming grin having abruptly mutated into a predatory scowl.

"Eat shit, pal. Whatever you tell her, you can tell me. I'm hip on the subject matter being discussed, a subject matter of which I have considerable interest, right Slim?"

Her back still turned, LeAnn's response was a hoarse, barely audible whisper.

"We'll finish this tomorrow, Doctor McClintock. I do understand the need to come to a final decision as soon as possible. Maybe...tonight I can organize my thoughts. In the meantime, I'm guessing it wouldn't hurt if you began sketching that outline."

In four quick steps, she turned sidewise and squeezed through the door Jorgensen had left slightly ajar.

Doctor and newly arrived patient exchanged a blank stare before the former broke an awkward silence that in reality lasted no more than thirty seconds but seemed to stretch out at least three times that long.

"So, Mister Jorgensen, while you're here, would you mind providing urine and blood samples? I think you know the drill…"

Huffing, Jorgenson trampled over to the metal tray and picked out a freshly wrapped syringe.

"Sir, yes, sir!" he blurted with a mock salute, "oh, and by the way, I feel it only fair I congratulate you on the effectiveness of whatever magic elixir you conjured up to take us out of the game a while back. Best damn shuteye I've had since walking into this dump. Yep, you surely know your chemicals, Doc."

"I, um, I'm afraid I'm at a loss, Mister Jor…"

"Yeah, yeah, I know…not at liberty and all that. So tell me," he asked moments later while transferring the contents of the filled syringe into a tiny vial, "doctor to dad-to-be…which way is the old ball and chain leaning?"

McClintock winced as if having endured a sharp pinch to the buttocks.

"Ball and cha…leaning, Mister Jor…"

Jorgensen rolled the vial onto an adjoining tabletop while palming a plastic cup from same.

"Yeah, you know…is she going to pop the tot or nip the nipper?"

Reaching up to adjust his glasses, the doctor appeared, if anything, more perplexed.

"Is Slim going to have the baby or have it expunged?"

"Expunged, Mister Jorgensen? Really?" McClintock replied with open disgust. "Even if I knew the answer to such a…crudely worded inquiry, I'd be damned if I would share same."

"Oh, gotcha," Jorgensen retorted while reaching inside the opened crotch of his sweat pants and retrieved the tool necessary to provide the requested specimen. "Doctor-patient confidentiality and all that happy horseshit, right?"

"Yes, partly," the doctor answered curtly while watching the patient provide the needed sample, "though I must confess my refusal is based mainly on a certain insufferable jackass making the inquest."

Having tucked away his manhood, Jorgensen placed the half-filled cup next to the vial before stepping over to a digital scale located in a nearby corner.

"Damn if such honesty isn't downright refreshing, Doc. Anywho, on to more vital matters..." he prattled through a tight smirk, "...what's the authentic dish on that fucking blackout?"

~ * ~

"Faulty wiring. This much was divulged. Faulty inner wiring to the main generator. Spark begat fire begat smoke begat...well, lights out. Shit happens, big fella. I know this don't exactly feed your hankerin' for conspiracy, but these are the facts as I was told 'em."

The slightly fuzzy image of Gabe Maxwell, decked out in a sleeveless Oakland Raiders ball-cap and matching muscle tee, cut-off jeans and high-top Reeboks, levitated just to the left of the weight bench where Brian Jorgensen lay, the former casually stroking the edges of a newly cultivated handlebar mustache while the latter pumped fifty pound barbells at a slight incline.

"Whatever you say, sport. Who am I to cast doubt?" Jorgensen replied, having rolled the weights away on opposite sides. Leaning up, his massively pumped pecs, biceps and forearms seemed to have added bulk in the time it had taken to complete a single set.

"Besides, it isn't like you'd tell me the truth if you were privy, right?"

Maxwell nodded vehemently, his own meticulously chiseled arms crossing tightly.

"Nothin' to hide, boss. As Joe Weider is my witness."

"Hey, I get it, Goober, I get it. Can't be gnawing on the hand that signs the checks. What say we get on with what really matters? You see, the numbers are the numbers, no matter how I shove 'em around. Basically I got fifty-some odd days—less than two calendar months, to pack on the equivalent of a modern-day middle-schooler."

Floating over until he fronted the bench, Maxwell's aura surged and dimmed in spastic waves, as if trapped in an unremitting reboot.

"Same formula we already discussed, pretty much, only now ya put 'er in overdrive."

"Overdrive? Expound if you will, Goob."

"Two things, boss. Number one is the intake. Suck it all down like gangbusters, but save the biggest chow-down for just before beddy-bye, and steer clear of the junk-food. Its damn near impossible to pack on the pounds in the aftermath of a diabetes-induced major stroke, get it?"

Leaning back to obtain a proper grip on the heavy bar balanced directly across from his brow, Jorgensen grunted in lieu of verbal reply.

"Lastly, it's all about maintaining the lowest pulse-rate possible. Outside of chucking these weights around, don't even strain to *pee* if it ain't necessary. Think sloth. Be the sloth. Might help, *ahem*, to start sleepin' in your own cot as well, if ya get my meanin'."

Jorgensen bounced the two-hundred plus pound set off his upper chest to full extension eight times before resetting the bar and leaning back up with a resounding wheeze.

"No...worries there, pal. Shrinking mama has no doubt strapped on the ol' chastity belt and swallowed the key. 'Sides, I've learned my lesson, carnal desires be damned."

"Ugh, yeah. Only time will tell, I reckon."

Scowling as if to fire off a scathing reply, Jorgensen instead hiked a leg and farted loudly. "Whoaaaaa, baby...fire in the hole! Must be all the extra grains, huh Goob?"

"Very much likely, boss." Maxwell reached up and pinched his nostrils.

"Whew! These are the times I'm proudest to claim hologram status."

Ducking beneath a bar holding well over three-hundred pounds, Jorgensen paused with flared nostrils before commencing a rapid trio of reps.

"As damn well you should. That particular butt-missile could've peeled lead paint off a battleship. By the way, Mister pro-fessional train-or..."

He concluded the set with a huff and sidestepped away, gripping his neck on both sides and vigorously massaging as to sooth a bothersome cramp.

"...what odds you giving Big Mama on keeping up her end of the bargain? That is, how much of a burden might Junior be?"

Maxwell scratched his noggin beneath the ball-cap.

"Tough to say, boss, but being as she has less to lose than you have to gain, I'd rate the overall odds as glass half-full."

Twisting his neck from side to side to further loosen the tightness, Jorgensen raised a forefinger airborne.

"Don't tell me...diet and exercise."

"Affirmative. Ain't no magic here, hoss. Woman's got the required grit. No ifs, ands or rapidly-shrinking butts about it. 'Course, the newly acquired oven-bun does toss a shiny new wrench into the proceedings."

"That it does, bumpkin Bob."

Following the release of additional gas leakage from his hind end, this one equally drawn out and comically squeaky, Jorgensen assumed a renewed pose beneath the rack.

"So what say you, Rube? That is, if you were a betting man, on whom would you place your last George Washington?"

Clearly caught off guard by the inquiry, Maxwell paused for several moments, his image flickering from crystal clear to static blur as if effected by the strain of drudging up a response.

"I don't take to failing my clients, boss, so I'd love to call it even-steven, but ya see, Papa Maxwell didn't raise no mealy-mouthed fence-sitters. Sooo...at this juncture, I'd have to say the little lady has the edge."

"Well then, Goober my man," Jorgensen replied amiably enough, though his searing gaze and wholly artificial grin spoke otherwise, "what say you start earning your pay? In cracker speak, this translates to...this here boy don't cotton to losin'."

"Now you're speakin' my language, city-boy," Maxwell spat through an equally faux smile.

Eight

Residual Effects

Part One*: Notes to the Boss*
Narrator*: Miss Jeanine, Facility cook*

"Sir...Mister J...I-I just don't feel comfor...I just don't think you ought to...d-do this. Its...it's a fatal path you've veered off into these past few days. I mean, a man's...you got the right...certainly got the right to do what you feel you gotta do to...reach the goal, but what if...the present danger exceeds any you might meet up with if that goal ain't reached?"

The requests had started three days past, on the mornin' of day one-fifty of his...of their incarceration. It was like Mister Jorgensen had shit-canned, pardon my French, the original plan altogether. True enough, he was thirty days away from what he'd dubbed 'the big weigh-in' and was still a ways off from reachin' the desired poundage, but what he proposed...the new strategy he'd mapped out... was, in this ol' pancake flipper's considerable opinion, nothin' short of a suicide attempt. Wasn't no noose, knife, or firearm gonna stop his heart from beatin' or his lungs from fillin' up, but the heapin' end of a spoon or fork.

"Didn't request your opinion, lady," he barked back, barin' dingy choppers that, only a month 'afore, had been as lily white as a Colorado mountain snowfall, "and sure as hell didn't ask to be moistened with crocodile tears. Just do the fucking job Hanley is overpaying you to do, yes?"

"B-but Mister J, this is...this is madness. I know what you're trying to d..."

As was the case, even in his better moods, he didn't even allow me the common courtesy of finishing a blessed sentence.

"As I instructed...jettison the old menu and install the new by noon today. I'm off the gym...for whatever *passes* for a workout in this broken-down lard tub of a shell I'm lugging around these days."

I was finding it harder and harder to maintain a steady stare. As days passed and his condition deteriorated, it was like lookin' through one end of a spyglass straight into the eyes of death. The sweats that had once hung off his frame like sheets from a king-sized bed now fit like one of those diver's suits—all snug like plastic wrap on a rump-roast. He'd ripped off the sleeves at the shoulder and a few scattered strings hung down like bug feelers. Lord, but his arms were big as my thighs, and that ain't hay when you're talking tree-trunk proportions. The forearms alone would give ol' Popeye a run for his money. But as impressive as those Anacondas might've been, the rest of the man's physique had traveled the opposite path of fitness. From paunchy gut to crescent-rolled neck to multi-layered chin, it was hard to believe this was the same slim, chiseled-from-stone badass kung-fu dude from five months previous. So truly astonishing was the transformation, if I hadn't witnessed it in such gradual doses, I would've never believed he was the same person.

"I...b-but some of the ingredients required might be a tad hard to fin..."

His smile was sickly but still scary as hades.

"Don't bullshit a bull-shitter, lady. Sub-sti-tute if you must," he snarled, the top lip rolled inward like a rabid canine. I came to the conclusion that no amount of fibbing or double-talk was gonna alter the man's course for potential self-destruction.

"Yes sir, will do. I'll...find a way. I do wish you'd speak to Doc McClintock before undertaking such a...reckless diet. I'm sure he'd disapprove even more fer..."

"McClintock's a fraud, bitch, much like yourself, that rube Maxwell and anybody else on Hanley's payroll, so you can kindly drop the 'oh I'm so concerned for your welfare' bit. It's not just growing old...its downright moldy."

'Tween the man's stained choppers, dark, puffy eyes, yellow-tinted flesh and a homemade buzz-cut so uneven it appeared styled by a team of crooked-tooth beavers, to choose the most frightening of the bunch was quite the chore. Regardless, in his mind, troubled beyond all reason, the jig was up.

"Whatever you say, Mister J. I'll...have those...the meals ready per your request, as best I can."

"You do that," he grumbled weakly, the flames of his rage extinguished in a blink as he pushed himself up from the table with what appeared to be extreme effort.

"You...take care now," I mumbled as he limped away. I didn't expect a reply save maybe an obscene phrase or gesture, but got neither. Sounds kinda gruesome I know, but the notion I'd just conversed with a ghost didn't seem at all farfetched.

~ * ~

Crazier than fiction, it is, to watch a full grown human being struggle to consume a handful of grapes. Might as well been a truckload of melons, or an orchard's worth of red D applies as far as Miss J was concerned. Repulsive as it was to watch her grimace and groan like she'd just gulped down the last in a twenty-course meal, what followed was equally disturbing if not more so. Once that last, plump raisin rolled down the hatch, she appeared, lying if I'm dying...nauseated to the point of heaving. Skin white as chalk and with just a thin layer of drool coating her lower lip and chin.

"Sure I can't whip up a fruit bowl for lunch, Miss G? Some peaches and pears just arrived on site—so fresh the dew ain't yet dried. Toss in some cherries and chopped Gala apples, maybe a strawberry yogurt dip...non-fat of course."

"Sounds like a winner, Jeannine, but make it dinner."

"But, what about lunch then, hon? Soup maybe...chicken broth and a buttermilk biscuit maybe?"

She frowned and nodded but neither act held much in the way of energy, understandable considering these days she wasn't eating enough to keep a jaybird alive.

"No, I'll...believe I'll skip it. On a tight schedule, you understand, mostly consisting of much napping and dozing...dozing and napping."

"But three, four days in a row, Miss G? Y-you think that's wise? I mean, I got to be honest. You're looking mighty piqued. You been keeping your appointments with the doc?"

"Indeed. Each and every day like clockwork," she mumbled, leaning back and grimacing like she'd just finished off a full roast with all the fixings instead of a handful of finger fruit, "for the most part. Appreciate the concern, Jeannine, whether it be sincere or scripted. I'm just...I can't deviate from the plan with the finish line drawing so near. McClintock says as long as I keep my water intake at its present level to prevent dehydration, all is well. Besides, I've discovered some definite positives in maintaining such a piss-poor energy level. Time flies when one spends the majority of it zonked out. Crazy...and I used to depend on handfuls of downers for the same effect."

Loose skin hung from her neck like mud flaps; mud flaps riddled with jagged stretch marks, and the only thing droopier than her drawers were those haunted, deep-set eyes. If one were to view before and after snapshots without knowin' the story behind it, they would surely label Miss Garner a cancer victim rapidly approaching the final, fatal stages. Liver…maybe even pancreatic—the most merciless types that, by the time one finds out about 'em it's too late to do anything but purchase a plot in the nearest cemetery. Saddest of all, in her case, two coffins would be more symbolic, one regulation size and the other no bigger than a shoe box.

"But, don't ya think you're, well, pushin' it to extremes a mite too early? I mean, there's thirty blessed days left, child. And, uh, speakin' of child, you gots to think about that bun warmin' in the oven. Little darlin' needs…requires nourishment. At this rate, you…well, you're gonna vanish off the charts long before you're able to collect the reward…takin' that unborn angel with ya."

She blew me a weak kiss before departing, the sweat pants that had once been as snug as a second skin hanging noticeably loose in the seat.

"Jeannine, real person or virtual reality entity, you are a sweetheart. I'd give you a hug if not for two things; hugging a vapor of static electricity might come off as damn strange…and to be honest, I just don't, at the moment, possess the required juice to do so."

As much fear as I held for Mr. J and his tight-rope walk to self-destruction, the level of trepidation tuggin' at my gut was twice that for Miss LeAnn and the little miracle currently takin' shape in that fast-shrinking tummy of hers. No mystery as to why. Whereas my concern on his part was more from a professional standpoint, with her it was, well, more personal, thus a mite more worrisome. Over time, I'd grown mighty fond of her. For a young woman whose legend spoke to a lifetime of laziness, indifference and chemical abuse, she'd displayed a warrior's grit, a grappler's moxie.

Sadly, several weeks back she'd given hints of a breakdown. A breakdown that had eating disorder written all over it—a gravely serious disorder that had a full month yet to eat away, pardon the choice of wording, at its source 'til all sanity had been consumed and nothin' was left but skin and bones.

~ * ~

Part Two: *Notes to the Boss*
Narrator: *Darwin McClintock, facility physician*

"Simply put, Mister Jorgensen, I'd estimate another seven to ten days is all that's required. That's on the outset."

"Gonna take all of a month, Doc. All thirty days...all six-hundred seventy-two hours...and every fucking minute therein...that being three-hu..."

"The exact math is hardly relevant."

"The *hell* it isn't. This here game is all about numbers, Doctor. Has been from the opening bell. Of course, only one really matters, right? I mean, when all is said and done and the dawn rises on day one-eighty, the scale tells the tale. Three little digits and the end credits roll. Only question will be who lives and who dies. As they say in Tinsel-town...to be continued."

Brian Jorgensen stood naked save a pair of white briefs (a faint yellow stain at the groin and more prominent brownish smear at the seat) just to the left of the digital scale, an instrument he had dubbed *'Satan's gauge'* several weeks previous. It was his first voluntary weigh-in since the previous Thursday, a span of five and a half days. His appearance, shocking to the point of disbelief, belied this fact. I would've thought such dramatic changes would have taken at least four times that long to execute.

"Are you listening to me, sir? On this pace...having adopted this...this *atrocious* diet, the odds are very favorable you're apt to lock up and power down weeks before the sun rises on day one-eighty."

"So says your employer, pal. You reading that horseshit from a cue-card he personally handed you?"

The expression on his red, bloated face defined dementia—a full-blown brain-pan gasket failure of irreversible fatality.

191

"He there with you, Doc? Standing right next to you tapping the keys? If so, I'd advise you watch those P's and Q's. From what I gather, you dare break wind in the old man's presence and it could cost you a fingertip."

To this, I simply could not conjure a suitable reply, if such a thing actually existed.

"I assure you, I'm quite al…"

"If you are watching, Hanley, and I'd bet my left nut that's an affirmative, allow me to present a sneak preview of things to come."

In lieu of simply stepping onto the scale, he practically leapt onto it heels first, his fleshy boobs and ample midsection bouncing and wriggling long after the deed's surprisingly graceful completion.

"Hey-hey-hey…its Faaaaatttt Albert!" he barked, executing a wild, mostly stationary boogie that served to reignite the looser portions of his physique to resume jiggling. "Check this readout, Doctor Worrywart, and in the aftermath, I challenge you to fire off those earlier health warnings with even a tenth of the previous enthusiasm."

Gliding over as he hopped from the scale with a raucous series of whoops and claps, I leaned over and noted the three-digit readout before entering said result onto his electronic chart.

"So? What say you, McClintick-tock? Share that pro-fessional opinion of which you're always soooooo cocksure."

"First off," I began, pecking out the words 'increasingly unstable' in the behavioral block of the weekly form, "mere numbers do nothing to change my opinion on the minefield you currently tread upon in terms of health."

"Not bad though, huh Doc?" he winked, flashing a mouthful of yellowish-green teeth whose lone semi-ivory inhabitants appeared to be the incisors—a borderline frightening footnote that.

"Very impressive, yes, Mister Jorgensen, considering the limits in time. I do congratulate you on the dedica..."

"Say it aloud," he insisted wide-eyed while flashing an imbecilic grin minus only the drool. He lumbered forward like a bull-ape sniffing the heated loins of a potential mate. "I wanna hear it."

"Um, what is it you wish for me to s..."

"Those three little numerical wordings I saw reflected in your specs just a few seconds ago."

"Oh...two-ninety-six."

"Again, please," he cajoled, pointing an ear my way with the palm of one hand tucked behind, "and crank up the volume if you don't mind. I know that's asking a lot from a tight-ass Brit such as yourself, but...*humor* a fat man, will ya?"

Following a rather awkward clearing of the throat, I did indeed manage to re-vocalize with a bit more fervor.

"Two...nine...six."

"Now *that's* what I'm talking about! Damned if I'm not on the verge of mounting the first successful boner in weeks!" he shouted, briefly reaching down to grope his crotch.

My frown was as genuine and naturally conceived as any in recent memory.

"Please, spare me, good sir."

"Got'cha, Doc. I'll save the carnal celebration for later when the lights in the old man-cave are dimmed and I'm surfing a few of my favorite porn suites. Now..." he sighed, backing away to eventually hop aboard the larger of two rolling gurneys. Lifting his enormous left leg a few inches from its padded surface, he broke wind for at least the fourth time since our consultation had commenced.

"...since I know I'm not gonna be allowed to escape without hearing it, go on and get your jollies."

"My...jollies? Mister Jorgensen, please refrain from clogging my ears with such jargon unless a part of you enjoys the endless translation."

"Oh, um...what I mean to say, old great scholar, is...go ahead and have your fun."

My severely creased brow fueled further explanation, to which Jorgensen's tone grew increasingly sardonic.

"Full steam ahead with the verbal flogging about how my arteries are gonna clog up and/or explode long before the final twenty-eight pounds are packed on. Go on..." he paused, gesturing with curled palms in the classic 'come-hither' pose that was once so common upon ring grapplers as a sign of fearlessness.

"...spew forth, old wise one. I'm thoroughly braced."

"Well, to be bluntly honest, the motivation to do so is quite minimal at the moment. Do what you must. You seem to have charted your course and I highly doubt anything I say will divert the planned trek," I replied with as much bland indifference as could be mustered, then adding a mild shrug for good measure. The forthcoming reply was exactly what I'd hoped for.

"Aw, c'mon McClintock, that's not the nagging jackass I've come to know and reveled in annoying," he pleaded while pouring himself into a skin-tight red tee and matching sweat pants, the latter clearly splitting at the sides "after all, just 'cause I'm not buying into your spiel doesn't mean I'm not bound and determined to hear it."

Still feigning disinterest, I paced the rear of the room while gazing down at the glowing device curled within my palm.

"So there's a chance, however remote, that medical fact might detour your master plan? If not, I believe I'll pass on the sermon."

"Remote, huh?"

Jorgensen scratched the thick growth of scraggy beard at his chin. With his grungy, disheveled looks, I couldn't help but muse that he resembled perhaps the portliest homeless man in history, albeit a homeless man with the bulky appendages of a lifelong power-lifter.

"Sure, I'll grant you that much. Odds equivalent to say, the Cubbies winning back to back pennants."

"Um, and those odds would be?"

Tilting his head slightly, he wore a mask of comic befuddlement.

"Damn near impossible."

Though secretly thrilled at the prospect, I sighed wearily.

"Fine, but only the abridged version."

"Fair enough," he said with an enthusiastic clap, the gurney shrieking its disapproval at the sudden movement of his mammoth frame.

"The latest blood result is quite grim, as in Type Two diabetes grim. Allow me a series of short inquiries."

"Shoot."

"Having any trouble nodding off or remaining asleep?"

"Affirmative on both counts. Nightly average is three, four hours at best, although...well, the napping and constant dozing during daylight hours probably doesn't help the cause."

"True enough, though I doubt it can be helped once exhaustion obtains a firm grip. How about muscle aches?"

"Like gangbusters. All the way down to the bone. Mostly my feet, calves and shoulders."

"Any numbness in the feet or hands?"

Suddenly wide-eyed, he nodded as if I'd just revealed the secret to immortality.

"Doc, I'd swear both are getting twice the amount of sleep as all other body parts combined. Once I do nod off, it's almost a surety I wake with dead limbs. What's up with that shit anyhow?"

"In a moment," I reassured with a raised palm, "any breathing problems?"

"Oh yeah, like somebody parked a Mack truck on my breastbone. Wake up gasping at least twice every night. Apnea?"

"More than likely, yes."

"When did you first notice this? Approximately..."

"Oh, two, three weeks back, I guess. Like waking up with a trash bag pulled over your face. Shit, even when I do manage to find coma-land, I'll usually fart myself awake. Truth be told, Doc, I'm of the belief I could provide the planet with an ample supply of natural gas. Must be mixing all the meats and grains, yeah?"

I nodded without reply in hopes of bypassing a surplus of bowel discussions.

"Anyhow, back to the numbness..."

As if to emphasize past reactions, he reached up with both hands to gently stroke his neck as if a noose had been loosened.

"So what's the deal again? Sometimes it seems to take upwards of a half-hour to get the feeling back in my toes and fingers."

"A circulation issue, Brian. This is what frightens me the most."

Hopping away in reverse, he sudden began a frantic session of shadowboxing, the timing of which I could not have found stranger.

"Because?" he huffed between jabs and combinations, all executed with amazing speed considering the added bulk. For a moment, I found myself utterly entranced by both the bouncing of his massive man-breasts and the deadly quickness of his punches.

"You could be experiencing the first signs of what might well mutate into a massive stroke. Of course, without the required neurological equipment, I can only speculate."

His breath coming in raspy spurts, he halted all movement and bent over with hands atop kneecaps.

"S-So what w-would...are the...o-odds of...the big cr-croak coming to...p-pass?"

"I don't give odds, Brian. I don't...won't guess when it comes to the subject of a man's mortality. All I can do is forewarn of the possibility. Now..." I paused, hovering near the man as he began to vigorously massage his breastbone as if attempting to ward off said coronary, "...though the forthcoming answer is probably of the painfully obvious sort, I must inquire... does this alter your thinking even a smidge?"

He blew out a final, labored breath and flashed the lunatic's grin that had become so prevalent over the past month—what I had begun to think of as his 'nutter-mask.'

"Not a single skid-mark does it alter, Doc."

"Skid-mark?"

He rolled his eyes and giggled maniacally before waving me off. He had clearly entered the familiar sarcasm-zone from which he obviously gained extreme comfort.

"I'm full throttle from here, McClintock. Little late to back out now, you think?"

He backed away and rotated both arms upward in a 'check it out' gesture.

"I mean, hell, the temple of fitness that *was* is nowhere in sight...cloaked by a suit of lard that's ten, shit, *twenty* layers thick. Take a jackhammer to dig down deep enough to find the specimen that was."

One final plea I did voice, despite a discernible lack of logic.

"Brian, all pride aside, it's your life we're talking about. The life you can have *outside* this damnable metal shell."

His ghost-pale complexion abruptly sprouted circular, maroon-shaded patches on each jowl.

"Doc, Doc, Doc...you are the card, you are. I know you bookish dudes are apt to grade out on the lower end of the scale when it comes to common sense, but that's really lame-o."

"Lame-oh...I don't..."

"You really think Hanley's letting me leave this burg unless its toes-up in a body-bag? Not a fucking chance, pal. Pigs will fly overhead and crap pork chops first. So you see, that only leaves me the satisfaction of watching him eat shit on weigh-in day. I won't....repeat...will not fail. Execution be damned, I can at least smile the smile of a winner as they gun me down."

"I...have no...you don't know that. He...I understand Mr. Hanley is, despite certain...shady contacts, an honorable man. I've had nothing but what you Yanks call 'straight up' dealings with the man."

"Horseshit, Doc," he cut in with a vehement nod, "got no time for the spiel. To a point, I understand loyalty, however misguided, to one's employer, but pardon me for preferring to walk at this point in the script."

I watched him lumber away. Literally, *lumber* away like an aged water buffalo on its last legs. As unbiased as I attempt to remain in regards to the ultimate outcome, now less than one full month away, the thought of just how much further his health might deteriorate over that time hatched a sudden chill.

~ * ~

As disturbing as both his attitude and appearance had been, the physical and mental ruination of Brian Jorgensen couldn't hold a candle to his female counterpart, who, in the week since our last session, had seemingly transformed into a sickly, walking husk. As pale and lethargic as she'd appeared those approximately one hundred fifty hours ago, compared to the present, she'd literally been the picture of health. In the aftermath of our visit, with admittedly shaky fingers, I'd retrieved several early photos of LeAnn Garner from my iPad with which to compare the shambling horror of present day. The first had apparently been taken at the conclusion of our initial visit, wherein the checkout guidelines had been set. The sweats she'd adorned on that faithful day, so skintight to appear sewn onto her chunky frame, now hung in billowing flaps. Even her sneakers, high-top joggers, appeared comically oversized.

Upon completing the prerequisite weigh-in, blood pressure and pulse rate readings and blood draw, she'd practically collapsed onto the nearest of two gurneys and even dozed off several times as we'd conversed.

"Miss Garner, I must ask and do not take offense...are you eating? I mean, daily and more than once? Considering your...delicate condition, this...weight dip is as frightening as it is astonishing."

"And what makes you think otherwise, Doctor?" she replied groggily, her left eye remaining semi-closed throughout, as if the droopy lid were sticking. The stark paleness of her complexion was beyond any I'd ever witnessed—what you Yanks might refer to as 'death warmed over.' As for her hair, once full and shiny and hanging just past her shoulders, it now appeared not only flat and lifeless, but roughly half the quantity—missing in clumps as if either the recipient of recent chemotherapy treatments or the victim of nuclear fallout.

"LeAnn, whenever I am visually witness to such a...what appears to be such a dramatic weight loss in less than a full week's time in a patient who is, pardon the dust-coated cliché, eating for two, professional curiosity compels me to query the patient regarding their feeding habits."

She responded between gnawing sessions of the fingernails of her left hand, the fingers of which appeared eerily, creepily elongated, much like the narrow appendages of a spider.

"Dramatic loss? Hmmm, sweet talk will get you everywhere. But then, the proof is in the pudding, I suppose."

She paused to shoot the digital scale a pained glance.

"Yes, Doctor McClintock, I have consumed daily nourishment."

"Of a sort, yes indeed. I have obtained the menu from which you have fed over the past three-plus weeks. May I say, Miss Garner, that upon close inspection of said list, consisting mostly of sliced fruits and various nuts served up in such microscopic rations to hardly keep a rodent alive, it is indeed a medical miracle you are able to sit upright."

Unfazed, her chin dropped and her head briefly swiveled about like a loose ball-bearing on a stick. Abruptly snapping to, she replied as if no delay had occurred.

"Yeah, well, gotta say I'm kinda in awe of myself as well. Brother, it wasn't...it ain't easy surviving on the gerbil-diet plan. Group everything I chocked down in the past week and it doesn't measure up to a single midnight snack from the olden days. Shit, what a glutton I used to be. Sloppy, cottage-cheese layered sow. Disgusting."

"Quite the achievement. No argument here. Such a woeful lack of calorie intake surely explains the blood pressure and pulse rate readings as well. You do realize such miniscule numbers present a clear danger for your unborn child."

"Do I reali...? Take a good, long, leisurely gander at your patient. Does it look like sleep and yours truly have been regular acquaintances of late? I got ulcers atop ulcers, buddy-boy, breeding like horny hares on a three-day pass. Yeah, I do possess a faint understanding of the predicament at hand."

If not for jabbing my own thigh with the clicker-end of a ballpoint pen, I'd have surely guffawed aloud.

"Very well, LeAnn. You are an adult and thus able to make your own decisions, however reckless."

Yawning, she was apparently without sufficient energy to cover her mouth. In turn, the act revealed teeth stained canary yellow. Teeth that, perhaps due to a massive loss of weight around her cheekbones and jowls, appeared freakishly oversized and squared—like woefully misfit dentures.

"Doctor, I'm waaayyyy too beat for double-talk, so whatever tongue-lashing you've prepared, just spill the beans already. Energetic deportment aside, 'fraid this girl's in dire need of a power-nap."

"You *don't* say? Well, considering your BP and pulse numbers, it's nothing short of miraculous you're even conscious."

Expecting either casual indifference or outright insolence, what I got instead was an agreeing nod.

"Truthfully, it's no cake-walk, Doctor. But then, one has to suffer for one's art, yes?"

"One's ar...? The art of dying perhaps. My dear, this is serious. Though I'd hardly consider a blood pressure reading of eighty-four over fifty-six as robust, it is the resting pulse rate of forty-three that has me the most concerned. Are you taking the iron supplements I recommended?"

"Every meal without fail," she stammered, reaching up to massage her temples with a thumb and forefinger, "unless, um, well, I might've skipped a few doses. I'm afraid the ol' memory is about as sharp as a dull butter knife these days."

"Shocking," I chastised with little or no effect as she appeared to doze off again. "Cohesive thought is, after all, as dependent on stored energy as physical exertion. Ready to step up on the scale? That is, are you able?"

She snapped to with a dull, perplexed gaze just as I'd prepped to repeat the latter query.

"Wha-whazzat? Ugh, y-yeah, sure. What you s-said. Uh, which w-was?"

I gestured toward the digital scale and she frowned as if I'd requested she walk barefoot through a minefield.

"Y-yeah, sure. Can't avoid it forever, I suppose. Face the music, as it were."

Amazing. Simply astonishing the psychological warping an eating disorder can evoke, never mind the catastrophic toll on the human body.

Once she'd rolled from the gurney with all the verve of a woman forty years her senior, the short trek to the scale was accomplished in a zombie-like shuffle, truly as if an electric chair awaited.

She stepped up and onto the scale with the release of a resounding, apprehension-filled huff and her head thrown back as if to avoid the readout at all costs. Once I'd successfully recorded said entry, I noted she'd fallen asleep standing, her chin having dipped onto her upper chest and her arms slumped at her sides.

"Um, Miss Gar-...LeAnn, you can dismount now. LeAnn?"

Obviously startled, she literally hopped back as if goosed. Even before totally regaining her balance, a rather unsettling rant began in earnest:

"Sooo, um, just h-how doomed to failure am I? You know, I have to admit, it's a hell of a relief really. Chances were slim to start, right? Slim and none, and Slim just rode a cobweb coated *Minute-Man missile* right outta this hole! Now maybe I can get back to what I know best: donut and ice cream binges, beer by the case, chicken wings by the bucket...and that was usually just the appetizers."

"Miss Gar..."

She began to pace. Limping slightly and leaning forward with her chin tucked within her right palm, she appeared to mimic the classic Yank comedic actor Groucho Marx.

"You recall our first meeting, Doctor? How these damn donated sweats stuck to my rolls like a layer of swathed margarine? Took me a good half-hour just to peel 'em off. Yes sir, a double-wide mama who owned more chins than tits, yes? Fingers like link sausages. Lemme tell you, brother, that physique was years in the making and a shitload harder to construct than it looked..."

"LeAnn..."

"...well, maybe difficult isn't the right word, but not everybody can be as shiftless and sloth-like as to mutate so recklessly, agreed?"

"One-thirty-eight, LeAnn. One...three...eight. You're down...sixteen pounds since last weigh-in. Good god, that's over two pounds a day."

With that, she stopped in her tracks and regarded me as if my nose had just lengthened in true Pinocchio fashion.

"Pardon the French, Doctor, and I hate to go all Brian Jorgensen on you, but...are you fucking with me?"

"No, ma'am. If you have doubts, feel free to remount the scale and see for yourself. All you have to do is...well, look down this time."

"I was...thinking more along the lines of...maybe one-fifty, one-forty-five at best. My, my, my...damn."

For the first time in several visits dating back at least a calendar month, I detected a spark of life in those normally dull, misery-laden eyes. Neutral emotions be damned, I must confess a twinge of joy at the mere sight. That is, until cold-hard reality retook its hold in the realization that as horrid her appearance and condition were at that moment, an additional month and fourteen pounds of further deterioration remained.

"I'm going to do this, Doctor," she beamed with a smile I could only describe as gruesome—a grinning skull. Lightly patting her midsection, she peeked down to address same, "excuse me...*we're* gonna do it."

Peering back upward, I noted building moisture at the corner of each of her drooping eyes.

"I...didn't think...I mean, I just f-figured I was...it was a lost cause. That's why I'd been avoiding this room...that damn scale...like the plague. I was just...I just couldn't face the...I couldn't face failure. Not after all the suffering, all the...torture in just getting this far."

"LeAnn, deserved elation aside, and as with your cohort in transformation, I feel compelled by the oath I've sworn to uphold to caution you of the dangers of...continuing down your current path."

Her normally ruddy flesh still flushed with newfound vitality, she flashed a double-fisted 'scouts honor' gesture.

"I'll take my vitamins, Dad, promise, and work in a bite of two of baked fish or tuna."

"Drink more water," I instructed blandly with the begrudging acceptance that additional warnings and/or advice was likely to be ignored. "Dehydration at this point in your weakened state might well be fatal, understood? Six to eight glasses per day if not more. Remember, you're drinking for two as well."

"Check."

"I think we should schedule, if not daily exams, at least every other day until the...this trial is over, agreed? I need regular blood work in order to determine how the fetus is developing."

"I'm cool with that. Day after tomorrow, then? Same time, same Bat-channel?"

Practically dancing from the room in a drunken, wobbly gait, she drowned out my reply with a glee-filled yelp.

"Catch you on the flipside, Doc 'Tock! Got plans to make and victory speeches to write!"

As with her male counterpart before, I was overwhelmed with equal doses of both professional concern and personal dread as to what the next thirty days would bring. Time and circumstances had created a certain fondness for Miss Garner and, to a smaller degree, Mister Jorgensen. Perhaps professional pride plays a part as well.

Regardless, as the finish line to the contest drew near, it was going to take extreme effort to mask such feelings, especially in the wake of recent premonitions that veered lopsidedly to the side of pain and tragedy.

Part Three:*Face to Face with the Warden*

Upon booting up his PC the morning of day one-seventy, he'd read the message typed out in bold, bright yellow lettering across a pitch-black screen. Later that morning, the casual act of powering up the big screen plasma resulted in a repeat of same. The message read simply:

Your presence is requested at 10 AM of day one-seventy-three for a private on-line chat session via SKYPE with your cordial host, Peter J. Hanley.

Please access the web fifteen minutes prior to appointment time and click on the SKYPE icon already saved on your desktop. From there, log in using the following username and password:

Username: BJorgchopsocky123 (not case sensitive)
Password: twentysixtofreedom (all lower case)

At approximately 10 AM, you will receive the signal for an incoming call. Please remain patient in case the call is delayed.

"Yeah, well, what if I stand you up, prick?" he'd barked at the monitor before punching the enter key with an overabundance of necessary force and thus forcing a fresh screen from which to peruse. "What you gonna do about it, huh? Arrogant son of a bitch. Haven't heard a peep in over four months and suddenly you wanna shoot-the-shit with the inmates? Could it be the cocksure a-hole is growing, dare I say it, nervous? Staff reports must be spelling out a fairy tale heap big boss finds less than enchanting. Either that..." he paused to lift a leg and fart noisily, "...or he's changing the rules to better the odds in his favor."

Jorgensen appeared to spend the remainder of the day in a brooding funk. Of late, he split the majority of his wakeful hours either in the dining hall, or mounting the throne from the effect of the latter. "Trash in, trash out" he'd often quip to the staff when struck by a sudden cramp that required a hasty departure.

Other than the four daily gorging sessions and suffering the natural aftereffects of said stuffings, the few remaining hours spent upright and conscious usually consisted of staring at the boob tube's increasingly inane offerings or on-line surfing.

Workout sessions with Gabe Maxwell had become an every other day affair at best, depending on several unique qualifiers, the most vital being whatever positive energy he could muster to force the issue. Motivation to hit the weights was not, and had never been, an issue. Problem was, a fourteen to sixteen thousand calorie-a-day diet overflowing with starches, sugars, fats and carbs, had served to effectively exterminate the will to pump iron while providing the ultimate in slumber therapy. In the matter of a few short weeks, he'd gone from averaging less than three hours a night to just over eleven, usually waking in a mild panic with the realization that prime scarfing time was passing him by.

Though not purposely, at least from his perspective, he'd spent precious little time with his partner in incarceration. They still shared the occasional movie-night and an alcohol free nightcap on floor four, sans the prerequisite roll in the hay that had become the norm several months prior. Rich, relaxed dialogue, never a strong point in the relationship, had of late been replaced by mostly wordless nods and gestures. There was, however, an unspoken understanding—verbal rooting or any variation of the proverbial 'pat on the back' would constitute downright campy, that each stood in the other's corner.

Waking at just before six on the morning of the scheduled chat, Jorgensen rolled from the bed and sat motionless on its cornered edge for several moments, as if pondering whether or not to attend.

With hours to kill even after the day's initial (usually the first of a half-dozen or more) bowel movement, he'd made his way to the dining hall. Soured stomach or no, a dozen eggs and half as many sausage biscuits were going down.

Arriving at just before seven, though there had been no sign of the facilities hologram chief, he found the dining hall occupied nonetheless.

"Morning, Slim. Little early for your morning grape, isn't it? Or is today double-peanut day?" he'd quipped, sauntering slowly by the table from which she appeared to be picking unidentified fruit from a tiny white bowl. Peeking into the fridge, he found his previous days' order wrapped tightly in clear cellophane atop a massive serving plate.

Trudging back into the dining area, he chose a table directly across from hers.

"Fueling up for the chat?" she asked wearily between sips of water from a clear plastic mug with the words 'Avian Ultra' stenciled across its midsection.

"Yep. I'll need every ounce of energy I can muster just to stay conscious once he commences to preach. Man just adores the sound of his own pipes."

"No argument. Here's hoping he talks himself out loooong before he gets to me."

They had spoken the day previous, sharing the news of the planned SKYPE interviews. LeAnn's was scheduled for three that afternoon. Jorgensen had joked of the fear that such a lengthy stretch between chats might indicate he might be forced to endure a five-hour conversation.

"Have no fear. I'll do my best to exorcise the majority of his anger. By the time your old man gets to you, he outta be Teddy Bear timid."

LeAnn lipped what Jorgensen was able to identify as a slice of strawberry, chewing as tentatively as if it were a sliver of glass.

"So what's your best guess?" he continued before shoveling in a heaping spoonful of cold scrambled eggs and sausage, to be followed by an equally jaw-stretching bite of buttered, grape-jelly-filled biscuit.

"No clue. Good luck wishes perhaps?" LeAnn had replied with a wink following a lengthy pause.

Somehow he managed to avoid choking as an uncontrollable giggle surfaced from deep within, the tabletop littered with specs of semi-chewed biscuit that had sailed free from between pursed lips. He was only able to respond after chugging down a full glass of chocolate milk and releasing a trio of echoing belches in the aftermath.

"Yeah, sure…that's it. What was I thinking? What else could it be? Good luck and god-speed. Mighty white of 'im, don'cha think?"

LeAnn nodded while holding her mug airborne as if to propose a toast.

"Indeed it shall be. Here's to us, then, big guy. Give 'im hell."

Jorgensen raised his own newly refilled glass.

"Will do. You do the same."

Moments later, they exchanged nods and she left him to clean his plate. He did so with great difficulty, nearly regurgitating the last few bites.

~ * ~

He logged in at nine-fifty-six a.m. Precisely ten minutes later, he was prompted to answer an incoming SKPE call. He did so while wearing a wide, mischievous grin while facing away from the monitor with his bare buttocks exposed to same.

"Good morning, Brian. Why, in visualizing what is unarguably your *best side*, I must say you're looking no worse for wear. If I may offer a suggestion, however, a shave might be in order. Shouldn't hide those cute little dimples from the world."

His smile having abruptly faded to be replaced by a sour grimace, Jorgensen pulled the snug-fitting sweat pants back into place before sliding a chair over.

"What's this about, Hanley?" he spat bitterly while avoiding eye contact with the image parked less than a foot away, choosing instead to focus upon a far wall, where a small pastoral-themed painting hung.

"I'm a busy man. Meals to eat and naps to take."

"Now, why does it have to...be about anything in particular, Brian? Can't we just sit here and jaw without it constituting some sort of conspiracy theory? Folks tend to be far too suspicious, don't you agree? Example: let's imagine simple mechanical issues arise with...say, a main generator. Rumor and innuendo ensue and before one knows it, all types of fictional malfeasants rear their ugly heads."

Jorgensen released a hearty belly laugh before regarding his video guest with a prickly smirk. In taking in the man's meticulously trimmed eyebrows, slicked-back hair and unblinking, reptilian gaze, he felt an unfamiliar tug at his gut that faded abruptly. Abruptly enough to dismiss as being even remotely associated with the word fear; an emotion he'd forever exclaimed to never having experienced.

"Damn efficient spy network you have at your disposal, Hanley. For my next half-cocked theory, I'm thinking microchip camera implants, possibly in one or both butt cheeks."

Hanley's expression remained stoic, eerily unchanged, no doubt somewhat affected by the iffy transmission.

"Not in the budget, I'm afraid."

"Yeah, right. You're low-budget all the way, warden. My heart bleeds. Actually, more like my hemorrhoids."

Clearing his throat, Hanley's tone lowered to a throaty whisper.

"In all honesty, Brian, the change...the physical transformation you've undergone is...to understate quite horribly...*simply...astonishing.*"

"Beyond your wildness dreams, is it?"

"Pardon?"

Scooting back several feet as the chair beneath squealed its disapproval, Jorgensen kicked out both legs while simultaneously eagle-spreading his arms.

"Oh come on, Hanley. I'd imagine just the sight of this fucking abomination has you ready to spew a nut. No need to hold back the joy, man...I can see it twinkling behind those beady little eyes."

Hanley cocked a brow and squinted into the camera.

"You truly think me that small-minded, Brian?"

Mocking the man's comically stoic expression, Jorgensen planted an open palm over his heart.

"I solemnly swear that would be a resounding...yes."

"This isn't just about retribution, Brian. Well, not entirely."

"For real, pal 'o mine? Pray tell then, what is...*was* the main thrust behind this perverted game of human torture and debasement? Just honing your natural-born talent? Keeping razor-sharp for future endeavors?"

Hanley leaned back, tucking a clenched fist beneath a smooth-shaven chin, a gleaming, thick-banded gold loop adorning the ring finger. With his arms and the majority of his upper torso suddenly on display, Jorgensen noted a palpable measure of bulkiness he hadn't noticed all those months earlier. He quickly shrugged it off as just another side effect of a second-rate SKYPE connection.

"A man of your...ilk would...*could* not understand the logic of my methods, Brian. You might be able to comprehend from an intellectual standpoint, but hardly from a moralistic one."

Jorgensen slapped a knee in mock jocularity. "Oh yeah, you're legendary for a high moral code, Hanley. A real role-model for the kiddies, you are. Shiiiiit, it is to laugh...hysterically."

"Regardless, how are you feeling, Brian?"

"How do I...feel? Surely you jest. Warden psychoanalyzes inmate? Well, not on my dime, Doctor Skull-fuck."

Standing, Jorgensen shoved the chair into a far corner, where it ricocheted off a far wall before overturning.

"So, we done here or what?"

Wringing his hands, Hanley's tone and expression descended to an even lower level of dour.

"Please sit, Brian. There is a particular matter we need to discuss. Something...vital to both our futures."

A short, silent pause ensued, wherein Jorgensen stood with his chunky hands propped atop massive hips. Eventually he retrieved the chair, obviously with no small level of reluctance considering his slumped deportment.

"Uh-huh. I thought so. Here we go, then. Talk to me, old great dictator of the underground kingdom. I had a feeling some kind of drastic rule change was in order now that I'm within striking distance of showing you up."

Hanley waited to ensure the other man's rant had ceased before offering his reply in a throaty whisper.

"As usual, you assume too much. There will be no such supplemental alteration to the original agreement, Brian. Instead, a minor stipulation I thought it only fair to share now that a...completion date is so near."

"Sure, sure. Tell you what...how about letting me decide just how minor a stipulation?"

Straddling the chair with its rounded backrest pressed against his ample bosom, Jorgensen's arms draped over like pale, meaty tentacles.

"Oh, it's fairly simplistic. Weigh in less than the required goal...and there is no deviation from the original agreement."

"Point of order, Hanley," Jorgensen barked with a forefinger raised in rebuttal, "I didn't agree to shit."

Running splayed fingers through a perfectly shaped coif, Hanley appeared to flash, ever-so-briefly, the tinniest of smiles.

"Point taken."

"So basically, I crap out on weigh-in day and the only way I exit this metal suppository is toes up. That about sum it up?"

"In a nutshell, Brian. The slight alternation comes into play if the set goal is successfully met."

"Oh, lemme guess...castration? A chopped off digit or two? Eye-ball extraction? Don't even hint of my walking away unscathed. I may look like a dumb-shit, but it's just a disguise."

"You're the father of my grandchild, Brian. A grandchild I'd prefer to be raised without ever meeting or knowing of you."

Left temporarily speechless, Jorgensen's wide-eyed gaze locked on the carpeted floor at his feet and remained for a full minute and a half.

"Sounds to me like we're back to the toes-up solution."

Hanley waived him off, the glittering ring almost blinding within the otherwise murky transmission.

"Not at all. Like I said, you keep your end of the bargain, so will I. You meet the goal, you walk...and keep walking, as far away from my daughter and unborn grandchild's life as my money will take you."

With that, Jorgensen regained the power to blink, as if snapping free from a deep trance.

"Your money?"

"As before, you'll be awarded travel expense to the locale of your choice. I'm adding an additional fifty thousand dollars in cash, as long as the aforementioned locale is outside the continental U.S. Needless to say, you are never to return or attempt contact with LeAnn or the child in any way, shape or form, to include social media. If this agreement is breeched, Brian, it won't matter if you've chosen to take your mail at the base of an active volcano in the Amazon rain forest, I will have you found and exterminated. Now, are we clear on any and all parts of this particular insert to the original pact?"

Jorgensen shrugged, exposing bare palms. The sad smile on display was that of a woeful resignation—a feeling of complete, utter powerlessness.

"Like I have a choice? What's next, want to prick my finger and get that in blood?"

Leaning back again, Hanley sighed in apparent relief. Jorgensen again marveled in how much...thicker the man appeared, like a miniature version of himself.

"I must say I'm pleasantly surprised at your attitude, Brian. Good show. Here's hoping LeAnn is equally in favor."

"Rest easy, Grandpa. Your daughter wants about as much to do with me as I do with her and the...the kid. I'm sure you know she considered aborting. Wouldn't listen to a damn thing I said on the subject. Shut me completely out."

Jorgensen hugged himself across the midsection, quite the chore considering the bulk involved.

"LeAnn is nothing if not extremely stout of mind, Hanley. Stout as steel and with about as much give. Maybe she inherited a bit of that from the bloodline, but I'm of the belief it's mostly a recent development."

The big man slid the chair forward until the only thing visible from Hanley's point of view was his grotesquely bloated, ghostly pale face.

"Don't be surprised if she tells you to fuck off, Grandpa. You and the whole Hanley organization. In fact, if she's half as sharp as I believe she is, she'll travel as far away from your rancid clan as you're hoping I do."

To that, Hanley openly grimaced before quickly regaining the icy composure that was his trademark.

"*Now* we are done here, Brian. See you soon."

"Oh, I'm counting on it, Hanley. Dreaming of it, in fact. No hired muscle standing between us. Just you...and me."

In a blink, Jorgensen was left staring at his own reflection from a black screen.

"Perchance to dream, you smarmy sack of shit...perchance to dream," he muttered as a faint gleam briefly illuminated each of his bloodshot eyes.

Part Four:*Face to Face with the Warden, the Sequel*

"Can you state, once and for all, what it is you expect from me? I must say, these mixed signals are quite...confounding."

"I'm serious, LeAnn. Dead...of the stone-cold variety. I've read the doctor's notes and studied the most recent of his findings. Another month of this and, at the very least...irreconcilable damage could be done."

"Aw, that's so touching. I'd all but forgotten you even possessed a soft-hearted side. So rarely rears its mushy head. Better not allow any of your many subordinates to ever witness such pansy-wansy emotion. Such perceived weaknesses are undoubtedly frowned upon."

Upon initially viewing her image, a full-frontal view to include head, shoulders and upper chest, Hanley had openly winced, the segmented, slow-motion imagery of the SKYPE video transfer actually enhancing the expression to comical proportions. Wide-eyed and slack-jawed, his cheeks had instantly drained to a chalky shade.

"Good g-god, you're...you're practically emaciated," he'd managed before a quick throat-clearing and straightening of the shoulders ensued in a pathetic attempt at regaining a semblance of composure.

"Great to see you too, sire. From the extreme opposite side of the spectrum, you're looking mighty buffed."

"I'm serious, LeAnn. I've seen the blood-work. You're practically anemic. All the symptoms of anorexia are present and accounted for. McClintock's belief, and I trust the man's knowledge to a fault, is that another week or so, never mind a full month, and you're apt to collapse into a coma from low sugar alone. Even if, and this is a colossal if, you *do* manage to survive to pass the set goal, the unborn child will most definitely not."

"Bingo," she exclaimed with a weak snap of the fingers, "just as I suspected. Therein lies the gist of your worries."

"LeAnn, don't be th..."

"Heaven forbid any prenatal harm comes to the heir to the throne of Hanley!"

"Correction, young lady," he retorted sternly, "that title belongs primarily to you."

Having lowered her head like a scolded child, LeAnn fell silent while avoiding eye contact. This lasted only until her father attempted a follow-up reprimand.

"As I was say..."

"This baby is none of your concern, Father. Regardless of its future health and well-being, I will not allow him or her to be...integrated into the family business. Whether he or she is ever introduced to her...kin at all."

"I...LeAnn, I didn't mean...that is...I di..."

"Unlike this forced imprisonment, that call will be mine and mine alone."

"Enough!" he roared, a loud thump ringing out from where a clenched fist met an unseen tabletop. "I've made my decision. This...regrettable project ends...right now. I'm pulling you out. I have a medical team on alert to fly in for extraction within the hour."

"You do that..." came the whispered reply, delivered in a guttural growl her father hardly recognized, "...you dare even attempt it, Father, and you will never again lay eyes on your only child, or the grandchild she carries. If you consider this a bluff of some sort, please consider what miniscule part we've played in each other's lives in the past decade plus. My sudden vanishing won't be a radical change, for *either* of us."

His mouth opened to reply, closed and opened again, though actual words never materialized, only a slight nod that verified comprehension.

"Twenty-some-odd days," LeAnn resumed, her voice noticeably hoarse but otherwise normalized, "we do it my way until this is finished. You understand? I will, for once in my miserable life, conclude what I've started. I would think you would feel immense pride in this...stand I've taken. After all, you pointed me down the trail."

"Promise me then," he replied meekly, "you'll eat bet....healthier. Take your vitamins. You promise me this...and I'll promise you, *swear* to you, that no matter the outcome of our...deal, you and...the child will always be taken care of."

"Nope. Unacceptable."

"Excuse me?"

"Are you allowing Brian the same arrangement?"

"Of course n...no. Drastically different circumstances."

"The father of your grandchild does not rate special treatment?"

Sliding back with arms crossed, Hanley wore a mask of frigidity.

"It's personal, LeAnn. Does this mean you...proclaim some sort of attachment to the man? I...understood the relationship between you two to be a briefly physical one. A monumental mistake. A regrettable series of...trysts. Did I...misunderstand? Is there an undercurrent of fondness there? Loyalty? By all means, dear daughter, help me to understand."

Mocking his defiant stance, LeAnn leaned back to strike a similar pose.

"I'm not questioning the reasons for your biased attitude, Father. I'd say any man who manages to screw both another man's wife *and* only child shouldn't expect an annual Thanksgiving Day invite. That said, there is a matter of basic human compassion, yes?"

"I will not budge on this," he replied sharply, "Jorgensen makes the required goal or he doesn't. Period."

"And if he doesn't, Father?"

"I'm here to discuss *you*. Drop the subject."

"Will he swim with the fishes?"

"Enough."

"Will he be fitted for the infamous concrete shoes?"

Placing his hands behind his head, Hanley sighed deeply and remained silent.

"You know, Daddy, I worry...deeply in fact."

"So do I, Lee. You look....horrid. I implore you to alter the diet that..."

"No, no, no. I worry for my fellow prisoner."

"Goddamn it, LeAnn!" he bellowed, lunging forward with teeth bared. "I won't discuss the fate of Brian Jorgensen! Now drop the subject before...before I retract the earlier offer, am I being clear?"

As if to match his intimidation play, she slid forward in a blur and practically stuck her face to the tiny camera mounted atop the monitor.

"Honestly, Daddy, even if Brian makes the weight, are you really, *truly* going to allow him to just walk out of here?"

Visibly deflated, Hanley sat back and gazed downward. "I...implore you, Lee, to take care. Take care of both yourself and my grandchild. See you soon."

Offering no verbal reply, LeAnn smiled knowingly before reaching over to click and disconnect transmission.

That night, while lying in the dark, tranquil confines of her bedroom with both hands clutched at her abdomen, the floodgates opened; the haunting, retching sobs reverberating like small-arms fire.

Nine

Limp to the Finish Line

Part One*: Final Note to the boss*
Narrator*: Personal Trainer Gabe Maxwell*

Once, in a lifetime far, far away, I possessed one helluva gambling Jones. I'd wager on damn near everything, from sportin' events, mostly boxin', baseball and the gridiron, to snowfall totals and even Hollywood box-office returns. During the affliction's heyday there were the occasional treks to either Vegas or Atlantic City. Lost a small fortune during that ten to twelve year span, not to mention trashin' not one but two marriages. Thank the good lord above, I kicked the itch before online gamin' came along—an addict's wettest dream and worst nightmare, all rolled into one. All that in mind, I should feel a stout sense of relief no wagers were available at the outset of this little study of the limits of human endurance, 'cause I'd have surely lost my collective ass on what seemed at the time like a couple of money-in-the bank bets.

First off, I would've wagered the farm and all associated implements on the total collapse of Miss LeAnn Garner within the first few weeks of her incarceration. Hell, upon laying eyes on that Macy's day float physique and piss-poor attitude attached, I envisioned her carried out on a triple-X sized stretcher before dropping the first pound. This presumption was only enhanced upon hearing of her past drug and alcohol addictions. Drop half her body weight? Yeah...sure...maybe in the same whacky universe where sea-cows sprout wings or Democrats cut welfare programs.

Well, here we sit one hundred seventy-five days later, a mere five wake-ups and a bag drag away from the curtain falling once and for all, and this old bone-cruncher is wearin' a mask of dripping egg yolk. Now, it surely takes no more than an average IQ, perhaps even below average if you consider yours truly, to pinpoint her motivation to succeed.

The old ma...the boss had challenged her numerous times to clean up her act and rejoin the family fold, but from what I gather, the majority of said trials had been of the soft-pitch variety. This latest was no less than a major-league heater headed straight for the noggin. Surprisin...no, more like shockingly, his little girl had not ducked or cringed away, but stood her ground, eyed that ball'a flames, nailed it right across the trademark and sent it sailin' into the upper deck. Sure, she looked like hammered shit and probably felt worse, but there was no downplayin' the accomplishment, especially considering the change-up, think knuckleball on a windless day, tossed her direction about midway through the game.

Her workouts, or what had passed for 'em, had become less frequent these last few weeks. Can't say how she'd mustered the moxie to do as much as she did, usually a fifteen to twenty minute session on the treadmill at one of its lower settings and maybe a set or two of crunches or gradual stretch that made tai-chi look like ultimate fighting. Night and day from the rabid-banshee warrior woman I'd watched her morph into sometime around day sixty or so. Predictably, as her gluttonous conjoined twin melted away, so did roughly half the inner spark that drove those three, four, sometimes five hour sweat-an' scream sessions. I kinda figured she'd also begun to cut back once the news broke of the...extra package she was haulin' around. Regardless, you gotta give credit where credit is due. Kudos to perhaps the most driven female I've ever come across.

As for her assigned silo-mate, I'd have once bet my undergarments on certain loss, and once again...been left walkin' around cuppin' my privates to prevent an indecent exposure arrest.

If anything, Brian Jorgensen's accomplishments are even more impressive. Consider the man's legendary ego and self-centered ways—the whole 'my body is a temple of gold' attitude and his own admission to not giving a shit about anything other than satisfying his own jollies. To be able to not only accept a slow, painful demolition of that chiseled physique, the 'gold temple' he'd spent most of his adult life cultivatin', but to actually execute said demolition over five-plus months of self-imploding, well, he displayed the stoniest of wills.

Motivation-wise, well, that's kinda self-explanatory, considering the stakes. Han...the boss had been kinda vague on an exact punishment in case of failure, but it was fairly clear...like fine crystal in fact, that whatever disciplinary measure was chosen, it was gonna surpass a simple dressing-down by a country mile. I figure Jorgensen would give his eye teeth just to show up the boss, much less save his own hide.

His workouts, much like his fellow hostage, had dwindled severely in both quantity and quality over the past few weeks.

Oh, he'd steered clear of anything resembling cardiovascular since around the two-month point, sticking with a program I'd mapped out for many a power-lifter, that being limited sets completed in a progressive, pyramid style of starting off heavy and ending heavier.

The added bulk he'd packed on might've slowed his metabolism and drained his energy over time, but it hadn't prevented his level of strength from shooting straight up the charts. Cock-strong even in his thinner days, he'd tripled his bench press and squat totals much in the same manner as he'd doubled his body weight. The last few sessions had been ten, fifteen minutes at most, minus the half-hour stretch that, considerin' he could no longer even touch his blessed toes, had become kinda awkward to watch.

Once he sprawled about on the mat like a sunbathing sea-cow, he'd head over to the bench and pound out four or five sets, followed by a turn at the squat rack and then, if he was feelin' extra spry, maybe a few sets of barbell curls, the last of which was usually executed with seventy-five pounders.

Bottom line was this: I'd have no qualms 'bout challenging this new version of Brian Jorgensen to a footrace, but I'd sure as hell think twice about an arm-wrestling competition. Never you mind the lard-coated shell, the dude was carryin' twenty-one inch pythons and thighs like Sequoia trunks.

On the downside, his breathin' had grown more strained by the day, and he was stomping around with a noticeable limp. I also noticed 'im wincing quite a bit, normally while grabbing or pushing at his lower gut. When I'd bring it up, he'd just waive me off, chalkin' it to that maniac's diet he'd taken up.

To sum it all up in a nutshell, longwinded prelude aside, I'd no doubt borne witness to two of the most unlikely, underdog transformations in the history of mankind, and the damn shame of it was that the world most likely would never know.

Gotta confess to feelin' a surge of pride with the small part I played, no matter the final outcome. Unfortunately, with that comes an equally stout surge of fear concernin' the same. I've even thought of prayin' to help the cause, but then, I've got a sinkin' feeling that god turned his back on any and all parties playin' a part in this sad little stage-play. If so, can't say I blame 'im a single iota.

~ * ~

Part Two: *Final Note to the boss*
Narrator: *Darwin McClintock, Facility Physician*

As the faithful day of truth grows nearer, the professional side of me cannot help but voice my deeper concern on the aftermath for my two...um...the two patients.

Taken directly from her digital chart:

Miss LeAnn Garner will require prolonged Medical Nutrition Treatment for anorexia nervosa and quite possibly its evil twin, bulimia nervosa. I must note there has been no evidence to date of the latter disorder. This might include but will not be limited to regular Cognitive Behavioral Treatments and, if necessary, Cognitive Remediation Treatments. I estimate, conservatively, a two to three year span for full recovery time, depending on complications from giving birth.

In all fairness, I must note Miss Garner has shown a high degree of intestinal fortitude over the last six months. I believe this will aid her immensely in the healing process she must soon endure.

Similarly taken from his digital chart:

From a physical standpoint, Brian Jorgensen will require carefully mapped out diets and exercise regiments in order to gradually, thus safely, decrease the inordinate amount of body weight he's gained over the last five and a half months.

At least measure, his Body Mass Index, or BMI, had increased to a frightening count of forty-five point three. This from a beginning measurement of just over six. Literally, this constitutes one extreme to the other. Again, it is imperative this loss is accomplished at a cautious, steady pace to offset additional shocks to the system. Diet must be high in fruits, grains and fiber and void of sugars, fats, and carbs. Unlike the change in menu, which should commence as soon as possible, the exercise regimen should be instituted in carefully regulated segments as to not overtax the cardiovascular system.

As for probable psychological effects of his...forced indenture, since I am not qualified to properly diagnose, my only advice would be to seek immediate counseling. Mister Jorgensen's rather volatile personality has not, in my unqualified opinion, altered in any dramatic fashion since his arrival at the facility. Whether a noted lack of change, no matter the increased level of stress, indicates a deeper issue is unknown. My personal opinion, for whatever its worth, is that Brian Jorgensen was in great need of psychiatric care long before he and I were introduced.

Also of note, I would like to extend my best wishes to both patients in the rather lengthy healing process ahead. I cannot honestly state I enjoyed treating either under such...traumatic circumstances, though the experience itself was, without a doubt, a wholly unique challenge I won't soon forget...or choose to ever repeat.

~ * ~

Part Three: *Final Note to the boss*
Narrator: *Miss Jeannine, Facility Cook*

Thank Lord Jesus, it's almost over. I know I should be happy for 'em. Happy for myself, to boot. The pressure's almost off. Pressure like I ain't never experienced in all my days. The kind that weighs one down like steel-toed boots with concrete soles. Not only is there no happiness, I'm finding little in the way of simple relief.

I could fib and say I got no earthly idea why I'm feeling nothing but a black emptiness at my gut, but why bother? Maybe owning up is just the therapy I need to wipe the slate at least semi-clean in my own feeble mind. There's no way to sugarcoat this, I reckon...and no reason to at this juncture, but if Miss G and Mister J either one had suffered some sort of collapse in those final weeks, I'd have surely bore a deep guilt. Fact is, in my fears that one or both weren't gonna make it to the end without a potentially fatal health crisis, I had labeled myself nothing short of an accessory to murder. Might sound a bit melodramatic, being that I was just following orders to fulfill the pair's specific meal wishes, but in my mind I might as well have loaded up a couple'a gats and instructed 'em both how to use 'em for self-destruction.

Consider the average day's nutrition, or lack thereof, prepared for Miss Garner in those last sixty or so days. I kept good notes, old habits die hard, and the following captures a fairly typical snapshot:

Breakfast: small-sized bowl of sliced fruits (pears, cherries, apples, peaches). Fat content practically nil, calorie content damn near the same. In the last three weeks or so, she'd struggle to clean the bowl, usually leaving behind a handful untouched or perhaps, god help me, regurgitated, as they sometimes appeared pre-chewed. Liquid refreshment: orange or fruit juice had long since been banished from the menu, replaced by plain tap water.

Lunch: Though she'd order up a sandwich of some sort...thinly-sliced turkey or chicken, fat-free a'course, there were countless days it was left either untouched or with just a few tiny nibbles eaten away. Liquid refreshment: H...two...oh.

Dinner: Assorted salads, almost exclusively of the veggie-only variety. Green-leaf lettuce, cherry tomatoes, spinach leaves, maybe a wildcard tossed in for good measure every few moons like sliced red or green bell peppers, or ham cubes no bigger than my pinky-nail. Much like breakfast, the last few weeks saw 'em picked at and tossed about plenty, but never completely consumed. I swear that girl was operating on less fuel than your average swamp rat. I can only figure she must've been spending fourteen, sixteen hours a day snoozing, 'cause otherwise she was treading damn close to 'walking dead' territory for real. Liquid refreshment: water, water, and more water. I do recall she'd popped the top off a Diet Dr. Pepper one particular evening, though the can left behind felt as if it weren't missing nary a sip.

I'd venture the poor girl's daily calorie never passed the five-hundred mark those last three to four weeks…or basically comparable to the average four to five year old minus a bowl or two of cheesy macaroni.

That she hobbled into my kitchen this morning with only five days remainin' and scarfed down an entire hard-boiled egg along with the majority of her daily fruit salad certainly picked up this old woman's spirits, that is until I watched her sneak off to the ladies room and swore I heard a muffled retch. Let me state for the record and without shame that I'll be rooting especially hard for Miss G to first reach the set goal and second to recover from the hell that brought her to that goal.

As for Mister J, his was the exact opposite in extremes, as one might imagine considerin', well, the personal stakes involved. Stakes that he always voiced as being a nothing short of life and death. Can't opine on something of which I have no knowledge, but he surely believed it, and I guess that was all that was needed for proper incentive. Lord knows I've witnessed some mighty eaters in my time, of both sexes. I'd once held a temp job preppin' meals for a construction crew outside Dallas; a dozen healthy, hearty menfolk who could routinely wolf down a half a side a beef, twenty pound bag of taters and four dozen buttered biscuits per day. Company didn't hold back on meal money since these men were known as the best in the profession, and I'll be stitched if they didn't take advantage of that unlimited food budget and then some.

Closer to home, my ex was no pansy when it came to mealtime either. Saw 'im routinely clean the bones off'n an entire baked or deep-fried yard-bird, along with a pound or two of mashed taters and heapin' bowl green beans or black-eyed peas.

In those few salad days when we'd had the budget for dessert, my man would oft times finish off the feast with a slice or two of whatever cobbler-pie I'd prepared. In other words, he 'twernt no slouch with a fork and spoon, but on his most ravenous day, my dear departed couldn't hold a candle to Mister Brian Jorgensen in those last few weeks 'fore the end.

It wasn't just *how much* the man was puttin' away, but *what* he was packin' away that separated 'im from any I'd ever seen or hoped to see. He'd obviously done his homework on the World Wide Web and handpicked the fattiest, unhealthiest dishes from several continents. Wasn't just desserts neither, though such artery-hardeners as pecan or chocolate pie and caramel-swirl cake were present and accounted for on a daily basis. He was suckin' down ice cream by the gallon, with Rocky Road and Death by Chocolate bein' the main culprits. Believe ol' Doc McClintock might refer to that second choice as 'highly ironic.'

Anyhow, it was mainly chicken, pork or beef by the barrel, all but the latter deep fried in lard, the way his mama had made it, he'd said, along with butter-rich pasta dishes infamous for their power to widen the waistline and clog the main veins. Meantime, he continued to choke down two gallons of chocolate milk per day which, in those last two dreadful weeks, he used to wash down block after block of cheddar cheese.

Much as I was tempted to nip what I considered a slow version of suicide in the bud, it simply wasn't to be allowed. So I cooked my tail off and was never ceased to be amazed he'd never failed to clean each and every plate.

Those last two or three weeks, I just...couldn't...was unable to meet the man face-to-face. Couldn't stomach the alternation of both his body and sanity. Those in the know might well describe me as a tough old bird, but in truth I never was much for dealing with the mentally troubled. No disrespect to Mister J...sure if I'd been in his shoes I'd have surely slipped a noggin-gear or two myself. It's just that...it was just too...I dunno...reckon it was guilt, plain and simple. I felt like I was a conspirator, willing or no, in killing a man, whether he pass in his sleep while awaiting liberation from the silo, or by cuttin' his lifespan short by a decade or more with the poisonous stews I'd stirred up in what I'd begun to think of as my personal witches' cauldron.

As with Miss G, my prayers are favorable for his survival, both inside and out of this iron tube. Arrogant, blowhard racist act aside, I sum up Mister J as a better man than he portrays. Here's hoping that upon escape he can rethink and, oh, what is it the young folks say? Re-kick? No, *reboot*...reboot his life and in doing so, fill up that hole in his soul that presently serves to fuel his roguish act.

Lord, guide 'em both down the correct path. While you're at it, please do the same for yours truly. After this, I surely feel as though a self-cleansing of my own wretched soul is surely in order.

~ * ~

The trio of slumped figures dashed from beneath the chopper's swirling blade, a distance of four to five feet separating them. They remained in single file formation even as the bird ascended, bathing them in a whirling funnel of blown dust. While the lead and rear men sported Marine-style buzz cuts and were decked out in dark khakis, short-sleeved polo tees, one dark blue and the other tar black, and Oakley wraparound designer shades, the center figure struck quite the fashionable pose in a gray Italian suit, reflective Ray-bans and Gucci shoes. He was obviously the elder of the three, perhaps by a decade or more— his perfectly coifed, salt and pepper-shaded do miraculously unfazed by the previous bluster.

Upon reaching the facility's lone entrance, the lead man instructed the middle one to hold position a few feet back while the rear figure bellowed into a cellphone while peering upward into blazing midday sun to watch the helicopter circle the area.

Within minutes the double-glass door swung inward and the trio entered in the same order in which they'd arrived. They stood in a tight circle as a fourth member stepped from the shadows to greet them with a casual salute. Noticeably smaller in stature than the new arrivals, the stockily-built man wearing a black tee, blue jeans and a red ball-cap, stood at the formations center in a parade rest pose while commanding their full attention. His in-briefing was relatively concise, concluded with a slight bow clearly directed at the man in the suit. He then turned about on a heel and led the trio, once again trudging forward in single-file, to the back of the room, where a wall of squared shadow swallowed them whole.

~ * ~

So, here we are then. Seventy-two some-odd hours and a bag-drag."

"Bag-drag?"

"It's an old military term. Means moving out while dragging along an overstuffed duffel."

"Oh, yeah, well, only thing I'll be dragging around is my bony ass."

"Right back at'cha, Slim, though I gotta replace the word bony with *mammoth*."

Silhouetted within the ashen glow of the movie screen's garish light, Jorgensen's massive bulk appeared magnified to monstrous proportions. Decked out in a bright red wife-beater tee, with both arms draped over the chair-back, his grotesquely thick forearms actually appeared bulkier than the connecting biceps.

"Enjoy the flick?" he asked with a nod toward the screen.

"I find a woeful lack of attention span prevents my sharing an opinion one way or another," she replied, suppressing a yawn. "This one was a comedy, right?"

"Of the black as night variety, I believe. A genre of film I usually favor, buuuut, as you mentioned, there exists those bothersome outside issues that do tend to distract."

They sat in silence for several moments, wherein LeAnn reached up to scratch casually behind her left ear and, as had become quite the normal occurrence in past weeks, pulled back a hair-coated palm.

"You know, on occasion, your chosen dialogue reminds one more of, say…a snooty, bespectacled history teacher than an iron-fisted, steely-eyed Kung-Fu warrior. If I didn't know any better, I'd say this whole experience has actually boosted your IQ."

"Hmm, interesting theory that. Stuff the body and the mind will follow. If so, you, my dear should be suffering side-effects with the polar opposite effect."

"Meaning?" she asked drowsily, cocking a brow just slightly.

"To put it politely, Madam Toothpick, you should be dumb as a rock."

"Nice. You might have a point. Why, just this morning I attempted to brush my ass and wipe my teeth."

Whipping his head back like a baying wolf, Jorgensen howled, slapping a knee in the aftermath.

"You do make me sooo proud at times. Such razor-sharp adlib only goes to showcase my influence, unfortunately."

Waving a bony forefinger back and forth, her tone grew increasingly sluggish.

"Sorry, champ…but I was a lost cause long before we ever shared space or swapped spit."

"Point taken."

Several minutes passed as the screen gradually darkened until the lone existing illumination originated from a sporadically placed string of emergency lights.

"Let me ask you," she began sluggishly, as if regretting her choice of words almost instantly, "just…to confirm my own paranoia."

"Shoot. I'll be more than happy to verify what we already know."

"You…have you been…I mean, heard anything out of the ordinary the past three, four nights?"

Jorgensen stared intently into his glass as if to catch even a fleeting glimpse of his future.

"Like what, Slim? Geez, here's hoping it's not my nightly butt-cheek concerto you're speaking of. Raw veggies play hell with my gut. I'm consistently blowing the sheets off the b..."

"It's more...well, I've...I think it's banging or hammering. Usually faint but...enough to slightly vibrate the walls."

"Come to think of it..." Jorgensen replied with a vigorous scratch through his beard, "...nope...nothing. Sorry, Slim....but you are as nuts as you feared."

She shook her head and smiled grimly.

"Super-duper. A cracked egg whose yolk will soon ooze."

"Don't sweat it. Probably just that mystery janitor again...perhaps unjamming the toilets. Lord knows I've done my part to clog 'em. Anyhow, allow me to preach on weirdness on a major-league level: the other night I dreamed I stumbled into the john to drain the lizard and no less than a wolverine was sitting on the stoop smoking a big fat doobie. Wasn't no Hugh Jackson-style sharp-clawed-critter either..."

"*Jackman,*" she corrected between muffled guffaws, the palm of one hand cloaking the shaky grin beneath, "Hugh...Jackman."

"Yeah, that guy. Anyhow, the damn thing curses me out in a Brit accent for walking in on 'im and then, pretty as you please, spits out the joint and lunges at me with a mouthful of bloody fangs leading the way. I woke up to discover a fresh change of underpants was in order."

"Thanks, Chubs," she said once the giggles had subsided, "I do feel somewhat relieved."

"I have a novel idea, Miss Garner," he blurted suddenly. "Might I interest you in a toast? I mean, while the lounge is so conveniently located."

"Oh, I don't know," she gently patted her midsection, "better not."

"C'mon," he chided, "Mellow Yellow on ice then."

Appearing frighteningly pale and drawn even in the surrounding murk, she leaned back with a heavy sigh and closed her eyes.

"Besides, in my present condition, I'm thinking just sniffing a beer tab might put me in a coma."

Suddenly wide-eyed, Jorgensen snapped his fingers as if overtaken by a sudden epiphany.

"Aw, I get it now...I get it. The *real* fear is that a little buzz might bring out the inner beast. No worries, Slim. I'll swear to you as a gentleman that I will *not* take advantage."

The raucous laughter that ensued, though brief in duration, was strikingly natural and considering the weakened source, surprisingly robust.

"Oh, heavens to Betty Boop but that is rich," she replied breathlessly while grasping her ribs on both sides. "Fat man, you are a true card. I swear your growth as a comic somehow coincides with that *other* recent expansion."

Pushing himself upright with a loud groan, Jorgensen sidestepped out from the aisle and stood before her with arms outstretched and legs spread wide.

"Whoa there, babe...you telling me you don't want a piece of this? Actually, you could remove *several* pieces and I'll be damned if anyone would notice at this point."

"Hey, don't talk yourself down, hot stuff," she said, standing to the sharp retort of popping knees, "you're every bit as sexy as yours truly. To properly translate: each of us might consider hooking up with the nearest monastery for all the action we're liable to see in the near future."

"I cannot disagree more, my lady. While my Jabba-the-Hut looking self would be wise to consider said advice, you are one smoking babe minus that chubby conjoined twin. A few weeks of proper R & R, breathing fresh air and snoozing in your own bed and they'll be crawling out of the woodwork to sign you up for bikini shoots on Waikiki beach."

"Again with that newly found sense of humor, muscles."

She followed him out onto the walkway, silently marveling at the immenseness of both his backend and torso and the skintight sweats attempting in vain to hold each at bay.

Minutes later she sat at the bar while he loitered behind it, turned away from her, scanning the vast inventory of whiskies and assorted liquors lining the shelves.

"So what's your pleasure, Slim?"

"Shirley Temple on the rocks, beer-tender."

"Get serious."

"Fine then. Coke Classic on ice."

Wide grin intact, Jorgensen quickly located then plucked the fifth of Jack Daniels Black label from the shelf.

"Will do, sister. Meanwhile, me and Jack Black are gonna do some bonding."

Within moments, they sat side by side at the bar, sipping timidly from tall, clear glasses amid the sound of jingling ice cubes.

"So tell me true, big guy, how close are you?"

"Broaching the ultimate taboo. I was wondering who'd crack first."

"Hey, just you and me here.

"Sure, and whatever's manning the hidden camera audio back at HQ."

"Brian," she goaded, leaning in with a palm placed strategically over her top lip, "does it really matter now?"

"Once again, point taken."

"So, you got it whipped or what?"

"Poundage wise? Not a clue."

His 'cross my heart' gesture effectively cut off her impending reply.

"Haven't lain as much as a loose testicle on that scale in just over...six full days as of today. And you?"

"Can't say."

He raised his glass in mock salute.

"Now who's being stubborn?"

"Scout's honor. It's been…just over a full week."

Flashing similar smiles, they lightly tipped their glasses.

"Well, I wouldn't lose a minute's sleep, Slim. In looking at that loose-fitting sheet draped over your bod, I'd say you got it whipped but good."

"Yeah? Well, in taking in that scuba-suit you've painted on, I'd surmise the same in your case."

Pausing with the edge of her glass posed at slightly parted lips, LeAnn's eyes suddenly gleamed with mischief.

"Amazing isn't it? It's like we…we've traded physiques, sans all that damn muscle you've layered on."

He raised a bare forearm and flexed inward with a clenched fist facing out, instantly pumping the connecting bicep to freakishly bloated proportions.

"Wow…if they bring back circus strongmen, you're a shoe-in," she continued, reaching over with an extended finger to poke the grotesquely swollen forearm,

"Our chillin' will be so proud of their freak-show papa."

"Speaking of oven-buns, you, um, noticing any of the obvious symptoms yet?"

LeAnn replied between the sharp retort of ice cubes crunching between her clenched teeth.

"Some faint nausea, but that could be diet, or lack thereof."

He cocked a brow.

"Taking your vitamins?"

"Yes, ma," she replied, smiling.

They sipped without further dialogue until Jorgensen pushed away his empty glass and regarded it through a glassy, unblinking gaze.

"Gotta confess…I'm scared shitless, Slim. Can count on one hand how many times I've confessed to same in this lifetime."

"Brian, you're huge. I'd say ten to fifteen pounds over the go…"

"Haven't slept for shit in over a month…four hours is a good night. Tried napping during the day. Won't take. Not only that, but since instituting the seafood diet from hell, explosive diarrhea is now a thrice daily routine. Feels like my gut's packed with cement. None of these little tidbits are exactly aiding the cause, you know? No matter how much I stuff in over a twenty-four hour span, damned if I'm not spewing out an equal quantity, if not more."

"You tried sleeping pills? Maybe McClin…"

"I inquired. Against the rules, apparently. As were the steroids I'd hinted about a few months back. No chemical aid allowed…so says the king. But enough *Rip Van Winkle has the squirts* stories. Talk to me, Slim. Fill me in on side-effects from the opposite extreme."

Contemplating, LeAnn's brow creased as she spat a trio of icy chunks back into her glass.

"Ah well, easier to show than tell."

Using her bare feet to push away from the bar until the stool titled precariously, she gripped her long-sleeve green tee at the bottom edges and jerked upward in a single thrust.

"Attractive, I know."

"Well." He shrugged casually as she replaced the drapery and leaned back toward the bar, "such is normal when a medium-sized frame is cloaked in an extra-large sheet of flesh."

"Damn," she frowned as if detecting an offensive odor, "appreciate the visual, Tiny. Not that I was feeling goddess-like with my pasty-as-Elmer's Glue complexion and this bird's nest head of hair that recently has lost more deserters than the Titanic, but now I'm thinking my first act of freedom should be coffin-shopping."

"Sorry, Slim, but an abundance of loose skin following extreme weight loss is normal…as much so as, well, these…"

Instead of mimicking her stool-lean, highly risky considering his bulk, Jorgensen hopped off completely and faced her before raising his own tee to the nipples.

"A real turn-on, yeah? Maybe if I can find a chick with a fetish for Atlas road maps."

Stretch marks of assorted lengths and widths littered his bloated abdomen, a select few a shade darker than his ultra-pale flesh and thus resembling abstract tribal tattoos.

LeAnn stared at the tapestry of skin-art until the daze was shattered by his re-covering of same.

"Touché, big man," she mumbled, turning back to her drink and slurping a fresh cube of ice between moistened lips.

"My sleep's been...erratic at times but I can usually doze off a few hundred times a day from lack of energy. Guess you could say I'm a walking powernap. As far as bowel movements go, I'm lucky if I can squeeze out two packages a week...and even then, we're talking gerbil droppings."

"Geez, Slim," he grinned, briefly reaching up to pinch his nostrils, "little more info than was really necessary."

"Sorry," she replied wryly with a raised palm, "it seems this extended isolation hasn't exactly sharpened my social skills. Uncouth, knocked up and riddled with various physical and mental issues. What a prime catch I'll be to some lucky Lothario."

"You'll have to beat 'em off with a stick, Slim. You just wait."

Jorgensen propped his multi-layered, beard-coated chin atop a clenched fist.

"As for my juggernaut self, I have not a clue why I'm stressing out to the ninth degree. In the grand scheme, it's a moot point. Gotta state, just for the record, as final resting stops go, this is a pretty shitty one."

"Good god, you still riding the paranoia train?'

"Label me a skeptic, but I just cannot envision your father keeping his word. Sorry."

Tipping her glass, LeAnn then slid the empty down the bar and belched softly.

"Brian, allow me to preach on it one final time: harm will not come to the father of his grandchild. Big Daddy Hanley is allll about family, and like it or not, once you saw fit to plant this here seed," she paused to point a finger toward her midsection," you were instantly granted permanent residence onto the kinship tree. Rotted roots and all, you have secured a limb all your own."

Wincing, he regarded her through tightly squinted eyes.

"Slim, I understand you're trying to lift my spirits but you can sincerely...stop...now."

"Well, a load of bricks doesn't have to fall on this girl's head to know she's been advised to clam up," she squealed with both arms raised in surrender, inadvertently revealing prominent folds of loose skin at the triceps region of each, "by the way, you get Pop...um, Hanley's message?"

Jorgensen rolled his eyes and whistled through pursed lips.

"Hard to miss. Not exactly subtle, is he? Plastered across the plasma and PC monitor, as per usual, then that added invitation delivered in true old-school style. Wild shit, that one. I kept thinking it was gonna self-destruct as I peeled it off the door with shaky fingers."

"Weird, even for Father," she nodded, "written invitations delivered by the silo fairy."

Raising his meaty hooks airborne, Jorgensen clenched and unclenched in timed succession, his eyes bright and gleaming in the relative dimness.

"Wish I could've caught wind of the sneaky little fucker, whomever they might've been, tip-toeing down the hall in bare feet to tape 'em to the door. I would've mailed back what was left of 'em as my personal RSVP."

LeAnn reached over and gently nudged his elbow with her own, the size differential of starkest contrast.

"Whoa, big fella. Reel it in before you blow an artery for which there is no sealant. Besides, you really don't want me attempting CPR."

Within seconds, he seemed to deflate somewhat and his fists lowered back to the bar top.

"Six in the blessed a.m. Your dad the early-bird type, I take it?"

"That he is. Time wasted is time lost was...is but one of many of P.J. Hanley's creeds to live by."

"Slim, no personal disrespect intended, but your father is King Prick amongst a vast kingdom of dick-weeds."

"None taken....he wears said crown with pride," she replied between yawns, "whoa, naptime's calling but good. Plans?"

"Got a pineapple upside-down cake waiting in the kitchen," he answered, patting his own ample midriff, "can't be slacking just 'cause that end-of-the-tunnel light grows brighter, you dig?"

"I dig. In comparison, my dinner menu for the next three days consists of anchovies on salt-free crackers and a handful of Santa Rosa plums...yum-yum-*yum*."

Jorgensen nodded while flashing the forefinger to thumb 'okay' gesture with his pudgy left paw.

"Understand completely...better safe than sorry. I myself have Miss Butterworth slow-cooking a whole side of beef just to tide me over 'til D-day."

Less than five minutes later, they stood side by side at the elevator's open entrance. It was LeAnn who instituted the gesture, reaching casually over until the fingers of her left hand gently brushed the top half of his right.

"So, wanna do another movie night tomorrow or the next?" he asked as they stepped aboard.

She sighed as he cupped her bony fingers inside his own Polish-sausage-sized own.

"Nah, guess not."

"Yeah, me either. So what's the plan, Slim?"

"Hole up in my room and hopefully slumber the majority of the remaining hours away....you?"

"Eat, shit, attempt to sleep…rinse and repeat. Hey, if you do wanna stop by…"

As the elevator door whirred shut and upward movement ensued, she squeezed his gripped hand just a tad tighter.

"I know where to find you."

Before exiting the elevator for her sleeping quarters, LeAnn twisted about, wrapped both arms around Jorgensen's thick neck and delivered a surprisingly sturdy hug. In the near total silence, even the rustling of their respective clothing was magnified two-fold.

"It's been a ride, Slim," he whispered once they'd pushed away and she'd stepped out onto the walkway.

"See you at the dawn of the beginning, Muscles," she replied without turning, her barely audible dialogue almost drowned out by the whoosh of the elevator door as it closed behind her.

Roughly a half-hour later, while gnawing at the edges of the pineapple upside-down cake with little enthusiasm, Jorgensen glared into the darkened kitchen with great intensity.

Raising a crumb-smeared fork into the air, he held it there in apparent tribute.

"To you, Miss Butterworth, wherever you are, for at least acting like you gave a shit. Even if you didn't mean it…even it was just part of the old prick's script, we…both appreciated the effort."

Waddling off the elevator toward his quarters a short time later, the upper chest portion of his tee littered with fresh stains, Jorgensen hesitated as if fighting the urge to reverse fields and hop back aboard. Even with less than three full days to go, such extroverted types supposedly find the act of voluntary isolation increasingly difficult. *A dying man has much to say*, it'd oft been said during the heyday of public executions.

"Even a dying man of little substance," he spouted aloud, halting at the open entrance to the one-bedroom abode that had been his home for just under six months.

Once inside, he sat on the edge of the living room couch and stared blankly at his own reflection in the plasma's colossal, black screen.

"So how you going out, fat ass?" he blurted through eyes suddenly burning and bleary with building moisture. "Going to make it easy for 'em? For... him? I... think...not."

Leaning back with his massive arms propped atop his rounded midsection, he soon nodded off and slept sitting up, uninterrupted, for the next ten-plus hours.

It would be the last deep slumber he would experience until dawn arose on D-day.

~ * ~

"We're...its prepped and ready, sir, that is...if you'd like to inspect."

Stepping gingerly forward, the man scooted the heel of both shoes across the surface as he gradually covered its limited square footage.

"Excellent. Just the right amount of give. Fine job, Jason," he announced upon exiting back onto the concrete flooring.

"Thank you, sir. We'll be erecting the turnbuckles and typing off the ropes next."

"Fine, fine," the man replied, tugging at his shirt collar while pacing the outside of the platform, "my apologies for such short notice. I surmise your mates and yourself have signed the affidavit of confidentiality."

The other man, tall, rail thin and decked out in badly-scuffed work-boots and dust-coated coveralls, replied with such unabashed fervor he practically drooled.

"Oh yes, *yes sir*. Got Mack and Abe to scribble their John Henrys just this morning before faxing a copy to your administrative assistant. I did bring a photocopy as well."

"Appreciate the forethought, Jason. You know, we...I can't be too careful about keeping this operation as secretive as possible, at least until the grand opening."

"I can surely understand that, sir. Media-types got wind of it, they'd be swarming the area like flies on a honeypot. Grounds would be littered with news-choppers and network-owned Cessnas."

The man nodded vehemently while checking his wristwatch.

"Indeed, Jason, indeed. I trust the bonus for such a hurried request is sufficient."

"Yes, sir, without a doubt," Jason blurted enthusiastically, his Adam's apple bobbing crazily. "Sir?"

"Yes, Jason?"

"If you don't mind me asking, how much are one of those...your luxury suites gonna go for?"

"Thinking of investing are we?" the other man chided while backing toward the exit and giving the room a final once-over.

"Awww, shoot, I wish, sir. I get the feeling this is waaaaay outta my price range. Just curious."

"No set price just yet, Jason, but ballpark will most likely be in the area of half-a-million to seven-hundred thousand per."

"Wow."

"Too much?"

Jason shrugged, ringing chalk-covered hands.

"Naw, I guess not, considering we're talking, well, survival in the aftermath and all."

"Honestly, we're speaking possibly of the most upscale fallout shelter known to man. Setting a reasonable selling price has been quite the task."

"I can only imagine, sir. Um, just wondering also..."

The other man cocked a brow but remained mute.

"...wasn't there room in the gymnasium? I mean, it...this set-up kinda fits the same mold, doesn't it?"

"Actually, it would cause a bit of cramping, since we're planning on moving additional weight and cardio equipment into the workout room."

"Got'cha. Damned if I'd give a rat's hind-end about building my muscles if such a scenario did come to pass. I mean, at that point, who's left to impress?"

The other man smiled wanly and studied his watch once again.

"Well, thank you again, Jason. I'll check back tomorrow then. Afternoon, say, three work for you?"

Jason practically genuflected while reaching to scoop a tape measure from atop a nearby sawhorse.

"We'll have 'er on a platter for you by then, sir."

The man twisted gracefully about on his left heel and departed with a casual wave.

Peering about the otherwise empty space, Jason then bent down to measure off and mark the first of four corners to be cut to fit separate turnbuckle.

"Fuck that noise," he mumbled while proceeding, "even if I did have a half-million plus to piss away, be damned if a space in this underground tomb would rate a second thought."

~ * ~

Sprawled over the largest of three available leather couches, the man stared into the darkness as a light rain began to descend, spattering the glass walls in bb-sized droplets. He sipped from a steaming ceramic mug, his splayed fingers effectively covering all but the dark blue 'S' in 'METS.' So lost was he in thought that he paid no mind to the figure creeping up silently from the rear.

"Boss?"

"Um, yes, Myron...what's the word?"

"We're green on the mainland."

"Fine. What about...that other thing? Are we confirmed?"

Clearing his throat, the man sauntered slowly around until the two faced one another. Compared to the subject occupying the couch, whose gleaming, ocean-blue silk pajamas appeared to pulsate with a life all their own beneath harsh fluorescent lighting, he appeared positively ragtag in an overly snug suit jacket and equally tight-fitting khakis.

"Finally, yeah, he's officially on-board."

"So, offered accepted?"

"Affirmative. He did apologize. Said he'd been in South America settling up an old debt. You know Salvadore. Mister Incognito for at least a week or two after a job. Still, took quite the sell job to seal the deal."

"Just glad you were able to fly in to witness the epilogue. I was starting to worry. After all, Mutt and Jeff in there are obviously lost without proper supervision."

McKinley grinned.

"That they are."

The other man smiled politely in return.

"All's well that ends well then. I'm just grateful we didn't have to...go an alternate route. This is no time to accept second-best in case things get...well, messy."

"Not likely, but I guess it always pays to be cautious. Boss, it's, ugh, well past the midnight hour."

Yawning, the other man sat the mug aside and stretched.

"Thank you, mother. Beddy-bye is imminent."

"Sorry. Just figured you might wanna catch at least a few hours' shuteye."

"Tomorrow is a big day, Myron," he replied, stifling a final yawn before removing the pajama top and tossing it onto the back of the couch, "the biggest. I'm fearful sleep will be quite elusive this night."

He executed a series of finger to toe stretches and then stood erect, his chest and arms rippling from even such a minimal effort.

"Gotta say, boss, you're looking damn good—one well sliced dude."

"Well...sliced?"

"Cut up...y'know...carved...chiseled."

Flexing sizeable biceps while performing a series of isometric exercises, the other man cocked a brow.

"If I didn't know any better, I'd swear you're hitting on me, big fella."

"Aww, cut the sh...cut it out, boss," Myron McKinley shot back with a casual wave, his chubby cheeks having instantaneously reddening.

Following a brisk, minute-to-minute and a half in-place sprint, the other man struck a relaxed pose with hands parked atop hips, his breathing seemingly unaffected by the sudden burst.

"Myron, I've never known you to lie. Crude as you can be at times, your penchant for complete honesty no matter the circumstances is practically legendary amongst my lieutenants."

McKinley peered down at his own shuffling feet like a thoroughly embarrassed child. "Yeah, well...thanks, boss."

"With that in mind, old friend, let me ask straight up: if Vegas came calling, who's the betting man's favorite?"

"You serious? Boss, did you get a good look at the opposition? I've bet a few longshots in my time, but there ain't a limb narrow enough to crawl out on to go again..."

The man interjected with a rare jolt of sternness that caught McKinley off-guard, causing the veteran enforcer to openly wince, an equally atypical occurrence.

"Myron, forget for a moment if at all possible that I am your employer. If you personally had a stack of cash on the line, whom...would...it...be?"

"Boss....Pete...rest assured this man's last surviving penny would be placed securely on *you*."

Peter Hanley reached over and snagged the pajama top, folding it neatly over a muscled forearm.

"Without a moment's hesitation? Nary a doubtful twinge?"

McKinley nodded and then shrugged with comical skepticism.

"No and....no? Might need a translator for that second one..."

"Disregard, old friend, I got the gist. I do hope to live up to such confidence," Hanley concluded with a gentle tap to the shorter man's left shoulder before walking purposely away.

Moments later, Myron McKinley stood staring out from the silo's glass double-door entrance as sporadic bolts of lightning pierced the far horizon. Perhaps driven by a high level of apprehension, the back of his right hand lightly patted the leather holster secured to his hip. Occasionally his pudgy, slug-like lips would part or tremble beneath the caterpillar-bushy growth found beneath a bloodshot, bulbous nose as if on the verge of spouting actual verbiage, only to eventually clamp shut.

"Boss?" a raspy voice like jagged rocks over a blackboard abruptly implored, breaking his daze. It was McGinty, leaning half-in, and half-out from the lone entrance/exit-way at the rear of the rear.

"You comin' back to the table or what?"

"In a minute."

"I'm startin' to drift but damn if I'll be able to sleep anyhow, what with you pocketin' half my paycheck from that last hand."

"I said in a minute, lunk-head. Just shuffle the cards and pour me a Beam on ice, clear?"

"Yeah, sure, got it. Damn but I can't wait to fly off this burg tomorrow. Fucking place gives me the creeps...big time."

Myron McKinley tugged at his collar just as the room lit up from a nearby lightning strike. No doubt internally grateful that his subordinate hadn't borne witness to his flinching in the bolt's aftermath, he lowered his head and sighed as the glass walls were drenched in a sudden deluge, rendering visibility to practically nil.

"Me and you both, lunk-head. Me and you both."

Ten

One-Eighty

LeAnn Garner awoke at precisely three-oh-nine the morning of day one-eighty, hardly resembling the same woman from six months previous. Following a leisurely shower, she dressed in a fresh set of sweats and headed to the dining room, where she consumed the last of approximately five hundred planned meals since day one.

It was just past five once she'd departed, having successfully, though painstakingly, consumed a handful of grapes, a trio of strawberries and half an overripe banana with a glass of lemonade-flavored Crystal Light. With just under an hour left to kill, she split the next forty-plus minutes between the lounge/theater and gymnasium floors, as if on the final legs of some melancholy farewell tour. The sweats hung from her like full-length curtains from a mini-rod, flapping at her backside like a makeshift cape. Her feet moved about too freely inside a pair of (faded) maroon Reebok sneakers that five months earlier had felt a size too small. Wearing the full regalia from day one's phantom-fitting had come at the request of her father, a bizarre footnote found at the bottom of the message screen within that final day's itinerary. At around five-fifty one, she hopped aboard the elevator and chose floor ten, which had previously been sealed off from access. She'd taken note that the connecting floors, seven to nine below and eleven to seventeen above, had remained inaccessible.

The elevator whirred to a stop and she stepped onto virgin ground, tiptoeing bashfully toward an unmarked double-door that stood partially open, a bright stream of light creasing the walkway in a clear yellow stripe as if to beckon her forward.

Pulling the doors outward with great caution, she took a half-step inside and instantly froze in place, piercing the dead air with a throaty gasp.

~ * ~

Brian Jorgensen rolled from the jumbled ruins of his bed at precisely four-thirteen, sitting upright with a groan while lifting a cheek and releasing a lengthy, moist-sounding fart.

"At last...at last..." he croaked, standing and lumbering toward the bathroom in a wobbly gait, "...we can drop the curtain on this pathetic...fucking...charade."

Not bothering to dig out a fresh ensemble, he soon departed in the same skin-tight sweatpants and stain-splattered top he'd crashed in a few hours earlier, running splayed fingers first through close-cropped hair and then scraggly beard while slipping on a pair of well-worn flip-flops.

Breakfast consisted of a dozen strips of crispy-fried bacon, five eggs over easy, four heavily-buttered country-style biscuits and a quart of chocolate milk. Before departing, having missed his co-inmate by less than an hour, he toted the dishes to the kitchen, where he left them rinsed and neatly stacked. Definitely a first. Pulling a Sharpie from his sweatpants' left pocket, he scribbled out a brief message atop the dining table he'd made his personal favorite months earlier. It simply read:

Aunt Jeannine – sorry for all the spiteful shit I flung your way. Do yourself a favor and find a better employer. You deserve better.

B.J.

Exiting the elevator at five-fifty-seven, less than three minutes since LeAnn had gently shut the doors behind her, Brian stood at the threshold with separate grips on each handle. Turning an ear, he stood motionless for a bit, no doubt attempting to comprehend the muffled dialogue reverberating from within. Finally, he whipped the doors outward in a single, fluid movement and flung himself inward. No gasp this time; no slack-jawed moan or shock-induced squeal. Just a four word denouncement uttered between lips curled into the most sardonic of grins.

"What in...*the*...fuck?"

The room was conspicuously empty save four objects. Objects possessing varying degrees of importance, though the purpose of items one and two, a pair of woefully unpadded high-back chairs, had yet to be determined. Item three was a digital scale, the same tool of weight measurement that the inmates/patients had utilized since week one. Item four, the source of the aforementioned gasp and profane query, respectively, sat at the center of the space all its enigmatic glory...the ultimate elephant in the room. To the new arrivals, it must've stood out like the proverbial sore thumb, and why not? After all, though it might've appeared perfectly normal when viewed in its natural habitat, say...Caesars Palace or the boardwalk in Atlantic City, in its present state it was more akin to a viewing a great white shark splash around in an oversized Jacuzzi.

While Myron *'The Tracker'* McKinley and his trained monkeys, Ray McGinty and Kerry Cleaves stood side-by-side to the left of the object in question, their individual visages locked in similar modes of unemotional blandness, Peter Hanley stood at its center wearing an ankle-length red robe and black-laced sneakers. His ultra-moussed do its usual meticulously-styled self, he stepped forward with arms firmly crossed and beamed, flashing teeth so perversely white they appeared air-brushed. While his eyes had widened only slightly upon LeAnn's entry, accompanied by a faint wince most likely birthed from sincere concern at his only daughter's haggard looks, the response to Jorgensen's metamorphosis was, if anything, just the opposite. Showing little in the way of restraint, he'd practically squealed with unabashed joy, the flesh of his jowls and forehead taking on a reddish, blush-like hue.

"LeAnn. Jorgensen. I do appreciate your punctuality. It is no small relief to me that we keep this...rather dicey scenario...strictly on an adult level."

Whether consciously or merely by habit, LeAnn and Brian each side-stepped over until they were practically arm in arm. Strangely touching and sad in equal measure. Ducking between the top and center of three ropes, Hanley exited the squared mat and began to circle, vulture-like, while maintaining a distance of six to eight feet.

"My god, the irony. Amazing. Almost...breathtaking. Pardon the dramatics, but you see...video feeds do not do justice to this...the change in each of you. Not even remotely close to...viewing it up close—face to face."

"Try and control the hormones, will you, Hanley?" Jorgensen grumbled while tugging at the collar of his sweatshirt, so tight it appeared to be slicing into the lowest of his three chins, "neither myself or the daughter of your loins wants to see a boner popping through those fancy-smancy PJ's."

Ignoring both Jorgensen's dig and LeAnn's muffled snicker in the aftermath, Hanley centered the pair and stood stiffly with hands on hips.

"Such role-reversal from a physical standpoint has to...I say *has* to be a first in the history of modern mankind. Why, you could swap wardrobes for an almost perfect fit, as could have been so similarly accomplished way back on day one. I have to confess, I've been...blown away by the resolve...the almost inhuman determination. Less so from Mister Jorgensen, impressive as his...rapid expansion has been, but LeAnn my dear, once so slovenly and weak-minded LeAnn, whose willpower and inner grit I had...have so tragically underestimated. May I say the pri..."

"Blah, blah, fucking blah. Spare me the croc tears," Jorgensen broke in with a lazy gesture toward the object of said query, "so what's with the playpen, Hanley? Got to admit, I had imagined a shitload of scenarios, but this...*that*...doesn't fit into even my wildest scripts."

"Father, what are you doing? Wh-what is this?" LeAnn chimed in with a pained frown that only served to insinuate the gauntness of her cheeks. Beneath the harsh lighting, easily twice the brightness of any other room within the silo, she appeared nothing short of emaciated when compared to six months past.

Seemly unaffected by the double-dose of insolence in the face of his rah-rah speech, Hanley pointed to the scale, his unnaturally wide, borderline psychotic smile hardly wavering.

"Never you mind that now, little girl. It's time to step up to the plate, so to speak. Jorgensen, if you don't mind..."

"Well, there you go," Jorgensen quipped with a playful wink LeAnn's way, "so much for sentimentality."

Just as Jorgensen moved away, hopping out of and leaving a pair of well-worn flip-flops behind, the two shared a wordless nod that spoke volumes.

Jorgensen stood with his bare toes mere inches from the scale before pausing to peel away his shirt, a skin-tight green tee, the sweat pants and finally a badly-faded yet still technically gray pair of Fruit-of-the-Looms. As this impromptu striptease commenced, McKinley and the twin lugs moved forward until they'd formed a security perimeter of sorts between Hanley and his rival.

Hanley cleared his throat as Jorgensen, ghost-pale and naked as his day of birth, stood erect in all his roly-poly glory and appeared deep in meditation.

"Ahem...anytime you're ready, Brian."

Lifting his arms out from his shoulders as if to attempt flight, Jorgensen then flexed biceps so grotesquely pumped they resembled overfilled bladders on the verge of explosion. Before stepping onto the scale, left foot first followed by the right, he extended the middle finger of each hand in the general direction of Hanley.

"Read 'em and weep, Warden. Read 'em and cry your fucking eyes out."

From the time he'd firmly planted each foot, Jorgensen had never peered downward. Whether this non-gesture was out of fear or sheer overconfidence was a question only he could answer. A few moments into the standoff, McKinley locked eyes with his employer, who, tight-lipped and stiff of posture, executed a lightning-quick nod in lieu of a verbal order. With that, McKinley alone moved forward until he stood directly to Jorgensen's left. He bowed slightly as Jorgensen continued to stare straight ahead, the Tracker's expression best described as a mask of uncertainty—afflicted by the occasional tick of the left eye or twitch of the upper lip.

"Well?" Hanley inquired with great reserve, despite an obvious undercurrent of building tension.

Having backed away several steps, McKinley turned on a heel but hesitated to speak, as if he preferred to deliver a private whisper over a public announcement. Hanley, however, was having none of it, his cool demeanor rapidly deteriorating even as his tone attained a healthy measure of edginess.

"Speak up, McKinley. Good grief, Mister…it's only three numbers. Surely I didn't need to employ a mathematician."

"Um, it's…" the veteran enforcer mumbled, halting in mid-step at the inception of Hanley's berating, "…the reading was three-sixty-seven."

Hanley's forehead creased and his eyes squinted into floss-thin slits.

"Three…how much was that *exactly*?"

McKinley tugged at his collar and glanced briefly at the lunk-head twins, who could do little but appear utterly clueless, a look they'd obviously perfected through years of non-thinking.

"Three-sixty-seven point four, Mister H."

LeAnn's gleeful yelp and Jorgensen's piercing wolf-whistle were executed in almost flawless synchronization.

"*Five pounds*," Hanley whispered, barely audible beneath a cupped hand, "*made it by a sack of sugar. Mother of god…*"

Executing a picture-perfect about-face, Jorgensen nonetheless maintained his balance atop the squared box. With his lunatic's grin, rippling, ultra-pasty flesh, bushy brown beard and caterpillar-thick 'tache, he resembled a crazed Neanderthal.

"What's that, shit-stack? Couldn't…quite make it out. How's about twisting the volume knob so we can all savor each and *every* precious syllable, huh Mumbles?"

"Cleaves, check the scale," Hanley barked with inexplicable glee, matching Jorgensen's warped grin with an equally unsettling leer of his own.

"Nothing personal, Myron," he continued with a glance toward his long-time enforcer, "just need a second opinion to confirm. A…second set of eyes, if you will."

Cleaves did as ordered, lumbering over like a bull gorilla in a cheap, ill-fitting suit that appeared on the verge of splitting up the back, a conspicuous bulge near the left side of his ribcage.

He shot a resentful smirk at Jorgensen, who continued to face away from the digital reading, having never checked its numerical readout with his own eyes.

"So how's the knee, big guy? Rehab went well, I presume?"

"Eat shit, lard-ass," Cleaves whispered, hovering over the scale as the top of his slickly-waxed head reflected the overhead lighting like a rotating strobe.

"Same result, boss," he grumbled.

Hanley shrugged impatiently while gnawing his lower lip.

"That being?"

"Three sixty-seven point four."

"Thank you, McGinty."

As his hired muscle backed away to reclaim his previous space, Hanley hopped forward with a sudden burst, essentially cutting the distance between himself and Jorgensen to perhaps a dozen feet. He commenced to lightly clap, perhaps five or six repetitions, the sincerity behind the gesture as artificial as the *faux* smile accompanying it.

"Bravo, Brian, bravo. I must confess I'd rated your chances for success as minimal at best. You may, um, dismount the scale."

Defiant as ever, Jorgensen paused silently with arms crossed for an additional ten seconds before doing so. In the background, LeAnn fidgeted about as if she were on the verge of peeing her sweats—her hands and feet twitched and gyrated without pause. A study in barely restrained jubilation.

"Hope you didn't bet the family jewels, buddy-boy. Oh, and speaking of which…" he replied while reaching down to cup his manhood in both hands while sidestepping over to retrieve his discarded underpants, "…by all accounts I should've kept those damn scuba-slacks on and loaded 'em down with ball-bearings, but then you see, unlike certain mob bosses that shall remain nameless, this boy cannot abide cheating."

Given a brief respite as Jorgensen pulled on his underwear and sweatpants, the latter providing quite the struggle, Hanley chimed in while retying the robe tightly across his waist.

"Be that as it may, at first view I figured you to be ten, even fifteen pounds below the set goal, this despite the shocking...modification of your entire physique. Once again I must say that the Skype images did not do either of your transformations justice."

Standing with his tee and sweatshirt slung over opposite shoulders, Jorgensen smiled grimly and shot LeAnn a quick glance before turning back to his captor.

"Hanley, you keep yapping of transformations and modifications like some mad fucking scientist. Doctor Frankenstein ogling his newest creations poured fresh outta the test-tubes. Devout Catholic, my dick. More like a goose-stepping goddamn zookeeper checking out a pair of new arrivals to stick behind the glass."

Hanley turned toward LeAnn just as Jorgensen paused just long enough to pull the tee over his head.

"I'd advise you remain shirtless, Brian."

Jorgensen paused, the shirt wound around his tree-trunk sized neck.

"Say what?"

Switching his focus solely on his daughter, Hanley's concluding retort was noticeably dismissive.

"Entirely up to you, of course. Now for my dear, dear Lee..."

Jorgensen reared back, wound up, and tossed both sufficiently balled-up shirts into a far corner. In response, Myron McKinley and his bookended knee-snappers lunged forward to strike a strategic position between captor and inmate.

"Geez, but you mick orangutans spook easy," Jorgensen said with hands raised in surrender, "so, tell the truth, boys...what's with the boss's sudden infatuation with my nude bod?"

Cupping a hanging, bloated bare breast in separate palms, he jiggled each furiously.

"Could it be the newly developed fun-bags? They are *beauts*, aren't they? Hey, McKinley, you might find a hankie to wipe away the drool."

The man known infamously as the Tracker did not reply save a familiar double-barreled gesture of an extremely profane nature.

Jorgensen fell silent, bowing onto one knee while scanning the squared stage that looked so weirdly out of place.

Meanwhile, Hanley faced his daughter—careful to maintain a three to four foot space between them. "Guess you're up to bat," he said softly, tilting his head toward the scale. "Go on, little girl. Show me what I already know."

LeAnn stood motionless, regarding her father with a scowl and slight tilt of the head. "Not without an explanation."

Hanley cocked a brow. "Explanation?"

Sighing, LeAnn's eyes shifted briefly to the right.

"Oh, that. Soon enough, my dear. Please, step over and up. Formality or no, it has to be done so that we may move on to the final phase."

"Final...phase? Jesus, what final phase? This d-degrading spectacle..." she stepped back, red-faced with clenched fists at her sides, her voice crackling with anger, "...are you seriously informing us there is m-more?"

"Lee," Hanley replied in a soft, condescending tone more apt to console a teary-eyed child, "at ease, my dear. It does not concern you. Now, do as I say," he pointed to the scale, "there is much to do, many details to attend to, in the aftermath of your triumph."

In lieu of adhering to her father's incessant pleas, LeAnn instead slid back until she was able to peek around his stoic form to Jorgensen, who continued to regard the mystery object at the center of the room as if it were some enigmatic work of abstract art.

"You were right, Brian," she announced, snapping him from his daze, "you were...right about him all along. I...guess I was blinded by...some type of family-loyalty gene disorder."

"Wish like hell I'd been wrong," he replied with a shrug.

Leaning down, LeAnn casually removed each sneaker before placing them neatly side-by-side with the accompanying sock stuffed inside. She then stepped stiffly forward, past her father until the tips of her toes brushed the cusp of the digital scale's outer shell.

"A farce. Just like you said...a goddamned farce."

All was quiet save Hanley's exasperated exhale as his daughter stepped up and aboard.

"McKinley, the results please."

LeAnn raised a hand, exhibiting a bare palm in the general direction of the enforcer, who'd in turn immediately halted in his tracks and looked to Hanley for further instruction. She began to strip away her sweatshirt, its successful removal briefly slowed as the flapping sleeves tangled at her elbows and shoulders.

"LeAnn, I don't think that's at all necessary," Hanley blurted through a tight smile as he moved toward her from the rear. "I'm perfectly willing to subtract up to two pounds for the clothing."

Slinging the shirt to one side, she then reached down with searching fingers to seek out the bottom portion of the loose-fitting tee beneath.

"Lee, don't...um..." Hanley babbled, groping with an outstretched hand as to prevent the impending striptease, "...keep them on. We...I won't penalize..."

The shirt was over her head, revealing a woefully ill-fitting bra from which one shrunken, milky breast stared out from below the wire fitting.

"Damn it, girl...stop!" Hanley croaked, forced to secure his robe at the chest with one hand while gesturing frantically toward McKinley with the other. "Would you stop her, please?"

The plump enforcer winced and performed a comical two-step, the brief pause allowing LeAnn to complete the act of going topless.

"Boss?" McKinley inquired upon scooping up the discarded bra from near his left shoe.

His face glowing beet-red, Hanley retied the robe at his waist for the umpteenth time.

"Just retrieve the clothing and then read the damn scale, Myron."

Once McGinty and Cleaves had handed over sweatshirt and tee, respectively, he strolled over, careful not to make eye or exposed-breast contact with the boss's daughter, bent over and did just that.

"The verdict?" Hanley asked in a surprisingly bland monotone, as if LeAnn's insolent attitude had perhaps dug deeper than he'd wanted to admit.

"One seventeen point five, boss," McKinley bellowed through a grin so forced one would have surmised the barrel-end of a locked and loaded firearm were being jammed into his ribs.

"She made it with a McRib or five to spare, boss."

Jorgensen's latest wolf-whistle was abrupt but sufficiently piercing as both McGinty and Cleaves flinched in equal measure.

"Way to go, Slim. I'd had no doubts whatsoever. My oversized ass salutes you."

LeAnn dismounted in a single hop, turning with amazing dexterity as her sagging breasts bounced and gyrated. She tossed a scout's salute his way before reaching over to reclaim her clothing from McKinley's outstretched hands, the enforcer purposely keeping his eyes focused on her father, who was half-stepping slowly toward them.

"Right back at you, fatso."

"I'm actually surprised it read that high," Hanley replied, while gesturing to McKinley to return to his previous position. "I was thinking more along the lines of one-fifteen or less."

They waited as she redressed in bra and tee, the sweatshirt left folded over a forearm, her father standing less than a foot to her left. Once her head had popped through the neck of the tee, he'd outstretched his arms and leaned in to attempt a hug which LeAnn immediately rebuffed by slinking gracefully to the right.

His arms quickly retracted upon taking in her disgusted expression.

"Lee, I just...wanted to...want to express my...the pride I feel in this...your accomplishments," he stammered while unconsciously moving away with palms raised.

"Father, my only accomplishments are swapping one eating disorder for two—laziness and irresponsibility for unrelenting paranoia and sleep apnea—assorted chemical addictions and their accompanying urges to urging for nothing at all, a total, complete disinterest in life as a whole. All that, and now...emotional and physical wreck that I am, there's motherhood to prep for."

"Lee, I...the emotional trauma you're experiencing after such a dramatic transformation is, I'm quite sure a natural reac..." Hanley attempted to chime in, only to be cut off in mid-psychobabble, his mouth still hanging agape as his daughter leapt forward until the two were practically nose-to-nose.

"So congratulations are in order, *Doctor* Hanley," she whispered hoarsely as fresh tears streamed down each sunken, pallid cheek, "the shock therapy you prescribed indeed worked wonders. The good news is, this girl no longer gives a damn about pigging out at the nearest buffet, or popping handfuls of whatever prescription pain pill lands anywhere near parted lips. Unfortunately, there is bad news as well, as in..."

Leaning in, she concluded with cracked, chapped lips parked mere inches from her elder's left ear.

"...I can't honestly state I *do* give a good damn whether I live or die past this conversation. How's them apples taste, Grandpa?"

After delivering a light peck on her father's clean-shaven cheek, LeAnn stepped back and winked before collapsing full-force onto her back with a resounding thump.

Jorgensen instantly hauled himself upright, nearly tipping over in a clumsy attempt to reach her, the attempt quickly aborted as McGinty and Cleaves rushed over to block his path.

Instead of diving to her aid as a father might, Peter Hanley stood motionless with arms crossed, shaking his head slowly from side to side.

"My god, how did this...person evolve from my loins? McKinley, please have one of your subordinates obtain a wet rag...maybe a bottle of water. In terms of revival, perhaps a Twinkie or Ding-Dong would turn the trick, or if possible turn up a Xanax or Prozac to wave beneath her nostrils. Remind her of...better times."

"Holy hell, man...she's carrying your grandch..." Jorgensen began, only to be cut off almost instantly.

"No, actually...she isn't."

Hanley shrugged, a gesture so casual in its execution it only served to enhance the shock value.

"Say...what?"

"A vicious rumor."

His enormous fists clenched and noticeably shaking, Jorgensen appeared utterly shell-shocked.

"Vicious...what the hell are you talk...? You...you lied?"

"Let's just call it an added plot twist, Brian. A plot twist created for the sole purpose of adding to the challenge from a...psychological standpoint. Alas, as things turned out, said twist didn't amount to a hill of beans."

Jorgensen eyes narrowed to slits, his words laced with a barely restrained fury.

"Jesus, Hanley, how could you possibly exceed the ultimate prick rating I'd previously awarded? Against all odds, no matter how often I tried to hammer home what a douchebag she had for a sire, that woman held out a flicker of hope that your word actually meant something. She swore as much to me more than once.

"Showtime, I told her....that's all this was to you. The kind of sick mind-fuck follies only the Peter Hanleys of the world—so called "made-men" with an immorality complex—could wet-dream up and then have the brass balls to execute."

"Look at it from my perspective," Hanley replied banally, "I had little doubt you two would...hook up eventually. Lee is so...weak-minded and you...well, you're a reptile in human guise. It was bound to happen eventually. Once she lost substantial weight, I had little doubt you'd commence to stalk. I wasn't abou...couldn't take the chance of the aftermath of said union creating a Brian Jorgensen Junior, now could I? Thus Lee's meals were occasionally laced with birth-control pills...crushed into an inconspicuous powder, of course."

"But, the tests...the blood tes..."

Hanley first lifted then slowly waved a forefinger from side to side.

"Good grief, Jorgensen, are you truly that dense? The good doctor is, after all, on the payroll. If Lee spoke of, well, symptoms, I'm afraid they were of the psychosomatic variety."

Having donned a perpetual scowl, Jorgensen peered over at LeAnn's motionless form.

"She's...this is going to finish her off, you bastard, you do know that, right? If she hasn't already snapped, this will sure as fuck turn the trick."

As if to officially verify Jorgensen's final statement as fact, Hanley snaked around on a cleated heel and left the limp form of his lone daughter for the hired help to attend to, the congratulatory façade having been effectively wiped away and replaced by that of ruthless predator. A drooling, blood-thirsty predator holding all the face cards—its sharp-clawed appendage perched atop its victim's heaving throat. This was the Peter Hanley so many unfortunates had borne witness to in those last fading moments before life was extinguished.

"Point of order, then, Mister Jorgensen. Showtime *is* officially over. Execution shall now commence..."

Even from behind thick concrete walls, the man felt a cold breeze slap the exposed flesh of his neck, arms and hands. What else, he deduced, save a thick sense of dread that accompanied it, could possibly explain a sudden rash of goose-bumps coating the whole of his body?

Eleven

Turbulence

"She's...your daughter...seems to be coming too, boss. Looks kinda...pasty though, and she's sweating bullets."

McKinley had kneeled down and pulled LeAnn upright, cradling her by the upper shoulders while keeping her body at a distance as if she were a diseased animal.

"I dunno, boss. She's burning up. Might need a doctor."

Ducking between turn-buckles, Hanley responded only after reaching the center of the squared circle.

"She's just weak. Try fueling up on sunflower seeds and tap water and see how *you* feel. Where's McGinty with the water, for Christ's sake? Pea-brained chimp could get lost on a one-way street."

As if on cue, McGinty barged in with a towel draped over one shoulder and a frosty bottle of Avian in the other. As McKinley commenced to splash water on the rag and gently pat LeAnn's sweat-moistened forehead, Jorgensen stood with hands on hips wearing a familiar smirk.

"Soooo, let me get this straight, Hanley. The plan is to revive her so you can punch her ticket? Damn, talk about pouring salt in an open wound. Boy, you just ain't right..."

Hanley had just begun to untie the robe-belt at his waist as LeAnn reawakened with a wet gasp.

"Pray tell, Jorgensen, just what did my ex see in you? Surely not that post-juvenile prattle that you attempt to pass off as humor?"

"Not quite, King Turd," Jorgensen retorted while reaching down to grab his crotch, "simply put...the slut hankered for prime tube-steak, something it was beyond your means to provide, apparently."

Hanley snickered as the robe gradually separated. Less than a dozen feet away, his daughter, still dazed but coming around, was being escorted toward one of the two available chairs.

"Let me state for the record then—I'm going to thoroughly enjoy beating you to a bloody pulp, and once said beating is complete, to celebrate I will proceed to urinate on your broken, battered face."

"Kinky old devil," Jorgensen winked in response, "but then, I guess that shriveled old noodle of yours is limited to waste disposal *only,* these days, right?"

"Get him in here, McKinley," Hanley barked between gritted teeth. "If he resists, shoot him directly in the balls. That is, if you can find such tiny jewels within that surging sea of blubber."

Jorgensen lunged forward with an open palm raised McKinley's way.

"Resist? Did you...*resist*? You shitting me, Hanley? Son, I might need to slap myself to make sure this isn't a dream. A dream...come...true."

"Father, wh-what are you...what is...this?" LeAnn muttered, slumped forward in the chair while combing her sparse hair with splayed fingers. The front of her tee was soaked with a fresh mix of her own fluids and the soggy rag draped over her left shoulder.

"You..y-you promised...y-you swear...s-swore...if he...if we...met the goals..."

Hanley peeled away the robe in its entirety and laid it gently over a top rope, revealing a buffed, chiseled physique that caused even Jorgensen's eyes to briefly pull wide in shock. LeAnn rubbed her puffy eyes between death stares, as if testing the validity of what they were seeing.

"Take a breath, Lee. Regain your senses. This will only take a minute or so and then we'll talk."

"My...god. Explains the full-sized boxing r-ring, if nothing else. You...been preparing for this, haven't you? Y-you've been in...training while f-forcing Brian into the worst shape of his life. So is this a shining em-example of the Hanley integrity you always refer t-to?"

"I finally hopped off my lazy duff and got in shape, if that's what you're referring to. About time, am I right? As for my worthy opposition, I view his...fattening up as a way of...evening the odds a bit. After all, the man wa...is a martial arts master of some note. In fairness, how could a novice such as myself stand a chance in a fair skirmish without garnering an edge?

"Now, just sit back and catch your breath, little girl. Papa will be right with you and we'll jaw about the future until your heart's content."

As she spoke, a glistening globe of droll hung from her lower lip like early morning dew from a flower pedal. The dazed appearance was fading even as her voice grew stouter with apparent frustration.

"Jesus...and to think I...I spent years fretting about how I'd let you down by...not living up to...expectations. You...you've planned this. From day one...mapped it out...to just how you wanted it to end. You were...on a schedule...just like us. Brian was just a guinea pig...both of us were. Shit, all three of us."

"Awww, not to worry, Slim," Jorgensen chimed in with his normal dose of cockiness, though on this rarest of occasions laced with a faint undercurrent of unease, "Chuck Atlas *Senior* over there might be wearing a new suit of Nautilus-Best muscles, but this ain't gonna be about who can strike the prettiest pose, am I right, old man?"

Hanley turned away and began yanking on the top rope with both hands.

"Right as rain, Brian. Remarkably astute as always."

"By the way, Hanley, don't you have one other additional nugget to share with Lee...your daughter?"

"In good time," came the stern reply, "once our...this dance card has been sufficiently filled."

Jorgensen grunted disgustedly while tossing up both arms.

"Figures you wouldn't have the balls. No worries. I'll fill her in once I've extracted the majority of your teeth."

Hanley did not respond save a barely noticeable wink.

Squeezing through the ropes with a pained grunt, Jorgensen leaned against the nearest turnbuckle and performed a rapid series of neck stretches while simultaneously cracking the knuckles of both hands.

"Better give Doc Churchill a ring, Grandpa Adonis, and tell 'im to empty out his medicine cabinet, 'cause fat as a hippo and outta shape as I am, you're not gonna walk or even *limp* away from this—easily the most misguided, bone-headed decision of your life, hands down."

"The doctor...yes, this is true," Hanley replied while slapping a bare palm to his forehead, "in all the excitement, darned if I almost let it slip my mind completely. By all means, my tireless, loyal staff deserves nothing less than a front-row seat."

With that, the man felt his gut, already wound in a steel knot, curdle and churn with a fresh wave of dread. Not that he'd considered for a moment daring to deviate from the script. No, there would be no such luck, nor any chance of divine intervention for the terminally damned. Thus, in that single, terrible moment, the bell had indeed tolled for all involved.

"Myron, if you will, please round up the staff post-haste and escort, ahem, them in. Though such...base vulgarity and brutality might not be their cup of tea, at least not the *lot* of them, it just wouldn't be right to exclude such valuable contributors to this day's festivities. Besides, one has generously volunteered...to referee."

~ * ~

"Goob? Is that *really* you? Well, dung on a donut if it isn't Gabriel Maxwell, as I strain and huff. Check it out, Slim, the trainer to the stars...in the flesh and blood."

"Mister Jorgensen, Miss Garner. Pleased to...finally meet you. I do wish the circumstances were of a more pleasant variety."

Though decked out in familiar garb...black Oakland Raiders cap and matching tee, yellow spandex shorts and high-top sneakers, there were several, rather drastic changes in the man's appearance that neither Jorgensen or LeAnn could immediately pinpoint. A rather bizarre few moments passed, wherein Jorgensen leaned forward and stared down the stocky personal trainer through squinting, unblinking eyes.

"Damn if somebody hasn't stolen your twang, son. Shit, perhaps it was the same dirty-rotten scoundrel who made off with your chin whiskers and all the body art," he paused, shooting LeAnn a weary glance, "correct me if I'm wrong, but along with the missing tats, haven't you also lost a layer or two of bulk off the same arms? It appears mini-Popeye's sprung some serious leakage around the biceps and forearms."

Positioned directly between the duo of stone-faced goons who'd escorted him inside, the stocky man shrugged uneasily before locking eyes with his employer.

"Well, I, ugh, Mister Hanley? Would you prefer to take over at this...juncture?"

"Oh, I see," LeAnn interjected, standing shakily and taking a shuffling step toward the ring, "I-I get it. Yet another prime illustration from Peter Hanley's magical book of smoke and mirrors."

"LeAnn, please sit down. You're still very wea..." Hanley began while side-stepping over to the ring's far left buckle, where McKinley handed over a pair of fingerless, thinly padded puncher's gloves normally associated with hard-bag workouts.

"Tell me, Father, is there even a thread of truth in *anything* you say or do? Imitation personal trainers, for god's sake? For what possible reason?"

"Apparently for the fuck of it," Jorgensen chimed in sourly, "seems to me it's fairly safe to assume that whenever the bastard's lips even tremble, there's a bald-faced fib about to sprout forth."

Shuffling his black with red-striped Nikes from side to side, the trainer-for-hire's cheeks suddenly flashed a deep hue, as if he'd been stricken by a sudden fever.

"Mister Hanley, are...were you going to tell them now or...later? Or...*at all*?"

Jorgensen proceeded with his rant, thereby preventing the requested reply.

"So what's next, you lying sack? Is Miss Jeannine actually some string-bean built white chick with Klan ties? And how about ol' Doc Doo-*nothing*? Don't tell me; he's a decommissioned vet specializing in turtles, lizards and small rodents."

He tossed his head back and howled, snapping forward having magically donned a mask of fury.

"Old man, I'm gonna collect a tooth for every untruth you've told. At pounding's end, that outta leave you just enough chopper-age to comfortably chew a mouthful of pudding."

"Tell them, Mister Hanley," the Trainer insisted, hands on hips, "it's only fair...that they know as much about my situation as I do theirs."

Standing at the center of the mat like the ringmaster of a woefully deserted carnival, Hanley sharply punched the palm of each glove several times before responding.

"Why, Barrett, I wasn't about to forego your story. Now, kindly take a seat beside Lee, as there is no more time to waste."

The Trainer did this, side-stepping over as LeAnn eyed him distrustfully. She squatted onto her chair only after pulling it over several feet to gain some distance from the new arrival.

"Ma'am," the Trainer said softly with a tip of his cap, to which LeAnn merely nodded cautiously in reply.

Hanley raised both gloves airborne as to gain the full attention of all present.

"Fine then...the condensed version will have to do. However, despite the newly sculpted pecs, I find myself growing stiffer by the minute."

Having pulled on a similar set of fighting mitts, courtesy Myron McKinley, Jorgensen raised a curled fist into the air and wriggled it to and fro like a grade-schooler desperate for a bathroom break.

"So where's the doc and Miss J? Or should I refer to their stand-in's? Thought you said you owed 'em, Hanley. I'm thinking they'd both go positively orgasmic watching you get that pompous can dented."

"I'd always heard you reward loyalty, Father," LeAnn added with a vigorous nod. "Appears to me that going back on deals seems to be the new Hanley creed."

Hanley's unyielding stare focused solely on the Trainer, who in turn bowed his head in apparent shame.

"Why, not at all, little girl. I'm showing my deepest appreciation to the staff as we speak. Isn't that correct, Mister Cohen?"

"If you say so, Mister Hanley," the Trainer responded wearily, reaching up to rub his eyes with the forefinger and thumb, respectively, of his right hand.

Peeking past the Trainer's slumped frame, LeAnn and Jorgensen exchanged a puzzled look just as Hanley sucked in a noisy, strained breath and commenced.

"The man resting so uncomfortably to your left, little girl, may or may not appear vaguely recognizable, depending on your knowledge of the independent film community. He's altered his appearance for this, the latest of his many performances, but if you look closely into the eyes, it's possible a staunch fan of underground cinema might experience a twinge of familiarity."

Neither Jorgensen nor LeAnn bothered even a passing glimpse toward the Trainer, who had raised his chin and jutted his jaw in the possibility a facial study had been in order.

"I hadn't watched a motion picture in its entirety in ten years or more until coming here," LeAnn said blandly.

Jorgensen's tone held even less interest—a groggy mumble between yawns.

"Ditto, save the occasional Adam Sandler marathon."

Hanley leaned back against a top robe and folded his gloved hands across a bare, burly chest.

"I figured as much. After all, we're not exactly talking matinee idol. To be fair, however, Mister Cohen here did make quite the name for himself during the nineties as a character actor. Refresh my memory, Barrett, how many films did you appear in altogether?"

"I...can't say for certain," the Trainer mumbled, his tone as lethargic as his movements, "forty, fifty...along those lines."

"A slew of credits, yes indeed. Some mere cameos, true, but a few garnering Barrett co-star billing along such Tinsel-town dignitaries as Mel Gibson, Emilio Estevez and David Carradine. Remind me yet *again*, Barrett. What were some of those titles? Not the B-flick straight-to-video sort but the theatrical releases?"

As before, the Trainer's overall deportment screamed extreme exhaustion.

"I...its...what does it matter?"

"It matters because I'm inquiring, Barrett. Besides, wasn't it you who mentioned it was *only fair* to inform Lee and Brian of your plight?"

"But, I don't...you heard them. They're *not* movie people. They won't kno..."

"The *titles*, Mister Cohen," Hanley spat sternly, having wound each arm around the taut, only slightly giving top rope, "three or four of the works you're most proud of."

"Three or f-....ugh, well, I'd say, um, shit, well, there was, ugh..."

Stammering, the Trainer stared at the stone tiles between his sneakers and lowered his head, massaging his temples with probing fingers.

"*Hands of Stone* with Gibson. *Dragon's Fury* with Carradine. *Rock and a Hard Place* with Estevez, none of which exactly set the box-office on fire."

The Trainer leaned up and back, his arms going limp by his sides. His legs splayed out, he appeared on the verge of passing out. Hanley briefly turned his spastic, wide-eyed gaze to Jorgensen and then LeAnn, as if to detect a glimmer of recognition from either. When nary a hint surfaced from either party, he refocused on the Trainer, who had closed his eyes and lowered his chin as if full power-nap mode.

"How about that Civil War western? You played one of Gene Hackman's raiders? Sported a full beard and what looked like a fake beer-belly, if I recall correctly?"

The Trainer snapped to lazily, straightening his posture as to not tumble sideways from the chair.

"Oh...oh yeah...*Gray Area*. Just a cameo...bit-part really—killed off in the first fifteen minutes, as was...the case more times than I care to remember."

"You see," Hanley resumed, alternating brief gawks from LeAnn to Jorgensen, "Barrett's specialty in those days was mastering the thankless role of either a forked-tongue weasel or dialogue-challenged tough guy. Then, around the turn of the millennium, the acting offers began to dry up. He was soon relegated to cameos in cheap-O urban crime sagas or, heaven help him, soft-core porn teenage comedies. It was around this time he turned his attention to the other side of the camera—writing, producing and even lensing low-budget documentaries in the independent circle. How many you have under your belt, Barrett? Six, seven? A few of which did pretty well on the rental/instant download circuit."

"Five completed. I was...working on the sixth."

"Yes indeed you were," Hanley snickered, "more on that as we proceed. I will say this, as I've taken the time to view three of his directorial efforts: Mister Cohen is hardly predictable in terms of choosing his projects. They've run the gamut from the study of a juvenile boot-camp in Texas...um...what was that title again, Barrett?"

The Trainer shuffled his feet and scanned the whole of the capsule-shaped room as if searching for a nearby exit.

"*Desolate Formations.*"

"Fascinating, provocative, but also surprisingly humorous. I understand the state corrections folks weren't exactly thrilled with the negative publicity that followed and were even forced to alter several facility regulations.

"From there came, correct me if I'm wrong, a character study covering the life and career of a legendary Georgia high school baseball coach."

"Alabama."

"Oh yes, my bad. Equal parts sports and character study, ripe with humor and pathos, as the man had passed away from cancer just following his fiftieth spring of coaching. Barrett's film was instrumental in fueling the man's induction in the state baseball hall of fame. Holmes, wasn't it?"

"Haynes," the Trainer corrected wearily and with obvious disinterest, "Mack Haynes from...Mobile."

"Such a clever title: *The King of Diamonds*, and so very fitting."

The Trainer nodded faintly in acknowledgement just as Jorgensen stood upright and began swinging his bulky arms from side to side to loosen the building rust.

"Hanley, if part of your pre-bout strategy is to bore me into submission, congratulations are in order. Can we please just skip the film history lesson and go on to the main event?"

Hanley's stern stare remained firmly locked on Barrett Cohen even as he addressed this latest inquiry.

"My sincerest apologies, Brian, but I'm afraid the backstory detour is a necessary part of today's itinerary. Bear with me a few more minutes. The finish line grows near.

"To continue then: Mister Cohen's most impressive work to date, at least in my opinion, came next—a fascinating study of the Harpe brothers, whom many historians have dubbed two of the earliest serial killers to ply their bloody trade on U.S. soil. I openly confess to multiple viewings and to owning a copy of the Blu-ray release. Your skills as an interviewer were honed to a fine, artistic point, as was the masterful editing. Bravo again, Barrett...bravo.

"Now, lady and gents, we have reached the meat of our tale."

The Trainer squirmed in his seat, gripping the underneath of the chair on both sides and in the aftermath poised statue-stiff. He cleared his throat and peeked over at LeAnn, whose sole attention remained on her father.

"For Barrett's next project, he decided to...well, branch out a bit and, how shall I say this, court danger? Yes, I believe that appropriate. You see, he decided, most unwisely, to turn the lens toward yours truly, or to be more precise, those most closely associated with yours truly. What was the working title again, Barrett? Help me out here..."

"*Techo-mob*," the Trainer muttered timidly, a chorus of faint guffaws acting as backing vocals in the aftermath. Hanley's stabbing gaze quickly found the culprits, McGinty and Cleaves, thus ending any additional giggles at the Trainer's expense.

"*Techo-mob*," Hanley repeated, smiling wryly while turning back to the Trainer, "Yes, very clever. Hinting of course at how newfound technology in all its computerized glory has become both a hindrance and boon to those involved in organized crime.

"What was it you divulged as an alternate title? I found that equally effective, if not more so..."

"***Made*** in Twenty-First Century America."

"Emphasizing the 'made' in bold italics, correct?"

"Yes."

"Cute, and yet in retrospect I do favor the former. Perhaps since the latter sounds less a parody than a serious overview of the modern-day mafia. Problem was, to effectively cover said subject matter documentary-style, one must have his ducks in a row, so to speak, right, Barrett? I speak of course, of *facts*, as this would be mandatory in order to give your film any semblance of credibility with both the media and general public."

Dull of eye and tone, the Trainer's replies grew increasingly monotonic. "This...is true."

"Soooo, in order to gain said facts, Barrett and an associate who shall remain unnamed took it upon themselves to commit several crimes. Crimes to include not only misdemeanor trespassing, but felony wiretapping. Is this not correct, Barrett?"

"Affirmative."

"Excuse me?"

"That is to say, you speak the truth."

Hanley began to stomp around the ring like a peacock at mating season, occasionally pausing to shadowbox.

"Barrett's associate was nabbed while placing a sophisticated tracer device underneath the carriage of my personal vehicle, having so cleverly bypassed the many security devices littering the property. Soon after, around three-thirty in the a.m. on a chilly Thursday night if memory serves, Barrett himself was apprehended while monitoring all outgoing and incoming phone communications from the back of an aged, rather inconspicuous van parked just outside the fenced perimeter of the Hanley estate. Again, Barrett, please feel free to confirm or disagree."

"Guilty as charged," the Trainer muttered distastefully, his upper lip curled into a semi-snarl.

"Needless to say, the decision on how to treat such shocking malfeasants on relatively short notice fell to the family patriarch. Natural instinct was to call on local authorities. At least until Barrett effectively...well, *came clean* as to the reason behind the attempted surveillance.

"Problem was, I had...well, concerns as to what information had already been gained, despite both men's adamant denials to the contrary. Instead, I offered an alternative punishment to each man—one I assumed would be easily preferred over possible federal charges. There would be time served of a sort, true enough, but not the type involving razor-wire, daily inmate counts or random acts of sodomy."

As Hanley had paused to execute a flurry of jabs, hooks and uppercuts, LeAnn and Jorgensen had turned with similarly creased brows toward the man who had so effectively served as their personal trainer.

"So...Goober here was...*is* just another inmate?" Jorgensen inquired, his flabby breasts flexing in timed intervals, "what cockeyed deal you make him, Hanley? He go the last six months without wiping his ass? I ask only because something stinks here...reeks to the highest of heavens."

"What about his...the...associate, Father?" LeAnn added, while still studying the Trainer's slumped form, "the good doctor, I suppose."

"No bet, Slim," Jorgensen grinned, "just can't picture Auntie J crawling under a Lincoln without needing a crow bar to wedge her way out."

"No, no, no," Hanley scolded, nodding vigorously, "methinks forced solitude has somehow diminished the capability of logical thought with you two. The...Mister Cohen's partner in crime was deemed to be nothing more than a witless lackey and thus the...his punishment fit the crime. A simple but stout advisement to forget the incident had ever occurred or if not, increasingly severe repercussions would ensue."

Jorgensen snorted while flashing double-barreled birds Hanley's way.

"Yeah, yeah...you threatened to hack off the ankles of their entire family...blah, blah, blah...same old same old...and *methinks* you're a wiseass prick. Just spit out the main gist, for fuck's sake. This mental boogieing session is wearing this fat man out. Or maybe that's just *part* of the plan."

"Then let me spell it out for the simple and/or addle minded."

Hanley regarded his daughter with the tip of a non-existent cap.

"Nothing personal, little girl. In your case, I'll be kind and chalk it up to exhaustion."

LeAnn frowned, her nose crinkling as if detecting a particularly sour odor.

"Brian's right. It does appear you're purposely dragging this out."

After yet another abrupt session of shadow-boxing, Hanley inhaled deeply—his chest expanding to reveal the full, undeniably impressive growth near and around his pectoral region.

"To the chase then—Barrett's sentence was akin to your own. Technically, this is day one eighty-one for the former actor turned filmmaker. You see, his initial in-processing into my little silo penal-colony occurred the night *before* Jorgensen's checking in, and preceded LeAnn's by almost a full day. You may or may not have heard him scuttling about the silo—though his assigned living quarters on floor eleven were effectively blocked off. He alone had access to certain...hidden chambers which allowed him to complete his duties—mostly in the dead of night, as I understand it.

His task, you may ask? Pardon the rhyme...to provide caretaker services mainly, as in maintaining the upkeep of the generators...um, more on that momentarily. While meals were prepared and shipped in on a daily basis, he was responsible for food inventory levels as well as making sure daily toiletries were well-stocked.

"He was your phantom roommate, so to speak. Always near but never seen. Of course, there was an additional chore Barrett was tasked to perform that was, at least I mused, as being right up his alley and one I assumed he might actually enjoy if for no other reason than to break up the tedium of a long, uneventful day."

Leaning over the top rope, Hanley thrust out his neck, pursed his lips and spewed forth an ear-splitting catcall of a whistle, the result of which shook the Trainer from a slumbering doze—his legs stiffening and his arms wind-milling to prevent tipping from the chair.

"Look alive now, Barrett. I'll need you to intervene in case I accidentally misquote the facts as you understand them, yes?"

"Y-yeah...yes, s-sure," Barrett blurted drowsily, probing droopy eyes with extended forefingers, "gu-guess I...I dozed off."

Jorgensen howled and sharply slapped his right knee with a gloved palm.

"I can definitely sympathize, Goob. It's obvious Slick up there just adores the sound of his own voice."

"One would have to forgive Mister Cohen for these unintentional bouts of fatigue..." Hanley resumed sternly, "...due to his sleep schedule being so inconsistent. No doubt that...rather unfortunate issue with the main generator was probably due to a bit of snoozing on the job. I can only imagine the level of fright our other two guests experienced during those many hours of darkness."

"Spare me, shit-stack," Jorgensen grumbled, "groping around in the dark couldn't hold a candle to constant chest pains, migraines that could KO a bull-moose and multi-daily sessions of explosive diarrhea, a few of which were tinged in dark maroon."

"*Geez*, thanks for the visual, Sunshine," Ray McGinty said with a frown even as Cleaves giggled uncontrollably by his side.

Ignoring what he obviously considered mindless banter, Hanley paced the squared circle with gloved hands tucked at his lower back, "To conclude then...Barrett was instructed to both journal the proceedings and report directly to me via personal blog, but also to do what comes naturally to men of his profession—to act...to...*perform*. Of course, I'd often heard that voiceover work is considered any actor's dream job.

"Still, as much as I'd like to lavish the veteran thespian with praise for his mastery of accents in creating such a diverse gallery of characters, in truth I found them quite...over the top and well...even cartoonish at times. Saddest of all, I detected similar patterns of dialogue a regular occurrence, making it sometimes difficult to ascertain between said characters.

"I will, however, give credit where credit is due concerning the three-person team for creating the CGI holograms that helped bring said characters to life. Though we had considered practical make-up, there was simply no way. It would have meant employing the artists twenty-four hours a day in order to accomplish multiple makeovers, not to mention a truckload of uppers to keep Barrett from slipping into a coma. As it was, the computerized versions were, for the most part, flawless. To them I say...bravo. As for Barrett there, to mimic the late, great Roger Ebert, I must regrettably rate a borderline 'thumbs-down.'"

His left brow cocked dramatically, Jorgensen looked from Hanley to Barrett Cohen and back again several times, an extended forefinger following his shifting gaze.

"Waitaminnit, are you saying he's...that he was...there isn't any...the others are...were never...they *never* were..."

Meanwhile, LeAnn remained mute while studying the Trainer with a renewed curiosity, much like an archeologist eyeing an intriguing new find.

"Oh, so smoothly put, Brian, but I think I can successfully translate your exasperated babble and thus answer with a resounding no...*they* never did...they never were...they indeed did not...exist, that is. Doctor *Darwin McClintock*, personal trainer *Gabriel Maxwell* and Miss *Jeannine Sanders*, facility cook, were all created and given vocal-life by Mister Barrett Cohen, proud graduate of the actor's academy and entertainer extraordinaire. Feel free to give the man a hand, as you two are surely the most qualified of critics."

Stepping over with bare, bulky arms crossed while being shadowed on both sides by McGinty and Cleaves, Jorgensen eventually scooted to a lumbering halt a scant two feet to the left of and directly in front of Barrett Cohen's chair. In response, the smaller man instinctively leaned back as far as the high-back chair would allow, his bloodshot eyes pulled wide with apprehension.

"So, just another inmate, are we? It appears Hanley's into collecting whoever gets under his skin and molding 'em into something they'd rather not be," Jorgensen queried amiably enough through a slight smile.

"G-guess you could say that," Cohen spat with a nervous glance toward their keeper, "I...well, allow me to state I found no pleasure in duping you or Miss Garner. I was, like you both, doing as I was instructed in order to...well, so that I might be liberat..."

"Hey, you covered your ass, the reasons being obvious. No sweat off my balls. Only question is, *why* the hell did you ever quit acting? Computer generated outer shell or not, you had to switch from snooty Brit to Texas twang and then deep-south black chillin' in a blink, female no less, several times a day, yes? Despite Hanley's take, I'm thinking you pulled it off without a hitch."

"Practice m-makes perfect, I guess. Been imitating folks since grade school. Never in my wildest dreams did I think it would be used...or would be *necessary* to use...in such a...warped fashion. I stopped acting when the jobs dried up and the only offers were of the ultra-rancid variety. Our business is more about looks and youth than talent, sad to say. Making films I care about seemed a natural progression."

Breaking her silence, LeAnn leaned from the edge of her chair until she sat an arm's length from Cohen, her forehead riddled in deep worry groves with her chin resting atop a clenched fist.

"So let me get this straight...Shakespearian trained, veteran character actor and documentary filmmaker?"

"Yes, ma'am, guilty on all counts," he replied timidly, raising a hand in confirmation.

"The doctor thing then, was all accent and no experience? Don't know a hemorrhoid from a hernia?"

"Um, well, in terms of definition perhaps, but th..."

"All the medical advice and statistical info was just bunk? Mental tap-dancing?"

Cohen swallowed hard even as his pasty cheeks commenced to pulsate a deep maroon.

"Lee...um, Miss Garner, there is an explanation. Ugh, Mister Hanley? A little help here?"

Hanley sighed, tossing up both arms in apparent exasperation.

"Rest assured, Lee, Barrett wasn't merely, oh what's the hip vernacular again? Ah yes, blowing smoke up your anal cavity with his daily prognosis."

Jorgensen's raucous howl drowned out Hanley's final two words.

"Oh, you're about as hip as a rotary phone, Hanley. Anal cavity? *Really?*"

"Barrett was being coached from my personal physician via iPad. He would pass on your progress and complaints and in turn receive hourly updates which to study in order to properly advise further actions."

Her brow still a roadmap of creases, LeAnn's continued dissatisfaction was apparent in both body language and tone.

"But, the blood tests? How...I mean, how were they tested? The...family doctor have a portable lab plugged into his iPhone?"

"Not quite. They were mailed out overnight to him and the results emailed no later than the following day."

"Mailed out over...by whom exactly? I'm guessing this place is beyond the normal USPS route."

"Fed Ex Express picked up upon on-line request, with Barrett there serving as one-man fulfillment and shipping department."

"Ba...he was able to...greet the Fed-Ex man?"

"Indeed."

"So...he..." she stuttered, pointing a shaky forefinger toward Cohen, her ice-cold stare centered directly on her father, "you had access to....*he* could just walk out the front door anytime he damn well pleased?"

Turning away, Hanley danced a rapid jig in the classic pugilist style.

"Back to you, Barrett old man. I'm growing unnecessarily winded."

Unable or unwilling to meet her gaze, the Trainer instead stared just past the gleaming tips of his own perfectly shined boots.

"I...was given the access codes to...be allowed to exit, yes."

"You didn't...you didn't try to...escape? Maybe find us some help?"

"I...Miss Garner, there was...I did...consider it. Even mapped out a long-term plan on...several occasions, but...b-but it...there was no feasible route to ta..."

"Yellow motherfucker!" she croaked with shaking hands, clear snot dribbling from her left nostril, "chicken-shit c-coward..."

"Hey, take...take it easy, Slim," Jorgensen said calmly, obviously taken back by his fellow captive's shocking use of profanity, "I'm...sure the man had his reasons. Probably get shot on sight once past a certain demarcation line."

Twisting about in his chair until he faced her trembling form dead-on, the Trainer stopped just short of reaching over and gently tapping the nearest appendage.

"Miss Garner, there was...there was nowhere to escape to."

"Fine actor he may be, little girl, Barrett speaks the god's honest truth in this case. There is indeed videotaped evidence of his boldest attempt, wherein I'd estimate he'd hoofed it a good two, three hundred yards past the entrance before turning back. As for possible escape destination, well, there's a reason I chose this particular silo—first and foremost it's desolate, off-the-beaten path locale. Let's just say, Jorgensen's sharp-shooter assumption notwithstanding, a man would have to be superhuman to even attempt the swim.

"So, let's not be too hard on poor Barrett there. Given the circumstances, he had little choice but to play caretaker slash postman."

Wadding up the lower half of her shirt, LeAnn blew her nose into a wadded gathering of cloth and snorted away the remainder of the sinus buildup once her head had arisen. She fell silent and solemn, her eyes as bloodshot as a skid-row bum hugging a recently emptied bottle of rot-gut ripple to his ragged chest.

Barrett held position for several more moments, holding both palms upward as to plead for her forgiveness before scooting slowly about to again face front.

Bowing, Jorgensen covered the left side of his mouth with a cupped hand, the impending whisper still easily comprehensible by all present within the relative silence.

"So, just between us, dude...you think that murdering jackass offed your associate? You know—the old concrete shoes or execution-style bullet to the noggin...maybe a Sicilian necktie?"

Cohen instantly stiffened, his tone laced with angst.

"I, god I would hope not…I mean, it would be overkill to…th-that is to say…"

"Along the same lines, DeNiro, what're the odds that the three of us befall a similar fate?"

"O-odds? I don't…I've tried not to dwell on such grim ma…"

Dropping his hand, Jorgensen concluded in full voice—a booming yell obviously meant for the man occupying the boxing ring to his immediate right.

"Best gird those tinsel-town loins, Pacino, 'cause regardless of the bang-up job in keeping us stocked in crap-paper and munchies, I'd personally wager the tip of my beloved Johnson you're apt to wind up in the same body-bag as I—twin packs of sliced and diced lunchmeat who made the mistake of screwing with the wrong demon."

"Brian, *please*," LeAnn pleaded in a weak, sickly voice just as Jorgensen executed a gradual about-face, turning from his former Trainer to his current captor as the beefy sentinels on either side kept pace, each with a hand tucked snugly inside their respective vests.

"Sorry, Slim. I guess spending half a calendar year stuck in this suppository-shaped penal colony did little to curb my penchant for blunt honesty."

Three brisk steps brought him to the edge of the ring, his massive thighs pressed firmly against the squared mat. Placing pudgy hands on considerable hips, Jorgensen peered upward and winked playfully.

"So, muscles, we gonna do this or what?"

Hanley stood back, waving each gloved hand in the classic 'come hither' gesture.

"By all means, fat man, climb on in and get you some. Mister Cohen, if you please…one final assignment."

"Father? I have a question," LeAnn inquired calmly, standing and raising a pasty hand airborne even as Barrett Cohen, slump-shouldered and head bowed, followed the obese man into the ring.

Backed against the ropes as both his opposition and match referee stood at ring's center, Hanley's reply reeked with annoyance—as if he were dismissing a bothersome infant.

"Yes, my dear, but make it brief, please. I have...old trash to toss out."

"What if...he wins?"

"Come again, little girl?"

"What happens if you lose? I mean, what happens to Brian? Do you then fulfill the initial promise and release him? Or is yet another...double-cross in order?"

"Double-cross?" Hanley mimicked, cocking a brow before storming past both opposition and referee until his upper body draped the top rope.

"And who exactly have I...double-crossed thus far, Lee? I must confess that all this...the back-stabbing talk is growing damned tiresome. Have you been cheated in some way that I'm unaware of? Has Jorgensen? Mister Cohen? If so, may the object of said malfeasance speak now or forever hold their peace," he blared with barely restrained rage, gloved hands forced to curl around the top rope to cloak anger-fueled tremors. "This is hardly breach of contract, little girl. It is merely...an amendment to the original and strictly between Jorgensen and myself."

His daughter openly smirked before retaking her seat.

"An amendment you'd obviously mapped out soon after our incarceration, Father, considering the physical transformation you've undergone."

Stone-faced, Hanley backed to a nearby corner, leaning against the turnbuckle as Jorgensen eyed him with squint-eyed glee.

"Believe you pinched a nerve, Slim, located somewhere between 'ego' and 'tistical'...or is that testicle, as in lack thereof?

Think now might be the ideal time for that long-overdue confession? I mean, she's plenty pissed as it is…"

"As I stated, it will *wait*," Hanley replied with obvious disdain, glancing briefly toward LeAnn, whose clinched expression confirmed her confusion at the exchange.

Hanley nodded impatiently toward the Trainer, who was already digging into a front pants pocket.

"Mister Cohen, the legalities if you would."

The hand that held the note visibly shook, as did the Trainer's voice as he commenced reading from its beige-shaded background.

"The rules of the contest are spelled out as follows, gentlemen: effectively, there are *no* rules other than to incapacitate your opponent, a 'la the early days of Ultimate Fighting before terminal political correctness set in.

"Once complete unconsciousness is obtained and verified by myself, the winner shall return to the corner of his choice and the fallen tended to until such time he is able to verbally respond to simple inquiries."

"Simplicity in itself. I like it. Good call, Hanley," Jorgensen said, flashing a thumb's up. "Why get complicated, right?"

Stepping away from the turnbuckle, Hanley slammed the tips of his gloves together.

"Why indeed? Myron, mouthpieces please."

McKinley moved forward, pulling a pair of purple colored mouth-guards from a suit pocket and tearing away an outer layer of clear plastic wrap.

He handed one to each fighter and quickly backed away, taking up position directly between McGinty and Cleaves—each bag-eyed and droopy, as if on the cusp of napping while standing upright.

Each man stepped to the ring's center, separated only by Cohen's lingering, comically out-of-place presence.

"Barrett, ring the fictional bell when ready," Hanley mumbled between sucking noises while attempting a proper fit with the mouth-guard, "let's get this show on the road, as it were, and may the best man win."

"If not the man with the lowest cholesterol level, right *Godfather*?" Jorgensen quipped between nosy sucks on his mouthpiece.

As if cued by some unheard chime, both men turned at almost the precise moment to lock eyes with LeAnn, their mutual nods met with a squinty-eyed, stone-faced stare.

Stuffing the haphazardly folded paper back into his pants pocket, Barrett Cohen then stepped from between the combatants and raised a fisted hand.

Embarrassment and shame practically flowed from his pores as he pumped it downward once, twice, thrice—repeating a single word at the conclusion of each repetition:

'*Ding...ding*'.

Twelve

Grudge Match

Hanley's opening jab bounced off Jorgensen's right shoulder, followed by a looping left hook that whizzed past his trio of chins in a blur. Stumbling back, the larger man ricocheted off the ropes, leading with his face and thereby catching a surprisingly vicious poke squarely in the nose. He laughed aloud at his own clumsiness while reeling forward with his massive arms pinwheeling. A sticky warmth soon coated his top lip, followed by the coppery taste of his own leakage.

Able to skid to a brake before slamming head-first into a far turnbuckle, Jorgensen twisted about with arms upraised and was rocked by a fierce combination of body shots, the last of which effectively emptied his lungs of useable air. Bent over with both gloves tucked at his wounded midsection, he was subsequently battered with a flurry of rabbit punches to the back of his head, neck and finally the base of the throat, the latter sending him sprawling onto all fours.

Short bursts of tepid air massaged his left ear as he strained to suck in and store that initial, magically replenishing mouthful of oxygen.

"It is so tempting to toy with you, Jorgy—to inflict the optimal amount of damage and ending it only when what I consider a fair amount of retribution has been achieved."

His back hunched and his throat hitching loudly, Jorgensen spat out the mouthpiece and stared down through a blurry haze as the mat was spattered by an assortment of blood-droplets that flowed freely from each flaring nostril. Meanwhile, Hanley's long-winded whisperings continued to echo from what sounded like the deepest of chasms.

"With respect for my only daughter, I'll force myself to live with the satisfaction of merely loosening some teeth or cracking a few ribs."

He felt a sharp thumping sensation near his left kidney, a similar shot just below his jiggling man-boobs. Rolling onto his back, a thrusting kneecap grazed the tip of his nose. Reacting with predictable sluggishness, he raised both arms and started to cross them in front of his face to ward off the inevitable blows to come. Instead, his groin was set ablaze in the aftermath of a smashing heel. Upon curling into the fetal position, the hissed monologue returned, this time into the opposite ear.

"Giving credit where credit is due, Brian, I have to admit you've called it from the get-go—'it' being that it goes without saying you will never again see the light of day outside these silo walls."

A solid left landed at his right temple, filling his blurred vision with sparks of light akin to mini-lightning strikes.

"Once I've...gotten my jollies, so to speak, I will instruct one of my men to first blow your balls off and then to extract that pea brain with a well-placed nine millimeter slug. Thought it only fair you knew, in case, well...you feel the need to find religion in the brief time you have left.

Now, if you can stop bleeding long enough, tell me...who's your daddy, lard ass?

Following a short, merciful pause in the bludgeoning, Jorgensen lunged over onto his left side and then combat-rolled beneath the lower rope, landing on the cold tile outside the ring with his left hip and shoulder taking the brunt.

Struggling mightily for a substantial breath of air that would serve to properly reboot his voided lungs, Jorgensen rolled onto his back and massaged his wounded groin. Though his ears were as stopped up as his vision was bleary, there was no shutting out the screeching, wailing dialogue originating from the opposite side of the ring, the gist of which he could only comprehend as:

LeAnn: "...never planned...kill him first....Father? You...consider...baby might...need a father?"

Hanley: "...no pregnancy, my dear. It...a ruse...to further test your mettle..."

LeAnn (screams): "Test...mettle? Are...serious?"

Hanley: "...Clintock, please restrain...daughter, as I am a currently...tad busy."

LeAnn: "...conscience at all? My god...embarrassed to share...same blood! Why not...us now and spare...the trouble!"

Hanley: "...Dismissed, Mister Cohen...services no longer required...I can...dle it from here."

Barrett Cohen: "...ter Hanley...require a real doctor...plan for...immediate treatment? Is there a...copter waiting nearby?"

Hanley: "Mister McGinty, please assist...certain second-rate filmmaker in...claiming his seat. As trivial as...final results may be at this juncture...have to go through ...motions, yes?"

LeAnn: "Asshole! Murdering...lying....faced...cking ASSHOLE!"

Hanley: "Jesus, McClintock...three need my help in sitting that skeletal bitch down...her chair? Three must outweigh her...five hundred pounds...Just...it, damn it!"

McGinty: "You want...turn out her lights now, boss?"

Hanley: "Just shut her...muscle-headed lame-brains...can you manage...much without visual aids?"

The ruckus continued, though the voices involved were soon drowned out by that of a new, closer entry.

"Jorgensen, you...are you able to breathe?"

He peered up and over and directly into Barrett Cohen's scowling mug, from which sweat dripped from the chin and each flaring nostril.

Reaching up, he snared the smaller man's shirt collar and tugged, pulling him down until their noses sat mere inches apart.

"H-he's go-gonna k-k-kill...all...of us. W-when you see...g-get an o-opening, g-go for one...their g-guns."

Goggle-eyed, Cohen bit his lower lip nervously while breaking Jorgensen's grip just enough to turn his head in Hanley's direction.

"The...a gun? Bt...h-how did you know...this? He's swore to me I'd be relea..."

A furious jerk at the collar sent him sprawling atop the larger man's waggling, sweat-soaked frame.

"Th-think about it, B-Buttercup...y-you really, truly think he...let your associate j-just walk? Re-really? He c-can't afford witnesses...to this...ne-never could. I...kn-knew I was gonna die this day...k-knew it from the mo...minute they...tossed me into the back of that v-van."

The racket in the background had abruptly subsided and in turn Jorgensen released his grip just as quickly, the sudden shift sending Cohen wind-milling back to land on the stone floor with a resounding grunt.

From the corner of his left eye, he saw Hanley hop back into the ring. The man was whistling and clapping his gloves together in gleeful anticipation of inflicting additional punishment to his winded, wounded opposition.

Standing stiffly, Cohen backed a few steps from Jorgensen's prone frame, though a final plea from the larger man rang through loud and clear despite its markedly low volume.

"S-save the g-girl. Save LeAnn. I'll...do my best to provide...the distraction you'll n-need."

"Go retake your seat now, Barrett," Hanley instructed with a casual wave of the glove, "while Brian and I wrap up this rather disappointing debacle."

Cohen's lips parted to reply—to respond in pent-up anger at the blatant unfairness of it all. That a man of such means, obtained in illegal activities of the highest order no less, could actually revel in the bludgeoning of a man he'd so expertly set up to fail. A man he'd obviously taken great pains to humiliate in high order before pulping to a quivering pile of dehumanized mush, all the while utilizing a newly constructed physique built exclusively for the task at hand.

The *rant that would never be* might also contain a paragraph of two regarding the treatment of the man's own flesh-and-blood in the name of personal vanity. Unable to tolerate an heir whose black sheep status was mostly due to his own parental failings, he had decided to rectify the matter by means of abduction, psychological and physical torture, and if all else failed, at least according to her fellow inmate, removing said family embarrassment from the picture via a bullet to the head. That final thought triggered a fresh outbreak of frosty chills down his otherwise toasty spine, as any such extractions by extreme prejudice would surely include a certain has-been actor-turned-covert-filmmaker.

Trailing the outer perimeter of the mat with a hand sliding the length of the bottom rope, he watched Jorgensen struggle to sit up as Hanley hovered overhead like a circling buzzard.

In this relatively brief timespan, Jorgensen was able to not only reclaim the power of breathing, but shake the jagged blurriness from his injured eye. Having released his bruised testicles, he'd turned his attention to the throbbing ache at his midsection by sitting up and pulling his knees as close to his chest as was possible considering the multiple layers of sagging bulk trapped between.

"Care to rejoin me, Brian...or do you require assistance?" he heard Hanley belt out cheerily. He utilized the few remaining moments before reentering the fray by inhaling deeply and allowing a gradual exhale, wincing at the sharp, shooting pain that streaked up his left arm in the aftermath—leaving a faint numbness in its wake.

McGinty and Cleaves stood ringside with McKinley splitting the middle barely a step behind as Cohen lingered nearby.

"You heard the man, *Spielberg*," McKinley grumbled without actually glancing Cohen's way, "grab some pine and enjoy the rest of the show."

It wasn't until the Trainer side-stepped past the stoic threesome toward his assigned chair that the reason behind LeAnn Garner's sudden silence became horrifically clear. Her eyes streamed tears down a frighteningly gaunt jawline, the edges of which were layered in grayish strands of duct tape, the majority of which blanketed her lips from the tip of her chin to just beneath nostrils from which snot bubbles protuded. Lowering himself onto the chair, he then noted the hands folded at her lap had also been bound together, presumably utilizing the same roll.

Upon bearing witness to such barbaric treatment, an additional layer of ice formed at the Trainer's already frigid backbone. He could only assume that if Hanley had so casually approved such brazen mistreatment of his own daughter, the odds of Jorgensen's grim theory possessing a palpable layer of truth just leapt from longshot to sure thing.

"Be r-right with you, Slick," Jorgensen was muttering, getting to his feet with Herculean effort and stumbling back clumsily before righting the wobbly ship, "gotta c-confess…you caught me off-guard with both…the punching speed and force of same."

Hanley backed from the ropes to allow Jorgensen ample space to reenter.

"Well, I was trained by the best and told I was a quick study for a man of such…advanced age. Total commitment, complete dedication. Worked out three, four hours a day, six days a week, for the better part of five months. Dropped twenty-seven pounds of the same type goo-shell you now sport like an overcoat sewn from Jell-O and replaced it with thirteen pounds of solid muscle. Of my many achievements in this life, this transformation rates the pinnacle. Just between us, Brian, do you feel a similar *swelling* of pride, pun fully intended, in your own accomplishment?"

Resembling a pale, mutated human-slug hybrid, Jorgensen crawled into the ring headfirst, oblivious to the fact that, standing just a few feet to his left, Hanley smiled a lunatic's grin while methodically peeling off his gloves.

"Pride in knowing you didn't for a New York minute think I could gain the weight, Hanley? Fucking-A right." Jorgensen huffed, briefly posing on one knee before rising as to milk as many precious self-healing moments as possible. "As for your great achievement, I'd venture to guess chemicals of the illegal sort had as much to do with it as dedication or commitment."

The evil, toothy grin gained a slight tic, as did the older man's left eye, which twitched with a faint spasm even as he assumed a fighting stance and prepped to step forward. Reveling in obviously striking a nerve, Jorgensen resumed between huffs while freeing his own fists of their padding.

"Aw, c'mon, Pete ol' sack, 'fess up. What's the point in…lying at this point? I mean, look at those jowls, man…sagging like a squirrel…storing away a few too many nuts? I think…not, 'roid boy. You'd think after three or four decades, the modern day chemist could…eliminate such obvious side-effects, right? Tell me...they still shrink the man-jewels to grapenut size? Main reason...I never personally partook."

Teeth-gritted to the point of shattering a molar, Hanley moved gradually forward with arms raised and bare fists clenched.

"Time to shut you up for good now, Brian. Forgive me in advance if I get carried away in doing so..."

As the two men converged again, the outside of the ring produced its own drama, albeit of the silent desperation type. As Barrett Cohen carefully studied the universally slumped postures of Peter Hanley's hired guns, LeAnn Garner's incessant whimpering had subsided, as had the accompanying leakage that had soaked her cheeks, trailed down her narrow neck and found a suitable crevice atop her pronounced clavicles. Her dark brown eyes no longer reflected sadness, pity or exasperation, but an icy cold stare of uninhibited hatred—twin lasers directed solely at the man responsible for her very existence.

~ * ~

Perhaps fueled by brazen overconfidence, Hanley waded in with a left hook so horribly telegraphed in its drawn-out execution it appeared delivered in virtual slow-motion. Jorgensen ducked aside with ease and lunged forward in essentially the same fluid movement, landing a solid right to the smaller man's breastbone. Leaping back a step from impact, Hanley clawed at his chest, clearing ample space between the two and thus setting up Jorgensen's perfectly executed follow-up— the side kick caught a wide-eyed Hanley in the lower abdomen just as he'd bounded forward and bent him like a pretzel while simultaneously evacuating both lungs with a shrieking gasp. Hanley felt an impossibly stout grip engulf the back of his skull and push downward just seconds before the right side of his jaw was battered by an ascending knee that struck with the force of a fifty-pound sledge.

"Shit, boss….boss, you want we should intervene? Boss?" McKinley shouted through cupped hands as his two subordinates visibly stiffened at the sight of their employer lying face-first atop the mat in a pool of his own rapidly oozing fluids.

Unlike McKinley with his perpetual frown, neither McGinty nor Cleaves was able to completely wipe the smiles from their collective mugs as Hanley rolled to one side and spat out a jagged assortment of blood-coated, toothy shards.

The Trainer saw McKinley's right hand move toward his shoulder holster and the Glock tucked within while shooting his subordinates a dirty look. As inconspicuously as possible in case any of the gawking trio turned his way, he dug with sweat-slickened fingers into his back left pocket.

"Wanna share the joke, gents?" McKinley spat, his hand now resting uneasily on the holster's hard leather shell.

The two shrugged, each struggling mightily to wipe away their collective smirks.

Jorgensen had backed into the far ropes, grasping at his chest and leaning on wobbly knees, his breathing labored and his complexion beyond merely pale—a ghostly visage in search of a proper haunting. Meanwhile, Peter Hanley lay on his back, probing fingers reaching into his bloody maw as if officially surveying the damage.

His ample bulk perched on the outer mat, McKinley cupped a hand and yelled through it as if his employer had lost his hearing along with a handful of choppers.

"Boss…Mister H…you want I…we should stop this?"

Hanley lifted a maroon-smeared hand and waved him off, nodding in time as a fresh stream flowed down his chin onto the mat. Releasing the top rope, McKinley took a step back even as his hand fell away from the holster.

"Just give me a…the high sign then, boss."

"Shit, another shot like that and he's toast, Gint," the Trainer heard Kerry Cleaves whisper toward McGinty, who nodded in turn. Having freed the desired item, its trim, metallic handle slick in his palm, he feared it might actually squirt free if a firm enough squeeze ensued. Sneaking a peek LeAnn's way, he noted her fierce, unblinking glare had yet to abate—her breathing so controlled and calm to be hardly noticeable considering the relative non-movement of her narrow chest.

Over the next minute-plus, the majority of motion within the room wasn't tied to either wounded combatant or their ringside sentinels, but to Barrett Cohen's rising from his chair and baby-stepping over with his right hand clenched at the small of his back.

Hanley stood awkwardly, having climbed the ropes like a man scaling a mountainside. He stumbled ahead a single step, nearly toppling over from the forward momentum. His jaw was bloated to grotesque proportions, forcing him to breath from nostrils which spewed forth a reddish mist with each strained exhale.

From the opposite corner teetered Jorgensen, his left arm hanging limp by his side, his face a contorted horror of unspeakable pain.

They circled each other while displaying similar limps, the lower portion of Hanley's face appearing from a distance as if he'd donned a blackish beard while Jorgensen's left eyelid drooped as if it were gradually descending, melting down his jawline like heated wax.

Grunting in obvious pain, Hanley tossed a trio of weak jabs that were easily slapped away, finally lunging forward and clutching the larger man in a failed bear hug, his attempted grope sliding from Jorgensen's wide-load physique like butter from a hot blade.

Before stumbling back in frustration, Hanley bowed his head and thrust forward in a blur, the impact of the proposed butt missing all but the top portion of Jorgensen's deadened left deltoid. Still, the force was enough to separate the two by a half-dozen feet, each bouncing into a far trio of ropes and hanging on for stability.

"Dead on their fuckin' feet. My kid brother's scout troop could wipe up the canvas with both of 'em about now," the Trainer heard Ray McGinty quip as Cleaves grinned his approval, each leaning against the mat with arms crossed. Meanwhile, their immediate supervisor remained poised like a stone gargoyle with eyes effectively glued to the mostly non-action.

Having acquired adequate space to do so, Jorgensen hopped forward on his left leg, leaping airborne as much as his massive bulk would allow while simultaneously swirling about in a whitish haze. His right heel connected with a sharp thump at the back of the smaller man's skull, sending him sprawling forward in an awkward flip that saw him land crookedly on his right shoulder.

Rolling over onto his back, Hanley sucked wind like a beached fish, his pale lips squirming and his tongue flicking in a mad search for air.

After landing a bit crookedly in the kick's follow-through, Jorgensen quickly recovered via use of the nearest set of ropes. Stepping cautiously toward his fallen advisory, he nonetheless maintained a defensive posture save the hanging left arm, clutched tightly at his bloated side. His breathing was beyond merely labored—it was a freight train burning its final chuck of coal while climbing the steepest point of Pikes Peak. As each strained word purged itself to open space, there was an accompanying spray of fluids that had already painted a psychedelic scape across his heaving, bare chest.

"Hanley, you're probably a smart man in...a lot of ways. Figure you have...to be to organize the...empire you created. With...that in mind...I have to ask—did you seriously think...a few extra muscles, a few dropped pounds, and six fucking months of training would allow...you to compete *mano-a-mano* with...yours truly?"

To his surprise, as well as that of all witnesses present, Hanley hauled himself up in three quick movements, though in the final stage of standing upright he did stumble back into a far turnbuckle. As Jorgensen sustained his stoic stance at ring's center, his wobbly captor similarly maintained a slumped posture with his upper back pinned against the padded pole, a pencil-thin stream of fluids more black than red dribbling forth from the corner of his left eye, soon joining the gory kaleidoscope masking the lower half of his face.

"Boss...you...hanging in?" McKinley bellowed, slowly retrieving a silver-barreled Glock from his shoulder holster. A dozen feet away, Barrett Cohen used the razor-sharp edge of a scalpel he'd procured from the same supply cabinet from which he'd operated his false medical practice and cut free the duct tape holding LeAnn Garner's hands. Upon being awarded her freedom, she reached up and gingerly pulled away the remaining binds from her lips, all the while staring straight ahead through searing, partially squinted eyes that, as far as Cohen could determine, had yet to execute a single blink.

Back inside the ring, Peter Hanley exposed a bare palm McKinley's way and waved weakly to and fro, his eyes glazed and his lips quivering madly in an apparent attempt to form a reply that was not to be.

Grinning mischievously, Jorgensen gestured him forward with the continuous curl of an extended forefinger.

"Crave another slice of...misery, old man? Damn if you aren't...the glutton, though."

Hanley paused, raised fists dropping several inches as if he were contemplating.

"Tell you a secret if you...promise it won't...leave this room," Jorgensen continued, his droopy left eyelid either winking in time or racked with involuntary spasms. "I allowed you a free shot...just to...test the waters. You'll be...proud to know whatever HGH you...sucked down as part of your... everyday diet... did the trick. Yep... knocked my shrunken pecker directly into the dirt."

Hanley's chest instantly expanded, either with a renewed shot of pride or a continuing struggle to reclaim full lung capacity. Sensing the latter, Jorgensen quickly resumed, his periodically parting lips the lone movement in an otherwise statuesque stance.

"If you'd...known enough to follow-through with the right combo, I'd most likely...be dead as a hammer already. Luck...luckily for me, your *kind* has a habit of gloating when...they should be stepping on necks. Tell you what...even though it's more than...you deserve...I'll give you another shot. That is, if you're man enough to take it. Honestly, I have...my doubts...leastways..." he paused to cackle loudly before concluding, "from what your ex told me...the godfather's iconic noodle had...well, long since lost its...tinsel-strength—*cooked linguine* I think she'd said—right before I nailed her...again *and* again...*and* again."

"F-f-fugggh uwwwww!" the smaller man shrieked, plunging forward with fists raised at chest-level.

Crowding in with his head lowered, he tossed forth a flurry of jabs that Jorgensen blocked or swatted away with little difficulty, all the while sporting a tight-lipped smile. Hanley shrieked with rage as an attempted backhand was similarly dispatched—a looping, right-hand follow-up snagged in mid-punch at the wrist and crook of the elbow. Clutching the smaller man's arm in a double vise, Jorgensen abruptly released the elbow grip, using the liberated arm, curled at the elbow, to throw a ferocious uppercut that connected with a sharp crunch. Hanley cried out as his right arm was essentially snapped at the elbow, bent back until tendons ripped, bone splintered and muscles were flayed into jagged strips. The smaller man fell to one knee as fresh tears spewed from each eye, essentially flushing the blood that had come before and making it appear as if he were leaking light maroon-shaded mascara. Instinctively gripping the shoulder of his ruined arm, he left himself wide open for Jorgensen's secondary attack of choice.

"Jesus Crow....b-boss!" McKinley blurted, raising the Glock clumsily upward until the tip of its gleaming barrel slapped the top rope and nearly spilled from his grip. By the time he'd righted his hold and took aim, a duo of troublesome complications had arisen.

At the precise time Hanley's veteran hired gun had almost fumbled away the main tool of his trade, Jorgensen had side-stepped over, leaning down with his wrists crossed defensively over his lower jaw until he'd hovered over his whimpering opponent, whose head was bowed in obvious misery as his upper body shook and convulsed.

Meanwhile, Barrett Cohen had inched forward, gradually shortening the distance between himself, McGinty and Cleaves to just out of reaching distance, the scalpel held out chest level like a protective cross.

"Tsk, tsk, asshole...I never...said...I'd permit that second free shot...to land," Jorgensen quipped just a blink before Hanley had released his ruined appendage and tensed as if to rise, the larger man plunging downward with the speed and agility of a striking cobra. Giggling maniacally, Jorgensen had expertly and with amazing dexterity, wrapped one mammoth, blood-smeared arm around his screeching victim's neck while the other wound around his chest. Upon obtaining his grip of choice, he'd instantly tensed, flexing and curling like a contracting anaconda.

"Ssssshhhh, best calm down and cease the struggle, old man. This particular arm, you see...the one you're currently wearing like a bolo tie, is so fucking numb it's like somebody shot 'er full of Novocain. In other words, I can't feel a damn thing, as in...how much pressure I'm actually applying to your gullet. Could even spaz out any second and wring your neck like an old banty rooster."

Without losing focus at the bead he was trying desperately to obtain, McKinley barked out orders with the controlled rage of a veteran drill instructor.

"Execute plan B, boneheads, just as the boss instructed. You know what to do...do it!"

McGinty and Cleaves instantly sprinted in opposite directions, circling the ring while palming their firearm of choice—the former a Beretta nine mil and the latter a forty-four mag.

Temporarily frozen in place by an almost complete paralysis of his lower extremities, Barrett Cohen realized he was mere seconds from being spotted by either or both men, who were taking up positions on opposite sides of the ring. It was Brian Jorgensen's final proclamation that snapped him from his daze just moments later and in doing, assisted in mapping out a new, wildly spontaneous blueprint of self-preservation.

"Understand *this,* Prick," the holder of multiple black belts had spouted in a calm, matter-of-fact tone utterly void his characteristic cockiness, "*six*-hundred pounds, in a wheelchair and one arm glued between my...*these* enormous butt-cheeks, and I could still pound...your ass to...dust."

With McGinty stationed to his left and Cleaves to the right, both trying frantically to obtain a bead as they pointed their respective firearms through the ropes, Jorgensen was forced to sling Hanley's squirming form from one to the other as a human shield.

"You got 'im, Gint?" Cleaves queried, propping the elbow of his shooting hand flat against the mat as to gain additional control, "I...can't lock on with 'im slinging the boss around like a fuckin' ragdoll."

McGinty alternated waiving the Beretta first up and down and then side to side, squinting through the twin sights with a booted foot propped atop the mat and the short barrel splitting the top and middle ropes.

"Every...time...I line up...a prime spot on that... blubbery hide...he...swings him back around...damn near let loose with a head-shot...straight 'tween the boss's eyes..."

Meanwhile, from angle number three—dead center across from the target and his human blockade, McKinley stood in the classic shooter's pose—feet spread evenly with his shoulders and the Glock wired-in at eye level.

"Boss! Mister H! Can you break free? Are you...able to loosen his grip?"

At the sound of his voice, Jorgensen added a third obstructing pose, slinging his semi-coherent captive up and over until he could only be seen peeking over the tip of Hanley's right shoulder. The 'boss,' however, appeared mostly incoherent, blinking madly between brief involuntary naps, his tattered arm hanging at a grotesque angle while showing jagged, bloodless white bone just below the crock of the elbow.

"L-looks like co-command...decision is...yours, big guy," Jorgensen croaked between labored huffs, "but I'd...advise you...choose wisely...'cause the first...shot that rings out...is liable to...trigger a natural reflex...in this rubbery arm...of mine to twist 'n turn...if you...get my drift."

McKinley did not twitch other than a nervous swallow.

"Boys, you know the drill...just as the boss mapped it out in case such extreme measures were deemed necessary."

As if running off the same weakening battery, McGinty and Cleaves' feverish gun-waving temporarily halted in mid-aim before resuming in similarly synchronized fashion.

"Goes without saying, though," McKinley continued with his pudgy jaws pulled taut, "try like the devil *not* to damage the precious goods."

Following a single, eerie moment of deafening silence, during which time even the frenzied movements of the two indecisive shooters appeared to be lifted from some ancient silent film, a tidal wave of spastic activity flooded forth that would go a long way in determining the fate of all present.

~ * ~

The first shot rang out—an ear-splitting boom that echoed like canon-fire within the squared, stone walls, following quickly by a second that sounded positively muffled in comparison.

In response to that initial blast, Brian Jorgensen had instinctively yanked Peter Hanley's withering body upward, resulting in a Beretta slug digging a circular hole into the inner bicep of the older man's already shattered, lifeless arm. Even as the slug exited the opposite side, just grazing his left thigh, Jorgensen was already pulling the body in the opposite direction, though not in time to prevent his right shoulder from being lit ablaze by a forty-four round. Flailing back as his neck and arm were flooded in the sticky warmth, he somehow, miraculously, maintained his hold around Hanley's chest, this despite both arms experiencing similar numbness.

As he'd crept up behind McKinley, just seconds before the twin explosions had ensued, Barrett Cohen had prayed he could remain unnoticed until forced into action. Once the shots had rung out to officially signal that all bets were off, he had dashed forward in three quick bounds. In the aftermath of the shooting, a mere wink before they'd impacted, he'd been able to acquire a mental snapshot that, in retrospect, made the timing of his leap all the more vital. Between the sights of McKinley's Glock had been a wide-open shot at the center of Brian Jorgensen's fully exposed skull.

Crawling forth on all fours as all hell had broken loose, LeAnn Garner's grim, squinty-eyed expression hadn't altered a single crease since being forced onto a ringside seat and effectively taped into place. Reaching the edge of the ring, she peeked around a squared corner to see Cleaves hopping about as if a bucket of fire-ants had been off-loaded into his Fruit-of-the-Looms. She scuttled in the opposite direction, circling rapidly about without ever rising to mat-level, halting just in time to watch Barrett Cohen's feet depart the cool stone.

Pressed so firmly to the ropes he appeared to be attempting a reverse limbo, Jorgensen's entire, colossal frame visibly tensed. With the prime target poised perfectly for a follow-up shot, McGinty jumped back a few steps and took aim directly between the shoulder blades. The trigger was engaged at the exact moment that Jorgensen hauled Hanley up and over, slinging the limp frame over the ropes toward the shooter—headfirst like a human javelin.

Barrett Cohen's attempted body-block failed miserably as he bounced off McKinley's tree-stout frame like a pesky gnat off an elephant's hide. It was, however, effective enough to skew the man's aim, redirecting his shot until it sailed well over and to the right of the intended target's head to free a golf-ball sized chunk of stone from a far wall. With an angry roar, McKinley whirled about to lock in this newest enemy, only to have the pointed end of a surgical scalpel plunged deep into the base of his neck.

Approximately two hundred ten pounds of dead weight clipped McGinty at the knees, the most damaging contact having occurred when, upon descending, Hanley's undamaged right elbow had sunk deep into the other man's groin. Once his employer's flaccid form had effectively pancaked his lower legs, McGinty had tumbled forward, the Beretta sailing from his right hand as he attempted to break his fall with open palms.

With the dumb, youthful exuberance of a newborn pup, Cleaves hopped over the top rope and into the ring, his ear-to-ear smile showcasing a wide space between the two front, gold-plated choppers. A half-dozen feet away, Brian Jorgensen struck a side pose while staring down the unwavering barrel of Cleaves' blue-steel forty-four.

"What'cha gonna do, tough guy? Dodge it, block it or swipe it away?" the hired gun smirked, applying steady pressure to the trigger. Jorgensen shrugged good-naturedly, tilting his head slightly to the left. Remarkably, he began his dive to the mat a split-second before the shot rang out, such unworldly clairvoyance resulting in his right shoulder catching the brunt in lieu of his upper chest. Though technically a graze, it nonetheless dug a substantial groove from the tip of the shoulder to half-way down the accompanying blade. Jorgenson allowed the momentum of the plunge to push him beneath the lower rope, tumbling to the rock floor while leaving a dark, circular slug-trail on the mat.

Barrett Cohen resembled a drunken contortionist, bent backward until it appeared the top of his scalp might soon scrape the heels of his shoes. McKinley bore down with his full weight—easily outweighing the Trainer by seventy or eighty pounds—as the two men's arms and hands entangled like tentacles while wrestling over the Glock. McKinley's neck, chin and upper chest were saturated, a gradual but continuing stream pouring from where the scalpel handle protruded like a silver proboscis.

Cleaves leaned over the top rope, spewing a torrent of profanities at the necessity for an additional shot, while just below and to his left, Jorgensen rested on all fours, apparently too wounded and/or exhausted to even attempt further movement.

Utterly oblivious to the varying degrees of mayhem at his back, Cleaves extended both arms, the left hand cupping the right, stared down the Magnum's gleaming sights and casually lined up yet another head shot.

"That's it, fat boy. No reason to make this any harder. Just stay...right...the..."

In a brief moment of surreal shock, Cleaves considered the rather implausible possibility that the forty-four had backfired. What else, he mused crazily, his vision blurred with dark red spatters, could explain the thumb and trigger finger of his shooting hand vanishing as if seared away by a miter saw? It wasn't until the realization that his hearing was severely impaired that a second, infinitely more logical conclusion swam to the surface—someone had just blown off two of his fingers, knuckle and all, via gunshot while more than likely aiming a bit higher.

Accompanying this abrupt epiphany came a woefully delayed rush of fear in the odds that a follow-up attempt might well be in order. Taking a final, squeamish peek at his mutilated right hand, Cleaves paused a bit longer to scan the blood-stained mat for his missing Magnum and in doing so, lined himself up perfectly for the shot that pierced his right eye and blew out the back of his skull in a grayish glut of hair, bone and brain matter.

Myron McKinley growled and spat, essentially drowning from his own external hemorrhage. Still, he'd forced the Trainer onto his back with the tip of the Glock parked a scant few inches from the smaller man's left temple. McKinley straddled the Trainer's midsection, essentially pinning him at the hips. As the barrel-tip shimmied ever closer, Cohen felt the strength in each hand ebbing to critical mass. In desperation, he began flinging his legs about, bringing up each knee with as much force as he could muster to continually strike the big man's lower back and buttocks. McKinley gurgled in apparent glee, his lunatic eyes gleaming as the Glock's barrel sight finally aligned with flesh.

Realizing one or both hands were on the verge of complete collapse, Cohen freed his right hand and reached for the big man's neck just as the ricochet effect allowed the gun-barrel to smack the side of his face. Groping blindly, his thumb and forefinger were able to navigate blood-slickened flesh and gain a grip on the scalpel handle. A series of vicious jerks ensued, first to the left and then the right, followed by an uppercut slash that felt as if it had drilled to the core to find solid bone. His nostrils filled with a coppery stench, Cohen turned away just as the floodwaters poured forth from the dead man's ravaged throat. He heard the Tracker release a final, choking gasp before the larger man rolled away, collapsing like an overstuffed duffel.

Long after the clip had emptied, LeAnn's right forefinger continued to pump the trigger. Cleaves' lifeless form had thumped to the mat, minus a sizeable portion of skull, but this had hardly contained her need to continue firing. A fourth shot had pelted a far wall, while a fifth had initially grazed the squared tip of a bar-buckle and ricocheted from the ceiling to finally land no more than a foot from Brian Jorgensen's left thigh. A sixth had struck Cleaves' left heel and essentially spread it across the mat, mingled with shredded shards of Cole-Haan casual loafer. While scurrying the ring perimeter like a cockroach in search of shadow, she'd run across the discarded Beretta. Long ago, in what seemed like some alternate universe, she'd vaguely recalled her father taking her to a shooting range. He'd been adamant in her need to be able to 'handle herself' if the situation arose. There had been sporadic lessons from an assortment of Father's bodyguards, and she recalled even going as far as obtaining a permit to legally carry. As it was, that first shot had felt quite alien—the result speaking for itself. The second, less so. By the third, she'd firmed her stance, aim, and breathing technique, clearly shaking off several substantial layers of rust. She lowered the smoking firearm only upon visualizing Brian Jorgensen pulling himself upright at the opposite side of the ring.

McGinty lay on his left side, facing away from the ring as the severe ache at his lower abdomen slowly subsided. A dull numbness at his left ankle hinted at fracture, while in the aftermath of all the booming retorts, his ears rang like a continuous, chiming church bell. Peter Hanley lay sprawled to his immediate right, the man's complexion ghostly-pale—his eyes flickering madly as if he were falling in and out of consciousness every few seconds. Before rolling over, McGinty took grisly note of a rather conspicuous absence in his employer's appearance, thinking at first glance the man's horribly shattered arm had been severed at the elbow. Upon closer inspection, it seemed Hanley's awkward landing had resulted in the forearm and accompanying hand facing in the opposition direction as the rest of the arm, bent completely back Flamingo-style and thus invisible from the front.

Tossing the empty Glock aside, LeAnn had sprinted around the ring to Brian's side, planting a firm shoulder beneath his left armpit just in time to prevent his collapse back onto the cool, blood-spattered floor.

"Just...t-take it sl-slow...s-slow and easy," she roared in overcompensation for her own hearing loss, her neck, shoulder and arm instantly saturated.

"Y-you're...stouter...t-than you l-look, S-Slim...," Jorgensen slurred, his left eye twitching uncontrollably and a thick stream of reddish drool hanging from his lower lip, "...s-sooo, wh-where w-we headed? V-Vegas sound okay to you?"

Able to comprehend his muttered dialogue only because his moistened lips hung so closely to her ear, LeAnn giggled despite herself. They waddled the length of the ring, his working hand gripping the lower rope for support while she provided sufficient leverage on the opposite side.

"S-stop yapping, you big lug. I...we need to stop your...the bleeding."

"B-better f-find a fir-first a-aid kit f-full of c-corks," he quipped as they cleared the ring and made a beeline toward the nearest chair.

McGinty stood shakily, briefly stumbling back and almost planting a heel directly onto the throat of his fallen employer before righting the ship on a gimpy ankle. Upon rolling onto his back, he'd reached down and retrieved a vintage, multi-carrier Cobra Derringer from the same wounded ankle, from where a tiny, matching holster hung. The Derringer had been taken from the body of a former associate he'd been tasked to eliminate following the man's outage as a law enforcement narc. In the years and multiple shootings since, he'd never before been forced to remove it from its equally antique holster, for which he'd paid a pretty penny at an online retailer that specialized in relics from the Old West.

He limped forward several steps in order to obtain a workable bead on the back of Jorgensen's head. Group hearing loss prevented either the target or woman from noticing his approach, and he moved to within five feet of their position when, out of his corner of his left eye, he noted a flicker of movement.

Barrett Cohen was lipping the same three-word phrase repeatedly; the execution of each syllable comically exaggerated, as if addressing the stone-deaf masses—a necessity at the moment. He held the Glock in his right hand. It was directed at McGinty's chest and was unwavering despite its possessor's overly-animated mouth-work.

Drop it, asshole…
Drop it, asshole…
Drop it, asshole…

Like a broken LP. Like a video snippet stuck in rewind. McGinty openly smirked, nodding wordlessly as if to say *'really?"* It was to laugh…hysterically. A washed-up play-*ac-tor* turned Hollywood tattle-tale, actually daring to threaten a man who had made a rather prosperous living from the art of termination. Perhaps the ac-tor had concluded that, in lieu of an actual fast-draw dual to which he would surely lose, a little tinsel-town bluff was in order. Or perhaps he'd underestimated the Derringer as a toy gun with no more firepower than your average air-rifle, or deduced that if forced to decide on a target with only one available round, Brian Jorgensen wore the lone bulls-eye. In case of the latter, the king of make-believe was in for a nasty shock, as the multi-carrier Cobra derived its name from its double-barrel, double-round capability. Thus, the initial shot could derail a Hollywood dream while saving the second for the Karate King. He figured Mister Hollywood must've read his mind once the man's eyes widened and his lips had clamped shut.

Unable to detain the dual-upturn at the corners of his mouth, McGinty shifted the minuscule pistol toward the Trainer with casual aplomb, pulling back the hammer for barrel one just as his right collarbone shattered and a quarter-sized entrance wound opened in the newly provided space. The Derringer dropped from his trembling fingers, adding insult to pre-death blow by striking the right big toe of his Puma high-tops. Attempting in vain to plug the aggressive bleeding with shaky, probing fingers, he regarded Barrett Cohen with comic disbelief as if doubting the validity of the shooter.

The Trainer held firm, altering neither his squint, firing stance or aim yet instantly improving his accuracy as Ray McGinty stumbled back with the back of his throat blown out in stringy chunks.

Barrett Cohen lowered the emptied Glock to his thigh, feeling the barrel's feverish heat and bemused at the realization that all those times spent learning how to both strike the correct pose and fire weapons from assorted trainers on assorted movie sets had not been, as he had remarked countless times, a complete waste of time.

LeAnn had pushed the two chairs together and somehow managed to hoist Jorgensen onto them, his upper frame engulfing the first and his legs hanging splayed off the second. They appeared to be communicating, LeAnn gently patting his blood-smeared cheek while dominating the gist of the dialogue.

The Trainer stood motionless, unable or willing to fight the temporary effects of a full-body paralysis that prevented immediate movement. Without little choice but to do so, he scanned the surrounding carnage amid a stout stench of wet pennies and involuntarily released bodily fluids. He was instantly reminded of the one and only time, as a pre-teen child, he'd had the misfortune to venture inside the walls of an active bovine slaughterhouse, during which time he'd barely refrained from throwing up from a similar stench, an act that would hardly have endeared him to his tough-as-nails, war vet father.

To the Trainer's left, Kerry Cleaves lay spreadeagle atop the drenched mat in a wide, rapidly spreading puddle—a virtual sea of maroon within which he appeared the subject of a rather grisly portrait that, if given a proper title, might well read 'the eternal backstroke' or even more aptly 'blood angel.'

To his far right lay the infamous Tracker, Myron McKinley, basking in a red river of his own creation, face-first with his arms at his sides as if overtaken by a sudden urge to power-nap.

To his immediate right, Ray McGinty had breathed his last curled into a fetal position, nearly decapitated by the throat-shot the shooter had meant for his upper chest. Mercifully, the man's face had turned away upon final collapse, sparing the survivors a peek at what was most likely a wide-eyed, open-jawed, thoroughly haunting expression of extreme agony.

Just past McGinty's own pool of spillage lolled the man wholly responsible for the massacre. Like McGinty, Peter Hanley faced toward an opposite wall, just the slightest hint in the barely visible rising and falling of his upper torso that he'd retained the power of breath.

A sudden pounding at his temples, the Trainer briefly and without a shred of sincere conviction, considered walking over and stomping the man to death. The wicked thought passed just as quickly as it had come. Predictably, he soon found himself standing at LeAnn's side, bending down to first listen in and perhaps join their muffled conversation.

"You stow that kind of talk, Jorgensen. You're...we're all...t-the three of us are getting out of here...if I have to strap you to my bony ass and d-drag you," LeAnn was squalling, no doubt an ear-splitting siren-wail if not for the badly damaged hearing of her audience.

"S-Slim, you...you're a great k-kid to s-say s-so...b-but it...it ain't ha-hap-hap'nin," Jorgensen replied as loudly as he could manage, spatting forth a fresh eruption onto his already soaked neck and chest with each strained uttering, "s-something...vi-vital g-gave w-way e-even be-be-before that fi-first b-bullet f-found me... some... something...d-deep d-down... a-and any... anyhow... I... I'm fowl..f-fairly c-certain I stro-stroked out a-after Ha-Hanley's first p-punch l-l-landed."

As if to emphasize this point, the man's left eyelid drooped horribly, the same corner of his mouth obviously paralyzed and thus slurring his speech almost to the point of being incomprehensible.

"Just rest easy, Brian," Barrett Cohen chimed in, practically screaming and still unable to fully make out his own words through the continuous ring reverberating within each ear, "we're gonna get you some help. Get...all of us...some help."

To this, both LeAnn and Jorgensen stared over and up at him, respectively, their individual expressions similarly mystified at his very presence.

Barrett had already inhaled to attempt a suitable follow-up when he noticed Jorgensen's leaning over as to peek past him, the man's good eye abruptly stretching wide, his crookedly set lips suddenly atremble.

Barrett heard LeAnn cry out but was unable to translate her message even as she'd reached over and planted a firmer-than-expected hand on his right shoulder and shoved.

Lurching to one side, he became aware of a slight burning sensation at the small of his back synchronized with a faint popping sound—a sensation that soon shot up his spine like the gnawing flames of a blazing wildfire. He watched Jorgensen squirm and finally roll from the overturned chairs as LeAnn's cries grew in both consistency and volume. All the while, he found himself powerless to do anything save collapse weakly onto his back, flopping like a gigged crustacean as his vision gradually darkened.

Thirteen

Thicker than Water

Peter Hanley stood propped against a far turnbuckle, his face contorted with rage as he slowly lowered the Derringer, a thin tendril of smoke spewing forth from its diminutive barrel. Drifting in and out, Barrett Cohen was aware of an increasingly intense throbbing at his upper back, directly between the shoulder blades. Peering upward through a foggy haze, he stared directly into the haggard visage of LeAnn Garner, her eyes brimming with fresh tears as she alternated shrieked dialogue with hacking sobs. She was apparently holding his head in her lap while addressing the man responsible for her former trainer and fellow inmate's abrupt downfall. Though he couldn't make out the majority of her words, he was able to piece together a few choice phrases.

"How dare you...*YOU*...criticize anyone else for their actions? Peter Hanley...professsional racketeer, swindler, drug-dealer and murderer? Is this what you see when you look in the mirror,

Father? Do you see a heartless, cold-blooded killer?" she'd screeched between blubbering gasps. Sometime during yet another, similar in nature rant, Barrett Cohen had faded out like a dying star.

When he came to, apparently discarded with his head titled fully to the left while still parked on his back—a sticky warmness had enveloped his upper torso and outspread arms and it became apparent the scenario had shifted once again....dramatically, and definitely *not* for the better. Though his vision would blur slightly with roughly every-other blink, his hearing had improved greatly, as if he'd been out for days instead of a few scant moments.

LeAnn had, at some point, laid him aside and confronted her father. Her back was to Barrett, her arms waiving frantically, her voice a gravelly whine so hoarse from screaming she sounded less herself than a middle-aged man with the raspy tone of a lifelong smoker.

"Why won't you respond, Father? Have I finally struck a nerve...buried somewhere deep down in what once was a human soul? How about this for a radical change? How about we sew this little tragedy up on a positive note, Father? How about you reveal a *single* truth about what this shit was really all about, huh?"

She paused, her spindly arms, at least by comparison from five months earlier, flopping to her sides as if the inner battery had finally ebbed. Just beyond her trembling frame, Cohen could just make out Peter Hanley's slumped outline.

"Well? How 'bout it, Pops? One time...to prove you're *capable* if nothing else—regale your only daughter with a single, honest answer."

Hanley's undamaged arm shot out with the speed and viciousness of a striking viper, hooking beneath her chin to acquire a grip stout enough to instantly hoist her airborne. Leaning hard against the mat, he twisted her around by the neck until Barrett was able to fully visualize both father and daughter, and thus immediately began a mighty struggle to rise.

"E-enough, Lee….that'll be…just a-about *enough* of t-that," Hanley growled beneath a hideous grin, his dialogue noticeably slurred from the effects of a badly broken lower jaw, "I…can't…w-want ter…tolerate such blac…blatant d-disrespect…from a-anyone…m-much less a f-fack…fucking t-traitor t-to the family bood…bloodline."

Able to push himself upright with arms that felt nine parts rubber and one part muscle and bone, the Trainer briefly peeked back over in the opposite direction to see Brian Jorgensen attempting his own, however unlikely, resurrection.

Pale to begin with, LeAnn's complexion was positively specter-like while trying in vain to break her father's death-grip by slapping and clawing at his forearm. Low gurgling noises escaped her pursed lips and a thin line of bubbly drool hung at the center—her eyes bugged to monstrous proportions as if on the cusp of popping free from their respective sockets.

"You…c-choose that…pace…p-piece of gab…garbage o-over your own fis-…flesh an-and blood?" Hanley continued to warble, a low grating sound emitting between words, like jagged bone grinding together, "I…had…r-rai-…real hopes…f-for y-you, Lee…and this is hel-…how y-you replay…by bedding th-the sa-same pile of h-human excrement t-that s-swapped f-fluids w-with my w-wife?"

As the ranting and railing continued, Hanley appeared to actually be gaining physical strength, as if reinvigorated by rage. His spine straightened, as did his legs, the lean layers of muscle lining his upper torso suddenly pumped as his lower appendages flexed and contorted with renewed vitality. It appeared only a matter of moments before his mangled arm might magically heal itself.

"Y-you want…h-honesty? I…d-didn't pain…p-plan it th-this way, little gu-girl….th-hat you c-can believe. As t-things stain…st-

stand, y-you l-left me no chase...c-choice but c-cut ties in a r-rather...bra-brutal w-way, but th-then, f-fathers do sun-sometimes h-have hard decisions to m-make conser...concerning their children."

His arm and hand jerked up and out, muscle, bone and tendon serving as a combination tree limb and hangman's noose, the former stout as an oak and the latter tightening with deadly similarity. LeAnn's sneakers hung suspended a full two feet from the floor, her hands curling around her father's massively bloated forearm—twisting in opposite directions to little effect. Even as she began to kick out, landing solidly around her father's abdomen, chest and groin, the lack in effect was the same. Hanley hardly blinked through a frozen, maniacal grimace.

About the same time LeAnn had been hauled airborne, Barrett Cohen had managed to stand upright ever-so-briefly before stumbling forward and breaking his fall primarily with his chin. Sparks flew and he temporarily lost consciousness before snapping to and snaking forward on all fours. He crawled past the discarded Derringer, nearly reaching out to snare it before recalling its load had been previously spent.

He reached Peter Hanley's ankles just as the cap of LeAnn's knee caught her tormentor flush on his shattered chin—the sharp snapping sound of bone akin to walnuts crushed beneath a steel-heeled boot. Miraculously, despite his lower jaw hanging as horribly askew as an axed shutter, Hanley's grip remained vise-like.

For want of any other mode of attack, Barrett Cohen scaled Hanley's lower leg before reaching up with groping fingers to squeeze the man's testicles through his knee-length boxers. He heard Hanley groan, the man's legs instantly weakening a degree as LeAnn plummeted to the floor in a heap. Sprawled onto her stomach, she released a single, exasperated gasp while massaging her damaged throat with both hands.

Hanley whipped about like a wounded tiger, slinging himself and his mashed groin free before delivering a looping right hand that sent his smaller assailant spinning away like a top.

Satisfied that Barrett Cohen, now curled motionless in a fetal position a dozen feet away, would provide no further annoyance, Hanley limped back toward his fallen daughter, his busted arm flapping like a mutilated tentacle.

He loomed over her squirming form and nodded solemnly, pausing briefly to spat a mouthful of blood over his left shoulder, the gooey blob landing at the pit of Myron McKinley's back.

"It may not shee-seem like it at this m-mu-moment, little gu-girl, but I'm ral-really doing y-you a f-favor," he stuttered, a dislodged tooth spilling free to bounce off his daughter's left thigh.

Upon viewing her father's foot levitating directly over her face, LeAnn gasped, releasing her throat and crossing her forearms in a blocking pose.

Pointing his heel downward, he altered his aim slightly, targeting her throat in place of the center of her face.

"No need to fa-fe-fight it, Lee...it's far...for the b-best..r-really..."

The foot crashed down, LeAnn's upturned forearms taking the brunt while changing the blow's trajectory just enough to prevent a direct hit, while not quite enough to deflect the full force. As such, she cried out as the back of her skull smacked the stone floor with a distinct thud, rendering ineffective a rather feeble attempt to crawl away.

Her father had stumbled back in the aftermath, righting himself only after a clumsy breakdance during which he'd stepped into a puddle of McKinley's rapidly thickening blood and nearly took a flying header directly onto his former bodyguard's prone form.

Hopping from the spillage with a warped expression of disgust upon his distorted mug, he took no notice of the building hum at his back, that is, until it mutated into a harsh, animalistic growl that reached a banshee-shriek crescendo just before impact.

Hanley had twisted his head toward the source a split-second before being pelted chest-level and sent sprawling onto his back a full ten feet from the point of contact. During that single blink in time, he'd been able to identify little but a massive blur of humanity that held at its center an expression of unbridled fury. He felt immense weight at his chest and, instinctively reaching up with his working arm, snatched a handful of sickly slick flesh. Mercifully, he was unaware that the forearm and hand of his previously shattered arm lay pinned at his lower back, having been severed from its host upon landing. Blinking madly from the effects of the beaming glow of an overhead fluorescent, he was only able to piece together his attacker in sketchy fragments.

"You're an even...bigger...asshole th-than I thought, Hanley..." he heard a familiar voice whisper, the words sounding strangely garbled, as if the speaker's mouth were packed with gauze.

"...and I gotta tell you...that's a bung-hole the s-size of Manhattan isle."

With a final spurt of energy, Hanley's head shot forward and spat forth a reddish, glutinous blob that struck his captor's left cheek and stuck, resembling a flaming boil.

"...y-you're...no b-but...better than m-me..." Hanley hissed, practically leaking from every facial orifice, to include both ears, "...we'll m-meet a-again s-sum..s-soon in...a d-darker p-place..." his bloated, misshapen lips upturned in a hideous parody of a smile, "...and t-there, I'll...s-surely o-outrank you, momer- mother fa-cker."

With that, Brian Jorgensen's bent right arm ascended at breakneck speed, driving his elbow into the center of Peter Hanley's face with a resounding crunch and in doing so, ramming a sliver of bone directly into the soft tissue of the man's brain.

Before rolling off Hanley's lifeless shell, he was afforded a quick glimpse at the damage incurred from that single blow; his former captor's features so horribly pulverized as to appear utterly unrecognizable. Above the flattened nose, shattered teeth, two of which had imbedded into his upper lip, and jawbones smashed to jagged pulp, the man's dark brown eyes remained askew—pulled wide, gleaming and seemingly aware while frozen in a permanent state of shock.

Scampering a few feet from the carnage, Jorgensen's upper back began to tense, bucking wildly as he proceeded to projectile vomit.

"Oh…oh g-god….just…just…don't move…I'll find…I'll go…we have to st-stop the…that bleeding," LeAnn croaked frantically from somewhere nearby, the fatigue in her tone somewhat overcome by a palpable sense of desperation.

"N-no…go…go check on the b-big g-guy f-first," Barrett Cohen had replied weakly, sounding as if he were speaking from another room entirely.

Brian Jorgensen had rolled onto his left side, his breathing dangerously shallow through lips caked with a fresh coating of gore. As LeAnn bowed before him, he managed to execute a pathetic but wholly sincere smile.

"H-hiya, S-Slim…h-how's G-Goob? I s-saw 'im t-take a sh-shot to the b-back…"

"My god, are you two long-lost lodge brothers or something?" she said, her cheeks saturated with a torrent of tears both old and new. She glanced briefly over at the ruin of her father before turning back to her fellow inmate, now wearing a mask of agony.

"S-sorry, Slim. He…he gave us…m-me no choice. I m-mean…he…he meant to ki-kill you. P-planned it…f-from the b-beginning, I…I think…"

"He surely would have, yes. A-all of us," she conceded, wiping a bare forearm across both eyes, "now, it's high time we vamoosed this…what'd you call it? Rock-wall suppository?"

Jorgensen's involuntary grin better resembled a pained wince, the accompanying giggle akin to the sick, wet cough of the terminally ill.

"Y-you're a c-card, Slim. A-afraid I'm g-going down with the s-ship," he finally replied between hacks, "t-truth is...it m-might be a b-blessing at t-that."

Peering down into his fast-fading eyes as she held his head on her lap, a few stray tears dripped onto his chest and abdomen.

"A...blessing?"

She gently stroked his stubbly noggin, noticing the shallowness of his breathing. Glancing over, she saw the dark maroon remnants of his recent regurgitation and her heart instantly sank.

"S-sure. Think h-how I'd...have to...bust my...f-fat ass...to get b-back in s-shape. Hell...I'm t-too used to th-the s-seafood d-diet n-now to g-go ba-back to w-watching ca-calories."

His eyes finally clamped shut, his bottom lip quivering and his left arm and hand following suit, as if he were undergoing a massive stroke.

"Shhhh, be quiet now. You need to...just take it easy. I...we'll get...go get help. You just have to...breathe slow and take it...."

His right hand shot out, reaching over to clamp her left and squeezing with a surprising stoutness.

"You...you've...got a...second shot, LeAnn..." he hissed so softly it was as if she were actually reading his barely parted lips, "...pay-play it...for all it's...worth. I am a...w-*was* a...better man...just...from...knowing you. Better than...I...dese...deeaaaa...."

His final refrain choked off by a throaty gasp, Brian Jorgensen's eyes popped wide open for one terrifying moment, his upper body convulsing in a futile attempt at jerking upright, before collapsing just as abruptly and falling back into LeAnn's waiting lap.

She bowed her head and wept—a single, agonizing sob, while applying a final caress to his lifeless hand.

Sniffing away another potential blubbering jag, LeAnn placed Brian's head gently atop the stone surface and stood with her arms crossed, hugging herself tightly while taking a conclusive, forlorn look at both her deceased father and the man who had just saved her from him.

As if the most recent deaths served to fully awaken her senses, she became acutely aware of the overwhelming stench, an assortment of putridness that threatened to double her over before she ever reached Barrett Cohen's splayed form.

She forced herself to breathe through her mouth while tending to him—first turning him over and packing the circular, penny-sized entrance wound just above his left shoulder-blade with rolled strips of cloth torn from her own shirt—ditto the exit wound just beneath his collarbone. During this treatment, a dazed, semi-conscious Cohen babbled and stammered mostly incoherently while utilizing an assortment of accents so very familiar to the woman serving as his impromptu nurse.

As Miss Jeannine: "...how 'bout some nice, fluffy blueberry pancakes, hon? You just can't keep livin' on sliced pears and sunflower seeds, you hear me, girl?"

As Gabe Maxwell: "...meetin' that goal weight was damn near a miracle, little lady...now we can move on to the sculptin' phase...you're gonna love it, mainly since you can finally start gnawin' on some real chow again."

And most importantly, a brief message from silo medical specialist Doctor Darwin McClintock: "...packing the wounds, for now, is merely stop-gap to quell the bleeding. The med lab first-aid kit has antibiotic ointments and pre-filled antibiotic syringes...not to mention an assortment of painkillers the patient will find most useful. Off with you now, Miss Garner. The patient will survive in your brief absence. Make it snappy."

She did just that, accomplishing the round-trip to the med floor and back in just under eight minutes. Once hydrogen peroxide met open wound, Cohen snapped to long enough to converse in his own natural tongue.

"You lost a l...some blood," he heard LeAnn say, his vision clearing gradually until her haggard features formed in squared segments, like fleshy puzzle pieces.

"Jor-Jorgensen?" he inquired weakly, wincing at the sharp, dual stings at his back and neck.

LeAnn nodded without response, lifting a syringe eye level and squirting out an initial spray into open air.

"Antibiotic," she said matter-of-factly. "I'll be gentle."

She was just that—the execution akin to a slight pinch to his left shoulder.

In response, his smile was slight but sincere.

"G-good job, d-doc. C-couldn't have done...better myself."

She leaned back, discarding the emptied syringe with a casual toss over the shoulder.

"Cohen...I, um, well, did what I could," she gestured to his neck wound, "but, bluntly put...we're, well, kinda trapped down here."

She sighed wearily, flipping away a pesky strand of stringy hair that had taken up residence over her right eye.

"Like rats in a trap...fish in a barrel..."

Cohen raised a shaking hand as if asking permission to speak.

"L-LeAnn...I...c-can...go-got..."

Oblivious, she rambled on unabated.

"...sardines in a can. Pick a cliché, any cliché. I don't kn-know how, but we...I will get us out. Swear to g-god, I...I won't die here."

"LeAnn, listen...I...have the co-codes."

"...at least we have enough food and water to last until someone checks..."

She froze, her mouth hanging agape and locked eyes with her patient, who nodded in kind.

"Codes?"

"Do-door codes, yes…to enter the silo's entrance and…t-then to exit it."

There was an audible click at the base of her throat, followed by a hard swallow and an orgasmic, full-body tremor. Leaning down, she planted a light kiss on his exposed forehead, numerous sweat-beads be damned, and lingered there just long enough to fight off another potential sobbing jag.

"Well that certainly sheds a fresh, nova-stout light on the rather pessimistic attitude this girl was so efficiently cultivating," she blurted, raw with barely restrained emotion, "Mister Cohen, I do believe it's time you and I turned in our room keys and checked out of the Purgatory Inn. You with me?"

"All…f-four of me, yes…m-ma'am," Barrett Cohen replied with as much enthusiasm as a plethora of assorted pains would allow.

She leaned down yet again, applying a gentle peck to his left cheek.

"It's a date then. We'll pack a sack of essentials and go for a walk. Um…" she paused, gnawing her lower lip, "…my father mentioned you'd…ventured outdoors at least once. Any idea where we are or…how close we are to actual civilization?"

Her former trainer/cook/doctor and present patient managed a light shrug.

"N-not a clue, lady. G-guess we'll have t-to…w-wing it."

"Hey, whatever," she countered with a thumbs-up gesture, "fresh air will do us good, right? I'm thinking it must be late spring wherever we are."

Reaching down, she pulled him up by the shoulders until he sat up on his own in a semi-mantis pose. From this relatively simple movement, his complexion turned an even ghostlier shade of pale—virgin chalk encased in a freshly piled snowfall.

"T-think we can…f-find me a wheelchair? Better y-yet, a cot with w-wheels?"

LeAnn Garner stood upright with hands on hips, her jaw set tight with newfound resolve.

"Seriously, don't sweat it, Mister Cohen. If need be, I'll piggyback you to the promised land."

As the escape plan progressed, she was forced to basically do just that.

Fourteen

Fight and Flight, Part I

LeAnn's aforementioned survival pack had contained a half case of bottled water, a handful of hydrocodone for painkilling purposes, three rolls of toilet paper, gauze, assorted bandages and a fistful of power-bars—what we'd agreed were necessities in case of an extended trek from the silo grounds. As for myself, I'd insisted on but one personal item for extraction from that hellish cylinder. Fact was, I'd insisted most fervently, at least according to LeAnn. Personally, I cannot recall such a tantrum. As it were, other than my chosen stowaway, it was proven we'd actually over-packed.

All told, actual departure from said grounds took place approximately one hour to seventy-five minutes following LeAnn's 'piggy-back' remark. Of rather grim note were LeAnn's efforts in retrieving cell phones from the stiffening corpses of Myron McKinley and Ray McGinty, both of which were of absolutely no use as gaining a working connection proved impossible. Still, quite the valiant effort considering her mental state at the time.

What with gulping down a threesome of pain pills as we'd stepped from floor ten to the waiting elevator, details of our great escape grows a bit fuzzy soon thereafter. I do recall LeAnn's pained groans, grunts and labored breathing as she was forced to not only haul about our travel supplies, tucked randomly within a pillow case, but also yours truly. She'd wedged herself beneath my right shoulder and, though I was able to pick up my feet in sporadic waves of self-reliance, was tasked with bearing the brunt of my body weight.

At one point inside the dining hall, she'd leaned me against a wall and proceeded to use a chair to bludgeon its accompanying table, battering the frame until a pair of crude but fairly effective homemade crunches were formed from the wreckage.

Obviously, I'd had enough of my wits about me to pass on the required door codes, perhaps running on autopilot and simply answering whatever I was asked, like a victim of hypnotism or dazed patient with veins shot full of Twilight Sleep-type meds.

There was a moment of complete clarity upon entering the silo lobby and locating the keypad hidden away in a secret wall-panel—trailing LeAnn once the glass doors had parted and, most vividly, feeling the warm, fresh breeze slap the flesh of my face and neck.

Despite partly cloudy conditions, the heady rays of sunshine that did squeeze through were magical in their ability to instantly revitalize, that is, until the meds kicked in again and only foggy imagery remains—an image waddling along a winding dirt road bookended on both sides by shoulder-high sea grass, drooping elms and fully blossomed birch. Be it daydream or actual occurrence, I do remember peering back in order to obtain a final visual snapshot of the silo's upper, outer shell and thinking crazily that it resembled an oversized porta-potty—a gleaming, glass-encased shithouse for the eccentric, filthy rich.

No doubt fueled by an astronomical level of apprehension, LeAnn had talked continuously, a never-ending ramble of only partially comprehensible dialogue that, if I retained the gist, dealt with the weighty issue of *how* and *what* exactly to report to authorities once we'd successfully reached secure grounds. As for any reply or retort, be it amiable agreement or fevered disagreement that I'd conjured up during this admittedly fuzzy duration, the jury is still and will forever remain out. LeAnn, you see, hasn't a clue, as she freely admits to having little recall of her own words. I referred to it as *adrenalized amnesia*—a definition she's readily accepted on the condition she be allowed to reclaim a similar state whenever convenient.

I haven't a clue how long it took us to limp, stumble and trip our way to that coastline, as I'd apparently split my time either staring down at the jagged terrain or happily dozing as LeAnn had been forced to drag me along like so much dead weight. I do recall, quite clearly, her resounding sigh, followed by a whispered curse as we'd stood on a sandy bank, staring out into clear blue waters. I also recall a distinct scent of saltiness in the air as a continuous warm sea breeze caressed my cheeks. Though unsure of an exact time lapse, it was a short time afterward that a low hum was heard overhead—a hum that soon escalated into a roaring buzz that my dazed mind initially identified as an impending bee swarm. As LeAnn yanked me into a shoulder-high growth of beach-grass, I caught a faint glimpse of the whirly-bird sailing past. Crazily, while being flung roughly into the billowy weeds, I'm fairly sure I began to warble the theme from *Magnum P.I*, on which I had co-starred twice during its lengthy run.

Things grow increasingly hazy from there. Nearly drowned out by the ascending chopper, LeAnn had bellowed something to the effect of *there goes our ride* while pinning me down by the shoulders—a totally unnecessary gesture considered my extremely altered condition. I watched her reach into the case and commence digging before retrieving the Glock and tucking it into the waistband of her sweats.

From there, she had labored greatly in attempting to get me to my feet, a vain exercise being as I'd apparently whacked my noggin upon descending and triggered a total body paralysis of sorts. I had to look no further for evidence of this fresh malady than LeAnn's blood-soaked hands, drawn from the back of my head as she'd finally given up the struggle and laid me gently back down onto the grassy terrain. One wet towel placement and pain-pill booster later, and all recollections cease. That is, until I awoke atop clean sheets with IV tubes taped to the crook of my elbow and a BP machine beeping and blinking nearby.

Fight and Flight, Part II

The fact that I missed all the nail-biting drama of our liberation is equal parts soothing and infuriating—relief and anger in similarly heaping helpings. Admittedly, even if completely healthy and at the top of my game, I might've proved to be more hindrance than help. Still, a man can't help but ponder.

As it was, LeAnn Garner proved pretty damn formidable a foil as a solo act.

A full three days into my rehab—as the cobwebs began to clear without reforming just as abruptly—she was finally able to provide all the juicy details of how we came to reside at what I would later label *the MMC...mystery medical center.*

~ * ~

Upon leaving me to nod and nap in a drug-induced coma, she'd watched from afar as the helicopter set down on the lone designated pad—a flat, vegetation-free circle positioned approximately one-hundred yards to the right of the silo.

A lanky, bald man wearing an ankle-length black duster had exited the passenger side as the chopper's motor idled down and its blades gradually slowed. Though viewed from several hundred feet, she'd described the man as unnaturally sleek and graceful of movement, even going as far as saying he appeared to slowly *levitate* toward the entrance like some unworldly, vampire-like entity. As far as the pilot, she could just make out a faint shadow, bulky shouldered and sporting hearing protection and a ball-cap of some type. The passenger—LeAnn had stated his shiny head glowed like a sunlamp—had stopped short perhaps a dozen feet from the silo entrance, a cellphone stuck to his left ear. Following a short pause, he'd removed a firearm of some type from the duster's interior vest, punched the entry code into the outer keypad and vanished through the silo's darkened entrance.

Figuring time was extremely limited, LeAnn had practically sprinted to the chopper, empty Glock in hand, flung the passenger door ajar and ordered the pilot to dismount in order to assist in carrying me down the hill. From what I'd witnessed of her character in the past five months, this I can envision Miss Garner executing without hesitation. Her description of the pilot...a pot-bellied, sandy-bearded, fiftyish black male decked out in a gravy-stained wife-beater and Cleveland Brown's ball-cap brought to mind your typical tourist flyer, though she did state the ever-so-fleet rising of a red flag at his open lack of either fear or surprise at her sudden appearance.

Oh, he'd departed the chopper willingly enough, even toting my limp frame down that hill without so much as a grumble or groan. It wasn't until he'd loaded me inside, propping me upright and strapping me in like a busted marionette, and LeAnn had insisted at gunpoint he fly us out that old Mister Cooperation turned downright stubborn. Despite LeAnn's threats, hollow as they might've been while waiving an empty gat around, she stated that round-bellied flyboy reached down as calmly as you please and yanked a peashooter from underneath the pilot seat.

Pointing the weapon in the general vicinity of her forehead with unnatural calmness, she thought it a stub-nosed thirty-eight, he proceeded to spout a few orders of his own.

Identifying himself as Jerry Lloyd, a special agent for the Federal Bureau of Investigation, he instructed LeAnn to drop her weapon and join me inside the helicopter, the outer shell to which he announced was not only so darkly tinted as to disallow a clear view from the front, but also equipped with bullet-proof glass.

She stated he'd argued vehemently and didn't drop the Glock until he'd produced a badge and a brief explanation. LeAnn had ducked inside the 'copter with just moments to spare, as the man in black had reemerged from the silo, sprinting up the hill and gesturing wildly with his free hand, his other gripping a long-barreled revolver, for the pilot to restart the whirly-bird's engine.

Jerry Lloyd had, according to LeAnn, reached inside with his right hand to do just that while tucking the firearm to his lower back with the left. She recalled with astonishment that the man's trigger finger was set firmly in place as he maintained an utterly emotionless expression.

"What's up, boss? Where's the rest of the gang? Still packing up, I assume," Jerry Lloyd had bellowed over the building hum of the chopper blade, leaning out of the cab while resetting his sunglasses with the same unoccupied hand.

"Objective's changed. The Garner woman and Barrett Cohen have flown the coop," the man in black replied in a surprisingly high, shrill tone—entrenched in a deep, upper east-coast twang—LeAnn later confessed to finding quite humorous considering its physically intimidating source.

"Search and rescue, then?" Jerry asked as his passenger closed the gap to approximately twenty yards or so.

The man in black appeared to crack a smile, a gleaming, gold front tooth briefly announcing its presence. LeAnn said that as he grew nearer, he'd used the pistol's grotesquely elongated barrel to clamp the duster's lapels to his neck in the face of the swirling gusts created by the chopper's swirling blade. At closer range, LeAnn was able to ID said blue-steel baby as a three-fifty-seven Magnum.

"More like search an' *destroy*. Shouldn't take long…there's only so many hiding places on this 'burg."

Jerry Lloyd had waited until the man in black had closed to within perhaps ten yards before whipping the gun forward from the pit of his back and striking a classic shooter's pose.

"Floor the brakes and drop the weapon, Delnagro! Do it *NOW*!" he'd screamed, LeAnn declaring that other than the man's lips, his entire frame in fact, was as still and motionless as a granite statue.

In response, LeAnn stated the man in black had adhered only to the initial order, skidding to a stop in the loose sand even as the Magnum was slung up and out to draw an instantaneous bead. The man's smarmy smile had resurfaced—or at least what such as his type passed off as one. Having only LeAnn's description to go by, I can envision more a frozen grimace that reeked of pure malevolence—the stereotypical leer of a mad scientist.

"Flyboy, whoever you work for has surely handed you the ultimate in shit sandwiches …overloaded and dripping from every soggy corner of the bread."

"The federal government serves my meals, mister. Now drop the weapon or I…drop…you."

The man in black had neither responded nor wavered.

"Salvadore Delnagro, you are under arrest for solicitation of mur…"

"The Garner chick's in the chopper, isn't she? Cohen's tucked in there as well, yeah?" the man in black had interrupted while shooting quick glances toward the copter's round, reflective glass. LeAnn had confessed that at this point, she'd seriously doubted our chances of departing those grounds alive. It had appeared on the surface, she'd continued, a woeful mismatch. Young, sleek, professional killer versus middle-aged, pudgy, staid man of law enforcement. Call it shootout at the Purgatory Inn—the final showdown.

"One last warn..." Agent Lloyd had shouted, cut off by the Magnum's booming retort. Though he'd instinctively fallen to one knee, LeAnn stated the agent's aim had remained steadfast—his frozen expression equally unchanged. As for LeAnn herself, she'd cringed and crouched, precisely in that order, as the first of two shots ricocheted off the chopper's front glass, distinguished solely by a whitish spark and leaving a tiny, blooming flower-shaped crack in its wake.

Their impact a mere split-second apart, an additional round struck a few inches below the first, LeAnn noting that, squatted position or no, one or perhaps both would have certainly found pay-dirt if not for the protective glass.

She'd watched the man in black whip the three-fifty-seven around toward the agent just as a neat, dime-shaped hole appeared just above his left eye, followed by a similar imploding of flesh on the right side of his face, perhaps an inch beneath the opposite eye. While the first wound appeared strangely bloodless, the second spewed forth a single trickle down the man's narrow jawline. LeAnn swears the man in black wore a tight-lipped smile as the magnum slipped free from his grip and he toppled face-first into the sand.

"Delnagro," Agent Lloyd had divulged to LeAnn on the flight to the mainland, "employed by your...late father as a...what we refer to as a Cleaner."

She'd quickly interjected that the term was familiar, as was the accompanying job description. Child of the mob she was, after all.

"He was sloppy, careless," the agent had continued, "more so than his MO would have ever indicated was possible. Lucky for all of us—most notably yourself and Mister Cohen."

Moments following the incident and before our imminent departure, two additional helicopters had descended to land on either side of our own, ejecting separate trios of well-armed soldier-types LeAnn had described as SWAT-clones.

She said after clearing a sizeable body of water, the terrain we'd crossed was remote and mountainous, with only a handful of small towns made visible.

Upon landing at a remote landing site outside what she'd stated resembled an abandoned clinic—I'd insisted on 'haunted sanitarium' in an attempt to inject a note of ironic humor—a joke which, not surprisingly, fell instantly flat. Regardless, I was told a foursome of EMT-types exited the facility almost immediately and loaded me onto a stretcher.

From there, Agent Jerry Lloyd, a man I'd never been afforded the chance to meet or even visualize, steered a copter I have no memory of being a passenger of straight up and away...never to be heard from again. A man who'd saved my life, no less. Alas, I'm sure such a man, upon being thanked for such a monumental deed, would comment flatly 'just doing my job, sir." For the record and having spent some obviously tense moments with the man, LeAnn agreed with my analogy whole-heartedly. Just over twenty hours later, I awoke to the angelic image of LeAnn Garner leaning overhead while flashing, bar none, the prettiest damn smile I'd ever seen.

Epilogue:

Therapeutic Measures

Strange, but I feel a distinctive dull ache at the site of both scars—entrance and exit wounds throb with equal fervor—almost immediately upon opening the word-file and for the duration of the work being accomplished, be it a single paragraph or five thousand word marathon.

Psychosomatic symptoms perhaps akin to what LeAnn was feeling during her infamous non-pregnancy. Still, it's damn weird. What's more bizarre is how, in some *hurts-so-good* sort of way, John Mellencamp will surely forgive me, I do sometimes *savor* the now familiar ache.

As far as backdrops for a full-time writing chore, is there any better locale than a semi-desolate, snow-crested mountain range? LeAnn agrees, though she openly craves warmer climes. A natural complainer, she is, and damned skilled at the art of bitchery, but this I knew from previous stints as her cook, her trainer, her physician. During times of spontaneous levity, so rare at first but growing more frequent as time passes, she will request I dredge up the voices of my creations—mealtime with Miss Jeannine is normally the most popular.

Eight and a quarter months since we checked out of the Purgatory Inn. Eight-plus flips of the calendar spent tucked safely away in our very own winter cabin, sans of course, that initial thirty-day stay at the MMC.

Physically we're on the mend, though LeAnn is still finding it extremely difficult to satisfy the daily diet her personal physician has set. I watch her struggle to finish a single meal, must less three. Still, she's managed to pack on fifteen-plus pounds, this despite frequent hikes into the nearby mountains.

Meanwhile, I've gained personal ownership of twin scars—permanent reminders of an ordeal that I recall, thank god, only foggily.

Mentally, a level of healing is harder to gauge. Personally, my sleep is a bit sounder but the frequent nightmares have yet to abate. Nightmares that find me still playing the role of twenty-four hour silo caretaker—not only tasked with the everyday mundane...stocking, equipment checks, voiceovers...but several...*additional* duties pulled from a blood-spattered checklist created within the darkest region of my subconscious. There are fridges packed with assorted body parts—specters that rake jagged nails ever-so-gently, almost lovingly, across the nape of my neck—bloodied hand and footprints that lead to rooms filled with the coppery stench of death. The worst night vision by far? Sauntering into an otherwise deserted gymnasium to find Alexis Alpajando hanging by his ankles from the squat-rack with his throat cut from ear to ear and the exercise mat beneath him literally floating in a river of red. Alexis had been my co-writer, co-producer and co-conspirator in the mob documentary that was never to be. During the seemingly non-stop barrage of interviews with various government agents, I'd been informed that Alexis had been reported missing a few days following my own abduction. He was a twenty-five year old film grad with boundless energy and a sincere love for the industry's glorious past and held little hope for the young man ever being found, much less found *alive*. When questioned, the stone-faced fed did little to raise any hopes to the contrary.

Though I cannot speak for my bunkmate, the symptoms of deep-seated damage were obvious. Her moods shift as frequently as the mountain breezes—her expressions equally varied depending on the status of the former. There are the sporadic nights filled with the echoes of her sobs—wrenching, wracking and occasionally accompanied by the shrieking of a familiar name, be it a traitorous, recently deceased parent or loyal, murdered comrade. It didn't take a degree in head-shrinkage to ID Miss Garner as severely damaged goods. Understandable of course, considering. In fact, anything other than the inconsistent instability of behavior she'd displayed would worry the hell out of me. On the bright side, she has the capability to heal. Perhaps not completely, but enough to carry on with the rest of her days without ingesting daily handfuls of anti-depressants.

We get along well enough, an easy-going relationship full of natural politeness and good-natured ribbing that isn't the least bit forced. There are long periods of silence, followed by marathon talks that last well into the night.

Many might find it unbelievable to fathom, but not a single twinge of sexual urgency exists between us despite sharing close quarters for such a lengthy duration. I can speak only from my own perspective, of course, but if LeAnn does possess such feelings, she's been a Zen master of self-control. If forced to define our relationship, I'd have to say there is a definite *sibling* vibe.

It had been around day forty of our cabin stay that my creative side emerged from a long-dormant state of flux. As was usually the case when such ideas birthed, it wasn't a gradual hatching but an explosive, rocketed projectile-type delivery. Decades in the business, and this had always been the case, even more so since I'd taken up residence behind the camera. Literally bursting at the seams, I'd shared the notion almost immediately. Much to my delight, LeAnn had nearly matched my enthusiasm, though the technical aspects of the project escaped her. Over a two-decade span, I'd completed four screenplays, two of which I'd used to direct documentaries and portions of several unfinished stage-plays. I'd even dabbled with poetry and a short-story collection, the latter of which I'd briefly considered self-publishing. LeAnn joked she'd never completed so much as a *grocery* list without an extensive re-write. Still, her input was, and is, vital to the project's shelf-life, as is that lone item I'd insisted accompany me from the Purgatory Inn. A taped audio recording on two discs of my many sessions with LeAnn and Brian, nearly eight full hours of swapped dialogue and, as a free bonus, several clipped conversations with Peter Hanley. True, the originals had been overnighted to Hanley on a semi-daily basis, but I'd always been a bit anal in terms of backing up files. The feds have, I'm sure, confiscated the aforementioned originals, the gist of which will certainly exonerate us from any wrongdoing.

Regardless, in terms of reference material, we're talking pure audio *gold*—the proverbial Mother-lode.

Eighty-plus thousand words into the initial rough draft, we brainstorm daily—usually over morning and afternoon coffee—as we near that final, faithful, and undeniably tragic finale. While the feds continue their never-ending investigation at Hanley's estate, we continue to document what we lived, survived, to chronicle. Through countless interviews by various law enforcement entities, we've been forced to relive it numerous times from our individual points of view. Only the tragic, bloody ending is an exact clone—logical considering the only genuine 'face-time' the two of us can claim over that one-hundred fifty day span.

Peter Hanley's empire, already verging on collapse, might surely topple once the truth...the whole truth...is divulged. Just the fact that his ex-wife and LeAnn's biological mother, Judith Hanley Carlyle—had kick-started the investigation that eventually led to our rescue by Agent Jerry Lloyd, gave proof that its imminent demise was a definite probability. In the meantime, we bide our time under government protection. How much time? We've been afforded no timeline. Once freedom, *true* freedom, is obtained once again, it's likely to be under the condition that new identities are assumed. In some ways, the notion terrifies me, especially considering the career path I've carved through the years—in others, there is indeed a measure of excitement in being able to start fresh. The latter, predictably, thrills LeAnn to the point of transforming her into a giddy school-girl at the mere mention.

As for the story we hope to share in the near future, via either traditional publisher or the aforementioned avenue of do-it-yourself, we've decided it will be told in fictional terms with the names changed to protect the innocent, that of course being yours truly and his stalwart sidekick.

While LeAnn and I don't agree on everything in terms of exact order and specific details, two distinct facts are agreed upon without debate. The first? The title itself. We'd kicked around several, to include the obligatory 'Purgatory Inn' reference. In the end, it took little convincing for LeAnn to verbally sign off on a choice very near and dear to my heart—*Made in The Twenty-First Century.*

As for the second, to whom to dedicate the work and, just as importantly, choosing the correct phrasing to do so.

For this, I give Miss Garner full credit for both content and simplicity of same. Short and sweet, but filled with the deepest of meanings from its co-creators.

It will read, fittingly:

For B.J., without whom these words would not exist...nor would their co-authors.

As for the manuscript's opening line, that much at least, was a no-brainer:

The instinct to survive, it's been said, is inbred in all living things. It is, seemingly at birth, hardwired. My partner and I agree to an extent, though with some slight reservations.

Meet Terry Lloyd Vinson

An Air Force veteran, Terry Lloyd Vinson is the author of twenty published novels. He currently resides in Hendersonville, Tennessee with his wife, Liza.

Works From The Pen Of Terry Lloyd Vinson

The Purgetory Inn - Man's will to survive the most dismal of odds is well-documented throughout history. Many of the more miraculous entries into the legendary canon of such tales involve individuals of such stout inner fortitude—perhaps shaped in personal faith or simply a psyche forged of pure iron—that the chances of escaping the reaper's sharp-edged scythe improve by default. Welcome then, into the desolate, stony confines of The Purgatory Inn, where the limits of human endurance are put to the ultimate test in the form of two involuntary guests, each forced to overcome the most formidable foe of all...the specters of their respective pasts.

Sea Of Bones - For veteran man-and-wife Correctional Officers Zachary and Liza Gorman, their assignment to the penal colony Atlantis is in of itself no more than a glorified babysitting gig, that is until a series of gruesome inmate suicides rock the deep blue sea facility to its stone and sand foundation.

With a possible facility shutdown looming and a potentially destructive tropical storm approaching, both the staff and surviving inmate population are subject to a dark, deadly conspiracy that ultimately serves to reveal the responsible party as one of shocking familiarity.

Crimson Falls - On the eve of a high school football game of epic importance, the sleepy township of Crimson Falls, Kentucky will play host to a tsunami in human guise: a rage-filled returning prodigal son with a deadly score to settle.

Left to die only to emerge from a fourteen-year coma a bitter, paraplegic shadow of his former self, Gunther McCarron has arisen phoenix-like to track down the culprit or culprits responsible not only for his current state of both physical and mental anguish but the unsolved slaying of a former love that same fateful night.

With the unlikely aid of a similarly paralyzed police records clerk and the somber, tight-lipped uncle who represents his lone remaining kin, McCarron soon faces resistance both subtle and severe in his attempts to uncover the suspect or suspects responsible for the infamous cold case.

As game day arrives and a fevered crowd packs the stadium to witness two bitter rivals clash for bragging rights and a probable state playoff bid, the snow-coated streets of Crimson Falls, Kentucky will soon run red with its town's namesake color.

Letter to Our Readers

Enjoy this book?

You can make a difference.

As an independent publisher, Wings ePress, Inc. does not have the financial clout of the large New York publishers. We can't afford large magazine spreads or subway posters to tell people about our quality books.

But we do have something much more effective and powerful than ads. We have a large base
of loyal readers.

Honest reviews help bring the attention of new readers to our books.

If you enjoyed this book, we would appreciate it if you would spend a few minutes posting a review on the site where you purchased this book or on the Wings ePress, Inc. webpages at:
https://wingsepress.com/

Thank You

VISIT OUR WEBSITE

FOR THE FULL INVENTORY
OF QUALITY BOOKS:

http://www.wings-press.com

*Quality trade paperbacks and downloads
in multiple formats,
in genres ranging from light romantic comedy
to general fiction and horror.
Wings has something for every reader's taste.
Visit the website, then bookmark it.
We add new titles each month!*